KT-364-635

From the Butterfly Barn Series

On Butterfly Wings

KAREN POWER

COMERAGH PUBLISHING

First published in 2015 by
Comeragh Publishing
Co. Waterford
www.karenpowerauthor.com

All rights © 2015 Karen Power

CreateSpace paperback   ISBN: 978 1 911013 112
eBook – mobi format   ISBN: 978 1 911013 099
eBook – ePub format   ISBN: 978 1 911013 105
Paperback   ISBN: 978 1 911013 082

All rights reserved. No part of this book may be reproduced or utilised in any form or by any means electronic or mechanical, including photocopying, filming, recording, video recording, photography, or by any information storage and retrieval system, nor shall by way of trade or otherwise be lent, resold or otherwise circulated in any form of binding or cover other than that in which it is published without prior permission in writing from the publisher.

The right of the author of her work has been asserted by her in accordance with the Copyright, Designs and Patents Act 1988.

All characters and events featured in this publication, other than those clearly in the public domain, are entirely fictitious and any resemblance to any person living or dead, organisation or event, is purely coincidental.

Produced by Kazoo Independent Publishing Services
222 Beech Park, Lucan, Co. Dublin
www.kazoopublishing.com

Kazoo Independent Publishing Services is not the publisher of this work. All rights and responsibilities pertaining to this work remain with Comeragh Publishing.

Kazoo offers independent authors a full range of publishing services. For further details visit www.kazoopublishing.com

Cover design by Andrew Brown
Printed in the EU

WITHDRAWN
FROM
STOCK

On Butterfly Wings

For my mam and dad, Nancy and Paddy Galvin.

Karen Power lives with her family in County Waterford. She has spent many years working in the travel industry and currently delivers training in communications and adult literacy. *On Butterfly Wings* is her second novel.

Chapter One

"I cannot believe you have done this," said Monique, looking at the printout Garvan had given her. Her French accent always became more pronounced when she was stressed. She stood up from the grassy dune and looked away from him down Bayrush's long sandy beach.

"Monique, you've always known how much I want to go to Dubai. I thought if I just did it, you'd finally make a decision and come too."

"But I cannot leave Gran."

"But what about us? What about experiencing the world? We're young, Monique. Dubai is full of opportunities for me," said Garvan, scrambling to his feet. He went to touch her.

She pulled away. "Opportunities for you!"

At least he had the good grace to look down, she thought. She was so hurt. He had actually booked a ticket without even talking to her about it. They had been together for four years. "And it is for tomorrow … how could you, Garvan?" She could barely see the print her eyes were so filled with unshed tears but she'd be damned if she'd let him see her cry.

"I thought I was doing the right thing. We don't have jobs and both of us have a degree. Why not leave? I can get a job and you can follow."

She walked towards him. She could see by his expression that he thought she was giving in. Instead, she handed back the piece of paper.

"Goodbye, Garvan," she managed to say, turning swiftly before he could see the tears pouring down her cheeks.

"Monique, wait. We can talk about it," he called after her. She quickened her pace, trying not to fall on the winding trail down the dunes. A part of her was afraid if he came after her, she'd change her mind. How could he do this? Force her to make a choice between him or her grandmother. She really hadn't seen it coming. What a fool she was! She had thought they were going for a romantic early morning walk on the beach to finish off a wonderful June weekend, no more exams to worry about. Not this bombshell. Her emotions were all over the place. Anger and hurt welled up inside.

In the distance she could see people walking their dogs, surfers and kite-surfers out in the ocean, children building sandcastles. Sounds of laughter and waves breaking against the shore. Life going on as normal while, her world had just fallen apart. At the bottom of the dunes she began to run to escape the sound of his voice still calling after her. How could he do this? She could never leave Bayrush.

"Last day of school, Sam," said Jessie, kissing her eight-year-old son goodbye.

"See you at twelve-thirty," he called back, running across the yard. He was so excited about getting his summer holidays.

"I'm going to pick up feed for the horses. I'll be back at ten, we'll have a coffee then," said Geoff from the driver's seat of his jeep.

"Bye guys." She turned to go back upstairs to take a shower. At the top of the stairs she felt it. Her period had been two weeks late. Hope that filled her heart every month left her again. She wished their home was filled with little voices. Had her twin babies lived they would have been two years and seven months old.

She used the bathroom and went back into the bedroom. She picked up the framed photograph of her two baby boys from the dresser. No baby would ever replace them. She knew that. She held it to her heart as the tears began to flow.

She caught a glimpse of her face in the mirror. Geoff hadn't wanted to try again. He had said he couldn't go through the worry of another pregnancy. She had agreed with him but had secretly hoped it might happen. She hadn't taken protection. She looked at her reflection again. "No more," she said. Her long red curly hair was a mess and her green eyes were bloodshot and puffy. It was over. She'd go to the doctor and have the coil inserted. At least she'd feel she had taken back some control of her life. "I'm so lucky," she said. "I've a beautiful son and a great husband. Be grateful." She kissed the little faces in the frame and placed it carefully back in its place. "And I had both of you, even if it was only for a moment. You are always in my heart." She took a shower where her tears mixed with the water streaming from the shower head.

"Push!"

"I *am* pushing," cried Grace, with her legs apart on the maternity-ward bed. She was in her seventh hour of labour. Beads of sweat formed on her neck. Tendrils of her long blonde hair fell in front of her face. She had never experienced pain like it before. Her son Finn had been born by Caesarean section.

"Breathe. One, two, one two," said Jack, holding her hand in an effort to encourage her but he was just annoying.

"Shut up, Jack. Oh God. Never again. I am never doing this again."

"Not long more now," said the midwife in a soothing voice. "Just another little push."

Grace put all her might into it. Why hadn't she opted for an epidural? It wasn't like she was the earth-mother type. And then she heard the most beautiful sound in the world: "Whaaaah, whaaaah."

"Oh my God, Gracey. It's a girl," said Jack, beaming at her as the midwife placed their baby skin to skin next to her heart. It was a wondrous feeling.

"Oh Jack, she's so beautiful." Tears of joy ran down her face.

"Look at all her brown hair. No wonder you had heartburn!" Jack laughed and wiped the tears of joy from her face with his fingers. He kissed her and then leaned in to kiss their baby daughter. It was magical.

"Jack, would you like to call her after your mother?" His mother had died from cancer only two months previously. They had moved into his family home, Oak House, to look after her in her final months. Her illness had been a shock to Jack and his brother, Conor. She had refused treatment. Her wish had been to die at home looking out at the retired racehorses she had asked Jack to care for.

"Lily would be perfect." He stretched over and kissed her again. "Mum would have been pleased." Grace heard him trying to clear the lump in his throat. She knew how much he had hoped his mother could have lived to see this day. Her heart filled with love for their little baby. "Look at you, you little dotey."

"She's gorgeous. She's so like her father," said the midwife. She beamed at Jack. Grace smiled; the young girl was nearly batting her eyes at him. "How old is your little boy now?"

"Finn is two years and ten months," said Jack.

Grace could see his flash of annoyance. But the girl kept talking. "I saw him with your mother recently, Grace. He's the image of you."

Grace smiled. What she was really getting at was that Jack wasn't Finn's father. As the girl left the room, Grace whispered to Jack. "At least one of them looks like me after all my hard work."

"Nosy cow."

Grace laughed. "Oh my tummy is sore."

Kate Fitzgerald came out of the subway on Wall Street. She planned to meet Richard for lunch. He didn't approve of her using the subway. After eighteen months together, she insisted on living her life her way. She had conceded to use his town car at night, but she liked being like everybody else.

Richard Wynthrope had asked her to marry him a month after she had arrived in New York but back then she had thought it was a crazy idea. Yes, she was impulsive but not that much. He had been married before and had lost his wife and son in a horrific plane crash. It had taken him a long time to get over their deaths so Kate had suggested they take things slowly.

Until recently she had been happy in New York studying art therapy but since college had ended she had become very unsettled. Her phone rang as she entered the Wynthrope Communications Inc. building. It was Jack.

"Well." She paused. "A baby girl." She began to jump up and down in the huge marble-floored lobby. She noticed the receptionist smiling at her. It hadn't been like that the first time she had come into the building two and a half years ago. Richard was the CEO of a communications empire and it had been like trying to get an appointment to see the Pope when she had asked to speak with him.

"Jack, I'm thrilled for you both. Tell Gracey I miss her and I'll be home soon to see you all. Sophia will be so pleased too. I'm sure she'll come with me."

She hung up, and still smiling she said to the receptionist, "My sister just had a baby girl."

"That's wonderful news."

Kate smiled but as she got into the lift that would lead to her lover's top floor office, reality hit her. Sophia, Richard's mother, was the only close friend she had in New York and she was in California at the moment. She had made some friends in college but since her course had ended it had proved impossible to catch up. There always seemed to be some perfectly valid reason that one or other of them couldn't make it. Then there was Lisa, Grace's school friend who lived at the other side of the city. Lisa was busy running an events management company and hardly ever had a moment to spare. Richard worked long hours which she hadn't minded when she had been busy doing college assignments and projects. Everyone was busy, except her. When the lift opened, she clicked Sophia's number but it went into voicemail. She was probably in a meeting.

For the last few weeks, Kate's carefree breezy way had been off kilter. In truth she wasn't sure what she wanted anymore. She loved Richard but their lives were just so different, maybe that was why he had never mentioned marriage again.

Richard's secretary smiled as Kate opened the glass door.

"Hi, Colleen, is the meeting over yet?"

"In about five or ten minutes, Kate."

Kate flopped into the leather couch set a few feet from Colleen's desk, and asked, "How is your daughter getting on at her art class?"

Colleen had pinned some of her nine-year-old daughter's artwork on the notice board behind her desk and when Kate had seen it, she had recommended that Colleen should enrol her in an art class immediately.

"She loves it. Thanks to you, Kate. I've noticed her confidence is growing. She's such a gentle girl. Since her dad and I split up, it hasn't been easy for her."

"I understand how that feels," said Kate. Her father had abandoned them a year after he had given up alcohol. She had loved him so much. She remembered sitting in their hall for hours waiting for him to come back. He never had. By her sixteenth birthday, Kate's life had completely spiralled out of control. She had caused her family a lot of heartache. It had taken years of therapy to break her drug habit. Only for her sister, Grace, she might never have found her way.

The office door opened. Richard gave her a big smile. He introduced her to a tall, imposing-looking man in his sixties.

"Maurice this is Kate, my partner," said Richard. The older man looked from one to the other. His face said it all.

"Hi," said Kate, stretching out her hand. He shook it firmly.

"Nice to meet you … Kate," he said, looking her up and down, taking in her diminutive height, her nose stud and her completely off-the-wall bohemian look.

"And you," she replied, but she didn't mean it. Nobody actually said anything; they just looked at her as if to say how could *she* be with Richard? It was beginning to wear her down. She looked at Richard, her tall, handsome, caring man and she wondered what he saw in her? Then she smirked because Richard was making stupid faces behind the man's back to make her laugh. He turned quickly and nearly caught Richard, but, ever the professional, Richard managed to look poker-faced. The old guy made a hasty exit and when he was out of sight, all three of them burst out laughing.

"What are you like?" said Kate, grabbing Richard and turning him back towards the walnut door of his office to the sound of Colleen still laughing.

He pushed the office door closed with his foot and she jumped up into his arms. If only this was how it could always be, she'd be happy.

"Honey, I have the best news. I'm an auntie again. Grace had a baby girl. Did you miss me?" she whispered, kissing his ear lobe as he twirled them both around.

He laughed. "It's only been five hours. And hey, that's fantastic news."

"I'd like to go home for a few days. Can you take some time off?"

He set her down on the office desk. "There's not a chance in hell I can get away from here. But you go and I'm sure Mom will too."

She couldn't help feeling disappointed. He kissed her before she could reply and they began to make out on the office desk.

"You're a crazy woman!" he said.

"Crazy and lovable, come on, let's duck off for the rest of day."

"I can't," he said.

"Sure you can, you're the boss. Come on. It's a great day. The weather's perfect."

He hummed and hawed a bit more but she just gave him her puppy-dog gaze and pulled his arms.

"Okay, okay." He laughed as he grabbed his suit jacket.

"You won't need that, or that," she said, pulling at his tie.

"Where are we going anyway?"

As she opened the door she called to Colleen, "Colleen, cancel the rest of the day. We have to see a man about a dog."

"Fine, but is that the excuse?"

Richard laughed and added, "Who knows? But I won't be available."

Colleen laughed as they sauntered out the door.   ·

Monique's heart ached for Garvan. She stretched over and picked up her mobile phone from the bedside locker to turn off the alarm before it rang. She wondered why she had bothered setting it. She had hardly slept. She got out of bed and pulled up her jodhpurs. Putting on a polo shirt, her fingers brushed against the jagged lines of the scars that ran along her side. It was a constant reminder of the horrific car crash in Paris that had taken her parents from her. Garvan's leaving had stirred up all those old emotions.

She had wished she had died with them. Instead she had come to Ireland at the age of thirteen when the authorities discovered she had a grandmother she had never known existed. Her mother and father had always told her they had both been orphaned. How could Garvan think she could ever leave the only person who had given her the love and security she had desperately needed?

She picked up a blue rugby shirt belonging to him and held it to her face. It still smelt of him. She lay back down, curled up and buried her face into his shirt in a desperate attempt to silence her crying. She didn't want Gran to hear her through the walls of their tiny cottage. But life felt pointless again without him. She had been with him since her eighteenth birthday. Being with Garvan had added to the sense of security she craved. His family had been so welcoming to her; his Uncle Jack was even Grace's partner. As far as she had been concerned Garvan was "the one". What a fool she had been. She had better get up or else she would be late for work at Butterfly Barn.

Jessie hunched her shoulders against the rain as she ran across the yard. She stood in the shelter of the American barn, and she waved when she saw the dark-haired petite figure getting out of her gran's old red Audi. "Monique Chevalier." Jessie laughed. "We must be crazy to go out in this."

"I am glad Gran was still asleep when I was leaving."

Jessie looked up at the grey June sky. "Nora would be right. Let's go back to the house for a cuppa and wait awhile."

In the kitchen, Jessie moved the kettle to the hot-plate on the range. She noticed Monique was avoiding eye contact. Her normally twinkling brown eyes were red-rimmed and shadowed. Jessie was really worried about her, but Monique had refused to talk about Garvan's departure. Jessie just hoped that she'd open up because she was concerned that Monique would go back to the very dark place she had been in when her parents had been killed tragically. Jessie hadn't really known Nora, Monique's grandmother, back then, only to wave at as a passing neighbour. Nora had been the kind who kept to herself. Jessie had been shocked when she had heard about the crash and had called to offer her sympathy. After that, she had begun to drop in regularly because Nora's granddaughter had refused to leave the house and the poor woman had been at her wits' end. Jessie had eventually managed to convince Monique to come to the stables, telling her how they badly needed help. The ploy worked and thankfully Monique had fallen in love with horses. But more importantly Monique had made friends with Rachel and a few more young teens who had liveried their ponies at the stables. When she met Garvan Leslie it had been love at first sight. Their relationship had even survived college. He had chosen engineering in Dublin while Monique opted to study in Waterford. If I had my way I'd throttle Garvan for doing what he did, she thought. It was so completely selfish, and so insensitive to Monique who'd already been through so much. It made her mad just thinking about him.

Monique's phone bleeped. Jessie looked at it. "Are you going to check it?

"No, it is probably Garvan. Are the Butterfly Barn log cabins full this week, Jess?" asked Monique, putting two slices of bread into the toaster. Jessie took Monique's hint to change the subject.

"Yes, thankfully all four are full with families."

"And the self-catering in the courtyard?"

"Two of the four are full and they are completely booked out next week. It's hard to believe it is only eighteen months since 'Jessie's Angel' won her first horse race. I truly believe my babies are watching over us. I dreamed of Butterfly Barn but without Sophia and Grace it would never have happened so quickly or be rated five stars and accommodate forty people. They are both like whirlwinds," said Jessie, pouring tea for them. She noticed Monique looking at her phone again. "Is it Garvan?"

Looking up, Monique nodded; Jessie could see she was close to tears. She was just so glad Monique had the literacy weekend to get her teeth stuck into. Monique's passion for literacy had driven both her and Sophia crazy enough to host a weekend workshop.

"Come on girly, the rain is clearing," said Jessie, getting up. "The fresh air will do us good." Jessie's mobile rang as she walked across the yard. She looked at the screen. "Hi Jack." She listened.

"It's a girl," she shouted to Monique. "Oh Jack, that's fantastic news. Lily, ah that's lovely too. We'll be in later to see them. I'm sure Grace will need some rest now. Jack, I'm really delighted for you both. See you later." She clicked off and smiled at Monique who came over and gave her a big hug.

Jessie was so grateful for Monique's hug especially because of what had happened earlier but she'd never tell anybody about that.

"I am thrilled for Grace and Jack."

"I know you are," said Monique. "But you wouldn't be normal if there was not a piece of you that was, well, you know."

"Thanks for understanding. I'll be okay. I can't wait to see them."

"Me too," said Monique. "Let's ride out the horses and get over to the hospital as soon as we can."

"Don't forget you are going on the radio at eleven to talk about Butterfly Barn."

"How could I forget? My stomach is full of butterflies."

"Ha, ha, good one," said Jessie, leading Beauty out of her stable.

Donagh Mullally parked his jeep on Bayrush Beach promenade. He looked out towards the ocean where the waves were perfect for surfing. He was about to turn off the engine when he heard a radio interview about a place called Butterfly Barn. The girl had an unusual accent that made him want to listen. His friends were waiting for him and yet he couldn't move.

"So Butterfly Barn is up and running."

"Yes Steve, last weekend we hosted a group for parents who had lost a baby in pregnancy or very early childhood. It was a wonderful success. People found the weekend uplifting."

"I can't imagine how that could be, considering the topic you were dealing with," remarked Steve James, a presenter known for his bullet-shot interviewing technique.

"The concept of the weekend was to gather people together who had experienced this huge loss, not necessarily to speak of it. Just to be in a place with others who understand how it feels. The guests took part in a range of activities from hillwalking, to pottery making, to spending time alone. Some went horse riding but there were also people on hand who are trained to help people come to terms with loss."

"Mmm, so is that what Butterfly Barn is all about?"

"Our wish is to offer a range of workshops and activities to diverse groups of people. We plan to host summer camps for kids and adults with special needs, but also there will be workshops open to everybody. There will be writers' weekends, cookery courses. It is open to all sorts of ideas. For example, the weekend after next there is just one place remaining on a workshop which will help people who have problems with reading and writing."

"Don't we have a government service for that? What difference can one weekend make?"

Donagh felt himself getting defensive for her. He was never that fond of Steve James. He always seemed to be looking for an argument. She was one brave girl to go on his show, thought Donagh.

"Yes, we do indeed have an excellent service, which we plan to work in tandem with. We hope the weekend will help people who want to learn to read but are afraid to make the move within their local area. They have hidden their problem for years. We are offering a chance to attend Butterfly Barn at an affordable rate using various ground-breaking and interesting techniques to help them with their learning. The first step is always the hardest."

"I can't imagine there are many people affected by this problem in this day and age."

"Actually, the last report from the OECD showed that one in six people in Ireland have a problem understanding basic written information and one in four people find numeracy very difficult. This figure is similar in the UK.

"Well, I must admit, I for one am intrigued. So for all you listeners out there, this could be your chance to change your life. I hope you don't mind my asking but why are you so passionate about this subject?"

"I live with my grandmother who was a librarian. She has devoted ten years to volunteering as a literacy tutor. As soon as I was old enough I volunteered."

"So for more information contact this lovely young girl Monique Chevalier on 082-2112341."

"Thank you for inviting me, Steve."

"It's been a pleasure and I must say I love your French accent."

She laughed and said, "Sometimes I have a problem pronouncing the letter h."

"I'm glad you do." Steve laughed.

Donagh smiled – she had even managed to charm the bold Steve. Her accent had been the reason he had listened. He could hardly believe it when she had begun to talk about a problem that haunted him all of his life. He found reading difficult and his handwriting was awful too. He was twenty-five years old with a head full of dreams to someday own a surf school of his own. It would never come true if he didn't take steps to address his problem. Could this be his chance? But what if someone recognised him? The girl had said that the people on the course would not be from the local area. He'd think about it. He grabbed his surfboard and joined his pals.

Kate had arrived with Richard to yet another Manhattan cocktail party. She felt uncomfortable. Richard was talking to two elderly men, one of whom she knew was a complete sleazeball. With nothing better to do she wandered away from them to the restroom. She missed Sophia; if only more people were like her she could cope. Why the hell did it matter so much what people thought of her? She had enough of being looked down on. Their glances spoke volumes. She sat in the cubicle with the toilet seat lid down, forlorn. She heard women's voices. Then she realised they were talking about her.

"My, but what is Richard doing with her? His wife, Heather, was so beautiful, unlike her. She's like a little elf and her accent is just awful."

The other woman sniggered. "You mean 'leprechaun', that's what the Irish call little people. And what about the nose stud? I mean really. What can he possibly see in her?"

Outraged, Kate swung the cubicle door open and with her head held high, she said, "It's the sex. It's fabulous." She took her time washing her hands and checking her face in the mirror. She could see their stunned faces in the corner of her eye as she turned on her heels and walked out. Thankfully she didn't trip. Her eyes filled with unshed tears. She wanted to go home but her pride wouldn't let them win. She bit her lip to stop her tears. They were right. Heather was stunning and from what Richard had told her, she was also a great person and wonderful mother. How much more could her self-esteem take? Maybe she'd consider going to a stylist the next time she had to attend one of these blasted functions. But a part of her screamed inside, I am who I am and I don't want to change.

Chapter Two

Sophia drove through the gates of Oak House and continued up the long curving tree-lined avenue. Grace had suggested that she and Kate wait until she was home from hospital. Grace wanted to be able to spend some time with them.

"It will be fabulous if they are lucky enough to win the lotto. The setting is just beautiful," said Kate. Sophia smiled; Kate always spoke her mind but she was right. The Georgian house was painted a light shade of pink that was peeling in places. It had two long windows on either side of the white front door and five across the top floor. The area around it could be described as parkland with lots of mature oak and birch trees. One tree had a swing tyre hanging from it and another one nearest to the house had an old chipped white cast iron table and chairs under it.

"Grace said there was a herb and vegetable garden behind the house. I can't imagine our Gracey having time to maintain that." Kate laughed.

The front door opened and little Finn's blond head appeared. He tottered into Sophia's arms.

"Hey dude, I'm your auntie," said Kate just as Grace came to the door with the baby in her arms. "But I get to hold Lily first."

"Hi sis," said Grace, kissing Kate on the cheek and passing over the baby.

"Oh, you are so beautiful. Gracey you didn't get a look in."

Sophia laughed at Grace's expression.

"I was going to ask you to be godmother, but I think I'll change my mind."

"Oh no, you can't. I'm going to be your godmother, little girl. Lucky you. You'll get away with murder with me," said Kate.

"I'm regretting it already." Grace laughed. "Come in, thankfully Jessie is here making lunch."

"Hi girls, she has me run ragged here," called Jessie from the kitchen where Kate went to join her with the baby in her arms while Sophia had a moment alone with Grace.

"It's so good to see you," said Sophia. She surprised herself with the emotion in her voice as she hugged her friend.

"Me too. Finn is so excited all morning."

"See horseys," said Finn, pulling Sophia towards the lane leading to the yard.

"Give her a minute, Finn. Let's go inside and have some lunch. You can show Sophia your tractors and trailers."

Finn caught Sophia's hand and led her into the house. She hardly had a chance to see Baby Lily. "Oh Grace, she is so beautiful. I can't wait to hold her. Hi Jessie," she called to Grace's best friend, as Finn dragged her across the kitchen to where his tractors were stored.

"I'm afraid Finn is going to take you over for a while, Sophia. We'll get a proper hello in a few minutes," said Jessie.

Sophia spent the next ten minutes on the floor in the corner of the large kitchen with Finn admiring multiple tractors and trailers while the girls caught up.

"Did I tell you Mam started a computer course?" asked Grace as she chopped some tomatoes. "She has my head wrecked asking me questions about the internet, and apps I've never even heard of."

Sophia laughed.

"She told me the other day that I was useless and that I wasn't with it at all. I'm already feeling like I'm brain dead. She's just great for a girl's ego, not." Grace smiled, as she began to grate some cheese.

"Wait a sec, who's supposed to be making the lunch?" said Jessie, putting down the chopping knife.

Grace grinned at her. "Okay, okay, I'll get out of the way."

"I'm sure I'll hear all about it when I meet your mum later at Rose Cottage. Nora and Eoghan are coming too," said Sophia, as she finally managed to take Lily from Kate's clutches to coo over her.

"Come on girls, tuck in, while the mama is between feeds," said Jessie, bringing some plates to the table. "She's adorable." Jessie had leaned over to coo at Lily. Sophia's heart broke for her. It must be so hard for her, she thought. The look that passed between them spoke volumes. Sophia touched Jessie's arm. Jessie smiled gratefully.

"She's so like Jack. It's so nice that you called her after Jack's mother," said Jessie. Sophia could see Jessie gathering herself and sitting down.

"How is Jack since she passed on?" Sophia asked.

"I just wish she had gone to the doctor earlier. Things might have turned out differently. She wanted to see the baby so much. I'm glad we moved in though, it gave Jack a chance to spend valuable time with her."

"I'd say you miss Rose Cottage," said Kate. "Not saying anything, sis, but ..."

Sophia looked around. It was true; the place was in need of redecorating.

"Kate, having this place even in its ramshackle state has given Jack a chance to set up his own vet's practice. He has so many contacts from his time working in Dubai that many of the racehorse owners were prepared to pay well to home their retired racehorses here. That will help to bring in some income while he gets the business off the ground."

The back door opened. It was Jack with Jay. "Hi, girls, it's great to see you. You both remember Jay. He's working with me now."

"Of course, what a day we had when you won the horse race on Jessie's Angel!" said Kate. "How's Rachel?"

"She's in the office sending an important email to Pal Pacific," said Jay, taking off his kickers. "She'll be here in a few minutes."

"We converted one of the stables into an office. Girls, I'd be lost without Rachel. Since she finished college she has been working for me. It's just bedlam around here. The first cruise liner will be arriving on Wednesday and Eoghan is already tearing his hair out."

At the mention of Eoghan's name, Sophia smiled. She was so looking forward to seeing him. "Is Eoghan coming for lunch too?"

"No, he is out and about all day finalising things."

Sophia felt a hint of disappointment even though he was coming over to Rose Cottage later. "Lily is seven days old. Are you not taking maternity leave?"

"The joys of being self-employed and working from home, Sophia. Ah to be fair, Rachel and Eoghan are looking after things but I suppose it's hard to take a back seat."

"I'd love to help on Wednesday," said Kate.

"I thought you were only staying for a few days," said Sophia.

"Grace clearly needs a dig out. Don't you, sis?"

Sophia saw the look that passed from Kate to Grace. It said you better back me up. What was going on? Sophia wondered. Perhaps things between her son and Kate were not as steady as she had thought after all.

"Thanks Kate, that would be great."

"She thinks she's superwoman Sophia, with two small kids, a book that needs promoting, and running Ireland for Real. Something has got to give," said Jack, stirring sugar into his tea.

Grace threw her eyes up to heaven. "He's off again. Rachel is doing a great job with Ireland for Real. The book will just have to do its own thing. And I know I will eventually find the right person or place for the kids. It just takes time."

"And she still won't marry me," said Jack, buttering a slice of brown bread.

Sophia smiled. "Well, who has a bee in his bonnet today?"

"There's a marriage proposal every day in this house. I thought he'd have her worn down by now. If she doesn't say yes, I'll have to marry him myself," said Jay.

"Jeez, Grace, aren't you going to save me from that prospect?"

They were all laughing when Rachel walked in.

"Hi everyone, what's so funny?" she asked.

"Please don't get them started again," said Grace.

"God, I miss this in America. I miss the banter as well as everyone," said Kate, wistfully.

Sophia looked at her but she understood how Kate felt. She loved being back too.

"More tea, anyone," said Grace. Sophia knew it was to fill the silence after Kate's comment.

After lunch, she dropped Kate off at her mother Molly's terraced house, just off the square in Bayrush. She smiled when she saw Molly hug Kate. She knew how much Kate missed her. Kate had lived with her mother until she had moved to be with Richard in New York.

"Molly, I'll see you later at Rose Cottage," she called from the car and left them to catch up. She drove towards the beach and her heart lightened when Rose Cottage came into view. When she had first come to Ireland she had rented it with Grace. She couldn't believe her luck when the owners had decided to sell. It was a two-storey dormer thatched cottage with a cedar-wood deck running along the back of it. The view was incredible from the upstairs living room.

Sophia planned to stay in Ireland for the summer. She wanted to get involved with Butterfly Barn and to help with Grace and the baby. But she was beginning to wonder if Kate would need her more in New York. She unpacked and brought the shopping in from the car. She was looking forward to cooking for Eoghan and the ladies.

A couple of hours later she put the final touches to the table. She heard the crunch of tyres on the pebble drive. She opened the door immediately and her face lit up when she saw Eoghan was the first to arrive. She had been away for two whole months. Richard rarely needed her these days but he had wanted her opinion on a takeover bid he was planning and it had taken longer than she had anticipated.

As he walked towards her, she took in his handsome face. He wore his trademark deck shoes and jeans. He smiled and ran his hand through his

Leabharlann
6378047
Contae na Mídhe

thick grey hair. "Hello you," he said, walking towards her.

She had to stop herself from running into his arms she was so happy to see him. You are just friends, she told herself. There had been so many moments over the past few years when something might have happened between them but she had been still grieving the loss of her husband and Eoghan was the kind of person who would never put her in a predicament. Even so she couldn't help wondering if she had purposely staying away longer in the hope he would miss her as much as she had missed him.

"You look great. Your hair is a little shorter and lighter from the sun," he said, kissing her on both cheeks the way he always greeted her.

She was pleased he had noticed she had returned to her shoulder-length bob but it hadn't been the sun that had lightened it. Always good to have a fantastic hairdresser; she smiled but didn't share her thoughts. "So do you and you've managed to get a tan already."

"Weather-beaten!" He laughed.

Nora's old Audi came down the drive and a pang of disappointment at having to share him hit her.

"Always on time," said Eoghan.

Had she detected a small hint of regret in his voice, she wondered?

After dinner, Eoghan and Molly sat on the upper deck of Rose Cottage. Even though it was growing dark, there were still people on the beach barbequing, and sounds of laughter floated on the air. Sophia was just coming through the French doors with a Waterford Crystal tumbler for Eoghan, when Molly declared, "Well, you're a dark horse, Sophia Wynthrope!"

Sophia passed the glass to Eoghan and looked at Molly with a confused expression. "I'm sorry ...?"

"I was at my computer class learning all about the internet and the tutor said look up something that you are interested in. The others were looking up movie stars. I was going to look up about Lauren Bacall ..."

"What's this got to do with Sophia being a dark horse, Molly?" asked Eoghan, his tone defensive. He was always looking out for her, thought Sophia. But her heart was pounding. She knew where Molly was going with this.

"Aren't I trying to tell you, Eoghan?" said Molly, impatiently.

Sophia could feel Nora had tensed too.

"I looked up Wynthrope Communications because that's the name of Richard's business, and I wanted to know about it. Sophia, I think you're just brilliant ..." Molly kept talking about how Sophia and her husband had built their business into one of the top magazine publishers in America.

She was in the throes of listing off the names of the magazines. Nora was super impressed but Sophia could see Eoghan was not. He took two slugs of the brandy she had just given him. As soon as there was a pause in Molly's monologue, he turned and looked at her with an expression she had never seen before and said, "Well now, isn't that all very interesting? I think I'll call it a night. I'll see myself out."

Molly looked at Nora. Sophia could felt her heart sinking. She stood up.

"No need, I said I'll see myself out." She sat back down.

"What hurry are you in Eoghan?" asked Molly, oblivious to the effect her words had had on Eoghan.

Thankfully Nora intervened. "Goodnight Eoghan," she said, firmly.

"Goodnight Nora," he replied. Then he was gone.

"What's his problem?" asked Molly, looking from Nora to Sophia.

"Will you have another?" asked Sophia.

"I'll get it," said Nora, "I think you definitely need one, Sophia and so do I."

"Was it something I said?" asked Molly, completely confused.

"Oh Molly," said Nora, bringing the brandy bottle out from the drinks cabinet and topping up Sophia's glass and then her own.

"What about me?" asked Molly, holding out her glass. Sophia, and Nora exchanged a smile.

"Molly you're unbelievable," said Nora.

Molly continued talking about her computer class. Sophia knew that Nora was encouraging Molly to chat on, allowing her some space. Why hadn't she told them just as Richard had suggested two years ago? They would never have judged her. What was so terrible about being successful? Why had she had such a hang-up about it? Eoghan surely knew she had money. After all she lived between two countries and she drove a Mercedes. He knew she had invested in Butterfly Barn. Why was he making such a big deal?

"What do you think, Sophia?" asked Molly.

"I'm sorry." She had no idea what the women were taking about. "What do I think of what?"

"Of Eoghan."

"He's a gentleman."

"That he is," agreed Molly. "I often wondered had he ever married. Isn't it gas to think we know nothing about him! Sure, we all have our secrets. I don't know why he reacted that way to me saying all that about you. I hope I haven't offended you, Sophia."

"No Molly, not at all. I suppose I should have told you."

"Why?" said Nora. "It's not any of our business. We are friends and as Molly says, we all have a past and secrets that we don't necessarily feel we need to share. Isn't that what friendship is? Accepting people as you find them."

"Thank you, Nora," said Sophia. She had been terrified that Nora felt the same way as Eoghan but was too well mannered to storm out.

"I agree with Nora. Meeting all of you over these past years has lifted my spirits. It's important to meet new people and do new things at our age. Who knew I'd sign up for computer classes ..." Molly was off again. That was why Sophia loved her so much, she never let things bother her too much.

At the end of the evening when Sophia showed them out, Nora squeezed her hand. "It will be alright. I'll bet he'll be knocking on the door in the morning when he realises he overreacted."

"Thanks Nora, I really hope so."

Donagh had finally found the courage to make the call. He got the last place on the literacy workshop. On Friday evening, he parked his jeep beside a converted barn. When he walked around to the front entrance, it was like an architect's dream. There was a wooden deck with outside seating and a view across a large lake where the evening sun glistened. He even spotted a pair of swans. The whole gable end from floor to ceiling was glass. His heart was thumping so loudly he could nearly hear it. What had he let himself in for? It had taken all his power to step out of the jeep but he had no choice. He had to face up to his problem finally. A woman with long, curly auburn hair came out to greet him. She had a great smile, he thought.

"You must be Donagh. I'm Jessie and you're very welcome."

"Cheers, eh thanks, how did you know my name?"

"You're the last to arrive," she smiled again. "Come on in. There are just six in the group. Monique will host the workshop and Sophia and I will be helpers. So we will all be learning together. If it's any consolation I'm just as scared as you are."

Donagh smiled for the first time as he followed her into the beautiful building. Nobody spoke. He felt awkward and could easily have turned and walked back out. One woman in her fifties smiled at him. He half acknowledged her. What I am doing here? he thought.

"So you are all very welcome," said Jessie. "I thought it would be nice if you'd like to chat to the person beside you and then maybe introduce them to the rest of us. I think it is a nice way to get to know people. Also I would like everyone to respect one another and that anything people disclose here will remain here."

People seemed to relax when Jessie said that and they began to turn and chat amongst themselves. Donagh looked at the person beside him. She was a cool-looking girl in her thirties, he figured. She had an earring in her nose and wore a pair of Docs with a long flowery skirt.

"I'm Viv," she said with an English accent. She told him art was her thing but school hadn't been. "I'm not thick or anything, ya know what I mean. Just ducked it as much as I could. It didn't go down too well at home so I left and haven't seen any of them for years. That's life." She didn't seem to have any problems disclosing.

He just shrugged his shoulders and said, "Fair enough."

"So what's your name?"

"Donagh."

"What kind of name is that?"

"I was called after my grandfather. It's an old Irish name."

"How do you say it again?"

"Just say 'done' and add an a."

"So Done–a. What's the story? Why are you here?"

She was so direct; he didn't know what to say. Thankfully the time was up.

"We'll start with Frank. Can you tell us a little about Sonya?" asked Jessie.

Donagh looked at Sonya, a woman in her late forties with very dark hair and a closed-looking face to go with it. He could see how uncomfortable she was and he found himself empathising. She was an only child who had had to care for her sick mother and she had missed a lot of school. Sonya spoke about Frank, a man in his fifties, wearing a Ralph Lauren shirt and well-cut jeans. He was a successful builder but his sister had passed away recently. She was the only person who knew that he couldn't read. He was worried that his workers might find out and think he was stupid. Every head in the room nodded in agreement.

Trevor, a rough-looking character with a scar along his right cheek, introduced Imelda, a blonde good-looking woman in her late fifties who was happily married with five grown-up children. "They don't know she can't read," said Trevor.

"This is Trevor," said Imelda, gathering herself. "He hopes to get a taxi licence or a lorry driver's licence. His other dream is to be able to read bedtime stories to his two beautiful children."

Donagh felt guilty for judging Trevor.

Monique could feel a lump form in her throat as she listened to Imelda. Then it was the young guy's turn. When he smiled his blue eyes lit up. She had noticed that all the women, even the older ones, had noticed him when he came into the room. He was tall with dark blond hair that looked untameable,. He also looked extremely fit and although it was only early summer his sallow skin was tanned. There was a hint of mystery about him. As he spoke she noticed his front tooth was slightly chipped in otherwise perfect white teeth. It gave his face even more character.

"This is Viv, she's into art and school was never her thing."

"Dead on mate," said Viv, with a Cockney accent. "This is Donagh. Weird name! Doesn't talk much about himself! So I don't have much to say. I reckon by the look of him, he's into water sports, surfing and stuff like that."

Donagh smiled and nodded.

"Thanks everybody. I'm Jessie, as you already know. I've had a chance to speak to you by phone. I'd like to introduce Sophia, who is a director here and will be helping over the weekend, and Monique, who will be your tutor. She is passionate about literacy and it is thanks to her that we agreed to host the workshop. All we ask is that you keep an open mind and enjoy your time here; it won't be all about reading and writing. We truly hope it will make a difference."

Monique blushed and when she caught the guy called Donagh looking at her, she felt even more uncomfortable. She was glad when Jessie suggested showing people to their accommodation.

The next morning, Monique's head was full of thoughts as she rode Jasper, her black horse, along beside the lake on her usual early morning ride out. She was so excited about the day ahead. But she was tired too. Garvan had kept texting her through the night, telling her how much he missed her and that there were so many job opportunities for her too. Words she had so needed to hear. Although she was angry with him she still loved him. She sighed. It was so hard to walk away from their four-year relationship but it was something she would have to do either that or join him.

A huge part of her wished he'd come back, if he missed her as much as he said. But with each passing day that seemed more and more unlikely. Rachel and Jay were so supportive but she just felt like a spare part. She was so used to being part of a couple. It bugged her that she felt so needy. It was a side of herself that she didn't recognise. It had been easy to be independent when she had felt loved.

As she reached Butterfly Barn, she saw Donagh sitting on the end of the jetty smoking a cigarette. It was only seven o'clock in the morning.

He turned towards her almost as though he knew he was being watched. There was something about him that … What am I doing even looking at him? I'm going to be his tutor, she thought. "Come on, Jasper, let's go or I will be late."

Donagh didn't know how he felt about the course being run by someone his age or maybe was even younger than him. For some reason she bothered him. She wasn't the kind of girl he'd go for. There was something about her, all dark hair and dark eyes and that very sexy French accent. He preferred blonde uncomplicated types.

He blew smoke up into the clear blue sky. He liked the peace of the place, not like his parents' house. His father would be setting off for a day's golf, while his mother spent the day rushing and racing after his younger brothers. Jessie had suggested that he stay on site for the weekend even though he lived nearby. He hadn't disagreed because his father would hit the roof if he heard he was learning to read with a bunch of "misfits". If somebody saw him what would they think? His father was all about image. John Mullally, successful business man's son can't read properly. What a disappointment he had turned out to be!

Sophia woke and checked her phone just as she had done since Eoghan had walked out. There were no missed calls or texts from him. She walked across the bedroom and unlocked the door leading to the cedar-wood decking. The morning was sunny and the ocean was calm. The serious surfers would be disappointed, she thought, but the day-trippers would be joyous.

She looked at her phone again and searched for her favourite photograph of him. She rubbed her thumb across his handsome face. She had taken the photograph one day when they were sailing. His dark blue eyes danced out at her. It was a look she was used to, not like the last time she had seen him. Realising the time, she went back inside to shower. She had to be at Butterfly Barn for nine-thirty. She was glad to be involved with the literacy weekend. It meant she had less time to think.

Chapter Three

Monique set up the flip chart and connected her laptop to the interactive white board. She tidied the A4 notepads and fixed things for the hundredth time. Nervous tension filled her stomach. She was so grateful to Jessie and Sophia for allowing her to use the skills she had learned from one-to-one tutoring mixed with her degree in English and diploma in teaching and adult education. She had spent so long researching and attending training courses about the different ways people learn; it felt great to have a chance to put her ideas into practice. The group began to arrive and gather in the training room.

When people were seated, she took a deep breath and said, "Good morning everyone, I am looking forward to spending the next few days with you all. Firstly, today will be all about you building on your own strengths. We plan to divide the day into indoor and outdoor activities. I would like everybody to take a moment. Please uncross your legs and place both feet on the ground. Take some deep breaths. By that I mean, draw in your breath and feel it reach into the pit of your stomach. On the outward breath blow out any anxieties you might have about the next few days because this is your special time. It is an opportunity to look deeply into you and hopefully do some reconnecting. On the inward breath, think of taking in new air. Freshness, a new beginning, a new way of thinking, now blow out the negative stuff and take in the new." In, out, in, out. They continued in silence for about a minute.

"Anybody feel like sharing? How did that feel?"

"You're crazy." Viv was angry.

"Why do you think that?" she asked.

"Firstly, the breathing thing. I wish it were that easy to just blow all my problems away. It's not that simple, you know."

"I just want you to feel good about being here."

"I came here to learn to read and write. What's that supposed to be about?" Frank muttered.

"Would anybody else like to share their feelings about what we have done?"

There was silence. Monique's heart was pounding in her chest. It was all going terribly wrong. Why had she asked for this? She noticed Imelda, the blonde woman, shuffling in her seat as though she was going to say something. But another voice spoke.

"Yes, I would like to," said Donagh. "Last night." He looked around at everybody in the group, "Jessie talked about how we were going to experience something different. She said it was not going to be all about reading and writing. She asked us to be open. So how about it?" He looked specifically at Frank and Viv.

Both looked a little sheepish. Then Viv spoke. "Suppose you're right. She did say that. Hey, I'm sorry, just I get a bit angry at times."

He looked at Frank, who shrugged and said, "What have we got to lose?"

"Thank you," said Monique, trying hard not to show how ruffled she was. She caught Donagh's eye and he smiled. Her stomach fluttered as she continued speaking. "For the next exercise, I'd like you to pair up and sit directly opposite each other. Then talk for about three minutes about your expectations for the weekend. One person is to speak while the other must only listen. Then reverse roles."

Everybody paired up. There was a buzz of noise, settling chairs, embarrassed laughter and then people got into the idea of it.

"The time is up," she said. "Now, this time I want you to use body language to show that you are not interested and not listening to the person who is speaking. Then reverse roles.

She found it comical watching people pretending not to listen. Some were very animated and dramatic. Then she asked for feedback. "Would anybody like to tell me how it felt when the person listened?"

"Valued," Trevor called. She wrote the word on the white board.

"Worthwhile," said Sonya.

"Like I had found a friend," said Viv.

"I got a real feeling of empathy," Imelda added.

"That somebody cared and felt very similar to me. I was very, very anxious about coming here," said Frank.

She noticed everybody looking at Frank in amazement. He had been hard to talk to and gave the impression of being a little above it. She exchanged a glance of relief with Sophia who mouthed, "You're doing great."

Donagh hadn't said anything.

"And the feelings when nobody listened?" she asked.

They all laughed and she could hardly write down all the words that came from the not listening exercise. Worthless, piece of dirt, an inconvenience, uninteresting, boring, stupid, of no value.

"I felt like nobody's child," said Donagh. The words had come out while everybody had been shouting up.

Monique felt a chill at the back of her neck. What had happened to him? What was it about him that made her feel so …? She turned and wrote what he had said on the board. She did it slowly because she needed time to compose herself. "So these are the messages we send when we do not listen. This can be particularly dangerous with children. Parents often dismiss their child, not realising the effect it can have on their self-esteem. Let's brainstorm. Who do you think are the some of the most effective communicators in our world?"

"Bill Clinton," Trevor said.

"Why?"

"Because he's so handsome," Viv piped up.

She laughed and asked, "Do you think that's a requirement?"

"Ah, not really. But I suppose it comes in handy to be easy on the eye. He's – what's the word? – *carry* something."

"Charismatic," Frank said.

"Yeah, charismatic, that's the word I meant."

"He always looks like he's really listening," said Imelda. "Somebody told me they met him when he came to Ireland. The man said he made people feel like they were the only person in the room. Now that must be something special."

"Thanks for that," said Monique. "You all got the point completely and so quickly. Good communication is more about listening than we think. I'd like you to think about the activities we have completed and make an attempt to write down something about what you have learned from these exercises. You can copy the words from the board or simply tell one of us and we can help you. It is not a competition. Work at your own pace and it will be your personal opinion so you cannot be wrong." She caught Donagh looking at her; he looked away quickly and picked up his notebook.

"Monique, can you help me out here, please?" asked Imelda, from across the room.

"Of course," she replied, going over to join her. Sophia and Jessie helped too and the rest of the morning flew by as the class completed a series of other reading and writing exercises she had prepared.

In the afternoon, Geoff was in charge of activities. He had suggested kayaking. She had thought it might be a nice way to get the group to bond and just relax and enjoy themselves.

Her phone bleeped just as she struggled to get into the wet suit.

<Hi Mon, thinking of u. Are you going out tonight? I miss u>

What was he playing at? He had left her. She tossed the phone into the bottom of her kit bag.

As she walked towards the lake, Trevor whistled. She smiled and joined in. Everybody seemed to be getting into the spirit of it all. She was enjoying kayaking until Geoff suggested a relay race. As the relay progressed Frank had created a significant lead for their team. She set off to a good start. She could hear the team shouting her on in the distance; all she had to do was circle around the buoy and head back. No big deal until she heard the other kayak gaining on her. Stupidly, she turned around and must have done something with the paddle. The next moment she could feel the kayak wobbling,. The more she tried to balance the worse it got, and then she toppled over. She panicked underwater. It was overwhelmingly dark. She couldn't remember Geoff's instructions. She struggled to release herself from the kayak. She pulled desperately at the cover and just as she managed to break free, she felt an arm around her waist and then she was brought to the surface.

"I would have remembered what to do!" she spluttered.

"I'm sure you would 'ave," said Donagh, mimicking her accent. He grinned and swam back to his kayak. She didn't know if she was flustered from the fright of being stuck underwater or if it was his close proximity. There was no way she'd be able to get back into her kayak.

"Hey Mon, are you okay?" called Geoff from the rubber inflatable boat.

"Yes, yes, I am fine," she said, bobbing in the water with her life jacket. She felt like a drowned rat. She pushed her hair out of her face.

"Think you lost the race." Geoff laughed, nodding in the direction of Donagh, who was paddling back to the shore. He pulled her onto the boat.

"I'm afraid I have let the team down."

"I don't think they care too much. Take a look." They were all laughing and cheering on the jetty. Geoff put the boat into full throttle and she nearly went flying again.

"Are you trying to kill me?" She laughed as the wind blew into her face. "I love it. Faster, Geoff."

"Hold on tight," he roared above the noise of the engine just as he turned the boat to do a wide arc. It was thrilling. She was disappointed when she had to go back in. "I'll teach you how to drive it, eh!"

"That would be fantastic."

They all gave her a cheer as Geoff pulled up to the jetty. "I guess kayaking is not for me." She laughed.

"But speed boat racing is," said Donagh, holding out his hand to help her off the boat. She paused for a bare second before taking it. Touching his fingers sent electric shocks through her body. If she pulled away she'd fall in again. Oh God, had he felt it too? If he had, he didn't show it. He was obviously the kind of guy who was used to women falling at his feet.

"Stick to the day job, Monique," Trevor joked.

"Ah leave her alone," said Imelda, linking her as they walked up from the jetty towards the barn. "She can't be good at everything."

"Thanks, Imelda." She smiled.

"Lads, it's a perfect evening for a barbeque. Let's meet again at seven," said Geoff. Everybody agreed and set off in the direction of their cabins. Monique decided to go home to shower and freshen up and walk back later. Her gran's cottage was only at the end of the lane.

A couple of hours later, she strolled back along the lane. In the distance she could see Donagh helping Geoff. She hadn't been able to stop thinking about him. Twice today he had helped her. Once in the classroom and then in the lake, yet he hardly spoke to her. When she reached Butterfly Barn, she joined Sonya who was sitting on the deck sipping a Coke.

"Are you enjoying the weekend?" she asked. Earlier, she had noticed that Sonya had found kayaking extremely challenging because she was terrified of water. But with everybody's encouragement she had pushed out her boundaries.

"Frank was so supportive to me today, Monique. I can't believe I actually got into a kayak. I don't know what I expected would happen this weekend but I've been here less than twenty-four hours and I feel better about everything," said Sonya. "My mother was always poorly so I was the one who took care of her. I missed so much school it was hard to catch up and then I just gave up trying. I left as soon as I could. When my mother's sight deteriorated, she could no longer read. She asked me to rent some audio books from the library. Oh Monique, it opened a completely new world for me. I used to listen with her. My mother loved the classics, the Bronte sisters, Jane Austen, Charles Dickens. I can quote lines from them, if only I could learn to read the words."

"It will happen for you, Sonya. The literacy service is waiting for calls from people like you. They will organise one-to-one tuition. Coming here is just the start of your journey."

"Thanks Monique, I'll go and help Jessie set out the salads."

Monique wandered off towards the lake. She had tried to ring Garvan earlier but there had been no answer. It was pointless putting off the inevitable. She was not moving to Dubai. She tried his number again; it went into his voicemail.

"Hi, Garvan, please call me when you have a moment." She turned to walk back. Donagh was standing on the jetty, smoking a cigarette again.

"Hi," he said.

She stopped. "I owe you an apology. I panicked earlier."

"Water sports can be very scary when things go wrong. But you do seem to like the adrenaline rush of them. Have you tried surfing?"

"I have never tried. I imagine it is very difficult to balance, no."

"You should try it some time."

"Maybe. Horse riding is my thing. I would spend all of my time with them if I could. But I have to earn a living."

"Is this what you do all the time?"

"I should not admit it but this is a first for me. I have just finished college. I am job hunting. And you?"

"A carpenter."

"Hey, Mon, Donagh, food's up," Geoff called from the patio.

Jessie sat with Sophia on the deck sipping wine. The sun was going down and the air was balmy. She watched as people milled around chatting. In the distance Geoff caught her eye and raised his beer bottle in salute. She raised her glass to him and smiled.

"What a day, Sophia!"

"Monique is doing a wonderful job," said Sophia quietly. "It was fascinating to see how much people learn by observation, listening, doing, and interpersonal skills. It is amazing how people adapt without being able to read beyond the very basics. Imagine how much further they will progress with help."

"I believe by offering such a range of workshops and activities that can impact people's lives in a positive way, Butterfly Barn is becoming more than I ever dreamed of," said Jessie.

"Jessie, it is my ambition to bring Butterfly Barn further. I haven't quite figured it out yet. If we could bottle it and send it out, it could make a difference, couldn't it?"

"Yes, and if anyone can find a way it will be you. Now, on another note, any word from Eoghan?"

"Nothing."

"Did you ring him?"

"No."

"Why not?"

"Why should I! He walked out of Rose Cottage. He doesn't want to speak to me."

Jessie looked at her friend. Sophia's face was always alight and welcoming but since the incident with Eoghan she wasn't herself. She and Grace had always hoped that Sophia and Eoghan would eventually get together. They had something special.

"Go and see him, Sophia. Give him a chance."

"Will I top you up?" asked Sophia, getting up to get some more wine.

"Yes, thanks." Jessie smiled at Sophia's way of changing the subject.

The next morning Monique had already formed a circle with the seats before the group had arrived. "Good morning everybody, I hope you are all ready for the day."

There were a few groans and moans.

"Go easy on us now, Monique," Frank called out as he held his head.

"In that case how about us taking a few moments this morning to meditate. If you are not comfortable about it, please feel free to opt out."

"I'd like to try it," said Sonya.

"So would I," Trevor added.

So Monique talked them through the process. After it, eyes began to open. Frank was obviously bursting to say something. "Anyone like to share?"

"I was thinking if anyone saw me in here listening to birds twittering and sitting around candles in the early morning they'd have me locked up. But," Frank added, wagging a finger at her, "I got something from that." He leaned back in his seat, with his legs stretched out in front and crossed at the ankles, in a contented pose.

"Yeah Frank, I thought the same," said Trevor. "It was real peaceful."

The others nodded in agreement. She noticed Donagh didn't say anything.

"Now before we begin the serious work I'd like everybody to stand up and give their bodies a stretch and shake down, loosen up those limbs."

Everybody did so willingly.

"Next I want you to touch your left knee with your right hand. Like so." She demonstrated. "Now do the opposite."

"I can never figure out my left from right," said Trevor, laughing.

"I can't follow instructions very well," said Sonya, nearly falling over.

"Do it slowly. The idea is to bring your knee up to meet your hand. It can be difficult to balance."

"Sure is," said Frank. "Didn't think I had signed up for a keep fit class, not that I couldn't do with losing a few pounds." He laughed, patting his belly.

"So we have a flow going now, keep it slow. What's happening here is that you are sending signals across what is often referred to as your midline," said Monique, pointing with her fingers along the middle of her head. "The idea is to increase the connections between the left and right hemisphere of your brain."

She could talk about motor neurons, neutral pathways, corpus callosum, myelin sheaths and other neurological terminology that might bore them to death. She just wanted to keep it simple. "You see, it is generally accepted that we do not know how much the brain is capable of. But so far research tells us that the left side of the brain is responsible for our logic and reasoning, language and maths, seeing the detail. Whereas the right side is our creative side, the big picture, imagination, dreaming. People are generally either left- or right-hemisphere dominant. It would be ideal if we could draw from both sides of our brain which in turn would help to improve our ability to learn.

"Doing exercises which would encourage crossing the midline, that is using both sides of your body in unison, can help. Even as you sit in your seats you can touch your right ear with your left hand and then do the opposite. You can create as many exercises as possible using your own ideas. Off you go. Give it a try. Just make sure you are crossing the midline of your body."

Monique watched as people began to share their ideas and make it fun.

"Okay, feedback time."

"I could feel a kind of buzz here. What's that about?" Viv asked, touching the top of her head.

"The corpus callosum is a bundle of nerves located at the top of your head between the two hemispheres. It is responsible for sending messages from one side of your brain to the other. For the moment, let us just say that it is the part that fires up when you use both sides of your body. That is exactly what we want to happen. Do not worry if you did not get that sensation, not everybody does."

She wrote a word on the board. "Now I would like to explain a little about phonics."

"I've never heard of that word," said Frank, taking out his notepad and copying it down. She noticed he was absorbed in every element of the course.

"Years ago we learned by memory and sight. For example, we saw the word *cat* and memorised it. Today kids learn using phonics. These are the sounds of the letters. So the letter *c* sounds like – think of the word *cat* and say the first sound."

Everybody said, "Cat."

"Now make just the sound of the first letter."

"Cuh."

"Exactly. Place your hand under your chin and touch your neck and you will feel where the sound comes from. All letters have a sound. We'll go through them. Before we do I want to explain, there are three ways of learning and we use all of them, but one might be your preference." She explained about learning in a visual way, or by listening, or by actually doing something. Then she went through an individual evaluation to discover how each person preferred to learn.

At lunchtime Donagh lit a cigarette. When Monique had mentioned that some newspapers targeted their writing to a reading age of a nine-year-old, he could have cried. He could manage the headlines and a little way in, but after a short while, he got a headache and the words seemed to jump around the page. He felt he had a mountain to climb. No wonder he had become the class clown. Popular because he could swim and surf and pull the girls. And he had always given the impression that he never took anything seriously. If his friends knew he was here, he would lose face big time. He had so many ambitions and dreams, now was his chance.

"You doing okay, mate?" It was Trevor.

"Yeah, you?"

"You do that."

"What?"

"Answer a question with a question. I noticed coz so do I."

Donagh shrugged. "It's easier that way."

"True." Trevor sat down and began to roll a cigarette. "You enjoying the weekend?"

"Yeah, it wasn't like I'd imagined."

"Better than I thought it would be. She makes you think. I'm determined to get the help I need now."

"Yeah, me too." But she made him think too much. Someone like her would never be interested in a loser like him. A part of him was glad it was over. He'd get help from someone else. She made him feel … "Sorry, I missed what you said."

"I was just saying everything these days is about form-filling. I'm hoping to get my driving licence but I'll need help with the theory test."

Donagh had so many qualifications he wanted to get if he was to achieve his plan.

He saw her strolling towards the lake. She looked so sad at times. He wondered what was bothering her. He turned back and blew smoke up into the sky. "I need to pack these in; they're costing me a fortune."

"Why do you think I'm on the rollies?" said Trevor.

Jessie had asked Geoff to drop in at 4 p.m. to hear some feedback. "So it's time to say goodbye. Monique can connect you up with your local literacy service where there is free one-to-one tuition available. They are just waiting for the call. Is there anything we could improve on in relation to the course or Butterfly Barn itself?

Frank began to speak. "Since my sister passed away my stress levels have been through the roof. Finally facing my challenge and being here has given me hope that I never thought I would find. I'm very grateful to you, Monique, and to the entire group for making this the most enjoyable experience I have had in years."

"Well said, buddy." Trevor clapped him on the back. Donagh smiled and agreed.

"Come 'ere," said Viv, getting up to give him a hug. "You're just a big softie."

"Go away, or you'll ruin my image." He laughed, hugging her back. "I hope you all sign up in your local areas and the lads here might even let us come back in a year to see how we are all doing."

"So I take it you are all happy," said Geoff, smiling. "Any suggestions as to other types of workshops we could do here?"

"How about a workshop in DIY? I'd love to show people how to do various odd jobs like hanging doors, fixing plugs, basic household plumbing and other odd jobs," said Frank.

"Great idea, could be something we'd offer mid-week for local people."

"A furniture restoration weekend or you could rent the place for music jamming sessions?" said Donagh.

"What kind of music?" asked Jessie.

"I suppose all kinds. Why restrict it?" he replied.

"There are some great ideas to mull over. Before we finish I would just like to say I had a great time with you all and I'd like to congratulate Monique for convincing us to let her host this weekend," said Jessie.

Everybody cheered.

Monique felt pleased by the group's reaction. She'd miss them all. Her gaze landed on Donagh. He was coming up with all kinds of ideas. He must have noticed her staring because he smiled right at her and mortifyingly she blushed.

She hadn't heard from Garvan since she had left him a voicemail at lunchtime yesterday. She wondered why he had been bombarding her with messages and then nothing.

"Thank you so much, Monique," said Sonya, hugging her. She spent the next twenty minutes saying goodbye. Donagh was the last one left. He was chatting with Geoff, Jessie and Sophia. She began to tidy up.

"Thanks, Monique," he called from the other side of the room.

"You are welcome," she called back, and then he was gone.

"That was fantastic, well done." Sophia put her arm around her as Jessie high-fived her.

"What a weekend!" said Jessie.

It had been but it suddenly felt flat and she didn't know why. When she went home, she watched the movie *It's Complicated* with Gran. They had seen it so many times but they both loved it. Nora got a great kick from Meryl and Steve smoking the pot. She laughed every time.

Just as she was about to get into bed, her mobile phone rang. She picked it up and saw Garvan's handsome smiling face looking back at her. God, she missed him, but she was angry with him too.

"Hey Monique, you have to come out here. It's fantastic. The weather is hard to beat and I just met a girl who said there's a job going teaching English to a sheikh's children. How cool would that be?" His voice sounded slurred and there was music in the background.

"Garvan, I'm not leaving."

"Nora doesn't expect you to give up your dreams."

"It's not my dream. It never was." There was silence. Then she added, "We have to face reality Garvan, it's impossible to continue."

"Fine, Monique, I get the message loud and clear. Goodbye." The phone went dead.

It was over. She knew she had hurt him but she was tired of him going on about how great it was and she was angry with herself for living from one text, phone call or Facebook message to the next.

She lay in bed. A tear trickled down the side of her face onto her pillow. Her heart was heavy; their four years together were finally over.

Chapter Four

Grace woke to the sound of Baby Lily crying. It was 4 a.m. She picked up her little girl from the Moses basket beside their bed. Jack stirred.

"Grace, I told you I'd feed her," he said, sleepily, pushing back the duvet to get a bottle of expressed milk from its holder. "You've a big day coming up."

"I just want to hold her. We're so lucky."

He sat on the edge of the bed beside them. "Let me." She passed Lily into his arms and he began to feed her. "Get some sleep, honey."

"My mind is working overtime. I'm so glad Kate is helping today. She was the one who secured our contract with Cel Cruise's two years ago and we need it to be renewed for at least another two. It all rides on how today goes and Eoghan is insisting I take a back seat."

"He's right, Grace. You have to see that the team you have in place can do this. You've got to look after your health and this little one." Lily happily sucked her bottle in his arms.

"Now go back to sleep and stop worrying."

She turned over but she couldn't stop worrying. Jack's business wasn't secure. Oak House was a financial drain. Nothing had been done to maintain it for years. She needed this contract but she was also worried about Kate. She seemed to want any excuse to stay. Maybe things weren't so rosy in the garden with Richard and she hadn't wanted to say because Sophia was such a big influence in all of their lives. Oh God, go to sleep, she told herself. Worrying never solved anything.

Kate had rung Richard to tell him she was staying until Friday. He was up to his eyes as usual but promised to be free so they could spend the rest of the weekend together. At least she had that to look forward to.

She stood on the harbour and watched as the passengers walked down the gangplank to board the many coaches lined up to bring them around the south-east. Her group was setting off to visit Kilkenny Castle. It was always a popular choice with the Americans. She smiled at the first passenger to board the coach. "Fáilte romhat, you are very welcome to

Ireland. I hope you enjoy the day."

"Why, thank you. I'm looking forward to it so much."

"And you brought the sunshine," she added. She hadn't realised how much she missed the buzz of it all.

The day flew by and before she knew it, she was back on the harbour waving as the passengers disappeared into the huge liner. Eoghan stood beside her. He was delighted too.

"Let's go for a drink. That's a day worth celebrating."

"You're on," said Eoghan. "I'll just ring Grace and let her know how it all went. She'll be anxiously awaiting the call. It's impossible to take a proper maternity leave when you're self-employed. She'll be thrilled to hear that there is a ninety-nine point nine percent chance that Cel Cruises will be renewing the contract. Thanks for today, Kate. You're a star for helping out."

"Ah, you're welcome. I'll go order the pints. See you in Nutties."

Ten minutes later, he joined her in the corner of the bar.

"So how are things in New York?" he asked and then took a sip from the creamy pint of Guinness she had ordered for him.

"Oh Eoghan, the truth is I love Richard but I don't like the lifestyle that goes with him." Eoghan raised his eyebrows as she continued. "It's a different world. I am never going to fit in. I'm just a small town girl. I like the simple things in life. I don't own anything designer nor do I want to." She took a slug of her pint of Guinness.

"Are Richard and Sophia as wealthy as I am imagining?"

"Whatever you imagine and more, Eoghan! They have penthouse apartments. There's an estate in the Hamptons, a ski lodge in Aspen – which Grace said was absolutely massive – another house in LA., a private jet, and Sophia even owns an apartment on a cruise liner. I overheard Richard offering it to some clients of his. It's so different. Richard even hates me taking the subway, for God's sake."

"I only recently discovered from your mother who exactly Sophia is." Eoghan sipped his Guinness. It left a white moustache around his lips that he wiped away.

"What did my mother say?"

"On her new computer course she discovered that Sophia is considered to be one of the most powerful people in magazine publishing. But when I looked Sophia up, I discovered they also own radio and TV channels across America. I'm afraid I reacted very badly the other night, childish of me really."

"What did you do?"

"I saw myself out."

"Ah Eoghan. Will you have another one?"

"It's my round," he said, getting up and going to the bar. He came back with two more creamy pints and set them down.

"Have you seen Sophia since?"

"No, I just feel stupid. Of course, I knew she was wealthy, but not that kind of wealth. It never occurred to me to google her name. From the first time I met Sophia on the pier in Bayrush, I was smitten. She was a stranger passing by who asked me what language I was speaking."

Kate laughed. "Your English isn't that bad!"

"Very funny," Eoghan grinned. "I was attempting to speak Irish with some fishermen from the Gaeltacht. I couldn't believe my eyes when she turned up with Grace a few days later, here in Nutties actually, after a cruise call. We chatted all evening." Kate listened, intrigued. Eoghan never talked about himself.

"Sophia was still grieving her husband. I didn't dare make any advances and as the time rolled on, well, I was afraid to risk losing her friendship. Ah well, it was never to be."

"But it's not too late, Eoghan. Talk to her."

"You're the right one to tell me what to do." He laughed.

"Well, I know what I'm going to do. I love Richard. When I go back, I plan to find something that interests me and I'll just have to get used to life there. Thanks for the chat."

"Cheers. I wish you the very best always, Kate Fitzgerald," he said, holding up his pint. She held up hers.

"Ring her."

On Friday at lunchtime Kate's flight arrived into JFK. Richard had told her he had to attend a Gala ball in aid of "Children in Crisis" that night. Wynthrope Communications were the main benefactors. He had assured her he didn't expect her to go to it but he had to represent the company. She decided to make a better effort and surprise him by turning up.

If she was honest, she had always dreamed of walking down a sweeping stairs with a room full of people watching from the bottom. They would gasp in wonder, asking "Who is this exquisite creature?" There would be whispers of "Who, pray tell, is it?" and "My, what a beauty!" Well, that was never going to happen. She smiled to herself as she pressed the buzzer that allowed access to Richard's penthouse apartment. Lisa, her events manager friend, had lined up three people to transform her for the Gala.

Richard had told her he was going directly from the office and that he would be home as soon as he could. She looked at the three expectant faces and declared, "I badly need a makeover, fix me, please!"

The demoralising part was that none of them disagreed. Hairdresser, make-up artist and stylist, not surprisingly all three were men.

"So," said Kate, "tea, coffee, a drink?"

"Let's get this show on the road," declared Rod, the hairdresser. "We have a lot to do!"

"Heartening," said Kate. "So very heartening!"

Sophia still hadn't heard from Eoghan. She had arranged to meet Grace and Jessie in Alfonso's, a smart Italian restaurant in Bayrush. She joined the girls who were already seated. After placing their food orders, Grace asked for a bottle of champagne.

"What are we celebrating?" asked Jessie.

"We got the contract."

"That's fantastic," said Sophia. "Is Eoghan coming?"

"I didn't ask him. Well, with the way things are between you two, I didn't know what to do."

"Oh, does he know we're coming here?"

"Well he does now," said Jessie, inclining her head towards the door where Eoghan had just walked in with a blonde-haired woman. "Who's she?"

"I haven't a clue. Oh God, he's coming this way. I feel awful for not inviting him now," whispered Grace.

"I don't," muttered Sophia under her breath. Who was that woman, she wondered.

"Hello, ladies," said Eoghan, while his dinner companion followed the waiter to their table. The two girls were staring in the woman's direction, leaving her the only one looking at Eoghan.

"Hello," she said politely. At the same time, the waiter arrived with the champagne.

"Apologies, I'll leave you to it," said Eoghan. He went to join the woman who was seated four tables away.

"Moët, for you beautiful ladies," said the waiter. All his Italian charm and smiles were lost on Sophia as she tried not to stare after Eoghan.

Pop went the bottle. They were drawing attention from all quarters of the restaurant.

"Maybe one of you ladies have birthday?"

"Yes, yes," said Grace.

"We do nice cake."

"Whatever, thanks," Jessie added.

"Whicha one?"

"Which one what?" Sophia couldn't concentrate on a word the waiter was saying. Obviously nor could the girls. They were all so distracted.

"Whicha one hava the birthday?"

"Me," said Grace and Jessie in unison.

"Youa twins, very, very good!" he exclaimed. "I dida not knowa this … that … very good. You redhead and you soa blonde. I never knewa." After pouring, he shook his head and walked away.

"I didn't have the heart to correct him. Girls?" said Jessie.

It's definitely a date, thought Sophia.

"Girls?" repeated Jessie. Holding up her glass.

"What?" asked Sophia and Grace at the same time.

"We have to get it together. The night is turning into a fiasco. Cheers."

"Yes, of course. Cheers Grace. I'm so pleased for you. It will take some pressure off you."

"Thanks girls," said Grace.

"Cheers, everybody, and happy birthday to you too, Grace," said Jessie, attempting to make a joke. Sophia smiled graciously and chinked glasses but she wondered how she was going to sit through three courses. She did not intend to let Eoghan see that she was upset. They had only been friends after all.

"So, how was the weekend?" asked Grace.

Sophia appreciated her attempt to normalise the situation. She settled her table napkin across her lap and said, "Grace, the weekend was wonderful. I learned so much from Monique and the group. I met some great people whom I hope we'll see more of. Are you going to give a creative writing class?"

Grace took her cue immediately.

"Yes," said Grace. "We're going to do a series of four Sunday workshops starting around the middle of August when Lily is settled into a routine."

Sophia listened as Grace and Jessie chatted but she wished she didn't have such a clear view of their table. Later the waiter, true to his word, presented them with a tiramisu with two candles lit.

"Onea for each of you," he declared proudly and then broke into song in his broken English accent: "Happy birthadaya to you!"

She couldn't help but laugh at the stupidity of it all. Surely Eoghan knew it was none of their birthdays.

When Kate arrived at the venue, she saw Richard greeting the guests at the entrance to the ballroom. She wanted to surprise him and she could hardly believe it when she saw a sweeping staircase. She slipped in behind some guests in the queue that had formed and made her way upstairs to the powder room and waited. Her phone rang. She smiled when she saw his photograph. "Hey honey, I can't wait to see you. I plan to get away as soon as I can."

"I'm here," she said.

"Where?"

She smiled and said, "I'm about to walk down a sweeping staircase. See you in a moment." She clicked the phone off. Whatever you do, Kate, don't trip, she thought. She scanned the crowd below and saw him. His eyes were transfixed on hers. Her heart beat loudly. She nearly glided down the stairs wearing a version of the little black dress worn by Audrey Hepburn in the movie *Sabrina*, a slash-necked, short silk dress with only diagonal pin-tucks as decoration. Her stylist had told her the moment he had laid eyes on her that he could only think of Audrey Hepburn and so the others had agreed and turned her into a twenty-first century version. The cool thing about the whole experience was that she thought that she was actually going to lose herself but she was wrong. And looking at Richard's face now, it had been worth it.

"Hi, you," he murmured as he kissed her near her ear. "Let's get out of here."

"You've got to be kidding me," she giggled. "This took a while."

"Never. You're beautiful in every way."

"You say the nicest things." She batted her eyelashes at him. Even her hair had worked out beautifully. She always wore her black hair short. Rod, the hairdresser, had given her a short fringe and Flick, the make-up artist, had highlighted her dark eyes with black kohl and used a neutral lipstick on her full lips. She felt fantastic.

Sophia had tossed and turned all night. At seven she went downstairs and made herself a cup of tea. She sat in the rocking chair she had bought for Grace that first Christmas they had spent together. She kept thinking of all the times she had spent with Eoghan on the sailboat. Those days had been special to her. She had him all to herself, while at other times, they had always socialised in a group. Once on the boat she had wanted him to kiss her and another time they had danced together and she was sure he had wanted to kiss her, but the moment had passed. In the three years she had known him, he had never invited her to dinner. Last night when she saw him with that woman, she was so hurt.

She could feel a quiver inside her, a feeling she thought she would never experience again. She had loved her husband Bill so much and his sudden death had devastated her. She hadn't ever thought she'd feel anything for another man again. But the truth was she did. And now it was unbearable being near Eoghan but not being close to him.

She heard the crunch of pebbles and looked out the window. It was Grace. It was too early for a social call; she hoped there was nothing wrong. Sophia opened the door just as Grace was getting out of her car.

"I'm sorry to call so early but I think you need to clear things up with Eoghan. He is distant and avoiding the office and you're definitely not happy and I don't know who the hell that woman was last night. But he kept looking at you, so for once and for all, I want you both to sort it out."

"Why are you telling me? I'm not the one who was out on a date. Tell him," said Sophia, standing in the doorway of Rose Cottage with her dressing gown and slippers on.`

"I just did."

"Oh God, Grace. What did he say? Did you call to his house too?"

"Yes, and I'm not getting into it. I've probably interfered enough already. I have to get back. Jack is looking after the kids. I hope you'll forgive me but both of you mean the world to me." She hugged her and ran back to the car and drove away as quickly as she had appeared.

When Grace left, Sophia decided to go for a walk. Her mind was all over the place. She walked through the red gate at the end of the cottage and set off along the beach.

She stopped and took her cell phone from her pocket. She put it back in again and continued walking. She was too stubborn to ring him first.

An hour later, she was about to reach the red gate when her phone rang. When she saw Eoghan's photograph she took a deep breath before she answered it.

"Sophia, I have to apologise for my behaviour." He paused. She didn't say anything. He continued. "I'd like to meet up. There is something I need to tell you."

"If it's about the lady you were with last night. I wish you the best but I really don't feel the need for us to talk." That's telling him, she thought.

"I want to explain. I promise it won't take long. I thought we were friends."

"I did too, Eoghan, but I'm not so sure I want to be after the last few days."

"Ten minutes, that's all I am asking for."

"Bonita's at midday." She planned to make her feelings very clear to him.

*

"Donagh! Hey, wait up."

Donagh turned around to see Pepe running towards him with his surfboard under his arm.

"Hey, where were you all weekend? You missed the waves, it was mind-blowing."

"I heard. I was talking to Butchie on the blower. He said you held up well."

It was easy to put the lads off. He was good at avoiding answers. It was nearly an art form with him. He paddled out towards the rest of the lads.

It was the first time he had been able to get to the beach. He had been busy at work installing a new kitchen for a woman who kept changing her mind and he had been trying to practise reading. He had told his mother about the weekend. She had been delighted for him. She asked him to move home, that way she could help him and he could save money. He had declined. His father's insults had never stopped. They had become more snide and sly over the years. His father had the ability to cut in a way that a person wasn't sure whether they had been insulted or not. He was such a wordy bastard. There was no way he'd move back home and nor did he want his little brother to know how thick he was.

"Hey buddy, you were on the missing list!" Butchie called from his perch on his surfboard in the ocean.

He paddled out to join his best friend. He was glad to be back with the lads doing what he loved. Every night for the past week he had tried to read the newspaper but it was just too hard. He knew he should ring Monique but he didn't want to. He didn't want her pity. He was back in the same place he had been in before that blasted weekend, only now he felt even worse. Thicker than thick. He should never have gone. What was wrong with the life he had? Wasn't he lucky to have a job and friends? And his pick of girls.

"Lads, let's go on the piss, tonight," he shouted towards the two lads.

"Sounds good to me," roared Butchie, paddling like crazy to catch a wave.

Sophia sat in the bay window seat of Bonita's. She saw Eoghan across the street; someone had greeted him and had stopped to talk. By his body language she could see he was trying to get away. She smiled, he was just that kind of person, and everybody who knew him liked him. Her heart was thumping but she had made her decision, she was going to tell him how she felt. The air would be clear between them. She'd wish him the best with his new relationship and apologise for not telling him the entire truth about herself.

"Sorry about the delay," he said, nodding towards the window while sitting into the seat opposite her. She noticed he didn't attempt to kiss her in their usual way of greeting. The waitress brought the Americano he had ordered on his way in.

"Sophia, firstly thank you for agreeing to meet. I am terribly sorry for my behaviour over the last while. There has been a lot going on."

She raised her eyebrows; clearly there had been. What was the point in her telling him how she felt? He had moved on. It was too late for them. She remained silent.

"Sophia, I'm married."

She looked at him in astonishment. "Was that your wife last night?"

"No, no, she was my sister-in-law."

"I'm stunned, Eoghan. You'll have to explain because I can't believe the way you reacted in Rose Cottage, and I was feeling guilty for not telling you everything about me and now you tell me this."

"It's a long story."

"I have all day."

"Let's drink up here and go somewhere private to talk. I don't want to be overheard."

She put her head in her hands. "I can't believe you never told me."

"I think there are many things we haven't been completely honest about, Sophia. That's why I want us to talk in private."

"If you're suggesting what I think you are, I want to make it very clear. I have never been involved with a married man and I don't intend to start now."

He threw his head back and laughed.

"Don't you dare laugh at me, Eoghan Forrester. I'm not finding any of this amusing."

"Sophia, let's go for a walk along the promenade. Is that public enough for you?"

She finished her coffee and got up. They walked in silence to the prom and she found a bench overlooking the sea. She sat down. "Tell me everything."

"I married when I was thirty-five. I had a great job, a beautiful wife and we were blessed with two wonderful little girls. I couldn't have been happier. One morning I left a file I had been working on at home. To this day I wish that I had not turned the car around."

Sophia watched as Eoghan struggled to continue. Whatever happened that day had changed the course of his life.

"As I ran upstairs calling to Ellen, I was surprised to find our bedroom door closed. When I opened it, she was in bed with a … woman."

Sophia's eyes widened. "Oh my goodness, Eoghan. I'm so sorry."

"My girls were twelve and fourteen at the time. Ellen begged me not to tell them. She told me it had been a huge mistake and that she wasn't gay. Sophia, I stayed for another two years for my children's sake. But it had poisoned me. I started drinking heavily and I was silently raging inside. Finally, I woke up one morning with yet another hangover and there and then I packed my bags. I wrote a note telling her that she could keep the house and the car in Dublin. The girls could come and live with me when I found a place, if they wanted to." He paused and turned to look directly into her eyes. "I tried to see them but she told me they didn't want anything to do with me because of my drinking. How could I tell them what their mother had done? I wouldn't have expected her to tell them the whole truth but she didn't even try to defend me. If I had stayed, I was well on the road to becoming an alcoholic and what use would I have been if I couldn't provide for them?"

"How old are they now?"

"That was ten years ago."

"They are young women now. Surely you can talk to them."

"The woman you saw me with was my sister-in-law, Kathleen. She came to tell me that Ellen has been diagnosed with early-onset Alzheimer's. While she was packing to help move her to a nursing home, she found all the cards and letters I had sent to the girls over the years unopened and some journals belonging to Ellen. She came here to ask me what had really happened at the time. The girls are already devastated and she doesn't know whether to give them the journals or not. Do they really need to hear that truth now that Ellen is so unwell?"

"Eoghan, you have to speak to them. They are adults now. There should be no more secrets. Look at all the pain and angst it has already caused."

"I can't take their mother's character away in the process."

"You're very forgiving, Eoghan. You are going to miss out on the rest of their lives because of your wife's actions."

"I know, love."

Her heart skipped a beat when he called her "love".

"I should have told you, Sophia. I'm sorry, especially since I reacted so badly to you not telling me everything. You've always been out of my reach and just when I thought we had a chance and you were healing, I discover you're a billionaire. I'm just not in your league."

"Do you realise how antiquated that sounds, Eoghan Forrester? I don't need someone to provide for me. What I do need is honesty and openness." She laid her hand over his. "I want us to have a life together, Eoghan."

"Oh Sophia, I would love that too, but I can't leave Ireland because I live in hope that someday the girls will come looking for me."

"You are a complicated man, Eoghan. Why don't you contact them?"

"I want them to want me."

"Maybe they need you now more than ever. Have you thought of that?"

"Oh God," he said, putting his head into his hands. "Kathleen said to give it all time to settle. It's enough for them to get used to their mother's condition and maybe in the coming weeks or months she will give them the journals and we'll see what happens from there."

"Sounds like a good idea," said Sophia, taking his hand in hers.

"You don't know how good it feels to be sitting here talking with you again. I missed you so much."

"Eoghan, time is precious. We've wasted enough of it."

"Let's take out the boat. It's a perfect day for it."

She smiled; she had been hoping for a kiss, but maybe that would be just a tad too public for him.

"Great idea," she said, getting up. "I'll see you at the harbour in twenty minutes."

He stood up too and just as she was about to turn away, he took her by both hands and kissed her. She threw all caution to the wind and kissed him back. It was an incredibly liberating feeling and he was a wonderful kisser too. She pulled back from him and laughed. "Well, that took me by surprise."

"To the first day of the rest of our lives."

"No more guessing games."

The lines around his blue eyes crinkled. "I love you, Sophia Wynthrope. I don't know how it's all going to work out but I want you to know I do love you."

"I love you too. See you shortly." She leaned in and kissed him again. My God, it had been years since she had done anything like this. She felt like a twenty-year-old again. She couldn't wait to get back to him.

Chapter Five

"Dirk, don't you think that's a bit much? He's only two years and three months old and you want me to leave him with you in France for a week?"

"He's my son too, Grace." She had put him on speakerphone so that Jack could hear him too.

"And take me off speaker phone. I'm not stupid, you know."

"You could have fooled me," she said, clicking back while Jack shook his head at her. He was warning her not to lose her cool. But it was too late for that.

"If you're going to be like that, I'm going to hang up."

"Well good riddance so."

Jack was having a fit in front of her now, mouthing, "Don't."

"Look, Dirk, you'll have to be reasonable. Finn hasn't seen you for six months. That's a long time in a child's life. You are the one who decided to move to the South of France. If you want to spend time with him – come home."

"I can't get away."

"So you're telling me some stranger is going to be looking after my son, over my dead body." She hung up. She'd had enough. He was such an ass at times.

"Well, that didn't go well."

"Don't you start either. Men!" she said, storming out of the kitchen to go to her bedroom. She needed time to calm down. She hadn't planned any of this. She had become pregnant with Finn around the time she discovered Dirk had been cheating on her. It had been one of the worst times in her life. But finding Jack again and being with him had been the best thing that had ever happened to her. Why was she stalling about marriage so much? Her father leaving them had made her so afraid of commitment. Was she really going to let that hang over her whole life?

"God," she said, sitting on the edge of her bed. She was fair to Dirk; his mother regularly took Finn because both she and Dirk felt it was important that he know his extended family, but asking for him to be brought to France was too much. Dirk worked morning, noon and night in the hotel business in Cannes. He'd think nothing of leaving Finn with a stranger. My God, Finn would be traumatised. No way would she allow that to happen. She wasn't getting any calmer. She charged back out the door and pounded down the stairs.

"This is crazy. I'm going to ring him back and tell him to f …"

"Hold on a sec, babe."

"Don't babe me." She stopped when she saw the look of amazement on Jack's face. "What?"

"I've never seen you like this before. Breathe and calm down then ring him back and try to talk it out again."

"There is no talking it out. If Dirk wants to spend time with his son, he can come home."

"I'm going out," said Jack. He got up and left the kitchen. She stood looking after him. What had she done?

Monique walked along the busy harbour front of Bayrush with Rachel. They had planned to meet Jay and his twin brother Alex, who was home for the weekend in Fosters.

"There they are," said Rachel, pointing to where the boys were perched on bar stools around a circular high table. "We'll have to listen to the newly qualified architect about how great London is."

"Rach, you make him sound awful. I missed him," said Monique, going over to them. "Hey, Alex, it's great to see you," said Monique, giving her friend a hug. Alex and Jay had been like brothers to her when she had first arrived in Ireland. Their love for horses had bonded the three of them. Monique could never understand why Rachel and Alex could never get along. Jay grabbed some more stools and they all gathered around chatting and catching up.

Donagh and his mates sat at a table in Foster's. He saw Monique from the moment she walked in.

"What do you think?"

"Sorry, what?" asked Donagh, watching Monique hug a tall blond guy. He wondered, if he was her boyfriend.

"Are you with us or what? How about Nutties next? There'll be more life in it," said Butchie.

"Ah, sure we'll have another one here," he said. He couldn't help looking in her direction.

"Who's your one?" asked Butchie, following his gaze.

"My round," said Pepe, getting up to go to the bar.

Monique smiled at him but he barely acknowledged her.

"Do you know her?" asked Butchie.

"Not really."

"I never saw her around before. She's cute," said Butchie.

For some reason he was annoyed with his friend for commenting on her and even more pissed off that she was chatting so much with the tall blond guy.

"What's the story?"

Donagh made no reply at first and then said, "No interest."

"Really? Doesn't look that way to me," said Butchie. "She keeps looking over. Reckon she fancies me then?"

Donagh gave him a withering look.

"Where's your sense of humour, boy?" Butchie laughed just as Pepe placed the pints in front of them.

"Cheers Pepe. Butchie, can't we just have a pint and enjoy it? Do ya always have to be on the pull?"

"I'm going for a smoke," said Butchie, getting up and walking towards the outside smoking area.

"You okay?" asked Pepe.

"Yes, we'll finish these and head up to Nutties. Butchie's right. There will be more life up there," said Donagh. Another friend came over and started talking to Pepe. Donagh stole a glance to see if Monique was looking as Butchie had said. She caught his eye – what was it about her? She was so not his type. She broke eye contact and turned her attention back to her friends.

Twenty minutes later, he walked out past their table. She didn't say goodbye. And he couldn't understand why it annoyed him. He had been the one to ignore her first.

Monique wondered if Donagh was ignoring her in front of his friends because she had been his tutor. He might find it awkward to explain how he knew her. She'd have to respect that. She just couldn't help looking in his direction when he wasn't looking. Her stomach was in knots. Maybe it was something she ate earlier.

"Where do you want to go after this?" asked Jay.

"Tosh and a few of the lads are jamming in Nutties tonight. I told him we might call in for a few," said Alex.

"Why not – what kind of music are they into?" asked Rachel.

"Coldplay, U2, that kind of thought-provoking rock," said Jay.

The two girls laughed at Jay, more because of the intense look on his face. He was so into his music.

"Ah stop taking the piss," he said, laughing.

Half an hour later the four of them walked into Nutties Bar. Rachel offered to go to the bar this time so Monique had a chance to look around. It wasn't a pub she usually went to. Garvan had liked the rugby club bar and she had never really minded where they went.

The musicians were playing U2's "It's a Beautiful Day" and the place was jammed. It erupted with applause when they finished. She couldn't see the band from where she stood waiting for Rachel. She spotted Jack sitting at the end of the bar, alone. She was about to go over to him when she heard the sound of an unaccompanied male voice singing Coldplay's "Fix you".

> *When you try your best, but you don't succeed*
> *When you get what you want, but not what you need*
> *When you feel so tired, but you can't sleep*
> *Stuck in reverse*

The voice was so clear and beautiful. She squeezed between people in search of its owner and stood transfixed when she discovered it was Donagh. As he sang you could hear a pin drop until the last chorus when the whole pub joined in. The place went wild with shouts for more.

"Who's your man, he's gorgeous!" Rachel shouted above the noise. "He's looking at you. Do you know him?" Her eyes were locked on his. Monique's heart had gone into meltdown. He had done so much more than just sing the song. He was sharing from his soul. The look between them was so intense, it scared her. She turned away and said to Rachel, "Let's get out of here. It is way too crowded."

"What about the others? We have to find them," said Rachel.

"I will see you outside," she muttered, as she pushed her way through the crowd. Just as she got to the door Donagh was beside her.

"Are you leaving already?" he asked.

"It is not my scene," she replied, taken aback. She hadn't expected him to follow her.

"Just going for a smoke," he said, holding up the pack of Dunhill. "See you round." He walked away and went to sit on the low wall surrounding the beer garden.

She stayed by the door feeling suddenly deflated and awkward because she had to wait for the others. She played with her phone. Out of the corner of her eye, she could see some girls flirting with him. Then a fabulous looking girl, with long auburn, bouncy hair, the kind she regularly saw on TV commercials for hair products, came out of the bar. Every guy in the smoking area watched as she walked straight up to Donagh and kissed him on the lips. "That was fantastic," she said and took a cigarette from his packet. Monique saw the way he smiled at the girl as though she was the only girl in the place. Monique turned away just as Rachel and the boys came out of the bar.

"That was brilliant," said Rachel, linking her and leading her away.

"Hey, there's that guy. Jeez, he was good. I've never heard him before," said Jay, standing outside. "Why are we leaving?"

"Come on," said Rachel. "It's too packed. I can't hear myself think." Monique shot her a grateful look as they set off along the harbour. "The beer garden in The Moorings is another great spot."

Grace sat in the kitchen. It was ten-thirty and there was still no sign of Jack. She was really worried. He had gone back out to the yard to work and then she had seen his jeep disappear down the lane just after eight o'clock. He hadn't come in for something to eat or to say where he was going and nor had he answered any of her calls or texts. She boiled the kettle. She didn't know who she was more annoyed with now. Dirk or Jack?

The kids were finally asleep. Men, she thought, taking out a mug. She heard the sound of an engine outside. She looked out the kitchen window – it was Jack. He always parked around the back of the house. When he came in the back door, instead of shouting at him, which was what she felt like doing, she ignored him and proceeded to make her cup of tea.

"So you're ignoring me now," he said with a hint of a smile.

"No," she said. "Tea?"

"Yes please." He walked over and sat at the kitchen table. "So you've calmed down."

"Not really. I don't understand why you left earlier and didn't answer any of my calls."

"I'm sick of this, Grace. Even Jay is making jokes about me wanting to marry you. When are you going to normalise our lives? What is wrong with you? Why can't you see that I am not like Dirk?"

"Why are you saying this today?"

"Because I don't want to be like Dirk, asking you for the right to see Lily or Finn for that matter in the future because you have decided that commitment is not for you. That is what you are doing every time you ignore what I want for us. I'm sorry your dad left and Dirk was such a complete asshole. But I'm not like them, Grace. I want us to be a proper family. We have been together since Finn was just a few months old and it seems to me I have no rights at all in his life. It's just crazy."

"Oh Jack, I'm sorry." She could see the hurt in his eyes.

"I needed some space. I'm sorry to land this on you today especially when Dirk is making demands too. But when I saw how mad he makes you and how he has added to your fear of commitment, I just saw red. I had to get away. When I finished work I went to Nutties for a pint. I don't want you to feel forced into marriage but it is something I feel very strongly about. I never imagined I would be another divorce statistic. I believed I would be married for life. When Lynda cheated I was devastated. But there was something better to come. I found you again and we're here back where it all began for us twenty-two years ago. If I'm asking too much I will have to accept your decision once and for all. But Grace, this is the last time I will ever ask you to marry me."

She began to speak. He placed a finger over her lips to silence her and said, "This doesn't mean we are splitting up if you say no. It means I have told you how I feel and then I will have to accept how you feel about our future."

"Yes, Jack Leslie. I will marry you." Tears ran down her cheeks as she said the words.

"Oh God, honey, I didn't mean to make you cry." He kissed her eyelids and then tilted her chin with his fingers. He kissed her and swept her off her feet. He walked towards the kitchen door. "Ah shite," he said, realising it was closed. "Can you open it, my dear! So much for my dramatic moment."

She burst out laughing at how ridiculous they were trying to open the kitchen door with her in his arms.

"I'll be fine," said Donagh, trying to walk up the stairs. "Just another little bit to go." He started laughing.

"Donagh, you've had way too much to drink," said Evie, leading him into his bedroom. The rest of the lads were still downstairs drinking in the house he shared with them.

"I don't want to go to bed." As he said the words he fell backwards on to it. "I just can't stop thinking about her."

"Who?"

"Who what?" He couldn't figure out what Evie was asking him.

"Get some sleep, Donagh," she said and closed the door. He managed to get back up and puked into the bin beside the bed.

Sophia woke and pulled the sheets up to her chin. Eoghan had invited her for dinner last night and she hadn't gone home. She looked around the bedroom, taking in the unusually high ceiling for such a small house, and the very male surroundings. She lay in the large double bed, alone. She blushed when she thought of last night. It had been a wonderful evening. She pulled the sheet over her face, giggling at her thoughts.

She heard a noise at the door just as Eoghan entered with a tray.

"Breakfast is served, my lady," he declared with just his navy towelling robe on.

Oh but he was handsome. She had loved running her fingers through his short thick grey hair. His mischievous eyes were always ready to laugh. Life was never dull around him.

She sat up in the bed, pulling the sheet around her. She was completely naked underneath which had been all very well in the heat of the moment last night.

"Don't move," he said, placing the tray on the dressing table. He went to his wardrobe and took out an Oxford-blue shirt. "There you are and I swear I won't look." He laughed and turned his back to let her put it on.

"You had better not, Eoghan Forrester!" She laughed. Of course, he sneaked a peek.

"Caught you, you old rogue."

He walked around to her side of the bed and took her in his arms. "That's not what you called me last night." He kissed her to quell her reply. She kissed him back and with breakfast forgotten they made love gently at first, and then passionately.

The sun beat down on Monique as she arrived back into the yard with yet another group of horse riders. The flies were having a great time bugging the horses. The sounds of children's laughter floated through the air but none of it lifted her mood. She couldn't face another Saturday night out without Garvan. Her thoughts were miles away when she heard Jessie.

"Will you come in for a bite to eat?"

"Thanks Jess. I'll follow you over."

Jessie had dished up a plate of Thai green curry with Basmati rice. It smelt delicious. Sam and his friend Ollie had nearly finished theirs and Geoff was still out working.

"How's Nora, I haven't seen her for a while?" asked Jessie.

"She went to Cork with the Active Retirement group. Of course, Molly went too. They had a great time."

"I could do with a day out. It's so busy around here."

"Take some holidays at the end of the summer before Sam goes back to school. I can look after the place for you." Jessie looked tired, she was always so high energy but running the stables and Butterfly Barn was taking its toll.

"No replies to your CVs then?"

"Non, nothing."

"What about going to Dubai?"

"It's finally over. Oh Jessie, what if I missed an opportunity of a lifetime?"

The back door opened and Grace burst into the kitchen. "I have news." She had her left hand behind her back.

"You finally said yes," said Jessie, jumping up. "Oh, show me." Grace held out her left hand. There were three diamonds embedded in a yellow gold band on either side of a solitaire.

"It's fabulous." Jessie hugged her just as Jack came in the back door with Lily in her carry tot and Finn toddling along in front of him.

"Oh Jess, it was Jack's mother's."

"Oh that's even more wonderful. Congratulations, I am so delighted for you both." She hugged Jack, while Monique admired the ring too. "This calls for a celebration. I'll ring Geoff."

Monique sat at the kitchen table with Baby Lily in her arms while the others rang around to invite people over for drinks at Butterfly Barn. It beat another Saturday night out in Bayrush, she thought.

"Will you text Rachel, Mon?" called Jessie. Monique put Lily in the carry tot and sent a text to Rachel. She smiled when she saw a radiant Grace, with Jack's arm around her, speaking to Kate on Facetime. They were all so happy in their relationships. Would she ever get over Garvan Leslie, she wondered? She hadn't heard from him since the night she had ended it. What had she expected? She heard Jack on the phone to his brother. Oh no, she thought. Garvan's parents would be over too. She hadn't seen them since before Garvan had left. Her phone bleeped. Rachel and Jay were on their way. Jessie had opened a bottle of wine. Monique poured herself a large glass. It was going to be a long night.

Jessie was delighted to see that so many people had turned up at such short notice. At ten o'clock, there was a great atmosphere at the barn. It was a warm balmy evening and most people were sitting outside.

"That's what's lovely about the summer, just grabbing the moment when it comes," said Jessie.

"True, we couldn't have asked for a better evening. Look at Sam and Ollie playing with Finn. I don't know how he's still standing," said Grace.

"So much for a routine," said Sophia. "Lily is fast asleep inside. I think

Eoghan is finding his feminine side in there."

"Eoghan dotes on her. He comes in every morning to see her," said Grace.

Jessie left the two women to chat and went to make sure people had enough to eat and drink. She saw Monique sitting with Rachel and Jay. She had been in the middle of finally opening up when Grace had arrived in with the big news. Jessie hoped she was okay. She spotted Jack's brother and his wife, Marie, chatting with Jack and Geoff. Monique smiled at Marie but her smile wasn't reciprocated. Monique stood up and Jessie noticed a slight stagger; the wine Monique had earlier had gone to her head. Marie made a beeline for Monique. Oh no, thought Jessie as she overheard Marie ask, "Monique, can I have a word? Garvan is broken-hearted over what you did to him." Jessie couldn't believe her ears. Him broken-hearted! He was the one who upped and left without a by-your-leave.

"I'm sorry," said Monique, meekly.

"You're sorry. I don't think that's good enough. He was trying to make a life for you. You are still unemployed, wandering around aimlessly; at least he has a decent job. And he even tried to get a job for you. But you thanked him by ending a four-year relationship – on the phone." Marie was on a roll. Jessie was afraid she was going to attract attention and Monique was standing with her mouth open just looking at her. In the corner of her eye, Jessie saw Rachel getting up. If Rachel got to Marie first, there would be trouble. Rachel was a true fiery redhead. She wouldn't be long about giving Marie a piece of her mind. Jessie could feel her blood boil but it was Grace's special evening and she did not want a scene.

"So Marie, I'm delighted you came this evening," said Jessie, leading Marie over towards Grace and Sophia. "You haven't seen Sophia since she came back from New York." Jessie made a face at Sophia who noticed immediately.

"Come and join us," said Sophia, pulling out a chair. Jessie virtually pushed Marie into it. She glanced over her shoulder looking for Monique and Rachel. They were nowhere to be seen.

"I just want to make sure everybody is being looked after," said Jessie, walking away.

She found Monique and Rachel at the toilets. Monique was upset. She didn't want anyone else to see them, so she led the two girls into one of the small training rooms and closed the door.

"Tonight is not the night for this conversation. But I am going to say what has been on my mind since Garvan left. Monique, you are the daughter we never had. Follow your dreams. Figure out what they are and follow them. And always know you have a home wherever we are. Nora wants you to be happy. If being with Garvan is the answer, go." Jessie crossed her fingers behind her back when she said that. "But remember you only have one life Monique and you can't continue to be so unhappy. Come here, honey," said Jessie, wrapping her arms around her. Suddenly great, big, wrenching sobs came out from Monique as her body shook to its core.

After a few minutes, Jessie released her and held her face in her hands. Looking into her eyes, she said, "There is nothing like a good old cry. Now you know how much Grace and I love ABBA. Are you girls on for a night out? The new cinema is putting on a rerun of *Mamma Mia*."

"Absolutely," said Rachel. She smiled and mouthed "thank you" behind Monique's back.

Monique smiled through her tears and nodded. "Yes, I will come along and thanks, Jess."

"Now go and splash some water on that beautiful face of yours and let's all enjoy the rest of the evening."

Kate's phone had rung.

"OMG, that's fantastic news. I can't wait to tell Richard. Oh Gracey, I wish I was at home to celebrate with you. Congratulations. Love you." She hung up. "My sister just got engaged," she told the volunteers around her. They all smiled and said how nice it was. She walked to a quiet corner to speak to Richard. No answer from his cell, so she rang the office. Colleen answered. "He's in a meeting, Kate. I'll get him to call you back."

Since she had come back to New York, she had taken a more positive approach to living there. She had read an article in one of Richard's magazines about a gardening project in derelict areas of Manhattan. She had made some calls and had become a volunteer. It filled her days because her visa didn't allow her to work. She was making a huge effort to fit into Richard's life but she still avoided the cocktail parties as much as she could and had refused to go to any charity lunches, as they were usually women-only affairs. She preferred hands-on charity work.

Beads of sweat dripped down her back. It was an incredible one hundred degrees Fahrenheit in the late July heat. She found it very hard to cope but she wouldn't give in. Nobody else did. She loved the work because it mixed art and design with gardening and she was meeting nice people with a similar outlook to hers.

She was knee-deep in muck. She looked across to where two other volunteers were working hard.

"And I thought I was an artist," she called to one of them. "When did it all get so pear-shaped?" she said, picking up a pear tree and placing it in a hole she had just dug.

"You see, you're even thinking in plants."

"So funny I forgot to laugh."

Everybody laughed.

The goal was to develop derelict sites throughout Manhattan into places of visual beauty for use by the whole community. There was a tremendous amount of clearing and lifting involved but it was planting that she enjoyed. There was something so very primeval about getting her hands dirty and feeling the earth between her fingers.

Last weekend she and Richard had driven out of the city to a huge garden centre to choose some plants to create their own piece of heaven on their rooftop. Previously a designer had arranged it. Neither of them had taken a particular interest in it. It was quite streamlined and uninteresting with little or no colour. To her surprise, Richard had enjoyed the whole experience and they had spent an evening planting together.

The rest of the day flew by as she worked alongside the other volunteers. Richard hadn't called her back. Two of the guys suggested going for a drink to celebrate her sister's engagement. "Sure, why not!" she had said. They walked to the nearest bar on the block. Three drinks later and Richard still hadn't returned her call. She was getting anxious. It wasn't an area she fancied being around at night. So she bid her farewell and left. She took the subway home. When she arrived at Richard's building, Pete the night porter was on.

"Did Mr Wynthrope arrive yet?"

"No," said Pete.

"Thanks," she replied, not bothering to make her usual small talk with him. She wondered what he thought when he saw her coming in and out of the building day after day with old work clothes on. The private elevator door opened directly into the empty penthouse. She went straight to the shower. Afterwards she lay down on top of the duvet. There was still no word from Richard. She eventually fell asleep. She awoke to the sound of Richard tip-toeing into the bedroom.

"Hi honey, I didn't mean to wake you. I got held up at the office."

"I called to tell you Grace and Jack got engaged."

"That's wonderful news." He dropped onto the bed beside her. She didn't move.

"I'm sorry it ran so late and I didn't get a chance to ring you back."

"Richard, I get that you work hard but you have never not answered my calls. I'm not demanding but I do ask for your respect." She turned away from him.

"Kate, I'm really sorry. That won't happen again." He curled up beside her and they lay in spoons on top of the bed in silence. When she woke the next morning, he had already left. There was a note on the counter. <I'm sorry, I promise I'll make it up to you later.>

She made coffee and brought it out to the rooftop garden. The view of the early morning Manhattan skyline was incredible. She turned to go back inside. She stopped in her tracks. She just had an idea. She rang Vince, Richard's driver.

"Vince will you pick me up in twenty minutes and bring me to the nearest paint shop?"

"Sure, I will."

She ran into the bedroom and got dressed. She had five weeks left on her student visa – she planned to enjoy every moment of her time left.

Chapter Six

Monique left the cinema with Jessie, Grace and Rachel. They were all still laughing.

"I love that movie. I know you can watch it on DVD but it's not the same. I've been looking forward to it for the past two weeks. All I want to do is dance like a mad thing," said Jessie, attempting a jig outside the cinema.

"You're crazy," said Grace, pushing her towards Nutties, the nearest pub to the cinema. "There might be music on in here. It's a novelty to get a night out. I want to make the most of it."

"A trad night," said Monique, reading from the poster on the wall. Two weeks had gone by and she still hadn't received any replies to her job applications, but she felt better about so many things. She had such good friends and she was getting used to being single.

"It'll do, come on," said Jessie, leading the way in. Monique hung back; the last time she was here, she had heard Donagh sing. Their paths hadn't crossed since. What if he was inside? Jessie ordered their drinks while she and the girls found a quiet corner away from the musicians.

"Bit of a come down from *Mamma Mia*," said Grace, as they listened to a woman singing 'All the lies that you told me'.

"Nice singer," said Jessie, putting a gin and tonic on the table for Grace and three bottles of Coors for them. "Wasn't Meryl Streep fab? You know she reminds me a little of Sophia. What do you think?"

"Yes, she does actually," said Grace.

"She is positively glowing," said Monique.

"They are so happy together. Eoghan is full of the joys every morning," said Rachel. Grace nodded in agreement.

The music started again. It was a male voice singing Phil Coulter's song 'Scorn not his Simplicity'.

Monique recognised the voice immediately. When the song was over there was a burst of applause.

"I have to see the face behind that voice," said Jessie, getting up to look. "You are not going to believe it, Monique – it's Donagh."

"Really?" she said, but she didn't get up to look.

Rachel stood up to look, turned, and said, "It's the guy we heard weeks ago. He's gorgeous. I think he likes you, Mon."

She made a face. "He does not."

Jessie waved at him. "Oh great, he's coming over."

"Hi Jessie," he said.

"You were brilliant, Donagh. This is Grace, a great friend of mine."

"Hi Grace," he said, giving Grace the full blast of his smile.

"And you remember Monique and this is her best friend, Rachel!" said Jessie, beaming at him.

"Hi Rachel," he said and he continued talking to Jessie. "So what brought you all in here?"

"We went to *Mamma Mia*," said Monique, blushing. "The girls chose here because it is the nearest pub to the cinema."

"Oh," he said. She wanted him to know it hadn't been her idea.

"Well, I hope you enjoy the rest of the evening, girls." He was about to walk away when Grace asked.

"Donagh, do you write your own material?"

Jessie exchanged a look with Monique. Oh God, she wondered how he would handle that question.

"I'm working on something at the moment. I'd like to do more with it."

"That's interesting because I am running a writing workshop every Sunday over four weeks. You might like to join it."

"Sounds interesting. I have Jessie's number. I'll give her a call. Cheers," he said. If he was fazed he certainly hadn't shown it, thought Monique. Then he turned to her and said, "Maybe you'd like to come outside for some air. You look hot."

Jessie and Grace laughed, and Rachel nudged her.

"I am not hot … thank you very much for your concern," said Monique, blushing more.

"Oh, but you are," he said, winking at the others as he walked away.

When he was out of earshot, Jessie said, "He's into you big time, Monique."

"Go, girl, go!" Grace said. "If I was a few years younger I'd fight you for him."

"Girls, we were here one night and he couldn't take his eyes off Monique," said Rachel. "Monique, he's gorgeous."

"You are all crazy. Do you want another drink?"

"Yes," they chorused, still laughing.

"Ah Mon, we're only messing," said Jessie, but she was already halfway to the bar. She looked around. Donagh was with the girl with the fabulous hair. It looked like they were definitely more than friends. So much for Jessie's assumptions, she thought. When she came back with the drinks, the girls were chatting about Dirk, Finn's father.

"Does Dirk still want Finn to go to France?"

"I meant to tell you Jess, his mother happened to ring the very next day to invite Finn over to her house. I mentioned that Dirk wanted Finn to go to France for a week."

"What did she say?"

"Nothing, but I got a call from Dirk yesterday asking to have Finn the weekend after next. He is coming home and staying at his mother's house. Of course, I agreed immediately."

"Happy days," said Jessie.

Donagh rang Jessie. He had some questions for her. Firstly, he described how it felt when he was reading. He explained how the letters seemed to move up and down on the page and about how tired it made him feel. He was getting headaches and feeling stressed about it.

"Will you talk to Monique about this?" But before Jessie had a chance to say another word, he cut in.

"I was just looking for a contact for one of those, you know, psych."

"Of course, I'll get a name of an educational psychologist who specialises in a learning challenge called dyslexia. I'm not very knowledgeable in this area, Donagh. It sounds a little like that. Really, you should …"

He guessed she'd suggest Monique again. So he said, "That would be great; you might ring me back with it. Also Jessie, do you think I could join the class your friend spoke about?"

"Do you mind if I tell Grace? She might have some tips and advice that could help. Also, I'm taking part too."

"Cool but I'm not sure I'd like everyone in the class to know."

"Let me ask Grace, and I'll come back to you. I'll get a name for you too."

"Thanks Jessie."

"Donagh, if Grace says yes, nobody else in the class will know your business, okay?"

He let out a sigh of relief. "Cheers."

"Give me twenty minutes."

He sat on the floor in his bedroom and strummed his guitar while he waited for Jessie's call. He thought of Monique and smiled. She was just so tetchy around him. He enjoyed winding her up. She was so serious.

He had heard she was going out with an engineer who had landed some big job in Dubai. People said it was only a matter of time before she'd be leaving too. They were together for a long time.

His phone rang. It was Jessie; she gave him the name of an educational psychologist but she had heard there was a three-month waiting list. He took down the phone number and Jessie spelt out the woman's name. Then she said Grace would be delighted to have him on the workshop.

"Thanks a million, Jessie. I'll see you on Sunday the 14th of August."

He rang the number. He got an appointment for the 10th of November.

Sophia sat around the table at Bonita's with Nora and Molly. They had just finished a five-mile walk around the sand hills of Bayrush Beach.

"I'm so delighted for you Sophia." Molly patted her hand. "We've been watching you two for years wondering when you'd finally get it together, haven't we Nora?"

"We sure have. Molly never gave up hope. I must admit I struggled," Nora laughed.

"Every time you came back from a day's sailing, we'd watch closer looking for any auld signs of a bit of loving," said Molly.

"Really, you two are the limit," Sophia laughed.

"Sure there's nothing in the world like a bit of romance," Molly laughed. "Look at you, you're positively glowing. If you could bottle that, I'd buy it. What d'ya think, Nora?"

"I sure would."

"Have you told Kate and Richard? I know Kate will be so pleased," said Molly.

"Don't tell her yet, we're thinking of going to New York. I'd like to tell Richard in person. I really hope he'll be happy for us."

"Of course he will," said Nora, reassuringly.

Sophia hoped she was right. "It seems everybody else knew, but us."

"That's always the way. You can never see what's right under your nose."

"Wise words, Nora. What about Monique? How is she since Garvan went to Dubai?" asked Sophia.

"Up and down, I'm at a loss to know what to do. I want her to be happy. I'm just so worried. I hear her crying at night. I don't understand why she won't go and at least see if she'd like Dubai. She loves Garvan. She wouldn't be so heart-broken if she didn't."

"Nora, I think you need to talk to her," said Sophia, thinking that the reason Monique had refused to go was Nora.

"You're right, Sophia. I want her to experience the world, travel, live life to the full."

Kate sat on the nubuck corner suite watching TV, in Richard's penthouse, alone. Wynthrope Communications was in the middle of a takeover bid that meant Richard had been working late every evening for the past two weeks. She got up and opened the doors leading to the rooftop garden. She stood at the low wall and looked out into the Manhattan skyline. Lights twinkled all around her but she had never felt so lonely in her life. She was happy when she volunteered. The work on the gardening project was so physical she came home tired. Most nights she was too exhausted to think which was good. When Richard was there, life felt great. But when he wasn't, she felt her life was in limbo. He must know her visa would expire at the end of August – only three weeks away. Neither of them brought up the subject. Maybe it was his way of letting her go. The other night, he had commented on her hands. He had laughed and said they were like farmers' ones. She had laughed too but it had hurt. He was the kind of man who was used to women with nice manicured nails. She went back inside and picked up the photograph on the mantelpiece. It was one of Heather, his first wife. She was blonde and tanned with the perfect all-American smile. She had her arm around their six-year-old son, Billy, who had the same rich dark-brown hair as Richard's with a dabbling of freckles across the bridge of his nose. He was smiling too.

"Oh God, how could Richard ever get over losing them?" she mumbled. The authorities had been unable to recover their bodies after the horrific plane crash that had taken them and the pilot of the light aircraft. Kate sighed; she must be crazy to think that she could fit into Richard Wynthrope's world. She placed the photograph back in its place and went to the bedroom. She lay down on the bed and cried herself to sleep.

Donagh parked beside Butterfly Barn and walked towards the jetty. It had been his favourite spot back in June. The mid-August sun glistened on the lake and he saw the rubber inflatable boat (RIB) tied up and smiled when he remembered Monique's face the day Geoff had picked her out of the water. Her eyes had been bright and alive, not like other times when he had noticed how sad she had looked. He hoped he'd catch a glimpse of her at some point over the day. He had come early to sit at the jetty. He'd love a cigarette but he had packed them in when he heard the cost of the visit to the psychologist. He had three months to get some money together.

He was apprehensive, but not nearly as scared about taking the creative writing class as he had been coming here the first time. He set off in the direction Monique had come from the first morning he had seen her. Ten minutes along the path, he was so busy humming a tune in his head and taking in the view that he didn't hear the sound of horse's hooves until the last minute. The path was narrow with the lake at one side and a ditch on the other.

"Jesus Christ," he yelled, as he saw a big black horse cantering straight for him. He jumped to the side to avoid them but he caught his foot in the root of a tree and tumbled backwards halfway into the lake.

Monique was startled. Nobody ever walked on this path. The last person in the world she expected to see was Donagh. His jeans were covered in a mixture of muck and water.

"Why are you walking here? There is a sign," she cried.

"You mean, are you okay Donagh? I hope you're not hurt or anything." He glared at her as he tried to get up from his very slippery place on the bank of the lake. "Doesn't that thing have any goddamn brakes?"

"Pardon," she said. "Are you okay?" She jumped down from Jasper's back.

"I hurt my leg."

"Show me."

"Do you really want to see it?" Then he grinned.

She gave him a withering look.

"Ah no, I'm serious. I think I've sprained my ankle. I can't put any weight on it."

"I am so sorry. I thought you were joking. I will help you. Lean on me, okay!"

"I'll be fine." He began to limp back the way he had come.

"If you want to get on Jasper I can lead him back to the yard. We can get you seen to then."

"You must be kidding. I've never been on a horse. I value my life."

"Did you not see the sign?" she asked, as she walked slowly back along the trail leading Jasper.

"No, I'm a bigger fool than you already thought." He smirked.

She blushed. "Your clothes are ruined. Are you taking the writing workshop?" Jessie hadn't mentioned he had signed up for it.

"Yes. I have some spare shorts in the back of the jeep." He stopped and bent down to rub his ankle again.

"You are not okay?" She was genuinely concerned. "Look, there is a branch down over there. You can rest for a minute."

"I think I might need to."

She tied Jasper's reins to a branch. He was taking the class too. How could she cope spending all day in the same room as him again? She sat down on a rock opposite him. She didn't know what to say.

"It's beautiful here and so peaceful," he said.

"It is." But it was the least peaceful she had felt in her entire life. Her heart was racing.

"Do you come here often?"

She smiled. "Every morning actually!"

"So if I ever want to see you again, I'll have to come here!"

She smiled, thinking that was the last thing she wanted, or was it.

"So what part of France are you from?"

"Paris."

"Nice. How long have you been here?"

"I must go. I have to bring Jasper back to his stable or else I will be late for class." She didn't want to talk about France, or her past.

"Oh, you are doing it too!" He seemed very surprised. "I'm sorry. I've delayed you so much." He smiled.

Her heart skipped a beat every time he smiled. She never remembered feeling like this around Garvan. There was something edgy and dangerous about Donagh. Women of all ages seemed to be enthralled with him. Jess, Grace, Rachel and even Sophia thought he was divine. She untied Jasper and put her leg in the stirrup and swung onto the horse.

"You make that look so easy," he said.

"Maybe you would like to try it sometime." What was she doing? That had sounded so flirty.

"I think I'll pass on that offer. I like my life." Obviously, he had thought so too and had brushed it off. He was used to women coming on to him.

She laughed to cover her embarrassment and trotted away.

Grace had changed her mind so many times about giving the workshop because Lily was still so small. But Jack had insisted she take some time out to do what she loved. He had suggested she run it on Sundays so that he could look after the kids. He promised to bring them over at lunchtime.

Her biggest concern was about meeting Donagh's needs. She had no experience around dealing with a person with a reading difficulty. But she had discovered there were songwriters who couldn't read or write and had simply recorded their words.

She sat at a large round table and smiled at the seven faces looking back at her. "You are all very welcome to Butterfly Barn. I'm looking forward to spending time with you," said Grace. "Firstly, you've all met Jessie; she will be taking part in the classes too. The rest of you might introduce yourselves and tell me your particular area of interest."

"Freddie is my name and I'm interested in poetry," a bald man in his sixties offered.

"Alanna, I'd like to attempt writing a short story."

"Thanks." Grace smiled at the pretty twenty-something.

"Marie-Claire, I'd like to do the same as Alanna." This came from a wide, cheery-faced woman of about fifty who then added, "Although I'd like to try poetry too. I'm on for anything."

"That's wonderful," said Grace, smiling.

"My name is Donagh and I'd like to learn about song writing."

With a voice like his, thought Grace, and his extremely handsome face, he could take the world by storm.

"I'm Monique. I am interested in all kinds of writing."

"I'm Sally and I'm just curious. They say everyone has a book in them. Who knows, I might discover a deeply, and I mean deeply, hidden talent."

Everybody laughed. Grace had been pleased when Sally had asked to take part. She was Sam's best friend's mother. She had been a great friend to Jessie when she lost her babies and she had become one of their close friends over the years. Her eldest son, Jay, also worked with Jack. Grace felt her anxiety leave her.

"Thank you everybody. I guess it's safe to say we will need pens and paper. Some of you might like to use the voice recorder on your smart phone. If not, I have some Dictaphones. I'll just show you how this one works." She held it up and went through the steps. She thought it would help Donagh to express his ideas immediately and it might benefit some of the others.

"So let's start with a game." She placed seven small pieces of paper folded on the table. "I'd like each person to choose one. When you open it you will see one word. I want you to find somewhere in the room or outside to either write or dictate a few sentences to describe the word. Let your imagination run riot but don't use the actual word because the rest of us have to guess its identity."

Jessie sat chewing the top of the pen. It had only begun and she was already enjoying the process. She had decided to do the workshop because she had found a journal she had written when her babies had died. In it was an attempt at a poem. At that time, she could see no light. She had left it unfinished. Three years on, she wanted to see where it would lead her. When she opened the piece of paper she had chosen it said "hope". She smiled and began to write.

Kate sat beside Richard at Yankee Stadium. She had arranged to meet Lisa and Chad. Richard was a big fan of the Yankees while Chad, being originally from Cape Cod, was a major Red Sox fan. He and Richard could spend hours discussing tactics and the ins and outs of baseball. Neither she nor Lisa appreciated any of it, but it was her chance to catch up with her friend. The first time she had come, she couldn't believe the size of the stadium or how long the game went on. Lisa shifted in her seat for the hundredth time.

"I can't get comfortable," she said from the seat on the other side of Kate.

"Me neither. Give me a hurling match any day. Much more exciting," said Kate.

"Must admit, I'm more a rugby fan myself," Lisa whispered. "All that muscle and testosterone."

Kate laughed. "And I thought I was bad."

"Will you two stop talking?" Chad had become exasperated. The Red Sox were losing.

"Let's go and stretch our legs," said Lisa, getting up and massaging Chad's shoulders as she passed behind his seat. "It'll be okay, honey. Really."

"Yeah, yeah, don't worry your pretty little Irish head," he said just before he jumped up to roar, "Home run!"

"Come on, Kate. I can see we aren't needed here."

Richard turned his head to give Kate a kiss before she walked off.

"Love in a bucket," Lisa said as they climbed up the many steps towards the back of the stadium. "Doesn't last forever, you know."

Tell me about it, thought Kate. She had just spent another week of evenings at home. "You're a bit cynical today."

"Just realistic!"

"Do I need to take some happy pills to be around you? What's the matter? Is the shine going off after how long? Four years?" asked Kate.

"That's what I mean, we've been together for four years and he still hasn't asked me the big question. I ain't getting any younger. I'll be thirty-eight next month. My body clock is ticking. In actual fact it's beginning to sound like a time bomb."

"So do something about it."

"Like what?"

"Ask him."

"I'm still old-fashioned."

"Me too," muttered Kate. "My visa runs out on the 31st of August and I am not messing with the authorities. I have my flight booked."

"Does Richard know?"

Kate shook her head.

"Ah for God's sake, Kate. He'd marry you in the morning. You were only here a wet day when he asked you."

"If he really loved me and wanted to marry me he'd know my visa is to expire shortly." She slumped against a barrier near the coffee dock. "We're from different worlds. Look at me, Lisa. I'm not Mrs Wynthrope material. I'll never measure up to his last wife. That's the reality, this way we don't get to have a scene. I just leave."

"Forget the coffee, this calls for alcohol. I think you'd make a fine Mrs Wynthrope," said Lisa, marching towards the kiosk.

Kate smiled; Lisa was such a good friend. She wished she could see more of her. Life here didn't make it as easy as at home. Nobody just dropped in. She never thought she'd say it, but she missed home, she missed her mother. She missed the wisecracks and the banter. She missed Grace and little Finn. Lily was growing up without her.

Lisa came back with some beers and popcorn.

"Kate, I think you're crazy. Talk to Richard, together you'll figure it out."

She nodded; she didn't want to say any more about it.

"Let's find the boys and enjoy the rest of the day, and thanks, Lisa." She linked her friend and they headed back along the corridor to rejoin the boys. "Jeez, everything is on a mammoth scale in this country. I'd have climbed a mountain at this rate," she said as they reached the top of the steps only to go down the other side again.

Just as she was about to enter the row they had been sitting in, Richard was making his way along it towards her. She waited on the steps, wondering what was the matter.

"I'm sorry Kate, but we have to go. I just got a call from Bruce Philips. It's about the takeover I've been working on for the past few weeks."

"No problem, off you go! I'll see you later," She leaned up, kissed him on the cheek, and followed Lisa back to the seat.

"Aren't you coming with me?" he called after her.

"No," she said, and continued without a backward glance. When she reached her seat, she sat down.

"Are you okay?" asked Lisa.

She wasn't but she was hell bent on having a good time. She stole a glance and saw Richard walking up the steps towards the exit. There was no way she was going back to spend another day on her own in that penthouse while Mr Wynthrope changed the world.

"Chad, I'll see you at home later."

"Sure babes," he said, clearly not too put out.

"Let's go out on the town."

"Great idea," said Kate. She drank the remains of her beer and put the full popcorn carton in the bin. Then she set off up the steps again. "At least we'll be fit." She laughed although she felt more like crying.

Lisa knew everybody. Every club they had been to so far, they had been able to bypass the queue. "Comes with the territory," said Lisa, smiling as she flashed her business card at yet another doorman. It said that she was director at one of Manhattan's best event management companies.

"It's 2 a.m. and we're not even dressed appropriately," whispered Kate; she was wearing jeans and a Yankees baseball T-shirt and flat shoes.

"This is New York, anything goes. You're beautiful and have a fab body. Who knows, you might even set a new trend."

"I don't think so." She looked around at all the fabulously made-up girls around them.

"Two Manhattans," called Lisa to the barman. Kate's world was beginning to spin. She hadn't drunk so much in years.

"I'm just going to the Ladies." She looked for a sign and began to make her way down a steep staircase. She saw a man taking money from a young girl and slipping her a small packet. She kept walking. When she closed the cubicle door, she took a deep breath. She had been clean six years. She remembered her counsellor's words. Remember once an addict always an addict. It's your job to control it. The fear that she had buried for so long had finally surfaced. If she remained feeling as lonely and unhappy as she had been for the last few weeks, she was afraid she'd slip. All she had to do was walk back up that stairs and she could have a fix. She flushed the toilet, washed her hands and went back up the stairs. She saw him again. He smiled and with as much willpower as she could muster she walked past him. At the bar, Lisa was chatting to two guys. She introduced Kate; Lisa obviously knew them quite well. Kate picked up the Manhattan Lisa had ordered for her and drank it. She leaned towards Lisa and whispered, "Thanks, for today. I'm calling it a night."

"You sure you're okay to get home?" asked Lisa.

She wasn't but she told her she'd ring Richard's driver. The little white lie satisfied Lisa. Kate made her way back through the crowds. Just as she got to the door, the guy from the stairs was standing there.

"You sure you don't want it?" He must be a mind-reader or else he knew a target when he saw it. Fear welled inside her. He knew she was leaving alone and she had no idea where the nearest cab rank was. Oh God, what was she going to do?

She ignored him and stood beside a burly doorman. "You okay, lady?"

She looked over at the guy and said, "Yes, I'm just waiting for my friend. Do you mind if I stay here?"

"No probs." When she looked again the guy was gone. The doorman was chatting to his colleague.

"Excuse me, but could you call me a cab?"

"That's a cute Irish accent you've got there. I'll call my mate, Danny."

She let out a huge sigh of relief. "Thanks a million, that would be great."

While she waited, she chatted with him. He was from Harlem, his father was Nigerian and his mother was Italian. Her heart had stopped pounding by the time the cab appeared.

"Hey Samuel," said Danny from the driver's seat of the yellow cab.

"Hey Danny, will you bring this lady home safe? Come back again soon, Irish. It was nice talking to you."

"It's Kate and thanks so much, Samuel." But she'd never come back. She knew she had crossed her own line.

"What part of the auld sod are you from?" asked Danny, as he drove towards Park Avenue.

"A small town called Bayrush in County Waterford. And you?"

"I'm a Kerryman, Tralee. Been here ten years. You must be doing well, nice address! Are you here long?"

"I'm a childminder. Wealthy family, you know yourself."

"Nice to see how the other half live, eh!"

"True. Thanks, Danny." She went to pay him.

"It's on me, here's my card. Maybe you might give me a call sometime. It'd be nice to talk about home."

"Thanks, Danny." She took his card and smiled. She wondered if he was as lonely as she was. She had lied because she felt like an interloper in Richard's world.

"See ya," he said and drove off.

"Good morning, Peter," she said to the young night doorman.

"It's three a.m." He smiled. "Not like you to be out at this hour."

"A girl has to have fun, Peter."

She leaned against the lift walls to steady herself. It had been a narrow escape. When the door opened directly into the penthouse, she heard movement in the living room.

"Oh my God, Richard, you gave me a fright. Why are you sitting in the dark?" she asked.

"You didn't answer my calls or texts."

"I was with Lisa. I didn't hear the phone. We had a great night. It was long overdue. She's great fun."

"Goodnight, Kate," he said, not getting up.

"Goodnight, Richard," she said and went to bed.

Chapter Seven

essie had hardly slept all night. Today was her twin baby boys' third anniversary. So much had happened since their loss. She looked at Geoff who was still asleep. She wondered what she would have done without him. She had heard that many marriages or relationships hadn't survived the death of a baby or child. She hadn't been able to say the word death until the day she spoke to another woman who was living through the same grief. The woman had told her seven-year-old daughter that she had lost her baby and the little girl had looked up at her innocently and asked, "Oh Mummy, where did you leave it? You'll have to find it."

That was the day she realised just how powerful words were. She had been struggling with an ending for her poem. It had come to her during the night. She got dressed and then she picked up her mobile phone. She sent Grace a text.

<I will be late for class. There is something I need to do this morning>

Jessie's phone bleeped while she brushed her teeth. It was Grace's reply.

She went over to kiss Geoff. He woke.

"Hey honey, how are you doing?"

She tilted her hand from side to side. "So-so."

"I love you." Geoff reached up, took her in his arms, and held her. There were no words.

After a moment, she broke away. "I'm going to Matthews Point."

"Your special place."

She nodded.

"We'll have breakfast together when you get back."

"Good idea, I told Grace I'd be late."

She tacked up Jessie's Angel and set off towards the highest point on their land. When she reached the top, she dismounted and tied the horse to a branch. She sat on the same rock she had found two years ago and began to write the ending.

The day I let you go

I felt you closer than before
I finally now understand
Two angels by my side was the plan
Now I could talk
And I could feel
And I could love
Two angels by my side for all eternity
Lucky me
Now I see.

Birds twittered and in the distance she could see the ocean. In her head an orchestra played. It wasn't a poem. It had to be a song. If only she could sing.

"You are my little angels, help me find a way. You've helped with everything else. This song needs to go out in the world. I'll always love you both and I'm finding my way to accepting." She put down the pen and paper.

Monique woke at 6.30 a.m. She was looking forward to the second Sunday on the creative writing class. She jumped out of bed and, just like every other day, she pulled up a pair of jodhpurs and rummaged in the chest of drawers for a polo shirt. Garvan's rugby shirt's presence jolted her. Her sunny mood dissipated. She missed him.

Garvan had sent a text to apologise and had asked if they could still be friends. She had said yes and since then they were texting, and he had called her using Facetime, which was cool because she could see the places he had told her about. She loved being able to talk to him again. Especially because people kept asking how he was doing and when was she going to join him. She always managed to avoid a direct answer but if she couldn't find a job soon she might have to go.

She walked along the lane towards Butterfly Barn and wondered if Donagh would be sitting on the jetty. He certainly wouldn't chance walking along the trek again after what had happened last week. She wondered his was ankle better. He didn't seem to be limping so much towards the end of the day. She tacked up Jasper and set off towards the lake. She tried not to be disappointed when she passed the empty jetty.

After her trek, she was a little late for class. She apologised and slipped into the seat quietly. When she looked up, Donagh was smiling directly at her. He winked. She looked away quickly. She could lose herself in those eyes. Thankfully, one of the others began to read some of their work. She stole a look in his direction. He was listening intently.

He caught her eye again and smiled. This time nothing could stop the blood rushing to her face.

"So guys, now all of your imaginations are running riot. Each of you has a style unique to you. It's your voice. Some of you may want to hone that talent, or simply share with people who have a similar interest. A great read on the art of writing is Stephen King's book called *On Writing*. I personally found it both inspiring and fascinating," said Grace.

"Now, there's a man with an incredible imagination," said Freddie.

"Exactly, Freddie, and that is a quality you need to become a fiction writer. It's the ability to bring people on a journey through your imagination but using the reader's own."

"I see," said Donagh.

Monique noted how intently he listened to every word Grace said. He seemed so determined; she wondered why he hadn't contacted her to arrange one-to-one tuition as the others had. She listened to Grace again.

"After the coffee break, I'd like you to work on your chosen area. There are pens and papers here or feel free to type your piece on the laptops provided. I also brought a variety of books and, Donagh, I brought some lyric books too, both ballad and contemporary. Or you can use YouTube to listen to some of your favourites. From these you will get some guidelines as to the layout and format used in your area of interest. Write from your heart, relax and enjoy it. Let's have some coffee first!"

Donagh saw Monique answering her phone. She threw her head back and laughed in a way he had never seen her do before. Whoever she was talking to was obviously funny.

"Oh Garvan, that is so funny," she said. "I have to go. Talk to you later."

He overheard Sally talking to Jessie. "I thought it was over between Monique and Garvan."

"Four years is a long time, Sally. It's hard to walk away when you still love someone."

He went out to get some fresh air. Why did that bother him? She wasn't his type. He didn't like how she made him feel. It was okay to flirt with her and have some fun. But that was it. She was way too serious.

He was meeting Evie and the rest of the lads later. Simple and uncomplicated was his motto when it came to girls. Monique was definitely not simple or anywhere near uncomplicated.

He saw Geoff down at the jetty with the cover off the engine of the RIB.

"How are you doing there?"

"Blasted thing won't work. It's probably something small," said Geoff.

"Want me to take a look?"

"Sure why not? I'll just go back to the house. I left my mobile phone behind. I'll give a mate of mine a call, he's a motor boat buff."

Geoff climbed out and Donagh jumped aboard. He loved boats. If he managed to fix it, Geoff might let him take a spin out on the lake. There was a tiny island out in the middle of it. He'd love to take a closer look. He was tinkering away at it when Monique came over.

"You know about engines too?"

"Not a whole lot but often it's just something small. My friend Butchie has a rubber inflatable boat, well it's his dad's but he uses it mostly. They are great fun." He replaced the lid. "Fingers crossed." He pulled the string and it started perfectly just as Geoff came around the corner.

"Fair play to you, do you want to give her a good run?" said Geoff.

"Want to come too?" he asked Monique. She hopped in and sat next to him. He revved up and as soon as he was away from the jetty, he gave it full throttle.

"Lads, ye have no life jackets on," Geoff roared from the jetty.

Donagh pretended he didn't hear him. Monique threw her head back and laughed. The wind whipped her hair from her face and the boat threw up spray from the water. His breath caught in his throat as he did some of the arcs she had loved that day in June. When he reached the little island, he slowed down to take a closer look. It was overgrown with gorse and heather. He was using it as an excuse to stay out there longer with her.

"We are supposed to be in class."

"Let's call this research. Kneel up in the nose of the boat and hold onto the ropes at the sides."

He revved the RIB up again and aimed full speed ahead back towards the jetty.

"Wow! That was fantastic!" Her face glowed.

He smiled, slowing down to bring the boat up next to the jetty.

"I think you found a new passion, Monique," said Geoff, helping her out.

"Great power in that engine," said Donagh.

"You certainly checked it out. Thanks for fixing it," said Geoff, slapping him on the back.

"Better get back to class." Monique had already run on ahead of him.

After Kate's night out with Lisa, things between her and Richard were better. It might have been because the takeover had been a success and Richard was home every night. Whatever the reason, she didn't question it and nor did he. She just knew that her partying days were over. There was way too much temptation out there for a former drug addict like her.

She was curled up next to Richard watching a movie, when the buzzer went off. She nearly jumped out of her skin. Richard laughed.

"Flipping hell, what was that?"

"We have visitors."

"Well that just goes to show how few people call to us. I didn't recognise the sound."

"It's probably maintenance," said Richard, pressing the control on the coffee table. "Yes," he said in a bored voice.

"It's me. Can we come up?"

"Oh hi, Mom, I didn't expect you for another few weeks." He laughed. "Kate is jumping up and down with excitement here."

"Hi Sophia," shouted Kate.

"I wonder who's with her, she said *we*," said Richard.

"I hope it's a man."

"Funny ha, ha."

"And what would be wrong with that? Oh imagine if it was Eoghan."

"Don't be so silly, Mom is nearly sixty for goodness' sake."

"She's not dead, Richard. I hope we'll be still doing it in our sixties."

He laughed, catching her as she jumped off the back of the couch and into his arms.

"You are crazy, you know that."

The lift doors opened and Sophia laughed when she saw them.

"I told you," said Kate, jumping up and down and running over to hug them both. "What the hell took you two so long?"

"And hello to you too," said Eoghan, grinning.

Meanwhile Sophia went to Richard. He put his arms around her and Kate heard him whisper in her ear. "I'm really happy for you, Mom. He's a good guy."

Kate could see the relief on Sophia's face. "Thank you for saying that. I love you, son."

"Let's celebrate," said Kate, leading Eoghan to the bar.

"Oh my goodness," said Eoghan, "what an incredible view!" Kate opened the doors to let him explore further. "The garden is fantastic."

"Do you really like it?" said Kate, taking out Waterford Crystal champagne goblets while Richard opened a bottle of Moët.

"It's all Kate's doing," said Richard, pouring the champagne.

"Richard helped too."

"Not as much as I would have liked to. I've been so busy lately."

"Well done, that was a good ploy, that takeover will be very good for Wynthrope Communications," said Sophia.

"True but let's not talk business tonight."

"To the happy couple," said Kate. They all clinked glasses and Richard chatted to Eoghan about Waterford's recent performance in the GAA Championship. Kate grilled Sophia about how exactly she and Eoghan had got together. Richard smiled over at her. She felt all warm and fuzzy inside. She fully intended to make the best of the time she had left. But she really couldn't see a future for them. She loved him with all her heart and she knew he loved her. It just wasn't home or the life she wanted to live. Why was life never straightforward for her?

The next morning Sophia wandered around Richard's rooftop garden. Richard had offered to take Eoghan on a helicopter ride around Manhattan. It was a perfect opportunity to talk to Kate alone. She had been concerned about Kate being so unsettled but when she saw them together last night, it had been a great relief.

"Oh Kate, this is fabulous." She stood transfixed. Kate had painted a mural of Bayrush Beach on one of the walls. "My goodness, I feel as though I am standing on the beach with the ocean lapping at my feet. You've managed to capture the essence and depth of it, the cliffs, Everest Rock and the sky. My husband, Bill, loved Ireland. He always said the skies there made heaven feel close to the earth. It was one of the reasons I went there when he died. Oh Kate, what an incredible gift you have."

She moved a sun chair to a spot under the shade of the banana tree to continue her admiration. "You've done a wonderful job here," said Sophia. "I love your use of colour and light. Can I commission you to do my garden?"

Kate laughed. "Sure, I'll pop over and take a look but you don't have to pay me. So tell me, are you going to live here or in Ireland?" asked Kate.

"Between the two."

"Wow! Lucky you!"

"But you are more settled here than before? Richard told me all about the gardening project. Sounds like a worthwhile concept. Will you take me to see it?"

"It'll have to be soon, just like my visit to your roof garden."

"Kate, what's going on with you?"

"My student visa is up and I'm leaving in ten days."

"Richard never mentioned it."

"That's because he has probably forgotten." She took a sip of her iced tea.

"The least you can do is talk to him about it. Don't just disappear. That would be a very hurtful thing to do."

"I don't want to hurt him Sophia but if he really cared he'd remember. It has taken me a long time to find me. I'm not going back to that place of addiction and if I stay here, I'm afraid the loneliness will overwhelm me. Sophia, he was hardly home for three weeks, it's not his fault, he just works so hard. Look at what I did." She pointed to the garden and the mural. "I'm trying my best to keep busy. I just don't fit in here."

Sophia said nothing. She knew how loneliness felt. When her husband of thirty-five years died suddenly from a heart attack, it had a devastating effect on her. The previous year Heather, Richard's wife, and her grandson Billy had died in a plane crash on their way to the Cayman Islands. Richard had been on a business trip and they had planned a surprise visit. His way of dealing with his grief had been to immerse himself in the business. Now it might be the reason he'd lose the only woman who had reached him since their deaths.

"I've managed to silence you. Now that is a miracle."

Monique was pleased when Donagh disappeared to the jetty to work on a song. After last week's boat ride, she found it increasingly impossible to focus when he was around. Her phone bleeped; it was Garvan. He had been checking out jobs for her. He had asked her to consider going over for a few months. She could make enough money to buy a small car and she'd get some teaching experience for her CV.

The money she earned giving lessons at the stables covered Jasper's keep and she gave money to Gran. Although Gran never wanted it, she knew it helped towards the little extras they had. Thankfully Gran had suggested she set up a Credit Union account when she was sixteen to save a small amount of money every week. She could apply for a loan to pay for the flight to Dubai. If she still hadn't received a reply from her job applications she would have to go.

Monique was so preoccupied she hadn't been listening to what Grace had said about writing a short story.

Her story could be about a girl who loved a boy but he didn't love her enough and left her. Then another boy came into her life but he didn't particularly notice her and had many girls vying for his attention, especially a fiery stunning redhead. The girl tried everything to be noticed but it wasn't to be. He sailed into the sunset with said redhead – whose hair, by the way, was the same colour as sunset. That was the most ridiculous story. This writing lark was not for her. Thank God, she didn't have to share it with the group.

She sat twiddling the pen. She wished she had listened.

"Why don't you try writing free flow, Monique?"

"I don't know how to start."

"I notice you're speaking to Garvan again. Write about your impressions of Dubai. Or else write about the most exciting thing you've done recently, and if you haven't done anything exciting – make it up."

Kate showered and dressed. When she went to the kitchen, Richard had already made breakfast and was eating it in the garden. Her heart was pounding. Her flight was leaving JFK later today. She took a deep breath. She had hardly made it to the huge glass doors when she said, "Richard, I'm leaving today."

He had been reading the New York Times. He folded it and laid it neatly down on the table beside his espresso cup. He remained in his seat.

"Are we going to talk about this or have you made your decision?"

"My visa is up, Richard."

"So it's not your decision to leave me, just this country."

She walked over and sat in the seat opposite him. He poured her coffee into the cup he had already brought out for her. It was their tradition – no matter what happened they always started the day with breakfast together.

She leaned her elbows on the table and put her head in her hands. After a moment she looked up and said, "I'm leaving the country. I can't settle here. I'm not Mrs Wynthrope material, Richard. You know it and so do I."

He put his hand up to his chin and rested his head on it. "Since when did the Kate Fitzgerald I know care so much about what other people think?"

"I don't. But you do. You don't invite me to events anymore." He made to object but she continued. "For the past few weeks I've spent too many nights here alone, Richard. My God, I nearly had a heart attack when the buzzer went off the other night. I didn't recognise the sound of our door, which is not even a proper door, it's a goddamned private elevator. Nobody visits. Everything is by prior arrangement and if I brought any of my college friends here, I'd be accused of breaking and entering."

He smirked.

"I'm glad you find it all so amusing. We are too different, Richard. I'm not happy here and you can't live in Ireland and work the way you do. I want us to be friends but I'll understand if you can't forgive me. I do love you, Richard but …"

"Not enough to stay."

She got up. She was blinded by her tears. "I have to pack."

She went to the bedroom and took out her suitcase. Even after two years, she hadn't accumulated much. After a few minutes, he stood in the bedroom doorway. His face was filled with sadness. She walked over to him. Tears flowed down her cheeks. He wrapped his arms around her and held her tight. He was so tall her head only reached his chest. He tilted her chin and kissed her full on the lips. "I love you, Kate Fitzgerald, and I always will." And then he left.

She said goodbye to Peter, the doorman. She asked him to wave down a yellow cab but he told her Richard had left the town car for her. Vince, his driver, got out and put her suitcase in the truck. She got into the back seat and put on her dark glasses. At the airport, she waited in the queue. A little boy kept turning around to look at her.

"Mummy, why is that lady wearing sunglasses indoors?" he asked.

"Don't ask silly questions," said his mother, turning around.

"She's probably famous," said his sister, with the tone of the all-knowing older sister. Their mother was mortified. "Turn around," she said, physically twisting the two kids towards the check-in desk. Kate half-smiled; it was a perfectly good assumption. She always thought people who wore sunglasses indoors were either famous or had something to hide. Her eyes were puffy and sore from all the crying she had done.

Eventually, she boarded the flight to Shannon. She made her way to her economy class window seat and she swapped the sunglasses for the eye mask. What had she done?

She peeped out from under her eye mask to look for some headphones. Just then a flight attendant appeared.

"Miss Fitzgerald, we have a small problem."

Kate raised her eyebrows in question, waiting.

"We're actually overbooked."

"Oh, do you need me to get off?" said Kate, trying to get out of the seat. The woman beside her was looking at her as if she were mad.

"Not at all, we would be very grateful if you would accept an upgrade to first class," said the young girl.

"Oh." She was disappointed. She had thought this was her chance to get off the plane.

The poor girl began to apologise profusely for the terrible inconvenience. She got up in a near trance. She picked up her things and followed the girl to the nose of the aircraft.

For one mad moment, she actually thought that Richard might be here. Instead a thin, bald man in his sixties smiled at her. She acknowledged him with a small nod and flopped into the window seat.

In the meantime, the flight attendant had made a quick exit. How ungrateful she must seem – a free upgrade and she had hardly said thank you.

Kate picked up the headphones, pressed the controls a couple of times and sat back to watch *The Simpsons* on her personal TV. It might make her laugh or else she'd make a fool of herself bawling her head off the whole way home.

Two hours and three gins into the flight, she reclined her seat and pressed the control to look for some relaxing music. She needed to sleep or else she'd be half-jarred arriving home. She stopped her search when she heard "Bring him Home" from the musical *Les Miserables;* she shifted in her seat to get comfortable. The song had a new meaning for her. She wished with all her heart that she could "bring" Richard home. If only her world could be so perfect. A tear trickled down her cheek.

She eventually slept and woke up to the sound of the captain's voice telling them that they would shortly be descending into Shannon. She looked out the window and saw the green patterned fields of Ireland atop the rugged cliffs. She loved this country so much. She loved her family and her friends. Unfortunately she loved a man who could never live here. At least she had tried his world. She could have no regrets. Imagine if she had said yes to his proposal. She would be returning an even bigger failure than she already was.

She went to the car hire desk and twenty minutes later she was on the road. Sophia had given her keys to Rose Cottage. She could hole up there for a few days before going to her mother's house. But when she saw the sign "Welcome to Bayrush", the only place she wanted to be was with her mam in their little terraced house off the square. She parked on the street beside her mother's Ford Fiesta just as the front door opened.

When her mother saw her, she stood gaping in amazement. What was it about mothers that they always knew when things were not right? Molly began knocking on the window and mouthing through the glass. "Is everything okay? What are you doing home? What's going on?"

Kate opened the car door. "Mam, relax will you. Let me at least get out of the car. I'll explain everything then. Don't go drawing the neighbours on us."

"Oh yeah," said Molly, looking anxiously from side to side. "Get out so, will you?"

Kate threw her eyes to heaven – twenty-nine years old and still bossed around by her mother. Thank you Sophia for giving me the keys to Rose Cottage, she thought.

She followed her mother inside where she began fussing around. Boiling the kettle, taking out the teapot, tidying things that didn't need it and all the while she bombarded her with questions. A real sign of her anxiety, the woman was in a whirl.

"Did he hurt you?" asked Molly, stopping dead in her tracks around the kitchen.

"No, Mam, don't be silly!"

"Why didn't you say you were coming home?"

"My visa is up."

"What? You're in debt. For the loving honour of God, how did you manage that? Were you trying to keep up with him? Didn't I always tell you to live within your means?" Her mother was on the rampage.

"Mam, you need a visa to stay in America."

"Did I get one of them when I went over to visit you?"

Kate sighed; she was too tired for this.

"I'm tired. Can I just get some sleep for a couple of hours?"

"Of course you can, pet. Give me a minute. I'll get your bed ready."

"Thanks, Mam, I'll give you a hand."

She followed her mother. They rarely did hugs in the Fitzgerald house but you never felt short on love. She had missed her mother even though she was off her head at times; people often said she was just like her.

"Mam?"

"What?" asked Molly, taking sheets from the hot press. When Molly looked at her, she put down the sheets. "Come here, love." Her mother wrapped her arms around her and Kate could no longer hold back her tears. "I know it's hard." Her mother squeezed her tight. Then she broke away and said, "Now, we'll get the bed ready and everything will feel better after a good sleep."

"Thanks, Mam."

Eoghan and Sophia were on the viewing point of the Empire State Building. Eoghan had wanted to do the tourist trail together. She looked at Eoghan's handsome profile as he gazed at the vista before him. She wandered away to another viewing point. Moments later, he stood behind her and wrapped his arms around her waist. She leaned back into him. He whispered, "Beautiful, isn't it?"

She couldn't answer because of the lump of emotion caught in her throat. She had never dreamed that she'd find love again.

"Come on, my love. I have a surprise for you. Let's go," said Eoghan.

They took the Fifth Avenue exit from the Empire State and walked hand in hand heading north. She had lived the town car life for so long she'd forgotten how beautiful Fifth Avenue was to walk along. But after a couple of blocks her feet began to ache. "I haven't been on the subway in years!"

"We'll have to do something about that." Eoghan led her down the next subway staircase.

"Where are we going? You've got to let me in on it."

"It's a surprise. Trust me, love."

"Okay," she mumbled. She had never liked surprises. Her heart was beating fast and she was intrigued and excited. They emerged from the subway on the corner of Fifty-Seventh Street and Fifth Avenue and walked to the entrance of one of the most famous jewellery stores in the world.

"We have an appointment, Forrester is the name," said Eoghan, to the pretty assistant who checked the schedule.

"This way please, Mr Forrester."

She could feel Eoghan's hand on her lower back. "Are you okay?" he asked.

She nodded her head but was completely overwhelmed. She knew they were being led to the diamond rings section.

"Good afternoon, Mrs Wynthrope," said the manager, recognising her immediately.

"It's good to see you again, Vincent," she answered.

"Claude will take care of you. Enjoy your viewing."

"Claude, would you mind if we browsed for a while?" asked Eoghan.

"Certainly, Mr Forrester, take all the time you need."

"Eoghan, what's going on?" asked Sophia.

"I don't expect you to take off Bill's ring. But maybe if you wore my ring on this finger." He picked up her hand and gently kissed the second finger on her right hand.

"Oh, Eoghan, I would be honoured to wear your ring."

He kissed her on the lips. She had never been one for public displays of affection either but when a handsome, kind, wonderful man wanted to kiss her she would be a fool to object!

They browsed for a short while and then they both saw it at the same time. It was a solitaire set on a platinum band, simple but beautiful.

"Oh Eoghan, I'll wear it forever with pride."

"Will we call it our commitment ring?"

"Till death do us part." She reached up and kissed him.

"I was planning to go for dinner, maybe we should just go home," he whispered. She laughed.

Eoghan turned to Claude. "Claude, we'll take this one." He pointed to the ring they had chosen.

When she walked out into the bright sunshine, she saw George, her driver, smiling at her from her limousine.

"Well, I couldn't bring you back on the subway. That would be too much for you in one day," said Eoghan.

"You mean you were too lazy."

"Oh, but you know me so well. Champagne, my dear," said Eoghan, picking up the bottle he had put on ice earlier. "And to top off this wonderful day, we are dining in one of Manhattan's finest."

"Wow, Eoghan, I'm impressed."

"Thanks to our man George here for the recommendation."

George laughed. "Glad to be of service."

Chapter Eight

Donagh sat on the jetty strumming his guitar. He had learned to play by ear. He loved all types of music. If he liked a melody after listening a few times he could play it. At the beginning of the summer, he wouldn't have had the nerve to join a writing group. Although he had been practising his writing and reading every day, he knew he needed one-to-one tuition. He just didn't want to ask Monique about it. He liked the fact that they were both students on this course and he didn't want that to change. Not that he might ever see her after today. Their paths never usually crossed. He kept strumming and humming.

> *It's the look of your face*
> *That makes my heart race*
> *I only see you*
> *In a crowded room*

"That's shite," he muttered but he still hummed it in to the voice recorder. Grace had told him to use it as though he were writing notes. The wooden planks of the jetty creaked, making him turn around to look.

Monique came towards him, barefoot and wearing a long light summer skirt that blew in the slight breeze as she walked. It revealed her gorgeous legs. She had that kind of skin that tanned easily. Jeez, he thought, how did she get so under his skin? He had kept telling himself she wasn't his type. She was quiet, unassuming and an extremely kind person. He had seen that in her when she had taught the literacy group. But he had also seen her on her horse or in the speedboat; she was like someone who was desperate to break free. Something haunted her and he couldn't figure out what it was. He didn't want to care. Anyway, she had a boyfriend who constantly rang her.

She smiled at him. He couldn't take his eyes away from her. She moved so gracefully. She sat down beside him. He returned to strumming his guitar in an effort to compose himself. But he couldn't. He packed up his things, muttering something about getting back to class. Being near her was screwing with his head. For God's sake, he was even writing a song about her.

"But we still have another fifteen minutes," she said, not moving.

"I'll be in Nutties tonight."

Jessie sat on the deck outside Butterfly Barn sipping coffee. She saw Donagh getting up just moments after Monique had sat down on the jetty. Monique's phone rang. Jessie had noticed the chemistry between her and Donagh from the start. But Monique was still too busy nursing a broken heart and talking to Garvan – that was probably him again. By all accounts, Donagh was a no-strings-attached guy but maybe Monique might be the one to change that.

Monique had only ever had one boyfriend and that was probably why she was finding it very hard to let go. If Geoff had done what Garvan did she would have finished with him on the spot. But Monique craved security and stability. Jessie couldn't blame her after all she had been through. She had the scars to prove it both emotionally and physically. The accident had been horrific. What that poor young girl had witnessed had caused her years of nightmares. She had refused to talk to anyone about it. Nora had been distraught, trying to deal with her own grief and that of a thirteen-year-old who had sustained injuries too. And then that asshole left her the way that he did. Jessie would love to give him a piece of her mind.

Donagh pulled out the chair beside her and sat down.

"It's hard to believe it's our last day," said Jessie, glad to be distracted from her thoughts.

"It's been a blast," said Donagh. "I love it here. It helps my creative flow."

"You sound like a real performer."

`"I don't know what that means but it sounds good"

"Just a creative type person and Donagh, you are welcome to come here anytime. Can I ask you a favour?"

"Ask away, I'd be delighted to help."

"I wrote a poem a few years ago and I have eventually come up with an ending. I'd like to turn it into a song."

"Sing it for me."

"That's the problem, I can't sing. I was hoping you could do something with it."

"The answer is yes. I will help you but only after you put a melody to it."

"Okay, but ..."

"No buts. You can do it. You know the message you're trying to put across."

"You're right, Donagh." She'd play around with it in her head and see where that brought her. "Thanks for the advice."

"Give me a buzz when you have the melody and we can take it from there."

She smiled and said, "Play me something."

He picked up his guitar and began to play. She didn't recognise the song. He stopped before it ended. She looked at him questioningly. "Keep going."

"I don't have an end yet."

"Donagh, it's beautiful."

He shrugged his shoulders. "I love music, Jessie. But it won't pay the bills. I need to get one-to-one help."

"Talk to Monique."

He looked up and saw Monique walking towards them. Without saying another word he got up quickly and went inside. Jessie had suspected the song might be about Monique but now she was sure. There was no way Donagh would ask Monique for help. Jessie would have to figure out another way. Thankfully, class ended at four. Some space might help them both to see things more clearly.

Kate drove along the pebbled drive of Rose Cottage. She had asked her mother not to tell Grace or anyone else she was home. She had needed time to think about her future. Anyway both Grace and Jessie were busy with the creative writing course. Her heart was heavy. She had been home seventy-two hours and Richard still hadn't called or texted. She felt awful. She should have told him how she felt earlier, not that it would change the outcome. She just couldn't live there.

The cottage came into sight. She loved this place. It was filled with happy memories of Richard and their first time together. The climbing roses were still in bloom around the little porch with its red half-door but she couldn't open it. She left her suitcase on the step and walked instead towards the red gate that led to the long sandy beach.

How did she think she could stay in the cottage without him? She kept walking.

Donagh drove up the winding avenue and took the fork in the road leading to the McGraths' house instead of the usual one that led to Butterfly Barn. When the course ended at four Geoff had asked him to call to the house later about some plans he had. He parked outside an old stone farmhouse. He noticed a trampoline, bicycles, toy tractors and trailers, swings and slides in the garden. A kid's paradise, he thought. Before he had a chance to knock, the front door opened.

"It feels strange opening the front door. Everybody uses the back one," said Geoff. "Come through, we're all in the kitchen. Will you have a beer?"

Who's all, he wondered.

"No, I'm driving. Thanks anyway."

"Donagh, this is Jack, and you know Grace, of course."

"We've met briefly at the barn," said Jack, putting out his hand.

He shook hands with Jack. "How's it going?"

"Sit down, make yourself at home." Geoff dragged a chair towards Donagh. "Jack, Donagh is big into water sports."

"Yeah," said Donagh, wondering where all this was going.

"I was thinking," said Geoff.

Jessie and Grace both put their hands on their heads.

"Oh spare us, please," pleaded Jessie.

"Women! They never give you a break, suppose you know all about that. Anyway, where was I? Water sports, I'm thinking of developing more activities down around the lake, maybe adding windsurfing. Basically, I'm open to suggestions and I was hoping it might be something you'd be interested in."

Donagh was amazed. He hadn't known what to expect when Geoff invited him over. He looked around him.

"Hey mate, I'm sorry. Maybe I shouldn't have asked under these circumstances."

"No, I'm just, well, I'm in. Whatever it is count me in."

"Great stuff, I'm also taking a trip to France to visit some wooded adventure parks. You know the kind, tree climbing and zip wires. I think we have the perfect location for it. You might like to come along."

"Sounds great."

"Right, can't you have a beer? We'll sort you out with a taxi later."

"Stay and have dinner with us?" asked Jessie.

"Sure, why not? It smells good." He smiled; it would save him picking up a takeaway.

He sat with them in the large kitchen, chatting, eating and drinking for a couple of hours. The atmosphere was lovely. They had obviously all been friends for years. There was no fussing about, not like when his parents had people over. It was all cut glass, linen, and catered food, with his father prancing around showing off his art collection and his poor, beautiful mother stressed out. If he ever settled down, not that he had any immediate plans to, he'd like to live like them. But first, he had to find a decent job. He wasn't sure what he had just agreed to. But his instincts knew it felt right, these people wouldn't put him wrong. He had never felt more accepted in his life. Three of the four people in the room knew his secret, and the world hadn't stopped turning.

"Where's Sam? I didn't see him all day. Usually we meet at the lake at some stage," said Donagh. He was very fond of the little guy.

"He's having a sleepover in Sally's. Her son Ollie is his best friend."

"I loved sleepovers when I was a kid," said Donagh, thinking how much time he had spent in Butchie's house to avoid being at home.

By the time Kate arrived back to Rose Cottage, the sun had gone down and she was cold into her bones. Her suitcase was gone.

"Oh my God," she yelled, wondering what had possessed her to leave it outside the door, not even safely in the boot of the car. Her laptop was in it, along with her phone charger and all her favourite clothes.

The door opened.

"Are you looking for something?"

"What the … did you take my suitcase?"

"That's a fine way to greet someone you haven't see for …" Richard began to look at his watch. "Seventy-four hours. What took you so long?"

"What do you mean?"

"Mom gave you the keys. I've been waiting for you."

"You are the limit, Richard. I can't do this shit. Why can't you be ordinary? Normal people just pick up the phone." She started to cry.

"Come here," he said, leading her inside. "I'm afraid you are going to have to put up with me forever. Remember you're the one who said we'll be doing it when we're sixty. I do hear you, you know."

"But my visa, Richard, you forgot about it."

"I didn't, I was waiting for you."

He laughed as he guided her to the couch and proceeded to kiss her and undress her slowly. "You are the love of my life. I never, ever thought I could love again after losing Heather and Billy. You proved me wrong, Kate Fitzgerald."

Monique's mobile bleeped; it was a text from Jessie.

<Where are you?>

Jessie and Grace had asked her to go out to celebrate the end of the course. She had been delayed at the stables. She went in the back door of Jessie's house. The last person she expected to see was Donagh.

"Hi Mon," called Grace, from where they were sitting around the kitchen table. "What'll ye have? We're on the wine. They're on the beer."

Grace was half shot already and so was Jessie.

"Beer anyone?" Monique asked, opening the fridge to help herself. She got a glass from the cupboard and opened the freezer to get some ice. She did it slowly, trying to compose herself. She couldn't believe he was here. Jessie was fussing over her and setting a place. The last thing in the world she wanted was dinner. "Thanks, Jessie, but I'm not that hungry."

"Ah, have a little bit. It was lovely, wasn't it lads?"

"Yeah," everybody chorused. They were all in high spirits.

"Let's take a walk down to the lake. You can give me some idea of what you plan to do, Geoff," said Donagh.

"Great idea, I could do with some fresh air. I'll show you where I am thinking about creating the park. We can talk about it as we walk."

"I'll come with you," said Jack, pushing back the chair to follow them.

"Jessie, why didn't you tell me he was going to be here?" whispered Monique.

"Geoff asked him over. I didn't know he was coming."

"He's gorgeous," said Grace. "And he can sing. What's not to love?"

"I am not interested. Anyway he has a girlfriend," said Monique, pushing the chicken in the Thai green curry around the plate.

"It's really tasty," said Grace.

"Are we talking about the chicken or Donagh?" Jessie laughed.

"You two are just the limit." Monique smiled.

"Ah let's just have a good night out. We could do with one," said Jessie.

"You're right. Cheers girls," said Monique, raising her glass full of ice and beer to their wine glasses.

"I definitely need to slow down," said Grace and then she took a sip from her glass.

Both she and Jessie laughed.

Monique sat on a bar stool in Nutties.

"I hope Donagh sings tonight," said Grace.

"Me too," said Jessie, hopping off the bar stool and heading in the direction of the band, dragging Donagh with her.

"This is for some new friends I've made," said Donagh and began to sing The Script song "Superheroes". In the middle of the song Monique followed his gaze. He was looking at the redhead who had kissed him in the beer garden. She saw him wink at her. He finished to rapturous applause. He went over to her and she stood up and hugged him. Then Monique saw him point towards where they were all sitting. A few minutes later, the girl left and he came back to join them.

"Nice one, same again?" asked Geoff.

"Cheers, thanks," said Donagh. He was talking to Jack and Grace who were encouraging him to write his own material.

"Are Rachel and Jay out on the town tonight?" Jessie asked, breaking into Monique's thoughts.

"I'm meeting them in Foster's."

"Can't they come and join us here?"

Oh God, thought Monique. She had lied, she wasn't meeting anyone. She just wanted to go home. "Em, they're with a group of friends from … school." Gran always said that one lie led to another. "See you tomorrow, and thanks for dinner," she said, grabbing her jacket and rushing for the door before Jessie had a chance to say another word.

Donagh wondered if she was leaving but Jack and Geoff were talking to him.

"I was just thinking, I'd love to try surfing sometime," said Jack, shifting on the bar stool to make himself more comfortable.

"Me and my mates surf regularly. Come down to Bayrush Beach sometime and I'll run through the basics with you."

"Count me in for that too," said Geoff.

"Can you ride a horse?" asked Jack. Donagh shook his head.

"Right, here's the deal. You teach us to surf and I'll teach you to ride a horse."

"Done," said Donagh.

"Call around to Oak House next Saturday. We're holding a one-day event. There'll be a barbeque after it. You'll see horses in action."

"What exactly is Eventing?"

"The day usually begins with dressage, then showjumping and finally cross-country jumping."

"I'll drop by as long as I don't have to get on a horse."

Jack laughed. Donagh looked around again. She had definitely left without saying goodbye.

Kate lay beside Richard in bed.

"Richard," she said, leaning up on one elbow to look at his face. "I can't see how we are going to make this work."

"I know how hard you tried to fit into my world. It was fine when you were in college and busy. But some of those events are just plain tiresome. I hate them just as much as you do."

"I'm sorry I didn't talk about it sooner. I love you but I was so afraid I'd fall back to my old ways." She told him about the night with Lisa. He sat up and listened to every word. She was open and honest about how hard it was living with addiction

"I can't deal with the loneliness. I'm used to people dropping in unannounced. I grew up in a tiny three-bedroomed house and shared a bedroom with three sisters. There was barely any room to move around the two four foot beds in it."

He smiled.

"I'm sorry. I really thought I could be everything to you. But I can't. My heart breaks every time I see Heather and Billy's little face. You had all you ever wanted with them. I can't fill her place. I'll never be able to host a party and say the right thing. Most of the time I say the wrong thing."

"I never wanted a replacement. I loved Heather with all my heart and Billy was everything to me. But they are gone. Remember I was not looking when I found you. So, honey, I can work from here for a while and you can figure things out too. Let's give it a try."

"Oh, Richard, come here."

Donagh decided to go to Oak House after lunch. Half a day would do him, he thought. He really wasn't interested in horses. He parked in a field next to the big old house. The place was buzzing with people, horses, jeeps and horseboxes everywhere. Who knew that there were so many people into horses around here? He walked towards the yard. The first person he recognised was Monique. The sight of her sitting on that big, black horse again took his breath away. She was all dressed up in white jodhpurs and a fitted dark green jacket with a blouse buttoned up to the neck. The horse was prancing around. He was a dangerous-looking thing. He must be at least seventeen hands and she was so petite on his back. She waved hello. He waved back, admiring her even more for taking her hand off the reins.

"Next in the ring is Monique Chevalier on Jasper," said the man on the PA system.

"Hey Donagh, glad you dropped by," said Jack, leading him towards the sand arena where Monique was about to showjump.

"How's it going, lads?" he said.

Geoff had come over to join them.

"We're pleased with the turnout. At least the weather held up." The boys chatted while he watched transfixed at the speed and the height of the fences Monique was jumping. Her face was set in concentration. She was so in control of the huge animal. He had never taken an interest in horses before. But she captivated him. She was so graceful in her movements. He could stay watching her all day.

"Donagh?"

"Sorry, Geoff, what were you saying?"

"Do you want to walk the cross-country course with me? I need to check the fences."

It was the last thing he wanted to do, but he nodded and followed Geoff. A small girl with short, dark hair came running towards them, followed by a very tall guy.

"Kate Fitzgerald, it's great to see you," said Geoff, giving her a big hug. "I didn't know you were coming home."

"It's a surprise." She laughed; it was a sexy kind of laugh.

"Kate and Richard, this is Donagh, a new friend of mine."

"Nice to meet you," said Donagh, shaking Richard's hand.

"Jessie and Grace will be thrilled you're here. Come on, let's find them." The girl linked Geoff while Donagh was left walking with the guy.

"Are you another horse man?"

"Not me. I'm into water sports," said Donagh, noticing his American accent.

"Me too. Only I've never tried it out around here."

"That's because he's never here long enough," said Kate. They had stopped at a fence to let some riders pass.

"Yes, you're right babe, but that's all about to change. We're on a long vacation …"

Donagh noticed that Richard looked at Kate as if she were the only person in the world.

"Richard has taken time off. Can you believe it?" declared Kate.

"No," said Geoff. "This guy is a workaholic. But if it's water sports you're looking for, he's your man. Jack and I are getting our first surfing lesson next week. Can Richard tag along?"

"Sure," said Donagh.

"Cheers. I'll look forward to it," said Richard.

Kate put on Bruno Mars and began to look for her next choice. It had been a great day. Grace had planned a barbeque for when the competition was over as a fundraiser for Butterfly Barn.

"Great party," said Donagh.

"Ah, my sister always plans a good party."

"Never would have thought you were sisters. You don't look at all alike."

"I'm like my dad's side. Grace takes after Mam to look at. I hear you are a musician. Grace said you're excellent."

He blushed. "Ah I'm just into it, looks like you are too."

"I play guitar badly and I've been known to sing a few tunes at the end of an evening." Kate smiled. She noticed a blonde girl hanging around.

"Hi Kate, have you seen Monique?" the girl asked.

"Last time I saw her she was with Alex."

"Hi," said the girl, batting her eyes at Donagh. "We haven't met before. I'm Vicky." Kate nearly laughed aloud when the girl pushed out her chest and did a hair flick that nearly caused her an injury. "I heard you singing in Nutties the other night. You were amazing!"

"Thanks very much," said Donagh.

"Here's my number, if you'd like to give me a call sometime." She sashayed off.

Kate leaned against the wooden rail and laughed. "If I hadn't seen that I wouldn't have believed it. Talk about offering herself on a platter."

He laughed and put the number in his pocket.

"You wouldn't?"

He laughed again. She threw her eyes to heaven.

Monique had been on her way to chat to Kate when she saw Donagh was already there. She overheard every word between Vicky and Donagh. She knew Vicky because she kept her horse at Jessie's stables but she wasn't a friend of hers. She had heard Vicky was easy but that was unbelievable. What kind of person was he to accept her number? He was going out with someone. God, she hated the thought of the dating game if that's how it was.

She had only ever kissed one other guy besides Garvan, and that had been a dare when they had all played spin the bottle as teenagers. There was no way she'd sleep with someone unless she loved him or at the very least really liked him. She was not the type to have one-night stands.

She leaned back against the wall of the stable and ran her hand along her side. It ached a little after the day. She took out her phone. She was so tempted to ring Garvan to tell him she would go to Dubai. No, she thought, maybe it is time to embrace being single. To stop wanting to be part of a couple. She shook herself down and went back to join Rachel and the rest of the gang who were dancing on a wooden floor thrown down on the grass. "Because I'm Happy" was blasting on the PA system. She joined in and danced just as enthusiastically as the rest of them. It was great fun. The music changed to an ABBA song. She turned to walk off the floor. Donagh was standing in front of her. She went to pass him but he caught her by the hand and led her to the middle of the floor. He put his arms around her. The manly scent of him made her knees weak. ABBA's words "I don't want to talk about it" had taken on a new meaning. She could hardly breathe.

The song ended and changed straight into "Take a Chance On Me." Without saying a word, she broke away and everybody started dancing in a big circle, with different people moving in and out. After a few moments, she slipped away. She was shaking. So much for her being independent. It was Garvan she wanted not this stranger. She needed steady and reliable not all of this … whatever it was.

The dance floor was full. Donagh couldn't see Monique. Had she felt it too? It was crazy.

"Donagh, I'd like you to meet Eoghan." It was Richard, the American guy with a tall grey-haired man.

"Nice to meet you," said Donagh, shaking his hand.

"Eoghan is involved with the sea rescue," said Richard, leading them off to the side.

"Really? I'd like to know more about it."

"Give me a call when you have time."

"What's your number?" asked Donagh, taking his mobile out of his pocket.

"Donagh is giving us a surfing lesson next Wednesday evening. Are you interested?" Richard asked Eoghan.

"Your mother wants me to give up the sea rescue. What would she say if I told her I was taking up surfing?" Eoghan laughed. "But I'll drop by to watch you all. Could be entertaining!"

"Sophia is my mother and Eoghan is her partner," said Richard. "And for the record she just wants him to stop going out in the boat and leave it to the younger lads."

"We're short on volunteers so needs must. But that might change," Eoghan said, patting Donagh on the back. "Maybe some of your pals might be interested. We provide full training. I'll look forward to hearing from you, son."

"I'll see you on Wednesday so."

Another person came to talk to them, so Donagh walked away. The sea rescue had always been something he felt he'd love to do. Previously he hadn't the nerve to ask about it. What if there were exams to take? When Richard had said Sophia was Eoghan's partner, Donagh figured he must be a good guy and he had liked the way he called him "son".

He scanned the crowd looking for Monique. He eventually saw her with her friend Rachel. They seemed to be deep in conversation. He decided to call it a night. He was over the limit to drive so he ordered a taxi.

He was about to put the phone back in his pocket when the blonde girl he had spoken to earlier came over. He smiled at her, not wanting to be rude.

"Don't forget to call me," she said, and then stretched up and kissed him on the mouth. She turned and walked away.

It happened so fast, he was shocked. He saw Monique and her friend looking over. They both turned their backs. What could he do? He shrugged his shoulders and set off down the lane.

Chapter Nine

On Wednesday evening, Donagh parked his jeep next to the promenade on Bayrush Beach. He spotted Geoff, Richard and Jack already in wetsuits on the beach. Butchie and Pepe would be along soon with their boards. He pulled up his wetsuit and was about to take two boards out of the jeep when someone asked, "Need a hand with that?" It was Eoghan.

"Cheers," said Donagh, passing him a gear bag. Butchie pulled up beside him and the two lads got out. "Pepe, Butchie, this is Eoghan." The two lads nodded at him.

"I'm looking forward to seeing this."

"And these two are looking forward to showing off," said Donagh. The two lads laughed as they all walked down the beach to where Jack, Richard and Geoff were waiting.

Donagh set out the boards in a row on the beach and began to explain the basic principles. Then he gave them a demonstration. "Now I'd like you all to try it."

"Are you an instructor?" asked Richard.

"No."

"You should be."

"Let's see how you do out here first."

"It's like reliving my youth," shouted Geoff, when he managed to catch a wave. He didn't get as far as standing before he toppled in.

"Toes curled just at the end of the board next time," Donagh called to him.

"Paddle now, Jack, one, two, three up. You nearly had it."

He turned to watch Richard. "Here's one. Paddle … yes … go Richard. That was great."

After an hour, Jack waded in and passed the surfboard to Butchie. Donagh and Geoff came in too. Pepe took the board from Geoff.

"Hey guys, watch out. You have strong competition out there." Donagh turned to the rest of them. "Richard is an experienced surfer. What part of the States is he from?"

"New York," said Eoghan.

"He definitely spent his summers on a beach somewhere." Richard was catching nearly every wave he attempted.

"I think you'll be seeing a lot more of him around here. He just moved into the cottage down there."

"Nice one, I've always admired that place. I love the decking."

"You being a carpenter, you'd appreciate it," said Geoff.

"Are you John Mullally's son?" asked Eoghan.

Donagh nodded but changed the subject quickly. "So when will you show me the sea rescue boat?"

"No time like the present."

"Right so." He went into the sea again to tell Richard he was leaving. He asked him to give his surfboard to Butchie when he was finished. "So much for teaching you to surf!"

Richard laughed. "Do you kite-surf?"

"Yeah."

"How about some lessons in that?"

"Sure, chat soon."

Ten minutes later, Donagh parked on the steep hill leading down to the harbour. Eoghan was already opening the boathouse. Although it was 7.45 in the evening the place was busy with a mixture of fishing and recreational boats.

"Jeez, that's some job," said Donagh.

"It's top of the range. We had to do an incredible amount of fundraising for it, along with applying for some government aid."

Donagh walked around the boat, running his hand on it.

"Tea or coffee?"

"Love a coffee, I didn't get a chance to eat yet."

Eoghan made the coffee.

"So, you interested?"

"I sure am. What's involved?"

Eoghan explained that he would need to be on call and to live nearby. That wasn't a problem. He lived within walking distance. Everybody had to train in first aid and be fully qualified with water safety training.

Donagh's head was buzzing, he wanted so much to be part of it all. He'd have to tell Eoghan the truth. "Look Eoghan, it's just … I find reading and writing hard."

"I didn't know what you were going to say for a minute."

"Eoghan, I won't be able to do those courses you are talking about. I'd love to. I have dreams and ambitions to own a surf school but there is so much paperwork involved. Everything is about qualifications. Years ago people could just be handy at something and that was it. But now" – he scratched his head – "it's just so frustrating."

"Right, I don't know about you but I'm starving. Come back to my place for some dinner. Sophia will be delighted to see you. I'll just lock up here."

Eoghan didn't wait for an answer and Donagh didn't object. He followed Eoghan up the hill, high on the cliffs overlooking the ocean. His house was a whitewashed fisherman's cottage.

"Hi honey! I'm home," called Eoghan, walking along the hallway with Donagh. "We have a visitor this evening."

"Donagh, come in. It's good to see you," said Sophia, walking across the small kitchen.

"Sorry to barge in like this, but Eoghan insisted."

"You're more than welcome here anytime," she said, setting an extra place for him.

"So … did you see his pride and joy?"

"I did, it's some job," said Donagh.

"It is that and more." Eoghan agreed.

Sophia dished up chicken chasseur and boiled potatoes. They chatted and laughed about the barbeque at Grace's house and the lads' attempts at surfing. Donagh couldn't believe how relaxed he felt. He asked how they had met.

Eoghan told him about how much he had wanted to be with Sophia for the last few years but it looked highly unlikely until very recently. The way they looked at each other really got to Donagh. They were so obviously in love. He was surprised to hear they had only moved in together six weeks previously.

"Eoghan bought me this ring," said Sophia, holding up her right hand proudly.

"Go on boy, you are some romantic," said Donagh, patting his new friend on the back. He wished to God he had been born to a man like Eoghan, imagine how different life could have been. He was enjoying himself so much, he didn't want to leave.

"I better go, don't want to be playing gooseberry to new sweethearts," said Donagh. He pushed back his chair as Eoghan stood up. "Thanks for the lovely dinner, Sophia. It was very kind of you to invite me, Eoghan."

"Our pleasure, son, and I'll talk to you very soon."

Donagh smiled as he walked down the little path to his jeep. Eoghan had called him "son" again.

*

Monique lay on her bed. The radio was playing quietly in the background when Coldplay's "Fix You" came on. She was even more confused since the event at Grace's house. Try as she might, she couldn't banish Donagh from her mind.

"Monique, you have some post," Nora called from the kitchen.

"Coming."

Monique sat down at the kitchen table. She opened the letter and began to read it while Gran made tea.

"Oh Gran, it is good news. I've been called for an interview," said Monique, looking upwards.

"Oh, thank you, God. That's great, love. Tell me about it."

"It's a job with the literacy service. It's the one I was hoping to be called for. I want to work in that area, Gran. It's so interesting. Let's go out for lunch to celebrate."

Monique noticed her gran's eyes had filled up. "Lovely, let me go and tidy myself up."

"We'll go off for a drive and stop wherever we fancy. We haven't done anything like that for ages," said Monique.

"Won't be long!" called Nora, walking down the little hallway to her bedroom.

Donagh drove down the long drive to his parents' house. His mother had asked him over because a letter had arrived for him. Although he had moved out, he still used his parents' address for post. He wondered who it was from.

He smiled when he saw her sitting in a garden chair on the lawn. His ten-year-old brother jumped on the trampoline. When Oisín saw him he opened the trampoline net and came running over to greet him. "Be careful Oisín," called his mother. She was so protective of him. There was a huge age gap between Oisín and the rest of the boys. He was the eldest and the next two were in college, one studying political science and the other three years into studying medicine. Devin was going into sixth year in secondary school and was brighter the other two put together than. And then there was Oisín, who was also very smart. Donagh often wondered where they had got him. His family were all high achievers.

His mother had told him his father was away; otherwise he wouldn't have come near the place. The less he saw of him the better.

He swung his little brother around and began kicking ball with him. He didn't get to see him half as much as he'd like to.

"How are you?" his mother asked. "You've lost weight."

"You always say that." He laughed. "I promise I do eat."

"I wish you'd move back. You could save money. You wouldn't have so many bills."

"Mum." He gave her the look she understood.

"He's never here."

He ran after the ball. Oisín had kicked it way off.

"I'll just get the letter. Will you have a coffee?" she called after him.

"Sure, thanks." He picked up the ball and went to chat to Oisín. "Hey buddy, how are you doing?"

"Good, I got a new inhaler. It's better than the last one."

"Cool." He high-fived him. "Let's get you a Coke or something."

"I might have a chance now that you're here. It's usually diluted orange."

Oisín's severe asthma had always been a constant worry. Donagh had lost count of the times they had nearly lost him. Donagh felt it had put a strain on an already strained marriage. He sometimes wondered why they stayed together. As far as he was concerned, his father only cared about material things.

Donagh sat at the marble worktop in the huge kitchen.

"Dad got a new car. A silver BMW 5 Series," said Oisín, missing the looks passing between Donagh and his mother. Donagh said nothing and opened the letter.

"I'm going up to my room to play on my Xbox. Will you come up?" asked Oisín.

"Sure I will, buddy. Give me a few minutes with Mum." He passed the letter to his mother.

"This is great – you've been offered a cancellation. The educational psychologist can see you next week."

"Brilliant, how much is it?"

"Four hundred and ninety euro. Don't worry, I'll cover it."

"Cover what?" asked his father, coming in the back door. Donagh startled, he hadn't heard a car and nor had his mother by the shocked look on her face. But she covered it well.

"Ah, it's nothing," said his mother, putting down the letter. "Will you have a coffee?"

"Yes." But before Donagh had time to pick up the letter, his father was reading it. "You're going to pay nearly five hundred quid to get someone to tell us how stupid he is. Are you crazy?"

His mother put down the coffee pot. Donagh got up and grabbed the letter from him and walked out the back door. By the time he got around to the front of the house, his father had come out the front door.

"You have some cheek coming here and sponging from your mother."

Donagh could feel the anger building inside. Years of it pent up inside. He never answered him back. He went to get into the jeep.

"Just like you still sponge off me."

"You mean this," said Donagh, pointing to the jeep his father had given him for his twenty-first birthday. "You gave me this to make you look good."

"You miserable little shit."

Donagh walked around to the back of the jeep and began to take his stuff out.

"What are you doing?" called his mother, running towards them. "Come back inside and let's sort things out for once and for all."

"No," they said in unison.

"Mum, I just want to leave my things in the garage. I'll get them later." He began to carry his surfboards and gear to the garage.

"You're just a lazy good-for-nothing. And that's my garage too."

"I only ever come here to see my mother and my brothers. I'm done with you. I never want to see you again. You might think you own half of Bayrush but you will never own me."

"We'll see about that. You wouldn't have got an apprenticeship without your old man. Have you even got your final cert? You think you can stand on your own two feet. We'll see about that." He sneered and went back into the house.

"I'm sorry, Donagh. I'll sort it out. I'll bring the jeep over tomorrow. It will blow over like it always does."

"Not this time, Mum. I'm done." He kissed her cheek and walked up the drive. It was just as well they had no immediate neighbours. He looked back. She was still standing where he had left her. He could see she was crying, but it was the little face in the upstairs window that broke his heart. Oisín must have heard everything.

Sophia sat on the garden bench. Eoghan had asked Donagh to drop by. He had a big plan he wanted to talk to him about. Donagh arrived on a bicycle.

"What's wrong with the jeep?" Eoghan asked.

"Long story."

"Coffee?" asked Sophia.

"Let me tell him my idea first. Then we'll all go inside. Take a look at the view." Eoghan spread out his arms.

Donagh looked out. The sun was setting on the ocean. The sky was a mix of oranges and reds. The only break on the horizon was Everest Rock. "It's an incredible view."

"I want to build Sophia a sunroom so that she can get a feeling of space. Looking out over that. Right here," said Eoghan, walking to the side of the cottage. "What do you reckon?"

"Good idea. You'll need planning permission."

"Have it. Got it a few years ago, but I never bothered to do anything about it."

"Okay, you're halfway there so."

"And I was thinking of a new kitchen. Are you interested?"

"Definitely."

Sophia got up. "I'll make a pot of coffee."

Donagh followed Eoghan inside and sat at the kitchen table.

"Donagh, there is something else we'd like to suggest. I'll let Sophia explain," said Eoghan, taking mugs from the dresser.

"I hope you won't take offence, but Eoghan told me about your conversation last week. We want to help. I'd like to tutor you. Eoghan knows about the exams you need so he can help too."

Donagh put his head down. When he looked up, his eyes were filled with tears. "Thanks," he managed to say.

"That's settled," said Eoghan. "Grab that coffee and we'll go back outside and you can give me some suggestions. I'll need a name of a good building contractor."

Sophia knew Eoghan had also seen the emotion in Donagh. She sat cupping the coffee mug between her hands. She hadn't realised it would mean that much to him. It was heart-breaking. If it hadn't been for Monique there would not have been a literacy weekend at Butterfly Barn. She had been in the magazine business all of her life and had never really thought much about reading difficulties. She intended to give Donagh her best shot and she knew he was more than willing, which would definitely make the task easier.

Eoghan was so impressed by Donagh. He couldn't stop talking about what a great lad he was. Sophia had noticed the way he called him "son", unknown to himself. He still hadn't heard from either of his daughters. He tried to hide his disappointment when post came and there was no letter or card. She noticed he checked his phone often too.

Two weeks later, Donagh sat in the front of the van with his boss.

"I'm sorry, there's just not enough business coming in to keep us both going. I have to lay you off. I'll pay you a month's notice. I feel terrible. You're a great carpenter. I can't believe this is happening, Donagh."

But Donagh could. His father was behind it. Jimmy couldn't look him in the eye. He kept staring out the window. His father had put a lot of work Jimmy's way over the years. He was such a shrewd businessman – even the last few years hadn't affected him too badly. Obviously, Jimmy didn't want to get on the wrong side of his father. He had a wife and two kids to consider.

"Sort out what you owe me, Jimmy. See you around." He got out of the van and walked up the street to the rented house. He opened the front door and went straight to his bedroom. He could hear the lads down in the kitchen but he wasn't in the humour for company.

What was the point in shouting and roaring about things? Thankfully, he had the kitchen to fit for Sophia and Eoghan. He had also recommended a builder to Eoghan who had no connection to his father. He might be able to pick up some labouring work with him. He looked around the room. He'd have to sell something to get the money for the assessment. He lay on the bed. His eyes rested on the guitar. No, he couldn't get rid of that. It was his sanity. Then there was his first ever surfboard but that wouldn't be worth much to anyone but him.

His kite-surfing gear – he'd sell that. He'd make a good few quid on that. A few calls and he'd definitely have a buyer. There was no way he was going back home. He knew that was his father's plan. Break him; just to prove that he was right all the time.

Monique sat in front of a three-person interview board. She was very conscious of her accent especially when she dropped the letter h.

"Monique, what qualities do you think you could bring to the position of tutor within our organisation?"

"For the past four years, I volunteer with the literacy service. I feel I can bring a level of understanding to the challenges that many people face today. Life is not straightforward. The current education system doesn't always meet the needs of people who learn in a different way." She paused to steady her voice; she was so nervous her heart was thumping.

The man with the grey beard spoke. "People drop out of education for many reasons. Our role in adult education is to show that we are adapting to help and encourage people back to learning. Do you think you possess the ability to encourage people?"

"Oh yes," she replied. "I believe encouragement is an essential part of any person's learning experience. To be encouraged is the ultimate gift one person can give to another."

"Well, thank you for your time. We'll be in touch soon, Monique," said the man who had asked most of the questions.

"Thank you," she said, addressing all three.

In the car park, she sat in her gran's old Audi rubbing her neck. She had a pain in it from turning and nodding at all three. The interview had lasted thirty minutes. They had also asked about her qualifications and her background and why she had moved to Ireland. She had tried not to be emotional. She really wanted the job – it would only be a six-month contract with part-time hours but it would be a great start.

She started the engine and drove off. It was such a nice evening she veered by Bayrush Beach – a walk would help to clear her head.

She parked. She had just bought new shoes for the interview. She took them off in case they would be ruined. She rolled up the legs of her black pants. In the distance she could see a kite flying. Kate had told her Richard was driving her nuts talking about "kites and shite". Donagh was teaching him to kite-surf. Kate had warned Richard that the wind was so strong at times he might end up wrapped around a tree inland and she hadn't been joking.

When she got closer she saw it was Donagh, with another guy. He was wearing jeans and a fleece. They were taking the kite down. He must be showing someone how to work it, she thought. Donagh saw her. She waved and kept on walking. He nodded and continued talking to the guy. She hadn't seen him since the night at Grace's barbeque three weeks ago. Whatever had happened that night obviously was a common occurrence for him but it had made her realise that she needed to experience more of life. She had been out with Rachel and the girls and had started to relax and enjoy herself more. She was enjoying her new independence. She didn't answer every call, text or message she got from Garvan immediately, sometimes she even forgot to answer.

"Hey Monique." She turned to see Donagh running up the beach towards her.

"Sorry I couldn't talk to you. I just sold that guy my kite-surf. How have you been? You're all dressed up."

"I had a job interview."

"That's great news. How did it go?" he asked, walking along beside her. She began to tell him all about it. He was so easy to talk to. It was like the Sundays they had spent on the creative writing course except then she had been dreaming about him in a different way. After the night at the barbeque her thoughts had shifted. It was time to be free, not alone, just carefree. She had even flirted with a guy the other night and he had asked for her number. She asked him why he had sold the kite-surf.

"Ah, I don't have time for it at the moment." He chatted about the boys' attempts at surfing. She laughed.

"Richard loves it, but Jack, I seriously think he's going to be injured before his wedding." Donagh laughed. "I think Grace will kill me if that happens."

She wanted to ask about the one-to-one tuition but changed her mind. It was none of her business. She had run out of beach. They had to turn back. It would be nice to be friends, she thought. There was a lull in the conversation. She couldn't think of anything to say.

"How's that guy you're always talking to on the phone?"

"Garvan, he's good."

They walked in silence and then they both started to speak at the same time. They laughed.

"You first," he said.

"Geoff let me drive the boat the other day." She was beaming. "I loved it."

"You should try water skiing."

"Sounds good, you should try horse-riding."

"The lads are working on me." He laughed. "I don't think they'll break me down. What's your favourite thing? Is it that dressage thing or some of the other stuff?"

"I love cross country, just giving Jasper his freedom and holding on."

Donagh loved her accent. He felt regretful when they reached her car.

"I hope you get some good news about the job." he said.

"Thanks, Donagh."

He stood awkwardly, not wanting their time together to end. She opened the car door and one of her shoes fell out. He bent down to pick it up and so did she. They bumped heads. "Mon, I'm sorry, are you okay?" he said, lightly touching the side of her head. He took her by the elbow to help her stand up.

"I'm fine, "she answered, but her eyes were locked on his. He leaned closer, slowly. She didn't move away. And then his lips touched hers, gently first and then they were kissing. He pushed her gently back against the car, all the while kissing her. He couldn't stop himself, he had never felt anything like this in his life. And then she pushed him back ever so slightly, but enough that he noticed. He stopped. "I'm sorry, I shouldn't have done that, you're in a relationship. I'm so sorry, Monique." He turned without waiting to hear what she had to say. He walked back down the beach. "What the hell was I thinking?" he muttered, mortified. She's in a relationship and I'm an unemployed carpenter with barely a roof over my head. What was I thinking?

She lay back against the car. It was the best kiss she had ever had in her life and he was sorry. She looked around. Thankfully, there was nobody around to witness her embarrassment. She got into the car quickly and caught a glimpse of her flushed face in the driver mirror. She gripped the steering wheel to stop her hands from trembling. She was glad he had pulled away because the truth was she hadn't wanted him to stop. Her phone bleeped. She glanced at the screen – Garvan's handsome smiling face looked back at her. "God, Monique, you are a fool."

With Garvan she had always felt safe. The earth shifted when Donagh was around. She didn't like that feeling at all – or did she? She turned the phone upside down and left it to ring out.

Donagh had cycled up the hill against the early October wind. His mother had begged him to take back the jeep but he had refused it. He had managed to get some work with the builder who would be starting Eoghan's extension shortly. His old boss had given him what he owed him and a bit more. Donagh figured it was guilt money, but he took it anyway. He needed every penny. Geoff hadn't come back to him about the trip to France yet.

In the meantime he was determined to improve his reading and writing and take the necessary exams to gain the qualifications he needed. Sophia and Eoghan had offered one hour every night for the past two weeks to help improve his reading. Eoghan had explained that there was a lot of practical training involved and he would be tested on that.

"Demonstrate how to use the defibrillator," said Eoghan. He was sitting opposite Eoghan in the dining room off the kitchen. Donagh showed Eoghan all the steps.

"Perfect." Then Eoghan asked him to perform the steps of resuscitation on a dummy he had brought up from the centre.

"Excellent. Donagh, I think you're ready to take the first aid test verbally next week. Why put yourself under so much pressure? At least you will have that completed. We can then focus on the other training. Sophia wants to teach you phonics, I don't know what that's all about but she says it will help with your reading."

"I have to meet the educational psychologist on Friday. Seemingly, I will have to complete some kind of assessment."

"Do you want me to come with you?"

"Ah no, but thanks for offering."

"How about a cuppa?" asked Eoghan, getting up to go to the kitchen. Donagh followed him.

"So when am I going to start on the kitchen? Let's talk about what you'd both like and I'll price it up excluding my labour costs. It will be my present to you for all you are both doing to help me."

"No way, there's no need for that," said Eoghan. Sophia came in to join them, while Eoghan made tea.

"We are going kitchen shopping for ideas, okay?" said Donagh.

"Sounds good to me, the sooner we get started the better," said Sophia.

"Sophia needs to go back to New York for a week or so. How about you work on the kitchen and oversee the building work for us while we are away?"

"No bother at all," said Donagh, stirring his tea.

"Here's the thing," said Eoghan, rubbing his hand across his chin. "We were hoping you might agree to let Monique help you with reading and writing while Sophia is away."

Donagh looked from one to the other. They were serious. "You haven't asked her already? I know she knows about my problem and all but ..."

"No. Of course not. We wanted to run it by you first," said Sophia. "Monique might not be available, but it would be a shame to stop while you're doing so well. You could come here for the lessons. That is if you want to."

He wasn't sure how he felt about their suggestion. "Tell you what. Ask her but don't tell her I know you are asking. I wouldn't like her to be under an obligation."

"Okay," said Sophia.

Chapter Ten

"Where are we going, Richard?" asked Kate.

"Just go with me on this, honey. Hop in." Richard held the car door open. Kate obliged. "You've been so busy painting and I've been doing things that I never took the time to do before. I think we need a day out, don't you?"

"Yes," she agreed. She was amazed at how he had immersed himself in life here.

But she knew they were only putting off the inevitable. He would have to go back to New York eventually and the longer she was home the more she was sure she didn't want to go back.

"I'd actually love to blindfold you, to stop you guessing and asking questions that I have no intention of answering."

"You couldn't cope if I stopped talking. You'd think there was something wrong with me."

"Well there would be." He laughed.

"Okay, I won't ask. What kind of music have you got in here?" she asked.

"It's a hired car, pet."

"You mean you're bringing me for a drive and you have no CDs. Bad start, honey. What were you thinking?"

"Quit complaining or I'll let you out here and you can walk home."

She laughed as he pretended to brake and so the banter went for another hour or so until they reached the mountains. He parked in exactly the same spot she had brought him to on their first day out together. She looked at him questioningly. He didn't say a word. He got out of the car and opened the boot. Then he came around to her side of the car.

"Now, darling, please can you wear these?" said Richard, presenting her with her hiking boots.

"Yes sir." She laughed. "Hillwalking. How original!"

"Don't be a smart arse," said Richard, mimicking her accent.

She smiled; he had brought her to her favourite place. The mountain air invigorated her. Hiking along, she watched the sheep as they grazed amongst the heather and gorse. Every part of her felt alive. After about an hour and a half they reached the summit. Richard set down a rug and she smiled when he took out shop-bought rolls from his backpack, just like she had done when she had brought him a few years ago.

"I don't 'do' kitchens. Those were your exact words the first time we came here. Do you remember?" smiled Richard, pouring coffee from a flask he had made up.

"Come here," said Kate, leaning over to kiss him. "I love you."

"Ahem, Kate," said Richard, clearing his throat.

"Yes."

"Kate Fitzgerald."

"That's my name. Don't wear it out," she joked, although she was getting a very funny feeling inside.

"Be serious just for a minute."

"Okay," she said, turning to look into his eyes.

"Kate, will you marry me?"

Kate jumped up, spilling her coffee. "Oh shite," she said and then pushed Richard backwards onto the rug and straddled him.

"I thought you were never going to ask me again," she said, punching him lightly.

"Take it easy," he said, laughing. "I hadn't quite expected this reaction. It's a yes or no kind of question."

"Don't get smart with me, Mr I'm so bright and intelligent."

"I ask a simple question and I get a lecture. Where is the fairness here?" said Richard, laughing.

She became serious. She paused and took a deep breath, stroking the face she loved so much. "Richard Wynthrope, I love you, but I can't go back to the life we had in New York. I have to be honest."

"Who said anything about New York? I asked you to marry me."

"Then yes." He pulled her down to him and kissed her. Then he wrapped his arms around her.

"What are we like, with these big jumpers and rain gear on!" said Kate and she laughed.

"I even have champagne here as part of my seduction plan. Look at those big grey clouds," said Richard, just as the first big plops of rain landed on them. They scrambled to their feet and began to run back down the mountainside. By the time they reached the car, they were both dripping wet. "And now for Part Two," said Richard.

"There's more," said Kate, hopping in. Richard drove for twenty minutes until they arrived at the country manor house hotel where they had had dinner the evening of their first day out.

He parked and went to the boot of the car while Kate ran through the rain to the front door. She glanced around and was surprised to see Richard walking through the rain with two overnight bags. For the first time in a long time, she actually didn't speak. She opened the door and he followed behind.

"Hello there. You got caught rightly in the rain. You're both very welcome. I'm Joe," said a friendly voice coming out from behind an antique reception desk.

"We certainly did," said Richard. "We have a reservation in the name of Wynthrope. We're a little earlier than anticipated. I wonder if the room is ready."

"Yes indeed, sir. Can I take your bags?

Richard handed over the bags.

"Follow me. Your room is the first one at the top of the main staircase. This weather is awful, isn't it?"

"It is, we're like drowned rats," said Kate, finding her voice again. "This is wonderful," she said, stroking the mahogany banister of the sweeping staircase. She gazed up at the ceiling from which a fabulous Waterford Crystal chandelier hung. A huge stained glass window spanned the two floors. The place was breathtakingly beautiful.

"If you'd like to have a pre-dinner drink in the parlour later, you are very welcome. There's also a library bar. Make yourselves at home," said Joe, placing their bags on the luggage rack. "What time would you like dinner?

"How's eight?" asked Richard, looking at her.

"Perfect, thanks," she replied, from where she was gazing at the fantastic view across the rolling hills towards the Comeragh Mountains. The sun was trying to break out again; she hoped a rainbow might appear. She turned around when she heard Joe decline a tip.

"Ah no, you're grand. It's all part of the service here. Enjoy!"

As soon as the door closed, she burst out, "Oh Richard, a four-poster bed, and look, there's an original claw bath in here. We could throw a party in the bathroom alone. This has to be the best day of my life. I can't believe it. You are such a romantic to bring me back to the place we had our first dinner together. Even though it hadn't been a date back then. Oh God, Richard. It sounds nuts but I am so proud to be Irish today. Just look at this, I don't know if I can ever leave it."

"Kate?"

"Yes," she said, turning around. Richard was holding a jewellery box in his hand. Lying in it was a gold ring with an emerald stone set on a bed of diamonds.

"Oh Richard, it's the most beautiful ring I've ever seen."

"I planned to give it to you on the mountain but the rain finished that idea. Kate, I know how much you love Ireland," said Richard, placing the ring on her wedding finger. "We'll figure it out. For now let's just take one day at a time."

"You are right." She smiled up at him and then dragged him toward the bathroom. Pointing at the claw bath, she said, "Let's not let that go to waste."

Monique walked up the main street of Bayrush and saw that Sophia was already seated in the bay window of Bonita's, their favourite coffee shop.

"Hi Monique," said Sophia, standing up to hug her. "Firstly, congratulations on your new job. When do you start?"

"At the end of the month. Oh Sophia, I am so pleased. Gran is too. I think she was very worried I might have to leave."

Sophia ordered an Americano for herself and a latte for Monique. Then Monique noticed her taking a deep breath, which always meant Sophia was going to say something very serious. "Monique, Nora just wants you to be happy."

Monique looked down; she wondered where this had come from. She felt very confused but she allowed Sophia to continue.

"Nowhere is far any more. Every place is accessible."

"Why are you telling me this, Sophia?"

"I'm trying, very badly I'll admit, to say that if you love someone, you need to follow your heart. Nora wants you to be happy."

"Garvan left, Sophia. He never asked me what I thought about Dubai. He made his decision. He didn't consider me at all. I loved him with all my heart but he obviously doesn't feel the same."

Sophia paused and then said, "Okay, Monique. I guess we are just worried about you that you are staying for the …"

"Who exactly was worried about me?"

"Your gran is and I am and Molly …"

"You were all talking about me?" Monique was incredulous.

"It's not like that. We're worried, that's all." Sophia put her hand on Monique's. "Please believe me. We are just concerned. You know how misunderstandings can happen. Look at Eoghan and me, how much time did we waste? Your gran wants the best for you, and you and Garvan, well you looked like you were both very happy together. So I suppose we all presumed that you stayed because of Nora. I hear by what you are saying that is not the case. Maybe you and Nora need to talk."

"Sophia, there are many things I need to speak to Gran about. My mother for one." She had not meant to blurt that out, but it was easy to talk to Sophia.

"Well then, Monique. Do it! Ask the questions you need answers to. Just make sure you're prepared to hear them. I want you to know I'm here for you. I always will be." Sophia smiled and added, "In actual fact, the reason I asked to meet was to ask you a huge favour. That is, of course, if you can spare the time."

"Of course, I'd do anything for you, you know that."

"It's about Donagh," said Sophia, leaning across the table and lowering her voice.

Monique's heart skipped a beat.

"I've been helping him with his reading. He's about to take a first aid test at the end of this week. After that I would like him to continue working on his reading. We're getting in builders and Donagh is putting in a kitchen for us along with overseeing the work while we're away. It would only be an hour a day and you can use our house. The living room will be undisturbed. You see consistency is important."

"Does he know you are asking me?"

"I'm sure he'll be pleased."

She couldn't say no, having just said she'd do anything for Sophia. What a fool she had been!

Kate dashed through the rain with Richard to Eoghan's front door. Moments later Sophia opened it.

"Well, hello strangers, I was wondering where you both had got to. I've been trying to contact you for the past few days to tell you we're going to New York for a week."

"Sorry about that, Mom. We meant to go away for a night, but ended up staying for three," said Richard. Kate could feel his hand on her lower back as he led her along the small hall. She was bursting to tell Sophia their news.

"Take off those wet jackets and tell us all about it."

"Cup of tea, anyone?" said Eoghan, getting up when he saw them.

"Maybe we might have something a bit stronger," said Richard, beaming at his mother.

"Oh my goodness, come here Kate Fitzgerald." Sophia held Kate's hand in hers. "It's absolutely beautiful."

"Well, congratulations!" said Eoghan, slapping Richard on the back.

Sophia put her arms around Kate and whispered, "I am so honoured and proud to have you as my future daughter-in-law." When she pulled back Kate could see tears in Sophia's eyes.

"Thank you, Sophia," she said, filling up too.

Then Eoghan caught her and gave her a bear hug. "I couldn't be happier for you both. This calls for a champagne celebration." Eoghan went to get some glasses. "So when is the big day?" he called, from the dining room.

"As soon as we can. Kate needs to get her American visa sorted out."

"Oh," said Sophia.

"Our plan is to live between Ireland and New York. That is until we have to make a more permanent decision," said Kate.

"You mean, kiddies and all," said Eoghan.

"Yes, something like that," said Richard, smiling.

"But seriously Richard, are you going to be able to run things from here?" asked Eoghan.

Kate could see the concern on Sophia's face. Was it all going to turn out a terrible mess? Richard obviously thought it was a possibility and she too was prepared to take the chance.

"I'm doing that already but I will have to organise things a little better. Eoghan, I've been on a treadmill for too many years …" He took Kate's hand in his. "And now I am having the time of my life with the woman I love."

"Life is not a dress rehearsal, Richard. You are one lucky fellow to have the hand of that girl beside you! Just like I am to be with your mother. Cheers, to the future Mr and Mrs Wynthrope."

Sophia hugged her. "I am so thrilled for you both."

On Friday morning Donagh could feel beads of sweat form under his arms.

Jeez, he hadn't been so nervous in years. You can do it. You know it off by heart, he thought, walking in to the centre where Eoghan had arranged for him to take the test.

Thirty minutes later, he took out his mobile phone and clicked Sophia's number. "It's me, I passed it."

He could hear both Eoghan and Sophia whooping in the background. "Well done, that's fantastic," said Sophia.

"No bother to you, son," said Eoghan from the background.

"I'll call round later."

"Come for dinner at seven," said Sophia.

"Thanks very much, Sophia. I'd love that. And thanks for the help."

"You are very welcome."

Later, Donagh walked up the hill towards Eoghan's house. A jeep pulled up beside him. It was Eoghan. He hopped in.

"Just on my way home. We have a busy day ahead of us tomorrow. One of the largest cruise liners in the world is docking here."

"Wow!" said Donagh. He was about to ask more about the ship when he saw an old red Audi parked outside the cottage. "I didn't know Monique was coming!"

"Nor me, the more the merrier, eh?" said Eoghan, opening the front door. "Hi honey! I'm …"

"Ah, jeez, that's getting old." Donagh laughed.

"Really?"

"Really, mate, I'm doing you a favour."

"HOME," shouted Eoghan while Donagh pretended to wrestle him in the little hallway.

"Will you two behave? We have company," Sophie smiled, as Monique appeared from behind her.

"Congratulations, Donagh," Monique smiled.

"Thanks," he said. He felt so awkward about the day on the beach. She seemed to be okay about it, he thought. Thankfully, Eoghan chatted about the cruise liner coming in. He was so excited by it all. Dinner turned into a lively affair. Neither Eoghan nor Sophia was ever short on conversation. Sipping coffee, Sophia explained how her new kitchen was going to look to Monique.

Eoghan was restless. "Liverpool are playing Arsenal! We'll just go in to see the score."

Donagh got up and followed him.

Sophia smiled. "You men love your sport!"

"What would you like me to go through with Donagh?" asked Monique, even though she was desperately trying to think of an excuse not to help.

"I'm so pleased you offered. It's about consistency. Donagh wants to do a range of courses over the coming months so he needs intense work. He is very committed. A friend in the UK recommended this book," said Sophia, getting up from the table to retrieve the book from the dresser. "It's called *Toe by Toe*. The theory is to break down reading into small steps hence the name *Toe by Toe*."

"Interesting!" said Monique, picking up the book and flicking through it, all the while wondering how Sophia had got the idea that she had offered. She had been tongue-tied most of the evening whereas Donagh seemed completely at home.

"It works using phonics and visual aids. Maybe you'll also blend your ideas."

"I will certainly look at this and incorporate some of the other resources I have."

"You can take the book with you."

"Thanks, so when do we start?"

"We're leaving tomorrow," said Sophia, getting up to go into the living room. Monique followed her and stood in the doorway. Eoghan paused the match.

"How's tomorrow for you both?" asked Sophia.

"Saturday?" said Monique, surprised. She hadn't expected such an immediate start.

"Ah sure it's only an hour. The time flies," said Eoghan.

"I'm working in Butterfly Barn all day. It will have to be in the evening around seven," said Monique.

"Seven's good for me too, thanks, Monique," said Donagh, giving her the full watt of his smile. She was mortified at the thought of being alone with him. What had she let herself in for? She was going to be a tutor to someone she couldn't get out of her head. Thank God he thought she had a boyfriend and that had been the reason he walked away. She did not intend to tell him otherwise. Anyway he had a girlfriend.

"Thanks for dinner, Sophia. I hope you both have a great time," she said, hugging Sophia.

Eoghan got up to hug her. Donagh waved goodbye from the other side of the room.

The following evening Monique rushed around the yard in an effort to finish.

"What's the hurry Monique, you got a date or something?" asked Vicky, passing.

"If you have and haven't told me, I'll kill you," said Rachel, smiling.

"No, I don't have a date. And if I had she'd be the last person I'd tell." She nodded in Vicky's direction. "Although I am in a hurry. I could use some help."

"Sure thing," said Rachel, taking up a brush. "Are you coming out later tonight?"

"What time are you meeting up?"

"Around nine."

"I don't know how long I'll be. I will text you. You can tell me where you are." She didn't like being secretive with Rachel but how could she explain where she was going? It was confidential. She hadn't thought about it when she had agreed to meet him on a Saturday night. When they finished, she thanked her and ran to the car. She still had to get home to shower. She was crazy to have agreed to do this. Her life was already busy. She didn't even have time to eat.

She drove to the cliffs above Bayrush and ran up the short path to Eoghan's house but there was no sign of Donagh's jeep. She decided to knock anyway and sure enough he was there.

"Hi, come in," he smiled. Her eyes were drawn to the slight chip on his front tooth. She wished he didn't have such an effect on her. He was still in his work clothes. He wore a T-shirt with high-cut sleeves, showing off his perfectly constructed strong tanned arms. She wanted to reach out and touch his skin.

"Sorry, I didn't get a chance to get home to shower and change."

"I did not think you were here. There was no jeep outside."

"I walked up today." He stood back to allow her to pass him in the small hall. She decided it would be safer to work at the kitchen table. It would be big enough to keep her distance from him. When she opened the door, she couldn't believe the sight that met her. She closed it quickly.

"We took out the old kitchen today," said Donagh, opening the door to the living room. "So I hope this is okay." He had set up a small table with two chairs side by side in the corner of the living room.

Why on earth had she agreed to this? She sat down and took out the book Sophia had given her. He sat beside her while she explained that they were going right back to basics. Retelling what Sophia had said. And so the work began.

About three quarters of an hour later, her stomach began to rumble. She was mortified.

"Excuse me. I did not eat yet."

"Me neither!"

"Let's continue until eight and we can resume tomorrow," said Monique, trying to sound as professional as possible.

"Sounds good," he said, continuing with the work.

Fifteen minutes later she said, "You have covered enough this evening. Well done. So I will see you tomorrow night. Can we start at eight instead? I am really busy."

"Eight it is. Thanks, Monique."

She got into her car and was about to drive away when she saw him locking the door and walking down the drive. "I'm going into Bayrush, if you need a lift," she said.

"I'll take a spin down the hill, thanks." He got in to the passenger seat and she drove down the hill as fast as she could.

"Here is great. Thanks again. See you tomorrow," he said, getting out of the car. As she pulled away from the kerb, she could see him in her rear view mirror saunter across the road in that way of his and into Murphy's Bar, still in his work clothes. Then she saw the red-haired girl walking up the road in the same direction.

On the outskirts of Bayrush, she pulled into McDonald's drive thru where she ordered a chicken wrap. While sitting in the car park eating it, she texted Rachel to find out where the gang were. She decided to join them for a while. She planned to take part in an event in Ballinamona tomorrow so an early night suited her.

Richard drove up the avenue to Oak House.

"I still can't believe how many people your mother managed to fit into her house yesterday."

Kate laughed. Richard had spent the day being gobsmacked as more and more family arrived to congratulate them on their engagement.

Her mother, Molly, had insisted on asking everyone over to share their news.

"You're still traumatised, thankfully the weather was great and we had the garden. But I will warn you, my mother would have done that even if it had been pouring with rain. She is nuts, I'll have you know."

Richard threw his head back and laughed. "You didn't lick it off the ground."

"OMG, you are even using the local lingo."

"I'm looking forward to a quieter day today," said Richard, smiling.

"Grace said something about having a 'real chat'. I wonder what that's about?" said Kate.

"Beats me. Jack has a new horse he wants to ride out and he said he could use some company."

Richard parked and went straight to the yard. She walked around to the back door and went into the kitchen, calling, "Hello."

"Hi Kate. Ah, Finn, give her a little space, pet," said Grace, adding in hushed tones to Kate. "He's killing her with kindness, kissing her all the time."

"Are you sure it's just kisses?" said Kate as Finn bent over Lily in the bouncer again.

"It's kisses. He loves her madly and deeply," said Grace.

Kate threw her eyes to heaven. "Whatever. Anyway I'm dying to know, tell me!"

"Tell you what?" asked Grace, confused.

"What's 'the real chat' about?"

"I was wondering if you have set a date. I'm not being nosy but ..."

"We haven't yet. I still can't believe it's happening." She twirled her ring around her finger.

"Me neither." Kate looked up quickly.

"No I mean about us – Jack and I getting married."

"I never doubted you two would."

"Yet you doubt yourself." Grace's expression of concern made her uncomfortable. She hadn't told her she had left New York.

"Boil the kettle, Grace. I've a lot to tell you." She told Grace about everything that had happened, especially how unhappy she was living in the penthouse. "It was cold, impersonal and lacked any character not to mention neighbours even." It still amazed her how much better it felt to actually verbalise her fears.

"Kate, do you love him?"

"Yes."

"Do you believe he can work between here and New York?"

"No."

"Well then, you will have to talk it out, maybe you could live somewhere else. I'm sure there is a solution."

"I was in great form and now I'm all confused again."

"Kate, problems don't disappear just because you choose to bury your head in the sand."

"Why are you always right?"

Grace laughed. "I'm piled up with problems here. I still haven't found a childminder. The bills are piling in. I'm chasing money we're owed. Life is never simple. Everybody has problems."

"I feel awful for making a big deal out of not wanting to live in a penthouse. Like what a problem to have!"

"Kate, it is a problem for you so please don't lessen it or compare it. Loneliness is a horrendous feeling. I've been there."

"Thanks, Grace. Finn, ah don't pet. Come here, let's play with the tractors. It was only kisses, my eye," said Kate, whisking little Finn off his feet and tickling him. Finn giggled.

Monique walked around Eoghan's house while she waited for Donagh. The week had passed by so quickly. Sophia had sent a text telling her they wouldn't be back until Wednesday. Last week she would have been annoyed but the truth was she looked forward to spending time with Donagh.

The builders had knocked the wall between the kitchen and dining room, making the area open plan to include the sunroom. When she arrived there were men tiling the roof. It amazed her how quickly the work was being done. Donagh had nearly finished the kitchen.

She noticed there were tools dropped on the floor and she nearly slipped on a yellow pencil. It looked like Donagh had either left in a hurry or else he was an untidy worker. Her phone rang.

"Monique, I'm sorry but I won't be able to make it this evening." He sounded breathless. "Are you okay for tomorrow night?"

"Em ... well ..."

"It's okay. I understand if you can't. I just ..."

"See you at seven," she answered, not waiting for his reply. She was annoyed with him for cancelling at such short notice. He could have called earlier. She had a life too.

"This is nice," said Eoghan. He sat beside Sophia on a bench in the garden project in New York where Kate had volunteered during the summer.

"It's such a simple idea to transform alleyways and derelict sites into little havens of peace and tranquillity. Look at that little boy chasing a butterfly in the middle of Manhattan."

"He probably never saw one up close before. I feel we are here for a reason. Are you going to share?"

"How well you know me. Richard and I were thinking about creating a version of Butterfly Barn here. In the Hamptons to be exact."

"Did you see a property you like?"

She turned to him. "We own a house there."

He nodded. "Of course you do. Your wealth has blown my mind, Sophia. Nothing could have prepared me for it. And you still want to live with me in Ireland." He shook his head.

She took his hand. "The Christmas after Bill died, Richard and I stayed in the Hamptons. It was the worse time in my life. Heather and Billy had, well, you know what happened and then Bill had died so suddenly from a heart attack. I don't know how we got through those days." He rubbed his thumbs along the back of her hand. "Will you come with me to see it? I'd love your opinion."

"Yes."

"George will drive us."

"No, I will drive. Let's just take some time together. We'll stop wherever takes our fancy."

"Long Island is a beautiful part of the world. I was thinking that house needs life. It was Bill's parents' house."

"I thought he had stopped speaking to them."

"After they denied Richard and me, he did. But when his mother died, his father changed the will and left everything to Bill. She'd turn in her grave if she knew I own it now." Sophia smiled.

Eoghan laughed out loud. "You're becoming more Irish than the Irish with your turn of phrase."

She got up. "It's unkind to speak ill of the dead but she was a dragon."

"We'll head off tomorrow morning. Sophia, look at the difference Butterfly Barn has made already. Donagh is not from a deprived background, just a negative one. It's not always people with limited means who are suffering. We should keep that in mind as we move forward."

She smiled, pleased that Eoghan was just as committed as she was to Butterfly Barn. She wouldn't do anything without his full support and willingness to be involved. Eoghan was such a natural teacher. It broke her heart that he still hadn't heard from his daughters. They were missing out on such a good, kind person. She slipped her hand into his. "We'll set off early."

Chapter Eleven

"Hi, Monique. Thanks for coming tonight," said Donagh, when he opened the door of Eoghan's house.

"Let's get started." She was still peeved with him.

She noticed his reading had improved significantly since she had met him back in June. She watched as his brow furrowed in full concentration, making him even more attractive if that could be possible.

"Well," he said, "I think that was better, wasn't it?"

She hadn't actually taken in a word of what he had read. She had been so distracted by him.

"Yes, yes, much better."

"Hey, look, I'm sorry about last night –"

She cut across him. "Forget it."

"But I'd like to explain."

"There is no need."

"No, I'd like to. I brought my little brother to the beach yesterday to hang out for a while. Everything was great all day but just as my mother arrived to collect him, he got an asthma attack. We had to rush to hospital."

"Oh my goodness, is he okay?" She felt awful for being so brusque with him.

"He has severe asthma. It's something we have to be very careful about with him. Oisín's only ten. Asthma is so common. But it's frightening to witness a severe attack. He's still in hospital. They will have to review the medication. He is getting too many attacks lately."

"Who is with him now?"

"My mum, my father is on a business trip at the moment."

She noticed his face had changed when he talked about his father. Then he continued. "I'm sorry about the last minute call and missing class." They were sitting side by side and his head was hanging down.

She felt so guilty and he looked so forlorn. She touched his shoulder in a gesture of sympathy. He turned to look at her. She could feel her breath catch in her throat.

"Ahem, it's eight o'clock, you have done enough for today." She began to tidy up.

"I'm staying on to work on the kitchen. I had planned to work after class last night." His phone rang. "I'll just take this call, it's Geoff."

"How's it goin'?" He went to the other side of the room to talk.

She didn't know whether to stay or go. She went to leave and he gestured to her to hold on. "Great Geoff, I'll talk to you soon."

He smiled as he hung up. His face was alight. "Remember that trip to France Geoff had talked about? It's happening next weekend. I'm really looking forward to seeing some of those adventure parks. It would be fantastic to have one at Butterfly Barn and to have water sports there too."

"They are always coming up with new ideas to develop the place."

"I'm really glad I 'eard you on the radio that day."

She laughed. "Are you mocking my accent?"

"Never."

"See you tomorrow night."

"Seven again?"

"Oui."

"Oh I love it! Say something else in French."

"Au revoir." She laughed as she walked down the hall.

"I reckon that means goodbye."

"Oui."

"And that means yes." She nodded and waved as she got into the car. He stood at the door to wave her off.

When she pulled up at the cottage, she wondered would Gran be home. She had gone off on another active retirement outing. She smiled; Nora had a better social life than hers. She checked the post box. She glanced through the usual bills and some junk mail and then she saw a cream embossed envelope addressed to her. It had a French postmark. Who could it be from? She threw the bundle on the table and opened the fridge. Whoever it was hadn't tried to contact her when she had needed them. Why bother with her now? She was starving. She took out peppers, onions, mushrooms, beansprouts and a fillet of chicken. She'd make a stir fry. Gran will have eaten, she thought. She cut and chopped, and then tossed the chicken and veg into the wok, adding soy sauce. She left it to sizzle while she turned on the TV to plan her night's viewing. She heard the front door opening.

"Hi Mon," called Nora. "That's a lovely aroma."

"Hi Gran, have you eaten?"

"Yes, we had a great day. I'm shattered."

"Put your feet up and I will bring you some tea."

"Thanks, pet."

She went to bed at twelve, but couldn't sleep. She kept thinking about Donagh and his reaction to his little brother. He was so kind and yet there was a roguishness that was so appealing. What was wrong with having a fling? At the moment, she thought, everything. She was his tutor so he was definitely out of bounds. But she wasn't exactly his tutor; she was just helping him out.

"Stop," she said. He was dating someone and even if he wasn't she would never be the kind of girl he'd find attractive. Men like him could have any girl they wanted.

Garvan's calls had cooled off too especially since she told him about her new job. It was inevitable that he had settled. She tossed and turned. At 5.30 she eventually got up. She padded quietly down the hall to make a cup of tea. She noticed the corner of the cream envelope sticking out from under the rest of the post. What the hell, she thought, she might as well open it!

My dearest Monique,

My name is Philippe Chevalier, I am your father's elder stepbrother. I realise this letter may come as a shock to you. I would dearly love the opportunity to meet you.

My dearest, it was a difficult decision to allow you to be raised in Ireland with your Irish grandmother, but I believed it was the best one at that time.

Monique put down the letter. She was completely confused. Why had her gran not told her she had an uncle? "Oh Gran, what have you done?"

I pray that you will find it in your heart to forgive me the lost time. I await you every day,
    With love,
    Philippe Chevalier

It was just too much. She went to her room and got dressed. She opened the cottage door. It was getting bright but a blast of cold air hit her. She grabbed her red jacket from the hall stand and shut the door behind her. She walked and walked with no idea where she was going.

An hour later she was on Bayrush Beach. She began to run in an effort to chase the memories of the car crash from her head. Her father's voice rang in her ears. He had called their names in a low whisper and then there had been an eerie silence. She had tried to move; blood had covered her top but she couldn't feel pain. She had been trapped. The sounds of voices and sirens had filled the air. She had seen sparks flashing and had heard the sound of the rescue service cutting the car open. She had screamed her mother's name but there had been no answer. She had prayed that her mother was just unconscious – she'd wake any second. So she had kept screaming until finally she had been cut out and placed on a stretcher. She had begged them to wake her parents up.

Her last glimpse of her mother had been with her head lying against the headrest. Her beautiful eyes had been wide open. But it was the emptiness in them that had shocked her the most. She knew her mother was gone. It was the image that haunted her every night for years. Her fun, lively, spirited mother with her strawberry blonde hair was gone forever. How could someone so full of life just disappear?

Her handsome, striking-looking father who had shared so much of his knowledge and kindness with her had left her too, leaving her a shell of the person she used to be. She remembered laughing, dancing, playing dress-up, having fun, and, as she got older, lively debates on world issues. Her parents' friends used to visit, eating, smoking, speaking, arguing, and fixing the world's problems. Gone. They were gone. She stumbled and dropped to her knees on the damp sand. She screamed at the sky. "Why, oh why did you take them from me?" Her body shook as more long held back memories flooded her.

"Are you okay?" a voice asked from behind her. She got such a fright she didn't recognise it at first. "It's 6.30 in the morning, are you crazy to be out here on your own?"

"I am not the only crazy one so. You are here too."

"I have a perfectly good reason." He pointed to the small streamlined surfboard under his arm.

"Donagh, will you just leave me alone?" She turned away. She felt so stupid. What must he think of her – crying on the beach like some kind of weirdo! "Please," she said when she didn't hear him move away.

"No. I'm not leaving until you are."

"You will have a long wait."

"I've got all the time in the world. Talk to me."

"There is nothing to say." She got up and began to walk back in the direction she had come. He caught her by the arm. She stopped and looked down at it. Something crazy possessed her. "Make love to me," she said.

His eyebrows shot up and there was a look of shock on his face. She walked away as though she hadn't asked.

"Wait!" he called after her. "You can't ask me something like that and walk away."

She ignored him and kept walking but he just walked beside her and said nothing. When they reached the entrance to the beach, he caught her by the hand and led her across the road. They walked up the promenade and turned the corner in the direction of the main street. He stopped outside a two-storey terraced house. He opened the door and led her up the stairs into his bedroom. Her heart was thumping; she had never done anything like this in her life. She could feel her nerve leaving her.

"Monique, I don't know what happened to you and you may never want to tell me but I'm your friend and there is no way I would leave you on that beach alone. You look exhausted, please get into bed and get some sleep. I'll be downstairs."

When Jessie arrived at the cottage, Nora was waiting for her in the doorway of the cottage. The sight of her brought back images of ten years ago when Nora's world had fallen apart. The poor woman was distraught.

"Is she back?"

"No." She handed Jessie the letter she had found lying on the table.

"Did you try her mobile phone?" asked Jessie, looking at the beautiful handwriting on cream embossed paper.

"It rang in her bedroom."

"We'll just have to wait. Are you sure you want me to read this?"

Nora nodded and turned to go into the kitchen. She sat at the table and waited until Jessie had finished the letter. Jessie looked up.

"Château Vieux De La Lac – who is this man?"

"I don't know."

"Nora, I think it's time to talk to Monique. She might need to speak to a counsellor or somebody who understands the grief she is going through. Between Garvan leaving and now this letter, it must have brought everything back."

Nora nodded.

"Oh Jess, what have I done? I should have told her about her grandfather. But what could I say? He beat the living daylights out of me and I stayed. What would she think of me?"

Jessie was stunned. "But he was the sergeant here for years."

"Who would have believed me, Jessie? I had no friends, he made sure of that. I came here from Cork. I was an only child with an elderly sick mother when I met him."

Jessie remembered him as a tall, handsome man, who always gave people the time of the day, whereas she had thought of Nora as a quiet, odd kind of woman who never bothered with anyone. Oh my God, she thought, does anybody ever know what happens behind closed doors?

"What about Eilish? Did he ever ..."

"No, but he threatened to kill her and me if I ever tried to leave. As soon as Eilish finished her Leaving Certificate I convinced him to let her go to France as an au pair for the summer. Of course he objected, calling it a skivvy's job, but I told him she could brush up on her French and it would stand to her in the future. He relented."

Nora paused.

"Nora, you don't have to talk if it's too hard for you." Jessie got up to make tea. "I think you need to eat." She put some bread into the toaster and took out butter and marmalade.

"I want to talk."

"It's not me who needs to hear this."

The kitchen door opened and Monique walked in. Neither she nor Nora had heard her.

"Hear what?" Monique's face was drawn and she looked dishevelled.

"Thank God you're back," said Nora, standing up. But Monique didn't move.

"The silence is killing me, Gran. Who am I? I have an uncle you never told me about. The address on that letter is a château, a castle for goodness' sake."

"Monique, I've never heard of him either."

"So what were you talking to Jessie about?"

Jessie put two mugs on the kitchen table. "Mon, will you sit down and have a cup of tea and some toast. I'm going to leave the two of you to talk."

"No, Jessie." Jessie stood frozen to the spot. She had never seen Monique like this before. Jessie looked at Nora – her life force seemed to have left her. "Please, I want you to stay."

"Is that okay with you, Nora?"

Nora nodded. "Jessie, I don't know what we would do without you. Please stay."

Monique sat down and so did Nora. Jessie took another mug from the cupboard and poured tea.

Nora told Monique what she had been telling Jessie. Monique was horrified.

"So that is why there are no photographs of my grandfather on display in the cottage."

Nora nodded. "He died a month before your ..." Nora's voice broke.

"Oh Gran, please say her name."

"My darling daughter, Eilish." Nora broke down and cried. Monique went and held her in her arms for what seemed an age. Jessie didn't know what to do so she took the cold toast from where it had been sitting in the toaster and began to break it up for the birds. She put fresh bread back in. She went outside and threw the crumbs to the wagtails and the lone robin and went back inside.

"Toast. I think you both need to eat."

"Yes," said Nora. "There is still so much more you need to know, Monique." Nora took the photograph from the mantel. "She was so beautiful. I took this the day she left. I never saw her again." Tears spilled down Nora's cheeks, she wiped them with the backs of her hands and continued talking. "Eilish became pregnant. She was both terrified and excited and so in love with a boy called André Chevalier. Eilish told me he was a local boy from a town called Bois Saint Etienne in south-west France where she had gone to a family called Dubois to care for their two young children. Of course, your grandfather went crazy, calling her horrendous names. He refused to speak to her and told me to tell her she was never to come home. If she did he would make my life hell and hers even worse."

"Oh Gran, I don't understand why you didn't leave him?"

"Where could I go? I had no family, no friends; he had made sure of that, and no money. He was so conniving. He even did the shopping and people used to say how good he was. He'd come home bragging about what so-and-so had said. When the truth was that he wouldn't give me the money to do the shopping. I couldn't leave nor could I see my daughter or granddaughter. But I did manage to convince him to let me volunteer at the local school to help with the children's reading. I met a lovely teacher there who became a trusted friend. One day she asked me why the Garda car was nearly always outside the school when I was there. Whatever way I must have looked that day, she knew something wasn't right. Over time I told her about Eilish and she suggested I use her address to stay in touch. Oh my God, Monique, I was so grateful to that woman, she has since passed away but I don't know what I would have done without her."

"He used to follow you!" Monique was incredulous.

"There is only one word I can use to describe that man and it's *evil*. When he died I could have danced for joy. Eilish and I had plans to meet. They were coming for a holiday as soon as she got time off from work. I can't. I can't go on."

"Oh Gran, I think you should lie down for a while." Monique helped

Nora out of the chair and led her to the bedroom. A few minutes later, she came back to the kitchen. She slumped into the armchair in the corner. "No wonder she could not talk. I'm so tired, Jessie. I just don't want to know any more. I want my life back. I want Garvan. I want everything to go back to normal. I cannot stand these feelings. Highs and lows and buried secrets – I feel like I'm going crazy. Why Jessie? Why did they have to die? It's not fair."

Jessie remained silent. After a few minutes, she asked, "Where were you?"

Monique had been sitting with her head in her hands. She looked up.

"I asked Donagh to make love to me." Jessie closed her eyes and waited. "He brought me to his house and put me to bed while he went downstairs." Jessie let out a huge sigh of relief.

"Monique, I think you need to find yourself before you start into something else with Donagh or Garvan or whoever. I'm just glad Donagh was such a gentleman."

"I'm not."

Jessie smiled. "Yes, you are really."

Monique smiled. "Kind of."

"Get some sleep. We'll talk about Mr Philippe Chevalier later. I love you," said Jessie, going over to give her a hug.

"So," said Monique, "the aim is to cross the midline."

Donagh smiled. She had such a cute smile, he thought. How was he going to be able to focus after what she had asked him this morning? She had arrived half an hour ago as if nothing had happened earlier. She was busy reminding him about the exercises she had told them about at Butterfly Barn. But all he could think of was what they could be doing right now instead. Obviously, she had other things on her mind. She was his tutor; it would not be professional to become involved. Anyway, she was much too complicated for him. He stood opposite her in Eoghan's back garden. He was copying the exercises she was doing.

"I brought a tennis ball and a basket with me. You have to throw the ball ten times with your right hand and then change to your left hand."

"Jeez, Monique, how old do you think I am, six?" He laughed.

"Humour me. I read that it is good practice for hand–eye coordination."

"Fair enough."

"As you get better you increase the distance."

"Monique, it's our last class. Sophia will be back tomorrow. Let's finish up."

"Okay, I hope you found the time useful. I would like to wish you the best of luck with everything." She picked up the basket and ball and walked inside to pack up her books and things.

"Monique." She stopped and looked back. He was standing in the garden. "Are you hungry?"

She nodded.

"You're not my tutor anymore."

"I know."

"Can we maybe watch a movie or something?"

"Oui."

He smiled.

Sophia stood on the balcony of the master bedroom looking across the ocean. She was just wearing one of Eoghan's shirts. It was a habit she had taken to. The white sand beach stretched for miles along the coastline. She heard Eoghan coming back into the bedroom. He had two cups of coffee in his hands.

"Sophia, this is not a house, it's a mansion. I can't get my head around it. I nearly got lost trying to find my way back from the kitchen. Bill's family must have been unbelievably wealthy in their day."

She nodded and went to sit on the white round-backed wicker chair. He placed the cups on the glass table and sat opposite her.

"It's just incredible. We're looking out at the same ocean from the other side."

"Do you think Kate would like it here?"

"You need to ask her. Does Richard like it here?"

"Yes, it was his idea. But have you noticed there is something missing?"

"Not really, my God, there are tennis courts, both indoor and outdoor swimming pools, even a pool house. What's that over there?" He pointed to a building. "I didn't notice it earlier."

"It's a garage with living quarters over it. When Bill was young the chauffeur lived there."

"Wow, what did his father do for a living?"

"He was a very successful banker, one of the few who survived the Wall Street crash."

"There's so much land around it too. And it has private access to the beach. No, I can't figure out what's missing."

"A barn." She laughed.

"Well, you'll just have to build one. That is if the lads want to."

"I really hope they will. Oh Eoghan, I'd love to hear the patter of tiny feet here."

"Sophia, remember you can't live their lives for them. How about we go back inside and live ours?" He stood up and took her hand.

"Let's stay here for a few more days."

"Sounds good to me." He kissed her.

"Here's looking at you kid," said Donagh jokingly when the movie had ended. Monique was sitting beside him on the couch. They had ordered pizza delivery and chose *Casablanca* from Eoghan's collection of old movies. She seemed to be more relaxed this evening. He had been worried about her all day and hadn't expected her to turn up for class this evening.

"Hey, you're upset?" She turned to look at him but this time, he just couldn't help himself. He leaned towards her slowly. She kept her eyes open. He paused and didn't move any closer but she did. He had never wanted anyone so much in his life. She was kissing him passionately. He couldn't get enough of her. Had he lost his reason … he didn't care. They rolled off the couch, all the while kissing. It was unbelievable. Then the living room door opened.

"Oh, em, sorry, lads. Sorry about that." The door closed just as quickly.

"Oh shite," said Donagh.

"That was Kate," said Monique. She was absolutely mortified, and so was he.

"God, Monique, I'm sorry about that … I … got carried away."

"Do not say another word, Donagh. This will not happen again." She picked up her bag and ran out the front door.

Kate opened the kitchen door. "OMG, it's fabulous." It was a huge open space. She ran her hand along the marble worktop. The units were made from oak painted off-white. Of course there was an Aga and an American fridge. But the piece for her was the handmade dresser painted an eggshell blue. The floor was mahogany, leading out into the sunroom. There was no furniture and the garden was still being landscaped.

She heard the front door slamming just as she put some fresh milk, cold meat, sausages and bacon in the fridge. She hadn't expected to find Donagh and Monique rolling around the sitting-room floor. She wouldn't have put them together. She liked Donagh but he was a lad. She hoped he wouldn't break Monique's heart. She'd been through enough. As long as it was just a bit of fling, that would be okay. But it hadn't looked like that.

"Hey, Kate," said Donagh. He was clearly mortified. "Em, sorry, em.

Sorry about that …"

"Forget it. Didn't see a thing. Say nothing. Between us and all that. This is fantastic."

"Cool, cheers," he said, still standing in the doorway.

He looked forlorn, she thought. "Are you okay?" she asked.

"No, you know. I'm not okay." He walked over and sat on one of the stools at the new breakfast bar. "Women, I can't figure you out at all. She just stormed off. What the hell was that about? I just don't know …"

"Did you say something to her?"

"All I said was that I was sorry for getting carried away."

"Oh Donagh."

"If you hadn't come in, who knows what would have happened? She's in love with somebody else, Kate. She's a nice girl. She's not … she's not someone you'd sleep with. For Christ's sake, she's someone you'd marry. I don't mean me but you know what I mean."

Kate nodded. For as long as Kate could remember Monique had been with Garvan.

"For your own sake, I'd stay away for a while. Let things cool off. Donagh, I don't know how much you know about her, but Monique, well, she has had more than her share of heartache for one so young. Love her or stay away. Don't mess with her." She could hardly believe she had said that but what she had witnessed for just a few seconds was more than lust and fooling around. It was electric and passionate and that only came from love. And most certainly she knew a thing or two about that.

"Have a beer and I'll drop you home," she said, nudging him to lighten his mood.

"I will so. Thanks for the chat, Kate. Where are you going?"

"To get the box of beer from the car, sorry it won't be cold."

"I'll get it." He brought the beer in and opened one. "Kate, I'm glad the lads are back tomorrow. It will be easier not to see her. I won't have any reason to meet her. Anyway I've too much going on. I need to find a job."

"I can assure you, when you can create a kitchen like this, you'll never be out of a job."

"Thanks, Kate."

"Didn't I hear you and Geoff are going to France?"

"Yes, but not until the weekend after next."

"Where's your jeep?"

"Long story." His phone rang and Kate heard him organising a lift from Butchie. He was coming up to collect all his tools.

She wondered what exactly was really going on. Donagh was in deeper than, he thought. But was Monique really over Garvan? And why had she been here in the first place? It was all very intriguing, she thought.

When Monique got home, she went straight to her bedroom and threw herself on top of her bed. The embarrassment of it all, it was excruciating. How could she face him again? How could she face Kate? She had made such a fool of herself. She would never allow that to happen again.

Sophia would be home tomorrow so she would never have to meet him again. She couldn't be in the same room with him again, never, ever, ever.

After a few minutes, she got up and went to her bedside locker. She took out the letter and re-read it. The strange thing was when she was with Donagh she had been able to put everything else to the back of her mind. She had been busy … busy just being happy … and apprehensive … and wondering … and hoping … hoping that he'd kiss her again, and then he kissed her and said he was sorry for getting carried away. She turned and buried her head in the pillow. The mortification had come back.

Eventually, she got up and took out her laptop. When she passed the living room, Gran was watching TV. She had slept for most of the day. Monique went over and kissed her. "I'm going over to Jessie's house for a while."

"Okay pet."

"Go to bed soon, Gran, it's been a long day."

"I will."

"I love you."

Nora smiled and patted her hand. "I'd be lost without you."

There, it was the truth. How could she ever leave her gran after all she had been through? She was too tired to walk so she took Gran's car. Jessie was watching TV when she came in but got up immediately.

"Hi Mon, now I can watch the match pundits in peace," said Geoff, grinning from the armchair. Monique smiled.

"Men!" said Jess, bringing her to the kitchen where she boiled the kettle.

"I've decided to go to France."

"I'll come with you."

"No Jess, I have to do this on my own."

"I don't like the idea of that. We don't know anything about this man. He could be a weirdo. Look, I know you're an adult now but there might be some sinister reason why he waited ten years." Jessie poured tea.

"Okay, you could be right, but I have just booked a ticket for Friday."

"I can't go. We have a group of special needs kids coming to stay. But I have an idea; Geoff is talking about going to France the weekend after next. He hasn't booked it. I'll ask him to go on Friday instead."

"I do not think that is a good idea. Donagh is going with him and after what I told you …"

Jessie didn't let her finish.

"Even better, because I know nothing bad can happen with them around. I'm sure there are parks they can view around there. Geoff …" Jessie was out of the chair and before Monique knew it, she had Geoff at the kitchen table with her laptop in front of her looking up adventure parks, flights and accommodation. Geoff was told to ring Donagh to make sure he was available. Three rooms were booked in a pension hotel in the middle of Bois Saint Etienne.

"I don't want Donagh to know why I'm going. What am I going to tell him?"

It was turning into a nightmare.

Jessie looked at Geoff.

"I'm sorry but I don't know what's going on here either."

Jessie looked at Monique. "Of course you can tell Geoff." Jessie explained about the letter and how Monique planned to visit her uncle to find out more about her parents.

"We'll tell him you are visiting some friends and you are also interested in the adventure parks so we decided to combine the trip," said Geoff.

"Perfect, you're a genius," said Jessie, leaning over and kissing him. Monique smiled; she felt a whole lot better. This way she could do it alone but she had some back-up if she needed it.

Chapter Twelve

Donagh heard the car horn beeping. He picked up his holdall and went downstairs. He opened the front door. Geoff's jeep was right beside it. Evie was just coming out of the kitchen. She was still in PJ bottoms and a fleece. "Have a great time," she said, kissing him on the cheek and continuing up the stairs.

Without looking he went to open the front passenger door. He stopped in his tracks when he saw Monique sitting there.

"Oh, eh, hi."

Geoff leaned over. "Mon is coming with us. Hop in the back. She's just visiting some friends who live nearby so I suggested she travel with us. She'd like to see the parks too, if she has the time."

"Fair enough."

It was 8 a.m. and the news came on the radio. "Just want to catch the headlines!" said Geoff.

Donagh looked out the window. He had been looking forward to the break away and now she was sitting in the front seat. It was bad enough that he couldn't get her out of his head. He had spent the last few nights playing guitar late into the night. He had gone surfing every morning at the crack of dawn, partly in the hope that she might turn up again, and now she was here.

"I'm looking forward to this. It's been a crazy busy time," said Geoff.

"Know the feeling," said Donagh.

"You did a great job on the kitchen, Donagh. That dresser is a fine piece of craftsmanship. We're also planning to build some more log cabins. There will be some work coming up when we get back. Eoghan told me Jimmy let you go. I hope that wasn't because of me offering you a job."

"Ah no, he didn't know anything about your offer. Things just dried up a bit." Donagh didn't want to tell him the real reason.

"That's strange. The building trade is picking up. Not to worry, his loss our gain. We'll have a busy few days ahead of us. It's something different. I've arranged to meet a guy who will show us around. It will be handy to have Monique to help with translation."

Donagh saw her side profile. She smiled for the first time since he had joined them. He couldn't understand why she was being so cool with him. She was the one who had asked him to sleep with her and she was the one with a boyfriend even if he was in Dubai. She'd probably be with her friends most of the time.

Kate took the roast stuffed pork steak out of the oven in Rose Cottage. She took the lid off and sniffed the aroma. She was beginning to surpass herself; if she wasn't careful she just might start baking. Both she and Richard had started to experiment in the kitchen.

She painted while he worked in the office upstairs. They went surfing and horse-riding. Every evening was spent together and they didn't have to entertain or attend anything. She knew it couldn't last forever. But it was perfect.

Richard came down from the office.

"Jessie has asked me to run an art therapy class for five days," said Kate.

He went to the wine rack and chose a bottle of red.

"That's great news. It will give you a chance to use your learning." He poured two glasses and sat at the counter.

"I'm thrilled about it. I've been so caught up with my own work. It will be a break from it and a chance to actually deliver a workshop."

"How many people do you need?"

"Anywhere between twelve and fourteen, not too big but not too small either. It's good to be able to break into small groups and then back to the bigger group, it adds perspective to it."

"Do people actually voice their problems?"

"Sometimes, but mostly it's about expressing through art, it's hugely reflective. People can often see where they are coming from with their thinking through what they create. It's fascinating, and sometimes it can happen that the person doesn't see it themselves until they start to talk about what they created. Then the listeners can often notice the person experience what I would call an 'AHA' moment in the midst of the conversation. It's like a light has been turned on."

"If you're not careful, you'll end up on the Oprah show. I think you're hanging out with Americans too much."

"Why, are you trying to get rid of me already? Is that the best you can do?" She laughed.

"Believe me, I've tried, but you are hard to shake off. But seriously Kate, we do have to make a decision about the future." She pulled up a high stool and joined him at the counter.

"I suppose it had to come to an end. We've been living in fairyland these past weeks."

He nodded in agreement. "So Mom went to Long Island."

"What has that got to do with us?"

"She's thinking about creating a US Butterfly Barn."

"That's … incredible. Do you think we could … be involved?"

"I think we could be more than involved but how would you feel about moving back? I know how much you missed everyone the last time."

"Since we came back, I get to see everyone but the reality is that they are all busy living their own lives. I've been painting and spending my time with you mostly. I think I needed to grow up and stop letting my insecurities swamp me. I will still never be comfortable with a Manhattan lifestyle but this way we get to do something of value and you can also get to the office to rule the world." She laughed. "Oh Richard, I would love it."

He leaned over and kissed her. "Come on, I'll show you. It was my grandparents' place."

"I'm sure I'll love it," she said, following him upstairs.

Monique had seen Donagh's girlfriend walking up the stairs. They had hardly spoken all day. She felt nothing but guilt for what she had done. Donagh might be on this trip but she fully intended to stay well away from him. Obviously, he didn't have a problem with two-timing, but she definitely did. She despised that kind of behaviour. She went to the check-in desk at the Hotel Pilate. Moments later, she passed the two other room keys to Geoff.

"The nearest restaurant is in the square. The receptionist offered to make a reservation for you. But there are also some along the seafront."

"Are you not coming with us?" asked Geoff.

"I'm meeting my friends."

"Oh right, yes, of course," said Geoff. He would make a terrible liar, she thought. "Make sure your phone is working. Let me ring it, just to check."

Donagh laughed. "She's an adult, Geoff. Come on." He went to the lift and pressed the button. When they disappeared, she went back to the desk. The young girl had been friendly and helpful. She spoke in French. She asked her about Châteaux Vieux De La Lac.

"Yes, it is very beautiful."

"Is it far from here?"

"It will take fifteen minutes by car. My sister works in the office at the vineyard."

"Oh, there is also a vineyard!" said Monique.

"Why yes, it has some of the finest wine in the region. The Count works very hard to ensure good quality grapes."

"The Count!" Monique's chin nearly hit the floor. "What's his name?"

"Count André Chevalier passed away recently and his son Philippe is now the Count."

Monique could feel her body go into a weakness. She leaned against the desk to steady herself. "Are you okay?" asked the receptionist.

"Yes, yes. Thank you so much. I am just tired from travelling. I need to lie down for a while."

Monique, picked up her carry-on luggage and went to the lift. She flopped down onto the bed in the tiny room. Her mind was spinning. Her uncle was a count. It was too much to take in. She picked up her mobile and was about to use the internet when she thought better of it. It would cost her a fortune. She had come all the way to France to visit an uncle without contacting him. Maybe he would be impossible to see. She opened the letter again. There was no mention of a count in it. The girl might be mistaken. In the top corner there was an address with a contact number underneath. She took a deep breath and tapped the number into her phone.

A woman answered in French. Monique replied in French.

"Can I speak to …" What was she supposed to call him? "Mr Philippe Chevalier please?"

"I'm afraid the Count is away at the moment. Can I take a message?"

"My name is Monique Chevalier." Monique could hear an intake of breath down the line. She wondered was the woman a secretary, or some relative. She didn't have the courage to ask.

"I am staying in the Hotel Pilate until Sunday. I will give you my mobile phone number." She called it out.

"I will try to reach him. Can I call you back shortly?"

After hanging up, she was full of nervous energy and she also wanted to get to the internet to look up some information about the château. The phone rang.

"Philippe will be available to meet at 11 a.m. He is sending a car."

"Oh, em, I can make my own way."

"He insists."

"Thank you." What else could she say? She hoped Geoff and Donagh would be long gone by the time the car arrived for her.

She went down to reception to ask about internet connection but it was down. The girl told her that there was an internet café in the square.

She wandered up the street until it widened out into a cobblestone square with a fountain and trees with leaves that had turned to the colours of autumn. A church imposed itself over everything else. It was a very pretty town centre. Even the businesses had discreet signage, maintaining the integrity of the place.

She looked for the internet cafe, but it had closed for the evening. She found a bench overlooking a kids' play area. There were a few swings, a slide and a couple of springy animal things in it. A young couple fussed over their little girl, taking photographs from this angle and that. Memories flooded her of the times she had spent in similar parks with her parents in Paris. A lump formed in her throat. Was she crazy to come back to France? What was she to gain by dragging up a past she could not change?

She had spent ten years avoiding these feelings. She never looked at family photographs, she couldn't bear to. She had no brother or sister to share memories with about how her dad used to read bedtime stories or how her mum always sang Irish ballads while she did housework.

She got up. She was driving herself crazy. She wished she were someone else. She wanted to be Rachel full of life, fun, happiness with the man of her dreams and working with her passion. She earned money working for Grace with Ireland for Real. But training horses was her and Jay's thing. They knew exactly where they were going in life while she felt she was dragging her way through hers. She reached the little hotel.

"What are you doing here?" She was so lost in her thoughts she started at the sound of Donagh's voice. "I thought you said you were meeting friends."

"I ... I have met them. See you tomorrow." She pushed the door open. Geoff was still in the lobby.

"Hey Monique, we're just going for a bite to eat. Will you come?"

She shook her head. "I hope your research goes well. I'll ring you when I get back."

"Okay, if you're sure."

By the time she opened her bedroom door, her phone was ringing.

"Hi Jessie."

"Are you okay? Geoff is worried about you. Can't you just go with them for something to eat?"

She lay on the bed and began to tell Jessie what had happened between her and Donagh in Eoghan's house and about the car coming to pick her up in the morning.

"I wish I was with you."

"I will be fine. I can watch TV. It will help me brush up on my French. It has been so long since I spoke it."

"Okay, I'm thinking of you. I'll ring tomorrow to see how you are doing. Love you."

"Thanks, Jess." She turned on the TV, put on her PJs and got into bed.

Donagh was keen to get to the seafront. Geoff had suggested they look around Bois Saint Etienne since the receptionist had said there were plenty of places to eat. Donagh spotted a sign for a surf shop.

"The evenings are getting darker. Winter is nearly on us," said Geoff.

"Yeah, it sure is. Let's check out this surf shop."

"Will you surf through the winter months?" asked Geoff.

"Sure I will. The waves are better in the winter. I'd love to be out there now," he said, pointing to the sea where there was some great surf. "Pity it's closed." He peered through the glass. So did Geoff.

"Maybe if we get back early enough tomorrow we could fit it in. We could hire boards."

"That would be great," said Donagh. He loved the place. There was something about it. He could live here if he had half the chance and it would be far enough away from her. He couldn't bear to think about her with anybody else. He had thought he was the one who was messed up but she definitely had problems. Asking him to sleep with her while she was involved with someone else. Did she take him for a complete fool? If only Kate hadn't walked in, maybe they could have just got on with it and then she would be out of his system. There was even a saying for it. The chase was always better than the catch.

"Any word from Geoff?" asked Kate, making coffee in Jessie's kitchen. She had hardly slept a wink and had come over at dawn to ride out Beauty. Her head was spinning at the thought of Butterfly Barn USA. She was so excited at the prospect of seeing the place. But there were visa issues to be sorted out and a wedding to be planned. Also she had her art therapy course to deliver. Her life was finally coming together in a way she could never have imagined.

"They are meeting a guy who creates wooded adventure parks this morning."

"Maybe we could do it in the States too," said Kate. She was so excited about it all.

"Sophia had mentioned she wanted to do something more but I could never have thought of a Butterfly Barn USA. I'm just over the moon."

"I know. Your idea to bring a small group of kids with dyspraxia over from New York to meet some Irish kids is fantastic. Colleen, Richard's secretary, will be thrilled when I tell her. She has always wanted to come to Ireland and this will bring together other parents of children and teens with dyspraxia. They can share their knowledge and ideas."

"It's fantastic, especially to merge fun and learning. Sometimes people just need to connect with others who are on a shared journey."

"Sophia knew I wasn't happy in Manhattan. That life is just not for me, Jess, and to be honest Richard living here isn't practical. This way will work better for Richard and I can do something worthwhile. I can't wait to see it for real. The estate has been in Richard's family for years."

"She is an amazing woman, Kate."

"We're taking flight on butterfly wings," said Kate, raising her mug. "Thanks to Sophia Wynthrope, Butterfly Barn is going global."

Donagh ate some cereal while Geoff made the best of a cheese and cold meat buffet breakfast.

"Would have loved a cooked breakfast, would you?" asked Geoff. "This is just not for me at this hour of the morning. Thierry said he will pick us up at 8.30. We'll have time for a coffee."

"Fair play to him for offering to drive us around," said Donagh, pouring very strong coffee into his cup. "Jeez, you could stand on this."

"Get it into you – who knows when or what we'll get to eat for the rest of the day? Maybe we'd be better off driving. We could find a McDonalds," Geoff laughed.

"Last night's menu being in French didn't bother me," Donagh laughed. "It saved me the embarrassment of having to read."

"If only we knew what we'd ordered," Geoff laughed. "Ah, good morning Monique."

"Hi," she said. "I'll just take a look at the buffet."

Donagh watched as she selected a range of cold meat, cheese and crackers, along with a homemade grape yogurt and some fruit. She picked up a newspaper and placed it under her arm. She was just so out of his reach. She could even understand a French newspaper. He could barely read an English one. She hardly even glanced in his direction. He was sorely tempted to ask her what her problem was. He wished he had cigarettes.

"I'll see you outside, Geoff." He couldn't stay a moment longer. He asked the receptionist where he could buy cigarettes. She began to explain. He nodded but was no wiser. Instead he went outside to wait for

Geoff and Thierry, the guy who was bringing them around for the day. He might know where he could get some.

When Geoff left, Monique sipped her coffee. It was good and strong just as she liked it. She was glad Donagh had left. Her stomach was in knots and it got worse every time she saw him. She had never felt that way about Garvan. Was she attracted to Donagh because he was so out of her reach? Stop Monique, she thought. My stomach is in knots because I am about to meet a count. She scanned through the newspaper in the hope that there might be some reference to the château. After ten minutes, she could find none. She went back upstairs to kill time and wait for the car.

At 10.40 a.m., the phone beside the bed rang. She rushed downstairs. There was a black jeep with blackout windows outside the hotel. She hadn't known what to expect but it hadn't been this. "Oh God," she muttered under her breath.

The driver got out. He introduced himself as Eric and seemed to be friendly enough. He didn't look French although he spoke in French. He opened the back door and she sat in.

Fifteen minutes later, the jeep entered the gates of the estate and continued up a winding tree-lined drive. The first glimpse of the Château Vieux De La Lac took her breath away. "Mon Dieu," she said. It looked exactly as she had imagined a château to be. Its stonework was a golden sand colour and it had turrets at the gable ends. It had beautiful manicured lawns and a huge lake to the left of it. It was magnificent.

She could feel her heart pounding. She should have brought Jessie with her. What if it all went terribly wrong? Maybe the reason her parents had never told her about her uncle was because he was a tyrant. What if it was some kind of hoax? "Stop," she whispered. "I'm here now. I am a grown-up."

Eric came around and opened the jeep door. "Come with me."

He must have seen the fear in her eyes. He smiled and said, "Philippe is so looking forward to meeting you."

She smiled and followed him up the steps and in through the huge wooden doors. They creaked. But the sight before her took her breath away. The floor was marble inlaid. A fabulous marble staircase with a brass balustrade led to the first floor. She gazed up at the detailed cornices in the ceiling from which a Venetian crystal chandelier hung. Antique chairs and tables from the Napoleon period were strewn around the huge lobby. She hadn't known what to expect when she heard her uncle was a count and that he lived in a château. She had thought it would be run down and in need of repair and that maybe he couldn't have afforded to take on his stepbrother's child. Not this. She followed Eric into a room off the hallway, which was equally impressive.

Donagh had just zip-wired from a platform fifty feet high and travelled a distance of at least one hundred metres. He had suggested they check out some of the activities before they discussed the costs involved. Both he and Geoff were excited by what they had seen so far.

He'd love to be involved in the building of it as well as working in it. So far they had seen two parks and both had quad bike tracks for adults and kids. Geoff was becoming more animated by the minute. Thierry had good English and was translating for them.

"Geoff, slow down. Have you won the lotto or something?" Donagh whispered to him.

"I get carried away. I suppose that's where Jessie comes in. She puts a stop to my gallop."

"Somebody had better or Butterfly Barn will go broke. First things first. Let's see how much we could get this for or even a smaller version of this to work at home," said Donagh, pointing towards the ropes and wires.

Eric had offered Monique coffee but she had declined. She sat waiting in what she figured might be called a drawing room. It also had a beautifully adorned high ceiling. Although it was impressive, the room looked used and quite comfortable. It had oak panelling with two large cream sofas opposite each other and a floral one forming a square in front of a huge white marble fireplace that thankfully was blazing. It had turned particularly cold since yesterday, or maybe she was feeling it because she was so nervous. She chose to sit on one of the cream sofas because it reminded her of Rose Cottage. It gave her a comforting feeling. After taking ten years to ask to see her, she wondered how long more her uncle planned to leave her waiting.

She fidgeted and moved around and became more edgy by the minute, until finally she decided if he didn't arrive soon she would leave. She looked at her mobile phone; she had only been in the room four minutes.

The door opened. She jumped up, startled. She had never been so nervous in her life. A medium-sized, fit-looking man in his early fifties appeared. He had dark hair peppered with grey and there was something strangely familiar about him, maybe it was her father's chocolate-brown eyes. But mostly he had a warm friendly smile. She could feel her body relax even before he spoke. It wasn't going to be so bad after all.

"Hello Monique. I am so glad you decided to visit us." He spoke with perfect English as he stretched out his hand to shake hers. She was surprised about the "us" but didn't ask for an explanation.

"Hello," she replied; her voice sounded formal and strange even to her.

"Some tea or maybe coffee?" he asked kindly.

"Coffee would be nice, thanks."

Seconds later, a little, rotund woman bustled into the room.

"Coffee for two, Rosario. Merci." He smiled and said, "This is my niece, Monique."

"Ah, oui, oui." Rosario smiled. "Welcome."

"Merci," said Monique, not quite knowing what to make of it all. He certainly didn't act like a count. He was very relaxed and courteous but her mind was focused on the word "us". Did she have cousins? She couldn't wait to hear more. It would be great to have cousins. She hoped they'd be nice. But what difference did it make; she had only planned to be here for an hour at most. It was just a courtesy call.

"Monique, can I ask if you would be gracious enough to stay a while? I have so much I want to tell you and I am so grateful that you made room in your schedule to visit while you are in France."

"The only reason I came to France was to meet you. I need to know everything. There are so many gaps in my memories." Her voice choked up. She had spent years blocking her memories. She needed to hear the story of her parents' lives.

"Oh Monique, for so long I have wished for this moment." He leaned back into the sofa and became visibly more relaxed. "I will tell you about the Chevaliers, about your heritage. About your father and what I know of your mother. About me and about your cousins. So Monique, let me begin."

Donagh sat outside a bar on the seafront smoking a cigarette. Geoff and Thierry were inside discussing the day. He looked out at the ocean. He could live here, he thought. It was a surfer's paradise. He blew smoke up in the air. He wondered how she was getting on with her friends. What kind of friends were they that she had been going back to the hotel alone last night? It was just weird, he thought.

"Thierry's friend works in a surf shop. One phone call and he can sort us out for gear in the morning," said Geoff, pulling out a chair to join him.

"Sounds great to me."

Philippe had driven her around the estate in his jeep. There was so much to take in, rolling hills of vines leading towards the lake. She had noticed unusual-looking grey cows grazing in the fields. Philippe told her they were Gascon cattle. He liked to breed them because they were specific to the region. But it was really the grapes and the types of wine they made that were his passion. He was warm and friendly and she had enjoyed speaking with him in French. He sounded so like her father.

They sat in a large vaulted wine cellar. He had offered her wine but she asked for coffee. She wanted to know about her parents but she didn't want to be rude by initiating the conversation. She wanted to have a clear head when he decided to tell her about them. He began to speak about her grandfather's devotion to her father.

"André Junior was everything our father wanted in a son. He was handsome, funny, warm, when he came into a room, it lit up. He was intelligent and extremely knowledgeable about wine and the business of selling it especially for one so young."

Monique had seen that Philippe was clearly passionate about the château too but there was a sadness about him.

"I was ten years older than André and you have not asked why, as the eldest son, I was such a disappointment to my father."

"I didn't like to."

He smiled knowingly. "And you have not guessed, non?"

She had but it wasn't her place to say.

"Monique, I am gay."

"When you said 'us' earlier, I wondered if maybe I had an aunt and cousins. But as we spent time together and you spoke so much about my grandfather's pride in my father, I wondered why he couldn't see all those qualities in you."

"Thank you, ma chére. But those were different times and there was a title and an estate. My father was forty when I was born. My mother died from cancer when I was five. A few years later, he married André's mother who was only twenty-five years old. When André was three, she was killed in a horse-riding accident. By the age of fifty-three our father had lost two wives and was left with a thirteen-year-old he did not understand and a three-year-old he idolised. Our father suffered from depression, he would spend days in his room or in the vineyard, completely ignoring us. André was so young he was unaware of what was happening. But Father resented how close we became. Of course, as soon as I was old enough, he sent me to Paris to university. I was happy to leave, except André was only eight. I worried about him being here with a man who had became more bitter and angry with each passing day. I spent the holidays here and as many weekends as I could. Thankfully, Henri Senoir, our father's cousin, and his wife Madeline lived in the lodge so André spent most of his time there. They had a young family, Henri Junior and Charlotte, whom your mother had come to as an au pair. At that time, André had just finished his second year of a business degree in Paris. He returned home to work the vineyard for the holidays. Oh Monique, when they met it was love at first sight."

Monique wiped away the tears flowing down her cheeks. Both her parents had terrible childhoods, one in a cottage in Ireland and the other in a château in France.

"Oh Philippe, they were so lucky to have met." Philippe reached across the table and took her hand.

"Monique, please will you stay ..."

Monique looked at him incredulously.

"I mean for this evening. Henri Junior and Mimi, his wife, would love to meet you. Thankfully it was Mimi who answered your phone call and but for her quick thinking I might not have been here to meet you. I was in Amsterdam with my partner, Eric. We came back immediately. They are waiting to hear how our time together went. What can I tell them?" He leaned back in his seat and smiled.

"You can tell them I'd love to stay the night."

"Fantastique! This calls for a celebration. Un moment," he said, getting up and walking towards the long cedarwood counter, behind which was a wall of wine bottles. "Come, sit here. It is where the tourists taste our wines." He browsed the rack and then chose a bottle of red wine. "This is our finest wine. It has won international awards."

He began to open it. She laughed. "Philippe, I'm afraid it will be wasted on me. I know nothing about wine."

"Ah, but Monique, ma chére, you have a lifetime to learn. We have so much more to talk about. Unfortunately Henri Senior passed away six years ago but his wife, Madeline, is also looking forward to meeting you. She has so much she wants to tell you about your maman and papa."

Chapter Thirteen

G race finished reading Finn a bedtime story. She kissed his forehead. He was growing up so fast. He loved Jessie's Sam so much he had wanted Liverpool FC in his bedroom too. She checked Lily – she was fast asleep. Fourteen weeks old already, she thought. She was so glad the cruise season had come to an end. Her mother had been a great support taking care of the kids on the days the cruise liners had come in but if she wanted to get back to her writing, she needed to find a child minder. When she opened the kitchen door, Jack was busy cooking. She was still breast-feeding so she poured a glass of water for herself and took out a beer for Jack.

"Saturday night, eh! Who knew we'd have two children asleep upstairs and a wedding to look forward to?" said Jack, placing crab claws in garlic butter with a sprinkling of lettuce in front of her.

"Thank you, honey. It smells delicious. Sometimes I feel like pinching myself to check if it's all real."

"So, now that the season has ended are you thinking about writing again?"

"That's exactly what was on my mind. You know how I like to write about real life issues. I was thinking about including literacy problems in my next novel."

"Interesting, it's not something I know anything about."

"Me neither. Recently I met someone who has a difficulty with reading and writing, something most of us take for granted. I was struck by how determined he is to get the help he needs. I'm hoping to chat to Monique about it soon. These are so tasty."

"Will we put them on the wedding menu?"

"You must be joking! It would cost a fortune."

"I'm so pleased for Kate. Butterfly Barn USA will be perfect for her. Have they decided when they are tying the knot?" He laughed.

"They are anxious to marry soon. She also needs to sort out her American visa."

"How about a double wedding?"

"Are you serious?"

"Why not?"

She put down her fork and knife.

"Have I said the wrong thing?"

"No, not at all. It's just I hadn't thought of it. I'd actually love that. I wonder how they would feel?"

"Ask them."

"Like now?"

"Why not? They can only say no and there would be no hard feelings."

"But what if Kate wants a big wedding? And maybe Richard would need to invite all his bigshot friends."

"We can tell them we are having a small wedding and if they want to join in – great. Kate always says what's on her mind so she'll tell you yes or no. It's very simple. Invite them over for a drink and we can suggest it to them."

She sent a text while Jack plated the salmon pasta dish he loved to cook. Her phone bleeped.

"They are on their way."

Fifteen minutes later, Kate and Richard sat at the kitchen table, eating dessert.

"I draw the line at baking," said Jack, munching into a banoffi pie he had picked up at the local cake shop. It was his favourite. "We have a suggestion. You know that we're getting married at Butterfly Barn. It's not going to a big affair, just family and close friends. We were wondering if you guys would like to make it a double wedding."

Kate jumped up immediately. "Richard, what did I say in the car on the way over?"

Richard laughed. "She said, 'I'd love to have a wedding at Butterfly Barn, only it wouldn't be fair on Grace'."

"Oh come here, little sis," said Grace, getting up to hug her. "Would you really love it? Now Kate, it's going to be small."

"I'd love it. How small is small?"

They all laughed.

"See what I mean, Jack? What have we let ourselves in for?"

Monique twirled the wine glass between her thumb and fingers. She was so glad she had accepted Philippe's invitation to stay. She had sent a text to Jessie to say she was fine and staying over. Jessie said she'd tell Geoff. It was 11 p.m. and Rosario, the housekeeper, was still bringing out food. She smiled at the little French woman whom Philippe treated like part of the family. She had joined them at the long table, which had been set up in the dining room. Philippe certainly did not act like a count, not that Monique would know how a count was supposed to act.

"I am so 'appy you are 'ere. It is like dream come true. You look like your papa, but have, how you say?" said Madeline, the woman her mother had come to work for as an au pair twenty-four years ago.

"Mannerisms ... traits," said Mimi, attempting to help her mother-in-law's English.

"Maman, Monique speaks fluent French," said Henri, her son.

"Yes, yes, but I practise. Her maman taught me." She smiled. "She was so beauty ... val. Inside and outside. They were so 'appy, so in love."

Monique bit her lip as Madeline continued. "The Count was very angry man, always so angry. Nothing make him 'appy except André. Then voom ... he turn against him. He even ... how you say?"

"Fired Henri Senior when he found out your mother was pregnant." Philippe finished her sentence as Madeline wiped a tear from her eye. "André had gone back to college to complete the third year of his business degree when Eilish discovered she was pregnant."

Madeline began to speak again. "Your maman told her mother but your grandpapa he ..." Madeline put her hand up to her throat and drew it away sharply.

Philippe cut across her. "He threatened to kill her if she came home with a ..."

"Baby," said Madeline.

"Mother, please do not make this worse for Monique," said Henri. He made a gesture to bring her away.

"Henri, I need to hear everything. The truth hurts but I would rather know exactly what my parents endured and why they had to leave."

Philippe continued. "My father was in a rage. Eilish's father had denied her too. Her life in Ireland had been horrific. None of that mattered because André loved her and wanted to take care of her and you. I convinced André to stay in Paris to finish his studies. In the meantime, Madeline arranged for Eilish to move to Paris to live with a friend until the baby came. I lied to my father. I told him that Eilish had gone home. When he cooled down, Henri Senior got his job back because the grapes were always the most important thing to my father. He also paid for André's last year in education. He had thought that was the end of it. But André refused to come back unless Eilish and you were accepted. My father threatened to disinherit him. André said he didn't care. They never spoke again."

"I remember you, Philippe," said Monique; the memories she had been so afraid of were flooding in. "You visited our apartment in Paris. But I was very young and I did not call you uncle."

"At that time, I lived in Amsterdam with Eric. I seldom came to Paris. We mostly stayed in contact by phone. Your parents told you they were only children who had been orphaned. They did not want to burden you with their history."

"What did they do for money? They were both so young."

"Both Henri Senior and I helped them financially until André found a job. Your father knew the wine business so well. He was very likeable. He became a sales representative for a wine merchant and over time worked his way up to become a regional manager. Your mother was also hardworking; when it was time for you to go to school she became a translator in a publishing company."

"I remember all of that." She decided to ask the question that she had being holding back all day. "Philippe, where were you when I needed you?"

Philippe put his head down. She had hurt him. She felt awful but she had to ask. It was wonderful to meet these people. They were warm and kind, but they were not around when she had been in hospital for weeks, orphaned.

"We were living in Amsterdam," said Eric. "We couldn't offer you the life you deserved. Your grandfather had also denied Philippe; he failed to tell you that he too was estranged. Madeline contacted Philippe to tell him that the Count was ranting and raving since André's death and that he wanted custody of you."

"Monique, he was bitter, twisted man," said Madeline, getting more and more distressed.

"Maman, you are upsetting yourself."

"Non, Monique must know this. It was not Philippe's fault. He made promise to André never to allow his child be …"

"Maman, let Eric explain."

"André made Philippe promise if anything happened to him you were not to be brought up here. André rang one evening very excited. He told us that Eilish's father had died and that they had planned a surprise visit to her mother in Ireland. They were so excited. When the accident happened, the police found the letters and records of phone calls to your grandmother. They contacted her and thankfully you were sent to live with her."

"I hope it was the best decision."

She nodded. It had been. "When did the Count die?"

"Two weeks ago," said Henri. "Six years ago the Count suffered a stroke and lost the use of the left side of his body. My father, Henri Senior, had passed away. Being a professor, neither I nor my sister Charlotte had any interest in wine-making. Charlotte has immigrated to Australia. The Count had to swallow his pride and asked Philippe to come back here."

"Philippe refused," said Eric. "Until Henri contacted him to tell him that things were beginning to fall apart."

"You see, Monique, many families here depend on the vineyard for their livelihoods along with my mother," said Henri. "So I convinced Philippe to come back to save this place. The Count still refused to accept Eric. Philippe has given up six years of his life to keep this business going while still commuting to Amsterdam to be with Eric. I think it's finally time for this family to unite and I hope that tonight will be the night for a fresh start."

Monique stood up and went to Philippe. She put out her arms and he stood up and hugged her tight.

"To new beginnings," she whispered.

"Merci, ma chére," he said.

"Philippe made promise to André that you be 'appy. You 'appy person, yes?" asked Madeline.

"Oui," said Monique, smiling. "I am happy."

Monique woke the next morning and looked around the bedroom. It had a high ceiling and beautifully draped windows. How could this be happening? She climbed out of the four-poster bed and went to the window that looked across the valley. Sunlight sparkled on the lake. She could see two swans. It was obviously a successful vineyard. The upkeep of the château alone must cost a fortune, she thought.

All she kept thinking about was the years that she had spent blocking her feelings but also resenting her mother for not telling her about Nora.

She had never visited her parents' grave. She had been unable to attend their funeral because she had been hospitalised for weeks. When she had finally been discharged, she had refused to go. She had never wanted to come back to France until now. She couldn't stop thinking about visiting their grave. Eric had told her last night that her grandfather had wanted to bring André back to the château for burial in the family vault. But Philippe had managed to hinder his attempts, ensuring that they were buried together in Paris.

It had been very late when she finally went to bed. Everybody had relaxed and they had told her stories of her father when he was young. Henri's mother, Madeline, had clearly loved both her parents and had delighted in telling her about mother's first attempts at speaking French. Eric, Philippe's partner, was such a gentleman. He had put up with so much over the years and always stood by Philippe.

She went into the en suite to take a shower. She decided there and then that she was going back to the hotel to check out. She was going to Paris.

Donagh and Geoff hired a couple of surfboards and wetsuits.

"Surf's up!" Geoff declared, as they walked along a windswept beach towards the ocean.

"You sure you're up for this?" asked Donagh.

"You suggesting I'm too old for it?" Geoff answered, laughing. "Don't you know life begins at forty, mate?"

"Whatever!" Donagh laughed. "Just make sure we stay near one another. The wind is blowing south. See that lifeguard post? Let's use that as a pointer."

"Fair enough."

The two of them threw the boards into the surf and began to paddle out.

Over breakfast, Monique told Philippe about her plan.

"I will come with you."

"I'm sorry Philippe, but I need to do this myself."

"Mais oui, but let me book the hotel I use when I am in Paris. It is centrally located. Please Monique, do not drive to Paris."

"My friends are staying in Bois Saint Etienne. They will be leaving for the airport soon. I can travel with them to Bordeaux. I'm sure there will be a train to Paris."

"I will check the time of the TGV. It is the fast train." Philippe went to make the arrangements. She took another croissant and began to spread jam on it.

"Monique, it has been a great pleasure to finally meet you. You have made Philippe happier than I have seen him in years. It is so wonderful," said Eric. He sipped coffee from his cup.

"I never expected this. It is all surreal, Eric."

"Yes," said Eric, smiling. "The first time I saw Château Vieux De La Lac, I was stunned by its beauty. I hope it can be a happy place now that the old man has passed. It is a chapter of life that is closed for the best, I think."

"Strong words, Eric. He judged my mother very harshly. It seems so crazy now."

"He was a terrible snob and land hungry, Monique. He wanted André to marry well. He had big plans for him. I am glad that André found your mother. They were so in love."

"Oh Eric, I remember you now too."

He laughed and rubbed his bald head. "I had wavy blond hair back then."

She smiled. "Eric, I was so afraid to remember anything, so afraid to cry or feel sad."

"Are you really sure about going to Paris alone?"

She nodded.

"Okay, but if you change your mind about visiting the grave, just call, we can come immediately."

Philippe came back. "So, I have booked the hotel. This is the address and the booking reference. I booked two nights. You might need the extra time. I also printed the train times. Eric, please tell her we can come too. I'm not comfortable about you doing this alone."

"Philippe, I have to do it by myself."

"She is a grown woman, Philippe, not the small child you remember."

"Thank you, Eric."

"I see you two are already ganging up on me."

Eric winked at her. She smiled and stayed chatting until it was time to leave. Both Philippe and Eric travelled with her to the hotel. Eric parked outside the small hotel. Both men got out.

"Please visit us soon. And bring your grand-mère, we would all love to meet her," said Philippe. "Be careful in Paris, Monique, and again, are you really sure about doing this alone?"

"I am, Uncle," she said.

Philippe beamed at her.

"You have made his day." Eric laughed. "He has longed to be called uncle."

Philippe smiled and wrapped his arms around her, squeezing her tight for the second time. "Safe journey, ma chére. I will see you soon."

"You are both always welcome to visit us too. We can make some room for you." She smiled.

"Merci, we will. I have always wanted to visit Ireland, now I have even more reason to."

Moments later, she stood on the pavement and waved as they drove away. She looked at her watch; there was still time to see the beach. It would be a shame to miss it and she could do with a walk. The past twenty-four hours had been an unbelievable experience.

At the beach there was a fair wind blowing as she set off towards the lifeguard stand.

She looked out into the ocean and noticed a group of surfers. She'd love to try it sometime, she thought, but not in those conditions. The waves were way too high for her. She watched as one guy caught a wave and skilfully travelled nearly all the way to the shore until he fell in.

Donagh had caught a huge wave and was negotiating it well when a red jacket caught his eye. Her long brown hair blew behind her. He'd recognise her from a million miles away. In the next instant, he fell in. When he emerged he swam to the shore. He turned and waved towards Geoff to let him know where he was. Geoff had caught a wave too so he had to wait until he acknowledged him. Moments later, Geoff appeared from the surf and waved towards him. Donagh dragged the board onto the sand, disengaged himself from it and ran up the beach to catch up with her. He had overheard Geoff talking to Jessie. It seemed she had stayed over with her friends last night. What was he going to say when he reached her? He felt silly but he had been really worried about her. It was all a bit strange. He stopped running and went back to his surfboard.

Monique turned back. It was colder than she had thought. She saw Donagh standing on the shore and Geoff coming out of the ocean. As she got closer, Geoff waved. Donagh looked towards her. He didn't smile. Her breath caught. He was so handsome, even wearing a wetsuit and with his hair wet and stringy. He was looking at her the way he had that first night she had heard him sing. Their eyes were locked; she couldn't break away. But he did. He bent down and picked up the surfboard and walked back up the beach.

"How was your night?" asked Geoff. He really wouldn't make a good actor. She smiled when he whispered, "That was for Donagh's benefit."

"Thanks, Geoff, for being here for me. I'm going to travel back with you to the airport and from there I'll take a TGV to Paris. I want to visit my parents' grave."

Geoff put his arm around her. "Are you sure about this? Maybe it would be better to do that with your gran or Jess."

"I'm sure, Geoff." He didn't say another word but just walked beside her back towards the surf shop.

Half an hour later, back in the hotel after she had changed and checked out, she sat in the tiny lobby waiting for them. Thankfully, Geoff appeared first; she was glad to have him to break the palpable tension between her and Donagh. Moments later, Donagh appeared, looking more gorgeous than ever. She went to pick up her carry-on luggage at the same time as Donagh. Their fingers brushed and she pulled away quickly. It was like getting an electric shock. Their eyes met for an instance and then he continued to pick up her luggage as though nothing had happened.

"Thanks," she muttered and joined Geoff as he led the way towards the car. She sat in the back seat.

Two hours later, they were nearing Bordeaux airport.

"So, what time is the TGV to Paris?" asked Geoff, looking at her through the rear view mirror.

Donagh turned around. "Paris?"

She nodded. "I'm taking the 16.24."

"How long will it take?" asked Geoff.

"Approx three and a half hours."

"It travels at speeds of around three hundred and twenty kilometres an hour," said Donagh.

"You seem to know something about them. Have you ever been on one?" asked Geoff.

"No, but I'd love to."

"Well, now is your chance. Monique could do with some company. Couldn't you?"

She paused and opened her mouth to say something but she closed it again.

"That's settled. I'll drop you into the city and head to the airport. Now I don't have to worry about a thing," said Geoff. "You'll be home tomorrow."

"I'm staying for two nights," said Monique, finding her voice again.

"The next day then. You're not working, so consider it my treat to you Donagh for coming on the trip. I'll cover the cost of the train, changing the ticket and whatever accommodation costs. You deserve a treat after all you've done for us."

"Sounds good to me," said Donagh, looking straight ahead. Was he actually smirking? she wondered. Two nights in Paris alone with him, she must be crazy not to disagree, but it would seem rude when he was so keen to travel on the TGV. Was that her only reason for not objecting?

Jessie set the fire and put her feet up. She was looking forward to hearing all about France.

"What time is it?" asked Sam.

"Five minutes since the last time you asked," said Jessie. She smiled at her son, who was lying on the sofa using his iPod.

"Jessie, Sam, I'm home," called Geoff, coming in the back door. Sam hopped up and ran out to the kitchen. She got up and went to join them.

"I didn't hear the jeep; we were snuggled up next to the fire." Sam was already in his father's arms.

"I missed you, Dad."

"Me too," said Jessie, stretching over Sam to kiss Geoff.

"Boil the kettle, love," said Geoff. "I've a lot to tell you later."

"Sounds intriguing!" she said, filling the big old kettle that sat on the Aga.

"Hey, little man, I heard you scored a goal at the match yesterday."

Sam launched into the detail of how it all happened. She smiled and thought how lucky she was to have them both. Monique hadn't answered her calls; she knew she'd ring when she was ready to talk.

Monique sat on the TGV. Donagh was fascinated with it.

"You are a real speed junkie."

"I am. I love it. I miss my kite-surf too," he said.

"Why did you sell it?"

"I need the money."

"I know the feeling. I'm so glad I have finally got a job."

"That's great. When do you start?"

"Next Monday, it's just part-time as a tutor to a small literacy group."

She shifted in her seat. She didn't want to talk about literacy with him. She wanted … Oh God, she just wanted him to kiss her so much. She wished he didn't have a girlfriend and that she had never been his tutor. But then she never would have met him and she certainly would never have thought she was capable of feeling so strongly about a man. Her relationship with Garvan had been so different – how had she thought that was love? But it had been in its own way. Garvan would always hold a special place in her heart.

"You're miles away."

"Pardon, oui, I mean yes."

"I love it when you speak French."

She laughed. "I spent the weekend speaking it."

"So you had a good time with your friends?"

"The best. Ten minutes or so left," said Monique, glancing out the window at the suburbs of Paris. She wanted to stay enjoying the moment with him. He was so easy to talk to, always making light of things. He brightened the world, she thought.

"Where are we staying?" he asked.

"Oh God, we need another room!" She took out her mobile and

rang the number Philippe had given her before Donagh had a chance to reply. She spoke in French. He smiled at her. "Hi, my name is Monique Chevalier, I have a reservation for tonight and tomorrow night. Do you have another room available please?"

"Just a moment, please. I'm afraid we are full. It will be very difficult to find another room at this late stage. There are three very large conferences on plus the usual tourist traffic."

"Can you check the type of room you have reserved for me, please?"

"Une moment! A suite, Madame."

"Merci." How could she explain that to Donagh? He was watching her expectantly.

"So."

"They are full."

"I don't mind, I'll find somewhere to stay nearby. I'm sure there'll be a hostel with a bed available. Don't worry about me."

"We'll figure it out when we get there."

At the hotel Monique spoke in French to the receptionist. She asked her to say in English that they had been offered an upgrade to a suite. The woman seemed surprised but agreed.

"OMG," said Monique, "a suite!"

"You must be joking. Are you for real?" asked Donagh. Then he muttered to Monique, "A suite, let's go before she tells us it's a mistake."

Monique laughed and mouthed a thank you to the receptionist as Donagh picked up the carry-on luggage and walked towards the lift. He turned back.

"Excuse me, what time is the next Paris by Night tour leaving?

"9.30."

He looked at Monique. She shrugged her shoulders. "Why not?"

"I will make the reservation for you."

She couldn't believe she was actually in a five-star hotel with Donagh and now she was going on a tour of the city of her birth with him. She hadn't wanted to make up an excuse when Geoff had suggested it because the truth was she couldn't resist being around him.

When they reached the fourth floor Donagh stopped at a window. "Can you believe we are staying in a suite in a five-star hotel on the Champs-Élysées? Look Monique!"

She leaned towards him and looked across the city that held so many memories. She swallowed a lump in her throat and said, "Thanks for coming with me." She must have been crazy to think she could do this alone. Moments later she opened the door with a key card.

"Oh wow," said Donagh, walking into the suite. "How did you find this hotel? An ordinary room must cost a fortune."

"There was a last minute offer on the internet," she said, crossing her fingers behind her back.

It was fabulous, all creams and gold with a parquet floor covered by rugs to denote different areas of the large room. A couch with cushions in different hues and fabrics acted as a centre piece in front of a huge wide-screen TV. Dotted around the room were different styles and sizes of antique chairs and pieces of furniture with a bureau in the corner. Strategic lamp lighting lent a warm feeling to the place. A door led from it. Donagh threw himself on the couch immediately, declaring to it, "Just you and me babe for the next two nights."

Monique turned away. She wished it could be different between them. He just saw her as a friend. Why would he see her any other way when his girlfriend was so beautiful and confident?

She opened the bathroom door. Donagh came in behind her. "Oh wow, a Jacuzzi. We could check it out together." She gave him a look. "You can always buy swimming togs. I have mine with me." He said it without a hint of guile. He went into the bedroom and threw himself across the king-size bed. "You'd need a search party to find someone in this thing."

She laughed. "The canopy is beautiful," she said, admiring the cream and soft-pink drapes hanging above the bed from the ceiling to the floor.

Donagh got up. "I wonder what channels we have." He began to flick through while she freshened up. She only had an overnight bag so clothes selection wasn't on option, she'd have to make do with her jeans.

She cleansed her face and applied some make-up powder to her face. Paris by night, here we come, she thought. She'd treasure every moment of it.

Jessie sat on the couch in front of the fire. Geoff came in. He had been upstairs tucking in Sam. He slumped into the chair opposite her.

"Monique and Donagh are gone to Paris together!"

"What!"

Geoff shrugged his shoulders. "Donagh really wanted to go on the TGV and to be honest. I didn't want her to go to Paris on her own. So I was thinking on my feet."

Jessie shook her head. "Geoff, did you not notice that there is something going on between them?"

"Of course I did. I'm not stupid. It's obvious they like each other. It might help to get Garvan out of her head."

"Donagh is going out with someone."

"Look Jessie, he might be and she might think it's Garvan she is missing. But there is something between them and they will figure it out or not. What better place to be than Paris? Anyway, Donagh's a good guy. I don't believe he would do anything to hurt her. If he didn't want to go, he would have made up an excuse and if she didn't want him to go she would have done the same."

Jessie listened. Geoff was right. "I suppose it's better to get whatever is going on out of their system."

Geoff looked at her. "Don't you think they are right for one another?"

"I'd like Monique to figure out who she is before she gets into another relationship and I also think Donagh has a lot going on at the moment."

"Since when did my wife get so sensible? We were young and foolish and had nothing when we met."

"We didn't have the issues those two have, Geoff."

"True. Let's talk about the reason I went to France." He chatted about the adventure parks they'd visited and what this fellow and that fellow had said. Then he launched into the health and safety issues involved and how they would have to talk to their insurance company about the Irish regulations and costs. He liked the idea of quad biking. She wasn't so keen on that.

"Overall, it was a great learning experience. We'll have to look into the cost and financing of it."

Chapter Fourteen

Monique enjoyed watching Donagh's reaction to the Arc de Triomphe, the Eiffel Tower, The Louvre and Pigalle. It was freezing; she would have done anything to cuddle in beside him on the front seat on the double decker tour bus. She loved every moment of just being with him. Crossing the Seine, she said, "Donagh, let's get off in Montmartre."

"Good idea, I'm hungry." She walked beside him around the famous streets for a while until he stopped outside a pretty French bistro with the sounds of jazz and blues and the aroma of garlic and herbs wafting from it.

"What do you think?" Donagh asked.

"Perfect."

The waiter led them to a candlelit table with a red and white check cloth. She explained the menu because it was in French. They ordered.

"Wine, Mademoiselle?"

"Why not?" Donagh said. "You choose."

"A bottle of the house red, merci." When the waiter was out of earshot, she whispered, "I have no knowledge of wine."

"Tut, tut, and you are French. Me neither, sure it will be grand. So, this is nice. I love the idea of live music playing softly in the background. It makes the place more intimate."

The waiter poured the wine.

"Do you know Monique, I really like France. Seriously, I could live here. Well, not here exactly but I'd live in Bois Saint Etienne."

She hadn't imagined he would want to live anywhere but Ireland. She saw how his eyes lit up when he spoke about his plans for the future.

"I'm going for the surfing and kite-surfing instructor's courses. I've started training with the sea rescue. If everything goes to plan, we will begin building the adventure park straight away. I'll get some money together and of course, the experience, and someday I might own a surf school either in France or in Bayrush."

She noticed his face had a dream-like look to it as he spoke. She could look at his face forever. He was pouring out his thoughts and all she could think about was how it felt when he had kissed her. She took another slug of her wine. Her glass was nearly empty. How was she going to get through the next twenty-four hours?

"Ah don't mind me. I'm thinking out loud." He poured more wine. "Suppose there is no harm in dreaming. What about you? If you had a fairy godmother what would you ask for?"

The question took her off guard. She didn't want to tell him what had happened yesterday. She was still trying to figure out how she felt about everything.

"I don't know. I came to Paris to visit my parents' grave."

His face dropped. "Oh Monique, I'm so sorry. I wondered why you lived with your gran. What happened to them?"

The waiter arrived with their starters. Monique began to talk about her childhood in Paris. Since last night she realised she was no longer afraid of what she remembered. She had had a lovely life with them. She talked about her mother singing Irish songs around the apartment as she did the housework.

"Do you have a photograph of them?" Her bag hung on the chair. She searched for her purse and took one out. She handed it to him. She had tears in her eyes that she didn't want him to see. Garvan had never asked to see them. Their starters lay untouched. "We had better eat."

"You're a mix of them. You have your father's colouring and your mother's smile. She's beautiful. They look so happy." He handed it back

He was about to eat a garlic mushroom when she blurted out, "I took that photograph just two weeks before the car crash."

He put down his cutlery. He stretched his hand over and covered her hand with it.

"I am so sorry."

"Oh Donagh, I am ruining the evening. Pardon. I will use the Ladies and when I come back we will talk about nice things again. Thank you for your kindness to me." She went to get up. He held her hand for a moment longer.

"Mon, can I come to the grave with you?"

"Thank you," she said, dropping her head to hide her tears. She went to the Ladies. She leaned against the cubicle door. Tears streamed down her face. Everything about Donagh Mullally was wonderful. She wished with all her heart that he could feel about her the way she felt about him. She vowed she would never settle for anything less again. At least she had glimpsed what real love felt like even if it was only for a moment.

Donagh watched as she walked towards him. Everything told him to stay away from her. He had nothing to offer but a head full of dreams. She deserved the best, she needed security, someone who could look after her in a way that he couldn't. He'd never be good enough for her. He'd visit the grave with her tomorrow and be a good friend. What had possessed him to come with her? But the truth was he couldn't say no. There was nowhere else he'd rather be than with her.

The next couple of hours flew by. They chatted and ate their main courses. He had chosen frites and mussels. She had seared duck with honey. They tasted one another's dishes. He told her about Butchie and his attempts at dating girls and how he always said the wrong thing. He asked how she was getting on with that big black horse. She laughed and offered to teach him to ride. He said he'd try horse-riding if she tried surfing. They shook hands on it. They had finished the wine and were well into the second bottle.

"That's a deal, so," he said, holding her a hand for a moment longer than he had intended. When he saw the look on her face, he took it away. "Come on, let's get out of here before I'm totally pissed. I'm not used to drinking wine. It's gone straight to my head."

He made to get up and wobbled. "See what I mean. Gents stop for me."

"Wait until the air gets you!" She laughed. "I'll get the bill and order a taxi."

"No, I'll get the bill. We have to sort out about the hotel room yet. I want to pay my share."

"It is not a date, Donagh. I don't expect you to pay."

"What's not a date, the hotel or this?"

"Any of it."

"Well that's putting me in my place. I know exactly where I stand," he said, walking towards the men's room. He diverted to the counter and paid the bill. He never drank wine. It had definitely gone to his head. The sooner they got back to the hotel the better. He needed to lie down.

Monique woke the next morning. He had hardly spoken to her on the way back to the hotel. She had changed in the bathroom and slipped into the bed. He had curled up with his clothes on and slept on the couch. She looked over to where he was still sleeping with his back to her.

"Oh GOD, I'm dying here." He groaned, and then his tousled head appeared from under the duvet. "I have the mother and father of a hangover. Need to use the loo."

She heard the shower running and a few minutes later he came out of the bathroom with just his boxers on. She couldn't take her eyes away from him.

"Right so, sleeping beauty. Get up, we have a busy day ahead of us. Will we order up some breakfast?" He pulled up his jeans and put on a clean T-shirt. He acted as if nothing had happened between them last night. She was relieved.

"Good idea, here is the menu."

"You order for us."

She rang room service and ordered fruit, cereal and croissants. She slipped out of bed when his back was turned. She took a shower and changed in the bathroom. They ate breakfast and the conversation between them was as lighthearted as earlier last evening. After breakfast, she took out a Paris Metro map to work out the route to the graveyard.

"Let's take a taxi, Mon. This is a special day, okay?" said Donagh, reaching to touch her hand.

"Okay," she said, getting up to get her coat. She couldn't cope with his brotherly affection.

When the taxi reached the graveyard, Donagh paid. He also took the driver's card. He linked his fingers around hers and walked with her to find her parents' headstone. Philippe had drawn a map. The cemetery was old and very well maintained. She felt an overwhelming sense of peace wash over her as she searched for their resting place.

André and Eilish Chevalier
Died as they lived
United in love

The words were in French.

It was simple and so very appropriate. Donagh walked away and sat on a bench a little away from her under an old oak tree. Sitting on the kerb surrounding the grave, she wondered if somebody would ever love her the way that her father had loved her mother. He had sacrificed everything for her; she must have been an incredible person.

"I'll make you both proud of me," she whispered, wiping a tear that had trickled down her cheek. She picked up two marble pebbles from the grave to keep as mementos. "I am going to enjoy the rest of the day in the city of my birth. Rest in peace, Maman et Papa. Je vous aime."

Donagh came over. "Mon, you've been here for over an hour. I don't want to invade your space but maybe you might like to talk about how it happened?"

She nodded her head. He led her over to the bench under the canopy of rusty leaves. She told him how her parents had said they were going on a long trip. Their destination was a surprise for her. She remembered being so excited. She had always loved surprises. The evening before she had helped her mother to pack the suitcases. Her dad had been delayed at work. When he came home, he had put the suitcases on the roof rack. She stopped talking. She couldn't tell him that the next time she saw those clothes was when they were strewn across the road.

"Donagh, we must have been going to visit my gran."

He put his arm around her and she rested her head on his shoulder. She was just so tired. She closed her eyes.

Donagh's arm was stiff. Monique was asleep over an hour. It all made sense. He understood now why she often looked so sad. Kate had warned him to stay away but he hadn't listened. He was in too deep. From the first time he had heard her voice, it had cast its spell on him and then in class, he had seen how compassionate she was to everyone. Monique Chevalier was one of those truly honest people. She didn't try to fit in, even the way she dressed or the fact that she didn't wear so much make-up you'd need a chisel to get it off. This morning she had been recognisable. He had slept with girls before and wondered was it the same one he had gone home with. Donagh Mullally, you are a man whore. You will never be good enough for this woman. Make the most of this day and walk away, he told himself.

It started to drizzle. He took his phone from his pocket. She woke when he moved.

"It's starting to rain, Mon."

"Donagh, I am sorry for falling asleep."

"It's been a tough day for you."

"I made a promise to my parents to enjoy the rest of my time here. I am alive. I survived even though there were times that I wished I had not. I am here. I have to move on with the rest of my life. It has to be okay to laugh out loud without feeling guilty."

"Come on, we are going to paint this town red." When he saw the look on her face, he added, "A joke, Monique!"

She smiled. "Just one moment." She ran back to her parents' grave. He saw her kiss the photograph of them. His heart broke for her. He didn't know what he would do without his mother.

What a girl, he thought.

*

Kate invited Sophia and Eoghan for dinner. Tonight's offering was more adventurous. She had chosen crab claws for the starter and stuffed pork steak for the main course. Okay, so it was roast again, but she had actually made the stuffing and she had made a Baileys cheesecake.

"Kate, the crab claws are so tasty. You'll have to give me the recipe for the sauce."

"Jack made them the other night so I thought I'd give it a go," she replied, full of confidence. "It wasn't a recipe as such. I fried off the crab claws in butter and then messed around with cream, brandy, white wine, garlic, mixed Italian herbs, salt and pepper to create a taste that I thought was nice and popped them on a bed of a mixed leaves salad with a homemade garlic bread to wipe up the sauce. Nice?"

"Fair play they're gorgeous," Eoghan said. "I'll try it myself."

"I wish you would. Since I moved in you've forgotten where the kitchen is," said Sophia.

"Ah, I don't know where anything is in that new kitchen. And sure you love cooking!" he bantered back.

"Not that much, sunshine."

Kate smiled. She loved listening to the way they carried on. Sophia was so happy here. "Guys, I'm so excited about the new project."

Richard laughed. "She's more excited by it than our wedding. Only for Grace, there would be nothing done."

"That's not true, who organised the menu? Who?" said Kate, poking Richard in his side.

He laughed. "Okay, I'll give you that."

"And the band?"

"Okay, I'll give you that too."

"See what I have to listen to, Sophia? The work gets done. I just can't help being excited about seeing the place for real."

Richard laughed. "Who would have thought that Kate Fitzgerald would want to go back to the States so soon?"

Sophia smiled. "I think a Christmas double wedding is fantastic and the first at Butterfly Barn. How magical!"

"So true, Mom. If we were to marry in the States, it might have turned into a corporate event and that is not what either of us wants."

"Any plans for your honeymoon?" said Sophia.

"Wait for this, Kate wants to go to … drum roll … the Hamptons."

Sophia laughed. "But it will be cold."

"Oh Soph, I just can't wait to see it."

"You'll love it, Kate," said Eoghan. "I'm even looking forward to spending time over there."

"Kate, I was thinking about the garden projects in Manhattan. Wouldn't it be nice to do something in relation to gardening and children from the inner city? Maybe some kind of summer camp where the children can experience country living and provide a sense of value around the environment and green issues?" asked Sophia.

"Yes, it's an idea. I can arrange a meeting with the foundation where I volunteered. They might be very interested in what we're planning to do."

"Kate, it's your project. You make the decisions. I'm a lady of leisure, these days," Sophia answered, leaning into Eoghan and smiling.

"Sophia, are you sure you want me to run the place? I've no experience to speak of."

"Yes you have. I've seen you in action, Kate Fitzgerald. Remember Miami? You closed a deal with a large cruise company even though you were late for people who don't wait," said Richard.

"Ah, thanks, pet. But that was pure luck."

"Honey, you have me. We're in this thing together."

"But Richard, you'll be busy with your own work."

"Kate, I'm running a business from a cottage in Ireland. The world is a small place and communications technology is so advanced these days. Most of the time, it doesn't matter where I am. It took your visa issue for me to realise that I don't have to do the events, meetings and networking to be successful. Not if it's at the expense of being happy."

"No truer words were ever spoken," said Eoghan, raising his glass. They all clicked and Kate leaned over to Richard and kissed him full on the lips.

"Time to go!" Eoghan laughed and winked. "We're in a bit of a rush ourselves. Aren't we honey?"

"That's too much information, Eoghan," said Kate.

"You Irish are insatiable but who's complaining," said Richard, taking Kate's hand. She smiled. She never dreamed that she could feel this happy.

At 8.30 p.m. Monique walked with Donagh along the Champs-Élysées. The day had been a rollercoaster of emotion. On the Eiffel Tour, a memory of her father stroking her head and pointing in the direction of their apartment had been as vivid as though it had only just happened. On the boat trip along the Seine, she had heard a mother asking her little daughter if she was enjoying herself. The child had gazed up into her mother's eyes and had nodded her head. In that moment Monique had remembered the feel of her mother's arms around her asking her the very same question, her mother's scent had been Chanel no. 5. She had desperately needed to smell it again. As soon as they had disembarked, she had looked for a perfumery to buy it. She was so glad Donagh was with her. If he noticed her sadness, he hadn't said. He had managed to distract her at the right moment every time.

"Okay, let's do something crazy," said Donagh. "There's a pizza parlour just down this street. Let's get a takeaway pizza and sneak it in to the hotel. We'll get some beer too."

"You are crazy." She laughed.

"Be a shame not to use that suite. We could watch TV and chill out. I've had enough culture for today."

"Why not?"

The whiff of pizza was unmistakeable as they crossed the lobby. The concierge smiled at them as they passed. Donagh gave him a cheeky grin. In the suite, Donagh moved the antique coffee table and put the pizza box on top of it.

"What were they thinking giving us an upgrade?" He laughed. "You'd need a small mortgage to buy a drink in this hotel. Do you want a glass for your beer?"

"No, it's fine." What would he think of her when he found out the truth?

"Cool chick."

"Smart ass."

He laughed.

They both plopped into the comfortable sofa. Donagh flicked the channels.

"I forgot that everything would be in French, so much for a movie."

"Ah, but look," she said, taking the control from him. She found the movie channel.

"*Love Actually?*"

"Are you serious?"

She gave him a puppy-dog look.

"You win." They sat munching pizza and drinking beer. Half way through she got a cushion and curled up at one end of the couch while Donagh sat at the other end. She fell asleep.

"Hey Mon, you're in my bed." He gently tapped her feet with his toes.

She sat up, disoriented. "I have missed the end." Their eyes locked in that way that happened between them. She got up and walked towards the bed. She turned her head to say good night but the words didn't come out. He was standing behind her. Her body ached for him to touch her.

He pushed her hair gently away from her neck and ran his fingers lightly against her skin and then he leaned in and traced kisses along it. She turned fully to touch his lips to hers. They kissed passionately and deeply. His hands held her head on either side. She wanted him here and now and to hell with all the consequences. He pulled back from her and looked deeply into her eyes as he began to unbutton her blouse slowly. It felt like he was giving her permission to stop him but she couldn't. She reached up to him and began to kiss him again as though she was trying to imprint the memory of his kiss in her mind forever. His fingers touched the bare skin of her sides and the cold reality hit. Her scar. She couldn't bear the thought of him recoiling from her. She pulled away from him and wrapped her unbuttoned blouse around her body.

"I can't." She ran to the bathroom. She sat on the marble tiled floor with her back to the door. She heard movement on the other side of it.

"Mon, are you okay?" She had expected him to be angry. To think of her as a tease – but Donagh Mullally was like nobody she had ever known.

"I'm sorry, Donagh. I'm messed up. I wish I hadn't met you. I mean, I wish we hadn't met yet."

There was silence. Then she heard a big sigh.

"I understand. I feel the same way. You were right to stop us. It's not our time. I don't know if it will ever be. But I want you to know you'll always be in my heart."

"You were in mine from the first day we met."

"I'm leaving now because if you open that door you and I both know what will happen. Take care, Monique Chevalier."

Her flight landed in Dublin at 11 a.m. Geoff had offered to pick her up. Thankfully she didn't have to stand around waiting for luggage. She scanned the sea of faces in the arrivals hall until her gaze landed on a familiar face. Her body went into shock.

"Monnie, I wanted to surprise you."

"Garvan," she managed to say. "What are you doing here?"

"I missed you so much. I came home. I know how hard it's been for you because of what I did. Please forgive me."

He was making a scene in the airport. She was mortified. "Where's the car?" she asked and began to walk towards the exit.

Garvan talked most of the two-hour journey home, which suited her because the shock of seeing him still hadn't worn off. "Monnie, I was so glad you were happy to see me," said Garvan.

Months earlier, she would have given everything for this moment. But now the only person she could think of was Donagh Mullally. Images of their time together kept floating in her mind.

"I couldn't wait to come home. Ah Monnie, life is not the same without you in it. We're meant to be together, Monnie, we always were."

He was the only person who ever called her Monnie. She had found it so endearing but now it irritated her. "I'm not moving to Dubai, Garvan."

"I know. That's why I came back. I'll get a job here. I want us to be a couple like we used to be," he said, patting her knee.

She felt like a child being pacified.

Donagh walked from the bus stop to his house. He opened the front door and called out. There was nobody home. He threw his bag into his bedroom and headed straight for Murphy's pub on the corner. He ordered a pint of Guinness and while he waited for it he rang Butchie.

"I'm going on the piss. Are you on?"

"What's eating you? How come you didn't come home on Sunday night?"

"Long story."

"Give me twenty minutes."

Donagh clicked off his phone and took a sip. He wasn't much of a drinker but he needed to blow off steam. From tomorrow on, he would figure out what to do with the rest of his life.

Chapter Fifteen

"The past eight weeks have flown by." Grace put the final touches to the Christmas table. "Thank God, Geoff, Donagh and all the team have finished the adventure park."

"I must admit I was getting worried," said Jack. He took the turkey out of the oven.

"It smells delicious," said Grace. "Here they come." She could hear the sound of a car crunching on the pebbled driveway outside. Finn ran to the door, excited to see his granny Molly, Kate, Richard, Sophia and Eoghan who were all spending Christmas Day with them.

The marquee was already in place to host Butterfly Barn's first wedding ceremony. There was such a buzz in the air about their double wedding, Christmas was being overshadowed.

"How's my little champ?" said Sophia, ruffling Finn's blond head.

"Santa, Soph, look," said Finn, grabbing her by the hand and leading her to the sitting room to see all his presents.

"And how is my godchild?" said Kate, picking up Baby Lily from her bouncer. "Imagine we are getting married in three days' time!"

"Isn't it about time!" said Molly, already fussing at the pots.

"Mam, it's all okay. Sit down and relax."

"I can't help it. I like being busy."

"Well today I'm looking after you. Jack, will you pour Mam a glass of wine?"

"At this hour?"

"It's Christmas Day!" The two girls exclaimed together and started to laugh.

"It's Christmas Day every day around here," said Molly, still peeved.

"Mam, what's wrong with you?" asked Grace.

"Marilyn didn't call from Lanzarote," whispered Kate. "But you know what she's like. She'll probably remember at midnight."

"Molly, get that into you. We're going to have a great day," said Jack, handing Molly the Waterford Crystal goblet nearly full to the top.

"We'll be wheeling her out of here later," muttered Kate. "Text Marilyn and tell her to get her finger out."

Grace threw her eyes to heaven. It was easy to keep their mother happy. It was the small things that threw her. Still, thought Grace, looking over to where Jack was talking with her mother, she must miss their dad on days like today. It was lonely being single and she had been for a very long time. Her mother never complained or burdened anyone with her problems. She was a get up and get on with it type of person. Some days, Grace missed her dad too. He hadn't been all bad, just when he drank. It was hard not to think about him now that their wedding day was looming. There was probably a lot more going on for their mother than she let on. Grace texted Marilyn. She and Kate had never really resolved their differences but at least they didn't let it affect the rest of the family.

"Here's to a wonderful day," said Grace, holding up her wine glass. "Merry Christmas."

On Christmas Day Monique walked along Bayrush Beach. So much had changed since her visit to France. She had started her new job and she loved every minute of it. Garvan had been offered a six-month contract with a local engineering firm. He seemed happy enough there. He said it wasn't as challenging as Dubai.

Since Garvan turned up at the airport her life had been in his hands. He had assumed she'd be waiting for him. She felt guilty because he had given up a great job for her. His mother kept telling her how wonderful it was to have him back and how she had always known they were meant for one another. She had added how glad she was that he had got all that Dubai business out of his system.

She felt trapped. Emotionally she hadn't had the strength to deal with Garvan at the beginning and with each passing day things were getting more out of control. She had managed to avoid sleeping with him. He thought it was because he had hurt her so much by leaving. It had been easier to let him believe that. How could she tell him she didn't love him anymore? She was afraid of the fallout. He kept mentioning commitment and making life choices. She had said they needed to take things very slowly. She had seen the disappointment on his face. After that she lost the nerve to take it a step further and end it. After Christmas and the wedding, she knew she had to make a decision that would be very unpopular.

She was in constant touch with Philippe. She had promised that she would visit again early in the New Year. They were getting to know one another by email and phone. She had asked Gran, Jessie and Geoff not to tell anyone about the château and the title. It was still all too surreal.

She had told Garvan that she had discovered an uncle in France but she hadn't elaborated.

She pressed her phone and moments later her uncle's face appeared.

"Merry Christmas to you all," said Monique, smiling. Technology was so cool. She was standing on Bayrush Beach using Facetime and the connection was good.

"Hello Monique, and many happy returns to you. I hope you have a wonderful day. Eric sends his love too." She could see him in the background.

"See you soon," he called.

"Gran is looking forward to meeting you all in the New Year. Enjoy the day and I will talk to you later. Au revoir."

She smiled as she placed the phone back in her pocket. She passed Rose Cottage. Richard's car was gone. They must be at Grace's house already, she thought.

Jessie had invited her for Christmas dinner as usual. She had been avoiding her since she had come back from France. Garvan had asked her to move Jasper to Jack's stables so that they could ride out together and she had also been so busy with her new job. But the real reason she avoided Butterfly Barn was because Donagh had been there building the adventure centre and she also knew that Jessie had a way of making her face the truth.

She wondered where Donagh would be spending Christmas. His relationship with his father was so tense. Stop, she told herself. But he was never far from her thoughts.

On St. Stephen's morning, Grace walked with Jack along Bayrush Beach. He had Lily in a baby pouch. She had Pluto, their golden retriever, on his lead and Finn toddled along beside them. When they reached Rose Cottage, Finn tried to climb on the red gate. She loved this place with all of her heart. She had been so sad leaving it. But when Jack's mother had taken ill, it had made sense to go and live with her. She walked through the gate and went to her favourite spot in the garden. The first time she had stood there, she had been pregnant with Finn and so very lost.

She reached for Jack's hand and said, "I love you."

His grey-green eyes twinkled in the early morning light. "I love you too, honey." He put his arm around her and they stood for a moment. Lily gurgled. "Every man should wear one of these. It makes you realise how heavy little ones can be."

"Red alert, there are two lovebirds in the garden."

Grace looked up to see Kate standing on the upstairs decking with just a T-shirt on. "Go put some clothes on, you nutter!"

Kate pranced back inside, laughing.

The French doors were open and when she walked in with Jack, Finn was already sitting on Donagh's lap at the kitchen counter. Donagh's hair was still damp.

"Have you two been out kite-surfing this morning?" asked Jack

"Yep," said Donagh, nodding towards Richard. "Every chance this guy gets, he's at it."

"The waves weren't great today," said Richard. He left his perch on the couch where he had his laptop open and the newspapers spread around him. "I meant to ask if you were happy with your new kite-surf gear?"

"So far so good," said Donagh, just as Kate came down the stairs.

"Two days left and our single days are over," said Grace.

"Your single days were over years ago," said Kate. "Do you hear her, Donagh? There is absolutely nothing going to change in her life."

"Are you implying that we have a boring life? We can't all be marrying billionaires, you know."

"No, but I have to leave here," said Kate, putting on a sulky voice.

"What's wrong with her?" asked Grace.

"Don't know. She's your sister," said Donagh. "It's probably cold feet. Wouldn't be me. The thought of settling down – don't know how you can do it."

"That's what we all said." Richard grinned.

"Someday it will happen to you, Donagh. You won't know which side is up," said Jack, passing Lily to her doting godmother.

"I shouldn't be saying stuff like that to you lot just before the big day. Sorry lads," said Donagh, getting up to boil the kettle. "Who's for coffee? Grace, Jack?"

"Yes please. The adventure centre is fantastic, Donagh," said Grace.

"Geoff was under wicked pressure to make sure that there wouldn't be a sign of building work or skips and the like around the place. I'm delighted with how it's turned out."

"It's a fine job, Donagh. Well done," said Richard. "And in the middle of it all he passed the lifesaving course, Jack. When is your surf instructor's exam?"

"In two weeks' time."

"Fair play to you Donagh. You've put the hard work in," said Kate.

"How's the song writing going?" asked Grace. "You've been so busy you probably haven't had a chance."

"I've being using the voice recorder on the phone like you suggested. Sure I'm always humming to myself."

"There's no end to this guy's talents," said Richard. "When do you sleep? I thought I was a workaholic!"

"Not any more. Thank God," said Kate.

"I don't have a woman in my life, Richie. No distractions boy."

Grace laughed. Donagh was the only person she knew who called Richard, Richie. He was so not a Richie. Kate had said that she reckoned Richard loved it because it made him feel like one of the lads. Donagh was a frequent visitor to Rose Cottage, he and Richard kite-surfed together and Donagh had even convinced Kate to have a go.

"I thought you were bringing that stunning looking girl, Evie," said Kate.

"I am."

"You're the pits, Donagh Mullally."

He shrugged his shoulders and smiled. Jack and Richard slapped him on the back.

"And you two are worse for encouraging him," said Grace.

Jessie's head was in a spin. The wedding which had started out as a simple affair had slowly mushroomed to over two hundred people from all over the world. Jack's ex-partner from his vet's practice Abdul and his wife had flown in from Dubai. Lisa and Chad had arrived from New York along with some of Richard's closest friends and associates from Wynthrope Inc. She hoped she hadn't forgotten anything. Being host and chief bridesmaid had kept her busy for the past few weeks.

"Everything is done, Jess. Relax, we can't do anything more. Except pray that the weather holds to get from the car to the marquee without getting soaked to the skin," said Geoff.

"Okay, you're right."

"Breathe, woman, before you start to hyperventilate. You'll get rosy cheeks and you know how you feel about that. Molly is funny. I understand why she wants Grace and Kate to stay in her house the night before their wedding. But you and Sophia as well, all trying to get ready in the morning – good luck with that."

"It's tradition, or so Molly tells me." A car pulled up outside. "That's Sophia. Okay. Sam." She ran into the sitting room to give him a hug. "I'll see you in the morning, pet. Don't forget to brush your teeth. Love you." She kissed his forehead and rushed back into the kitchen.

"Geoff, don't forget …"

Geoff put a finger on her lips. "Go, relax and enjoy yourself. Everything will be perfect."

"Thanks, Geoff. I just want to get it right for them."

"It will be. I love you." He kissed her.

The next morning Jessie watched as Molly beamed with pride. She had a lump in her throat. Grace was glowing. Her long blonde hair was pinned up; Jessie had always felt she had been aptly named. She oozed grace and style. Kate stood beside her, so opposite in her appearance but so very beautiful too. Kate's short dark hair was styled like Audrey Hepburn; Jessie had never noticed how much Kate resembled the fifties movie star until now. Both of them wore white.

"I wish your father was here to see you both," said Molly. "I'm so very proud of you. I know life didn't quite work out the way we might have liked it. But I want you to know, he loved you both very much. Girls, please remember nobody is perfect. We all have flaws and foibles, just promise me that you'll never go to sleep on a row. Sort it out. Now, that's all I'm going to say."

The girls hugged their mother. Jessie wiped a tear from her eye. "Molly, I'll kill you. My make-up will be ruined."

"Go on outta that. You're a big softie, Jessie McGrath."

"Less of the big, Molly. I've been dieting for months."

Molly laughed and took her face in her hands and kissed her on the cheek.

"Now I am really going to kill you," said Jessie, wiping Molly's lipstick from her cheek. "Okay, have we got everything? Bouquets!"

"Jessie," said Grace.

"What?"

"Relax, you're more nervous than anyone."

"Sorry girls," said Jessie, "Right so, we're off."

When Jessie opened the front door, the terraced street was buzzing with neighbours waiting to wish the Fitzgerald girls well. It was overwhelming. They finally set off in a row of vintage cars towards Butterfly Barn.

By the time Grace reached Butterfly Barn, she was overcome with emotion. Jessie had hired a wedding planner who already had a fabulous canvas to work from but the touches he had added were perfect. There was a fabulous marquee right beside the barn. The sun had even graced them with its watery presence. She could hear music gently playing. Grace could feel her heart beating faster. He loves me, she said over and over in her head until she felt her body relax. She looked across at Kate who looked relaxed and full of confidence. She felt Sophia's arm around her. "Take a deep breath and enjoy every moment of this special day."

"Thank you, Sophia. I will." She smiled, as the photographer took some shots. They had asked the photographer to capture the day in the most natural way possible. Finn ran over to her and hugged her. Sam was so excited and was busy telling Finn to hold his hand.

"We have to get this right," said Sam, trying to be the responsible big boy.

Moments later, Grace could hear an orchestra playing the introduction to the song they had chosen to walk up the aisle.

> *"I've dreamed of you*
> *Always feeling you were there*
> *And all my life*
> *I have searched for you*
> *Everywhere"*

It captured exactly how she felt about Jack and when she had played it for Kate, she had loved it too. Sam caught Finn's hand and the two little boys set off up the aisle. Heads turned to look and smile at them. Halfway up Finn began to run into Jack's arms. There was a collective chuckle. Jack mouthed the words "I love you" to her. She felt complete. Jessie walked up and joined Geoff and Eoghan who were Jack and Richard's best men. Molly and Kate went next and finally she walked up beside Sophia. It had been her mother's suggestion to ask Sophia to give her away. Molly had joked, "The three of us won't fit up the aisle."

She prayed her mother wouldn't be cross with her and Kate when she saw who they had invited. She heard a gasp when her mother saw their father sitting in the front row but then she saw Molly smile as she sat quietly into the seat beside him. Her eyes locked with Jack's and when he took her hand she knew nothing could ever compare to the overwhelming love she felt for him.

Nora read a piece from the New Testament. "Love is patient and kind …"

Then Monique walked to the podium wearing a soft-pink fifties-style dress. Her long chocolate-brown hair was held up on one side and cascaded around her bare shoulder. Grace had never seen her look more beautiful. She began to read in her wonderful, unique accent, Maya Angelou's poem "Touched by an Angel". She captured the essence of every word, so much so that there was spontaneous applause. She looked at Jack with eyes filled with unshed tears. The skin around his eyes crinkled as he smiled at her.

His smile had always been her undoing.

The wedding service began.

When the celebrant said, "I now pronounce you man and wife. You may kiss your bride." There was rapturous applause. Then the mini orchestra struck up an instrumental of The Beatles, 'All You Need Is Love'.

The marquee erupted with applause as the wedding party walked back down the aisle. People came from all directions to congratulate them. Waiting staff went around with champagne and canapés. When most of the crowd had dispersed her father came to her. She had Lily in her arms. "Thank you for inviting me."

She felt awkward. She hadn't seen him since she was sixteen years old. Over the years, money would arrive in the post but that had been as much contact as he had made. The postmarks had never been the same. Recently, Kate had seen a letter her mother had left open on the kitchen table. It had been from him. Kate hadn't read it but she had taken note of the address. They had sent a wedding invite. He hadn't replied. Instead just in the manner he had left, he had turned up. "Jack, this is my father, Jimmy Fitzgerald." The two men shook hands. Then he leaned closer to look at Lily. "She's so beautiful, just like you," he said. "Can I hold her?"

She passed her baby girl into her father's arms and felt an overwhelming sense of peace wash over her. Her mother joined them with Finn. Molly put her arms around her and whispered, "Thank you."

"We did it for you, Mam. I love you," she whispered into her mother's ear.

Molly pulled away and gave herself a shake. "Well, wasn't that some surprise! Wait till the neighbours hear." Then she took Lily and started cooing at her while Jack introduced Finn to his grandfather. Grace smiled as she felt Jack's arm around her. He knew more than anyone how much her father's departure had affected her.

Kate joined them and introduced Richard. She glanced around looking for the rest of her brothers and sisters. Gerry, Joe and Lauren had gathered but she saw Marilyn walking out of the marquee.

Sophia sat with Nora. "That was wonderful."

"It was. Look at Molly," said Nora. "It was lovely of the girls to invite their father."

Sophia watched as Molly fixed her dress. "Thank goodness she didn't go crazy."

Nora laughed. "It could have gone either way."

"This has been one of the best days of my life, Nora, and it's only just begun. Look at my son, he is positively glowing."

Nora hugged her. "You deserve all the happiness in the world."

"And so do you, Nora. Here's to a Happy New Year to both of us." A waiter appeared and Sophia took two champagne flutes from the tray. She passed one to Nora and chinked glasses. "To France."

"To no longer burying secrets."

Monique spotted Donagh from across the marquee. She watched as he introduced his stunningly beautiful girlfriend to Grace and Jack. The girl attracted admiring glances from all the men in the room, including Garvan. Beautiful people attracted beautiful people. It was hard not to stare at them.

"The ceremony was magical," said Rachel, following her gaze. "Mon, are you okay? You keep looking over at Donagh. You're with Garvan now." Rachel had lowered her tone because Garvan and Jay were within earshot.

Monique no longer cared. "I don't know anymore."

"Oh God," muttered Rachel. "Jay, just popping to the Ladies." She caught Monique by the arm and headed in the direction of the toilets. At the last minute she detoured and led Monique outside.

"Donagh is with someone else. Garvan is here. He came back. He loves you. Garvan is not blind. I noticed and so will he. Is that what you want?"

"Rachel, I had decided to be on my own to figure myself out and then Garvan came back. He was so confident I would still be waiting for him. Am I such a sure thing? So boringly reliable. Good old square, never puts a foot wrong, good girl Monique. Is that who I am?" She looked at her friend, desperate for reassurance that maybe, just maybe, she might be wrong in her summation of herself. Rachel said nothing.

"I do not want to be such a sure bet. I want someone to love me the way Jack loves Grace, and Richard loves Kate." She paused to take a breath. "And the way my father loved my mother." An unexpected tear trickled down her face. She wiped it away. Who did she need to be for Donagh to love her?

After today she'd finish with Garvan. It wasn't fair. She didn't love him. She couldn't pretend anymore. "Oh Rachel, I have come up with every excuse not to sleep with Garvan since he came back. He must know there is something wrong."

"I wish I could fix things for you but only you can do that. Just let's get through today. Come on, Joe Dooley is setting up the bar in the barn, we'll have a shot. Everybody will still be in the marquee until the bell rings for dinner."

She followed Rachel through the fabulously decorated room. It was hard not to be impressed by the beauty of it all, but the wedding had just brought up all the feelings that had been lying dormant in her. The poem she had read had summed up what being with Donagh had felt like. She wanted that kind of love. She'd rather be alone than settle for less.

"Hey Joe," said Rachel, to their old school friend.

"Girls, what will ye have?"

"Two baby Guinness," said Rachel. Joe made up the shots.

"What am I going to do? We're booked into a log cabin tonight. I just can't sleep with him, Rach."

Joe handed over the shots.

"For now, just get that into you and we'll figure it out."

"Same again, Joe," said Monique. Rachel looked at her.

"Girls, you're going to be in right form," said Joe, making up two more. Rachel went to pay.

"Free bar," he said.

"God help us, so. Thanks, Joe. See you later," said Rachel, leading her back to the marquee. She had never been much of a drinker. She bumped off a table and nearly fell. "Okay, maybe that wasn't such a great idea."

"It was one of your best," said Monique. The drink was already having an effect.

Donagh went over to Kate while Evie chatted to someone she knew.

"Congrats." He kissed her on both cheeks. "You look fantastic."

"You scrub up well yourself," Kate laughed. "So are you going to introduce me to your girlfriend?"

"Friend, you mean."

Kate laughed. "I could say something but it wouldn't be appropriate today. Donagh, she is fabulous."

"I noticed," he said, winking. "We can't all meet the great love of our lives and live happily ever after."

"So what do we do? Settle for less?" She looked at him questioningly.

"Maybe we never settle at all," he answered. He saw Monique coming back into the marquee with Rachel. He had heard her boyfriend had come back from Dubai. He had noticed him looking at Evie more than once. "Donagh, did you hear me?"

"Sorry, what did you say?"

"I said she's back with Garvan." He tore his eyes away from Monique, not before noticing she was a bit wobbly. Maybe she wasn't used to high heels.

"I'm really happy for you both, Kate. He's one lucky bastard," he said, nodding in Richard's direction.

"He'll love that. Richard, did you hear what he called you?"

"I can imagine," said Richard, joining them just as Evie came over.

"Evie, this is Kate and Richard," he said, putting his arm around the small of her back.

"It's nice to meet you both. The ceremony was just so beautiful," said Evie. "Your dress is amazing."

"Thanks," said Kate. Donagh had stopped listening. He watched as Monique knocked back a full glass of champagne. What was going on with her? He caught her boyfriend looking at Evie again. He was tempted to stick out his tongue at him.

After dinner, Kate looked around the room. It was an overwhelming feeling to be surrounded by people she cared about. She listened to the speeches and laughed at all the jokes. She caught her eldest sister, Marilyn, looking at her. She smiled. Marilyn smiled back and mouthed, "You look beautiful, I love you." Kate felt her eyes watering up. Then she mouthed back, "I love you too." She could see Marilyn was struggling not to cry too. Just because they could never connect didn't mean neither of them cared. Family was family no matter what, thought Kate. She could hardly believe her ears when she heard her mother's voice over the PA system. She threw her eyes to heaven and Marilyn burst out laughing. This had definitely not been in the plan.

"Is it on? Testing, one, two! I've always wanted to say that." The microphone wobbled in her hand.

"Oh God," whispered Grace. "What is she doing?"

"Making a show of us as always," said Kate.

"Now all of you who know me, know that this is not my thing. But I couldn't let this day pass without telling you all how proud I am of my family. Now, it hasn't been a bed of roses, especially these two, one of them even got pregnant at thirty-six, no less."

"Oh God, get the microphone off her quick before she starts on my drug-taking youth."

"Nobody is safe with that woman," muttered Grace. Jack and Richard were laughing their heads off.

"And as for my youngest, well we won't go there. Thank God, the rest of them are normal." Everybody laughed.

"I could tell a few stories about Gerry," someone heckled.

"You leave my boy alone." There was jeering from the tables.

"Seriously, when Sophia Wynthrope came into our lives, everything changed. She has brought our family such joy. Today our family has extended. I couldn't be happier. Welcome officially to the Fitzgerald clan, Richard and Sophia Wynthrope."

"What about Jack?" someone heckled.

"That fellow, it took him twenty odd years to figure himself out. But then again he had his work cut out with my daughter, Grace." There was another burst of laugher.

"From the first day I met Jack in my back garden, I hoped they would find their way to one another. All my dreams for my family have come true. I'm very grateful for my two grandchildren Finn and Lily, even if their mother did put the cart before the horse. Now let's get on with the party. Fr. Jim, will you do the honours and bless that cake? It's about the only traditional thing that will happen here today." There was a roar of laughter and applause as Molly sat down.

"Your mom could be a stand-up comedienne," said Richard.

"You don't know the half of it."

Chapter Sixteen

After cutting the cake, Grace returned to the top table. Jack held the back of the chair for her. As she sat down she noticed Monique watching them. Since Garvan had returned from Dubai, she was seeing more of Monique. Grace could see her heart wasn't in the relationship anymore. Poor Monique, she thought, she must be feeling so trapped since Garvan had given up his great engineering job in Dubai to return to Bayrush to be with her. Stop, thought Grace, her writer's head had created a whole story because, for a fleeting moment, a once pretty but now beautiful French girl looked forlorn.

She turned and saw Jack kissing their baby daughter's chubby cheeks. She had thought she'd look silly wearing a white wedding dress when she already had two children but she didn't. How could she when a man like Jack Leslie loved her? She leaned towards him and kissed him.

Monique saw Grace leaning over to kiss Jack. Her heart lurched. She glanced in Donagh's direction. She felt the most unmerciful kick under the table. It was Rachel making signals at her. She took a big gulp of white wine from her glass and mouthed "That hurt" to Rachel.

Garvan looked at her. "How many drinks have you had?"

"Who is counting? It is a celebration." She took another big gulp.

"Monique, can you help me?" said Rachel. Monique followed Rachel and nearly tripped over her handbag which had fallen on the floor.

"What's with those two today?" asked Garvan, while she was still in earshot.

"Don't know," said Jay. "Will you have another one?"

"I might as well, thanks."

In the Ladies, Rachel fussed around her. "It's my fault, I should never have suggested shots."

"I am a grown-up," said Monique, but she felt like getting sick. The door opened. Monique stood up tall trying to steady herself. She looked at Rachel and just as the girl closed the cubicle door, she whispered. "That's her, Donagh's girlfriend. She's so sexy and beautiful."

"Shush, Mon," said Rachel, pulling her out the door. "I hope she didn't hear you."

"But how can I compete with her?"

"Listen to me," said Rachel, leading her away from the ladies' room door. "You are beautiful, unique and special. Make a decision and stick with it. What's to be will be. I don't ever want to hear you comparing yourself to anyone else again, Monique Chevalier. Drink water and enjoy this very special day. You look gorgeous. Head up and let's go. Everyone is mingling around again until the band is ready." Rachel flicked her long auburn hair and walked confidently back into the marquee which had been set up for after dinner drinks.

She followed behind but because of her diminutive height, she couldn't see Garvan or Jay in the crowd. Somebody had stopped Rachel to chat. A waiter offered her champagne. She took it. Rachel would kill her, but so what, she thought. Then she saw Jay introducing Garvan to Donagh. She took another big gulp. Could this day get any worse? She was about to make a quick exit when Garvan spotted her.

"Hey Monnie, there you are. I was wondering where you were." He slipped his arm around her waist and pulled her close to him, making her feel like his possession. Her reaction was to pull away but she didn't.

"I believe you know my girlfriend, Monique?" said Garvan.

"Yes," said Donagh, keeping eye contact with Garvan.

"Evie, this is Jay, Garvan, and Monique," said Donagh, smoothly putting his arm around Evie, who had just joined him.

"Hi," she said, and then she turned her full attention to Donagh. She put her hand on his chest and gazed up at him. "I've met so many people I know here."

"I noticed," smiled Donagh. He turned towards Jay and said, "Catch you later, no doubt." He acknowledged Garvan with a nod of his head and walked away.

"Do you know that guy well, Jay?" asked Garvan.

"Yeah, he's sound. He's been around Jack's place a lot."

"Funny, I've never met him there."

"Actually, that's true. Lately, he's been too busy building the adventure centre with Geoff."

"Just going to chat to Sophia," said Monique, walking away.

*

Sophia saw Monique drinking the rest of her champagne and taking another one. She was wobbling in her direction. At first, Sophia thought it might be the shoes but as she got closer she knew Monique had exceeded her quota. She'd have to do something with her. She caught Monique gently by the arm. "I could use some fresh air. Let's go for a walk." She took the glass from Monique and left it on a table. Monique still hadn't said a word.

When they got outside and away from any prying eyes, Sophia asked, "What's the matter, honey?"

"Oh Sophia, everything."

Sophia glanced around. "Let's take a stroll up to Jessie's house. I could do with a break before the dancing starts." She'd get some coffee into her, that should help. She linked her as they walked along the lane. They had nearly reached the yard before Monique spoke again.

"I do not love him, Sophia. Today, at the ceremony, it was all too much. I cannot pretend anymore. I thought I loved Garvan. But now … I have felt love. It is when your heart beats that little bit faster and you feel butterflies in your stomach. It is when somebody looks at you and you feel like you are the only person in the room. It makes you feel all fuzzy and warm inside and that you can take on the world together. When you are together nothing else matters. You can't think straight … but … it is not to be. Oh Sophia, the person I love does not love me. It hurts so much it is worse than a physical pain."

"Oh honey. Come inside."

Firstly, Sophia poured a glass of water and put it in front of Monique who sat with her head in her hands at the kitchen table. She began to make coffee. The stronger the better, she thought. "Drink the water while we're waiting for the coffee to brew," said Sophia. "You have to get yourself together. Monique, life is not easy. You and I know that more than most. Today was a huge insight for you. Do the honourable thing by Garvan. You'll be doing him a favour in the long run. He might not see it that way for a while. Always, always live by your own truth. You are so young and on this day you have been blessed with the most wonderful insight and learning." Sophia poured two cups of coffee.

"What learning?" asked Monique, sipping the strong liquid.

"What it feels like to really love someone. Many people are not that lucky. They never experience love. Value it, remember it and try your very, very best to get over it."

"Oh Sophia, I never will."

"Why don't you consider going back to France for a while? Get to know your relatives. Learn about your heritage. The change of scene might be the best thing for you."

"Maybe Sophia, maybe I need to find me. I have been one-half of a couple since I was eighteen. Garvan was my first boyfriend. I always thought how lucky I was to have him until he left."

"My darling, go to the bathroom and raid Jessie's make-up drawer and come back to the wedding. Enjoy what's left of the day and deal with everything with a clear head tomorrow."

"Sophia, I hope you have not missed the first dance. I will drink more coffee and do as you said."

Sophia gave her a hug and rushed out the door.

Monique poured more coffee. What had she been thinking? It had been silly of her to drink so much. Today was special and she was ruining it. She brought the coffee upstairs and splashed water on her face. She drank the rest of the coffee. She put toothpaste on her finger to clean her teeth and then she used Jessie's make-up to redo her face.

She walked through the yard and she heard old Duke neighing. She stopped at the entrance and was about to go into the American barn when she saw Donagh. He didn't see her. She kept walking.

She heard a familiar voice calling her name. She ran towards the voice. "Hi. I was just on my way back," she said, linking Garvan's arm and leading him back the way he had come. She'd do what Sophia had said. Enjoy the rest of the evening and sort things out tomorrow.

Donagh had seen Monique leave with Sophia. He had wanted to apologise for ignoring her, but by the time he got outside she was already halfway up the laneway linking Sophia. She was definitely after having one too many. He was glad Sophia had noticed too and was looking after her. He had needed a break, that boyfriend of hers had just got right up his nose. He was an arrogant asshole. The way he had put his arm around Monique had really irked him and he had kept calling her Monnie. It bugged him.

He dreaded going back but he had left Evie for long enough. Thankfully, she knew people and she seemed to be enjoying herself. He wasn't much company and she had been great to come. They had been best friends since childhood. He hadn't lied when he said they were friends – people often presumed they were a couple especially because they shared a house. It was handy at times when neither of them wanted to be tied down. Evie had always been tactile by her nature but he had really played it up today because he was jealous. He couldn't stand seeing Monique with that ass. If only he could talk to her for just a few minutes to find out if she was happy. She had said she was messed up in France. He had thought that she might just need some time because of her parents, not that her boyfriend would come back from Dubai. He should never have kissed her that day on the beach. If he hadn't he was sure he wouldn't be feeling so shite.

As soon as he passed the surfing instructor's course he planned on leaving. There would always be work in beach resorts around the world for someone like him. No ties, no strings. He didn't need much. He couldn't stay around watching her with someone else. God, he thought, when did I become this person?

When he rejoined the celebrations, he spotted Evie almost immediately. There was no doubt but Evie turned heads. Over the years, she had been offered modelling contracts, but music was her passion. She was leaving for Verona on Monday to take up a place as a violinist in an orchestra. She was so excited about it and he was thrilled for her. Evie smiled as he whispered something in her ear.

"You have it bad," she said.

Grace felt Jack's arms around her as they slow danced to "This is the Moment". She spotted Sophia dancing with Eoghan and smiled. She wondered how life would have turned out if she hadn't met Sophia on a flight to New York three and a half years ago. She hugged Jack closer to her. "I love you with all my heart," she whispered into his ear.

He smiled and whispered, "Now that we're licensed, come on, let's get out of here."

"It won't be half as much fun since we're not breaking any rules."

"Oh honey. It's always fun with you."

"You won't be saying that when I'm seventy."

"Ugh. Now why did you go and ruin it on me?"

She laughed.

"Look at your mother!" said Jack.

Molly was dancing with Grace's brother, Joe, and her sister Lauren was dancing beside them with their father. Her mother's face was animated and glowing. Grace was so glad he had come. Life was too short. Her mother was right when she had said nobody was perfect.

Monique saw Donagh lead Evie to the dance floor. She sat opposite Garvan. She couldn't think of anything to say. She sipped her water. He sipped his pint.

"Do ya wanna dance?" asked Garvan. His voice was slurred.

"Are you sure you are able?" She smiled to soften the harshness of her words.

"I can hold my drink as good as any man," he answered, getting up.

He took her hand and led her purposely to the dance floor. He stopped beside Donagh and Evie. He put his arms around her in a possessive way. It wasn't a nice feeling. She did not intend to make a scene but she felt extremely uncomfortable. She prayed for the song to end.

"Am I not good enough anymore?" he asked, looking down from his six-foot-two height.

"Garvan, let's just enjoy the evening. This isn't the time or place to have this conversation."

"You can't stop looking at them?"

"Who?"

"Them," he said, pointing towards Donagh and Evie. Garvan dropped his arms and just stood in front of her. "You can't even deny it, Monnie." He walked off the dance floor.

The music changed to a fast track and Rachel came up behind her. "Keep walking towards the bar and pretend you haven't a care in the world. A Bacardi Breezer please, Joe, and a sparkling water."

"Oh Rach, did Donagh see what happened?"

"I don't think so. Monique, seriously we need to talk. I don't know what is going on but let's enjoy the rest of the evening. At least you won't have to worry about that other situation now."

"Here's to bad girl Monique, breaker of hearts," said Monique, holding up her bottle of water.

"Sorry to burst your bubble. But you could never do the bad girl stuff. It's not you."

"Here's to mending my broken heart so."

"I think I know who broke it," said Rachel, looking in Donagh's direction. "I hope he's worth it, Mon. Some guys can never be caught."

"What's the crack?" said Jay, putting his arms around the two of them.

"Will you go and see if Garvan is okay?"

"I will. But remember, Monique. Garvan always does what he wants. Surely you know that?"

Just then Kate waved to them. "Guys, come and meet Lisa and Chad from New York."

Monique was glad of the diversion. That was an interesting observation from Jay. She had never noticed that about Garvan. Maybe love really is blind.

She spent the rest of the night dancing and laughing. When the band finished, a DJ struck up. The next time Monique looked at her watch it was 3 a.m. and there was a singsong in full swing.

Kate spoke quietly to Jessie. "I'd like to sing your song, Jessie."

"It might not be appropriate."

"Jessie, the best songs are about heartache and Butterfly Barn would never have become a reality had it not been for your babies. Their coming into the world changed everything for you, losing them has made you who you are today," said Kate, taking Jessie's hand. "Please let me."

Jessie just nodded.

Kate went over to Donagh, who was sitting with Evie. She spoke briefly to them. Donagh walked over to the keyboard and Evie took out her violin. Kate picked up the microphone.

"I'd like to sing a song called 'Angels by My Side'," said Kate. "Jessie wrote it in memory of her twin baby boys, Anthony and Geoffrey." Donagh and Evie began to play as Kate sang.

> *The day you both were born*
> *Our lives were never the same*
> *Your beautiful faces remain*
> *Forever in our hearts and minds the same ...*

Monique wiped tears from her eyes as Kate sang. The song was beautiful. She looked over to where Geoff sat with his arm around Jessie. Her head rested on his shoulder. She loved them both so much, her heart broke for them all over again. She had prayed so hard that they might someday have another baby. But Jessie had always said, "One life can never replace another." She had added that she would always be the mother of three children and that she had finally accepted that it was just different. The words in her song reflected that feeling. *"I finally now understand two angels by my side was the plan."*

"Oh Mon, it's so sad, but filled with hope too," said Rachel, squeezing her hand.

Sophia sat beside Eoghan; she wiped a tear from her eye and saw that Eoghan was glassy-eyed too. Someone started to sing the "Wild Rover." She glanced at Eoghan again. He still hadn't heard from either of his daughters. Their silence was killing her. She couldn't imagine what it was doing to him. Weddings were such emotional days. They highlighted issues that were so often buried. Live in the now, Sophia Wynthrope. She slipped her hand into Eoghan's and felt a well of love for him. She overheard Evie, Donagh's girlfriend, asking him to sing.

"This should be good," said Eoghan.

Donagh picked up a Spanish guitar and began to play. Evie joined in on violin. Sophia thought her playing was hauntingly beautiful and Donagh's voice was incredible. It was the first time she had heard him sing.

I see your face across a crowded room
I can't think straight just wish you'd feel it too

I can't deny
This love inside
But I just can't stay to watch you walk away

Sophia followed his gaze. He was singing to Monique. What would his girlfriend think?

I wish you'd
Love me, like I love you
We'll make it through the hard times too
Love me like I love you
Together forever
Take a chance
Just hold my hand
Oh hold my hand

Then Evie began to sing.

I see your face across a crowded room
I want to care just scared to feel it too

I can't deny
This love inside
But I'm not enough to make you stay with me

"What's going on at all?" muttered Eoghan. "What a voice!"

I wish you'd
Love me like I love you
We'll make it through the hard times too
Love me like I love you
Together forever
Take a chance
Hold my hand

Just hold my hand.

Sophia noticed Monique had put her head down from the moment Evie had begun to sing. It was Donagh; Monique was in love with Donagh. Sophia closed her eyes for a brief second. When she opened them, Donagh and Evie were singing a big finale together, looking into one another's eyes, smiling. What was he playing at? Sophia was just cross now. How could he write something as beautiful as that song and be such a womaniser?

I love you like you love me
Together forever
Just hold my hand we'll make it through
For ever

The last words were.

Coz, I love you.

Sophia noticed he was looking at Monique again but her head was still down. There was a burst of applause. Then Sophia overheard Lisa's partner, Chad's, loud whisper. "Am I missing something? I thought they were a couple. That girl is stunning. She should be a model. Why was he staring at the little dark-haired girl?" He nodded towards Monique.

"Oh Chad, just look at her, she is so beautiful," said Lisa.

"Whatever!"

Sophia's heart broke for Monique. She was devastated and doing her best not to show it. Sophia looked around for Garvan. "Oh no," she muttered. "What happened?"

"What did you say, love?" asked Eoghan.

She didn't want to get into explaining everything. Instead, she said, "Will we have another drink?"

Eoghan raised his eyebrows. "We might as well. How about a Baileys?"

"Perfect."

"What a day and night!" said Jessie, stretching in the bed beside Geoff. "It was the best wedding I've ever been to."

"Thanks a bunch," said Geoff, turning on his side.

"Not including ours, of course." She laughed.

"Jessie, your song is beautiful."

She lay still. She had been afraid to let the song go. Kate was right. Songs bring people to places in a way like no other. "It's from my heart."

He leaned down and kissed her closed eyelids and then he kissed her lips. She could hear the sound of feet coming up the stairs.

"Mum, where's my Liverpool jersey?" They both laughed just as Sam came into the bedroom.

"There's always later," said Geoff, getting out of bed. "Come on, let's find it."

She showered and went downstairs. Geoff had taken out eggs and sausages and was about to start cooking.

"What is going on with Donagh? I'm really annoyed with him. I just don't like guys who mess women around."

Geoff stood still.

"What?" she said. "I know you are good friends and I really like him too. But Geoff, what does he want to do? Leave a trail of broken-hearted women behind him?"

"Donagh is crazy about Monique. Evie is his friend since they were kids. She just came to the wedding with him."

"Oh, so why can't he just tell Monique how he feels?"

"Why should he? She's with Mr Bigshot Engineer, who leaves her to go to Dubai, breaks her heart and comes back four months later and all is forgiven."

"Has Donagh said that?"

"No, I've never spoken to him about her. I'm just telling you how I see it."

"Well, I don't see it like that."

"How do you see it?" He started to laugh. "We're doing an awful lot of 'seeing' it."

She smiled and sat down. "I'm worn out. I actually don't know how I *see* any of it. I need breakfast."

"Coming up."

Donagh put sausages and rashers on the table. He had already gone to the shop to get some blaas. There was nothing he liked more than sausages with ketchup in soft, floury bread after a late night.

"Breakfast is just about ready," he roared up the stairs. Moments later, he heard Evie coming down the stairs. "No need for all that shouting," she said. Her long red hair was tousled and she had one of his T-shirts on.

"Loving the look, sexy lady. How about some eggs?"

"Yuck! I'd vomit. My head is so sore. What time did we get home?"

"After five, I think," said Donagh, pouring two cups of coffee. She pulled a blaa open and began to spread butter thickly on to it.

"I see you still take blaa with your butter."

She wriggled her nose at him. "Too right, any chance of a bag of Tayto crisps?"

He laughed and got up to look for some. "I'm going to miss you."

"You can come visit me."

"Evie, what am I going to do?"

"Honesty is the best policy. Tell her how you feel, Donagh."

"I tried to last night and she just ignored me for the rest of the evening. She wouldn't even look at me after the song. How clearer could I have made it?"

"Men, you really are stupid."

"Enough of the stupid. I'm hearing that all my life."

"Sorry, but Donagh, how can she possibly know that you wrote that song for her? Find her today and just tell her for once and for all."

"Will you come with me?"

"You must be joking. I think I've caused enough confusion. Anyway I have to pack."

Donagh watched as she bit into the bread. She had flour all over her lips. He smiled and passed her a piece of kitchen roll. "Thanks for coming yesterday. It would have been a long day without you."

"They are a great bunch of people. I really enjoyed it."

"Maybe I will take a trip to Verona, just don't expect me to go to the opera – unless you're playing in it. I suppose I'll have to suck it up."

She laughed and stretched a hand over to rub flour from his cheek.

Later Donagh drove to Butterfly Barn. Grace and Kate had decided that instead of a post-wedding party, they would host a sponsored ride fundraiser. They hoped to raise funds for specialised indoor play equipment for kids with special needs. His head was still hopping and he was planning to ride a horse. Since meeting all of them, he had grown a social conscience. There was no doubt but it was hard not to feel inspired by what they were doing. He had seen Garvan leave the wedding last night. He couldn't help hoping that he and Monique had broken up.

He had spent the past eight weeks on one hand hoping to meet her but also dreading seeing her with him. She hadn't been around Butterfly Barn. He had overheard Geoff telling one of the lads that she had moved Jasper to Oak House because her boyfriend's horse was there.

He found a parking space for the secondhand van he had bought. He went around to the back of it and took out riding boots. He sat on its platform and pulled them on.

"Garvan, you made your feelings very clear. We can still be friends. We have spent four years together. We have so many good memories."

Donagh froze. He didn't want to draw their attention. There was silence. Then it occurred to him that she must be on her mobile phone. He hoped she'd stay within earshot.

"Garvan, if you really cared you would be here. We both know it has not been the same since you came home. We have both changed."

She was obviously listening to what Garvan was saying. "Donagh!" Had she seen him? Then he heard her say, "He has nothing to do with us. Nothing whatsoever. I am hanging up now. Take care, Garvan." She clicked the phone off. He closed the van door and she startled when she saw him.

"What don't I have anything to do with?" he said, walking towards her.

"You scared me!" she said. "It is rude to listen to people's conversations."

"It is rude to speak about someone behind their back." He stared into her beautiful chocolate-brown eyes.

He was so close to her now. He whispered, "What has nothing to do with me?"

Her back was to the stud fencing.

From the moment she saw him, wearing cream jodhpurs and riding boots, with his blond hair tousled and jaw unshaven, he had never looked more irresistible. Her breath caught in her throat. She couldn't remember what she had said to Garvan. But Donagh was dangerous. She could never trust him. Yesterday had been further proof. He was in love with someone else. Why was he doing this? If that beautiful girl couldn't hold his attention, how could she hope to? "I said – it had nothing to do with you." It took all in her power to walk away from him. Flashes of all the time they had spent together in Sophia's and in France played in her mind. How could he be so kind and then hurt her so much?

"Monique," he called after her. Another man calling her name, hurting her again. She was done with them both. It was time she got on with her life and made decisions of her own. But unlike Garvan, Donagh ran after her. He touched her arm. She shrugged him off.

"Stop," he said. "Just listen to me. I wrote that song for you."

"But you sang it with her."

"Evie is one of my best friends. Monique, please can we go somewhere to talk?"

"It did not look that way."

"Please, let's talk."

She desperately wanted to believe him. "I have to tack Jasper."

"I'll get a horse. Meet me in ten minutes over there." He pointed to the stud railing where they had been standing.

She tacked up Jasper. She must be crazy to have agreed but she was sick of just existing. Everybody around her, Grace and Jack, Jessie and Geoff, Kate and Richard, Sophia and Eoghan, her mother and father, Philippe and Eric had experienced this great love. She had found it too. Surely it was worth listening to him.

She trotted Jasper towards the point he had said. She saw him on a chestnut gelding. "Donagh, are you sure about riding a horse? Maybe we can go for a drive and talk."

"No, no, I'm fine. I've been on this fellow before."

He didn't sound very convincing.

"Will I lead?" she asked.

"Whatever, you know where you're going."

Jessie passed by. Monique saw the look of confusion on her face. "We're hacking to Miller's Point."

"Lovely, enjoy yourself. Wait, who gave you that horse, Donagh?"

"I got him out of the stable over there."

"Donagh, he's one of the race horses Geoff is training." Jessie hadn't even finished the sentence. Donagh was off the horse and leading him back to the stable. Jessie and Monique burst out laughing.

"My God, that was a close one. He told me he had been on him before. I thought he was a new riding school horse."

"I'm so glad for you," Jessie whispered, passing close to Jasper. "Donagh, here's the right fellow for you." Jessie took out Caesar. "He's bomb proof."

"Ah, thanks, Jess. I was just in a bit of a hurry so I grabbed the first one to hand."

"Here's the thing, horses are like motor boats, and some are faster than others."

"Don't worry. I'll never make that mistake again. So we're off."

The yard was busy with people preparing for the ride. Geoff saw her from a distance and gave her the thumbs up sign. She spotted Vicky, the girl who had kissed Donagh at Grace's barbeque, gaping at them. "Hi Donagh," she called. "Looking good."

"How's it going?" he said.

She had decided to bring Donagh to Miller's Point, her favourite place on Geoff's land. She took the trek until she could see how well Donagh could ride. She trotted and looked back. Then she cantered on. Again she looked back.

"I'm fine," he shouted above the sound of the horse's hooves. After ten minutes, she stopped at a gate.

"We can continue on the trek or if you'd like we can canter across the field. I will warn you, Jasper will take off and Caesar loves a challenge."

"Let's do it. Who doesn't love a challenge?" He laughed.

She hopped down and opened the gate and led the horse through. Donagh followed. She closed it and got back up.

"Are we putting on a bet?"

"You'll never catch me." She laughed as she took off on Jasper.

Chapter Seventeen

Donagh's heart was in his mouth. He wasn't as sure of himself as he had pretended. He watched as she galloped across the field. It was a remarkable sight. So much had happened since he met her. He still had nothing to offer her but he couldn't let her go.

"Right so, Caesar. Just get me from here to the other side in one piece, okay." He gave him a little kick. Nothing happened. So he tried again. "Ah come on. I know Jessie said you're bomb proof." He tried a few kicks together. It worked. He was off. "Bloody hell." He yelled as the horse cantered across the open field. "How do I stop him?" he roared, wobbling from side to side. He considered throwing himself off. Surely the horse would stop when he ran out of field. He could see Monique's shocked face.

"Pull back the reins. Woah, Caesar, good boy. Stop kicking, Donagh."

"I'm not."

"Keep your hands down and pull back the reins. Woahhhh, Caesar." Her voice seemed to calm the horse. He stopped.

"Oh, Thank f … sorry," said Donagh. "I think we'll go home along the trek."

"You should have told me you can't ride."

"And miss being with you, no way."

She blushed. "I thought the boys were teaching you to ride."

"Yeah, but I only ever went on a trek. The horse just followed the one in front and I'd go up and down. It always stopped when the one in front stopped. But that was some buzz. I'd like to try it again."

"Not today, you won't. You crazy man." She laughed. "You should have seen your face."

"You should have seen yours. Where to next?"

"Up there." She pointed to the hill and said, "No more trotting or cantering."

"Aw."

Just before reaching the top, Monique dismounted. Donagh did the same.

"There is a stream just here. They will need some water and then we can tie them to some branches."

Her heart was pounding again. She was afraid if he came too close he'd hear it.

He put out his hand when she finished sorting the horses. "Come on."

Her fingers entwined his as she led him up to the top.

"Wow, what a view!" he said.

"It is my favourite place in the world."

"I can see why! We're surrounded by woods and then a patchwork of green fields, leading to *my* favourite place in the world – Bayrush Beach." He climbed up onto the large flat stone. "It's even better from here." He reached for her hand to help her up. She stood beside him and looked across towards the ocean. The sea stack they called Everest Rock loomed high. Neither of them spoke. After a few moments, she turned to him.

"Donagh, I'm moving to France for a while. I need to take some time to figure out who I am."

He turned to look at her. His blue eyes held her gaze as she tried to explain.

"I do not know if that makes sense. I should have ended things with Garvan when he surprised me at Dublin airport. However, I was so confused and unsure about everything. I could not think straight. I felt guilty because he had given up his job to come back to me."

"I understand. I can wait for you. You said 'for a while'. That's not forever."

"Donagh, when I'm with you, something crazy happens. I have never slept with anyone but Garvan. Girls are always vying for your attention just like Vicky at the yard."

"Monique, I don't want to be with anyone else but you. You said in France that our time is not right. I agree. I have goals I need to achieve and dreams I want to make come true. If I know you are part of it, well, I would be so 'appy."

"Donagh Mullally, you are making a joke of my accent again."

"Oh Monique Chevalier, I am," he said, leaning towards her. She reached up and kissed him. What started tenderly took off the way it always did. Eventually he pulled away. "Come sit beside me for a while. I just want to hold you in my arms." She rested her head on his shoulder as they sat on the rock looking across to Bayrush Beach.

"My special place is even more special now."

"Here's the deal, Monique. We meet here in six months' time no matter what has happened in our lives. That would be the end of June."

"Will we make it the first Sunday in June?" He nodded and kissed her again.

"Mon, can we be kissing friends until you go?"

She laughed. "I think I would like that too. Did you really write that song for me?"

He nodded and began to say the words. "I see your face across a crowded room. I can't think straight just wish you'd feel it too. I can't deny this love inside, but I just can't stay to watch you walk away." And then he sang the rest softly to her.

"It's beautiful."

"You're beautiful."

"Donagh, I have to show you something." She got up.

He made to stand up too.

"No," she said, gesturing for him to stay sitting. She stood in front of him and opened her jacket. His eyes remained locked on hers. She opened the top button of her jodhpurs and pushed down the band on the right side of her body. She raised her polo shirt. Finally, he looked at the part of her body she was showing him. He got up on his knees and pulled her close to him. His fingers traced the red and purple jagged scars that marked the right side of her body from her hips to just below her breast. He kissed the route his fingers traced and then he rested his head against her bare skin. She ran her hands through his tousled hair. It was silky to touch. Eventually he stood up. He allowed her top to fall back down. His fingers brushed against her stomach as he tied up the button of her jodhpurs. Electric shots pulsed through her body.

"Was this the reason you stopped in Paris?"

"Yes."

He wrapped his strong arms around her. "I love you. They say 'if you love someone you should set them free'. I'll be waiting. Let's go back and have some fun. I really like your friend Jay, and Rachel seems nice too. When she's not giving me cross looks."

"When did she give you cross looks?"

"How about all the time." He laughed and jumped down off the rock. He helped her down. "Now my only problem is how to get back in one piece on that horse."

"I am amazed that you were able to tack that young gelding."

"That was no bother; Geoff showed me."

"But they can be difficult to handle. I'm impressed."

"Don't get carried away, I still have to get back."

She laughed. She felt lighter. She looked up at the clear blue winter sky and thought about her parents. They must be watching over her. It had been a very long time since she had felt so happy.

*

Kate joined Jessie and the girls at a table in the marquee. Her head was full of ideas for Butterfly Barn USA.

"Girls, it was fantastic of you both to offer to do a fundraiser instead of having an after wedding party. Talk about a successful day," said Jessie, tucking into her turkey salad.

"It made sense to me. We might as well get full use of this beautiful marquee. The turnout has been amazing. It's hard to find a seat," said Grace.

"It will be interesting to see how much was raised," said Sophia.

"Well, with a twenty-euro entrance fee and I'd say at least two hundred horses and ponies turned up, sure that's four thousand euro, at least," said Kate, she took another sip of her soup.

"Others have made pledges when they heard what a good cause it is," said Grace.

"That's fantastic," said Jessie. "I can't believe how kind Aisling, the occupational therapist, was to offer one hour a week free of charge to work with the kids. All the mums are thrilled. They are also doing some fundraising of their own and Donagh offered to make some wooden outside play equipment too."

"Jess, how did this come about?" asked Kate.

"It all started when a mother invited another mother to her house for coffee. Both had children in wheelchairs. They had such a nice time chatting and sharing worries, concerns and jokes, that they invited others. Before long, there wasn't enough room in the house. That was when I heard about it. At the school gate, would you believe! So I suggested they could use Butterfly Barn, one morning a week."

"Brilliant," said Kate.

"One of the days Geoff dropped in. He had a football in his hand and one of the boys in the wheelchair asked him to throw it to him. The next thing was the little guy was bouncing it and throwing it to his pal. They were having a great time. That was when Geoff became determined to do something around activities for them. And you all know what he's like."

"Hence the low basketball nets he put up," said Sophia. "And the consideration both he and Donagh took in the design of the adventure park."

"Sophia, we can replicate this in the States," said Kate.

"Exactly, girls, it's just wonderful. I am so excited by all that has happened here. The adventure centre is going to add a new dimension to Butterfly Barn. We can host team-building weekends for community projects and other groups and organisations."

"Geoff wants to run a summer camp for kids with special needs."

"So tell me more about the specialised equipment," said Kate, leaning forward. She listened as Jessie began to explain.

An idea burst into her head. She needed to talk to Richard but she couldn't see him anywhere.

When Monique got back from the trek she untacked Jasper in his stable and went to see how Donagh was getting on with Caesar next door. He pulled her into the stable and kissed her. She broke away. "Someone will see us."

"I don't care."

"Oh but I do, it is not fair. I have only just finished with Garvan. It would not be kind."

"You are too nice. But I get it. Does this mean we have to be secret kissing friends for a while?"

She raised her head and tilted it to the right; looking upwards she thought for a moment.

Donagh smiled. "Are you looking for inspiration?"

"I just thought life shouldn't be about other people's view of me. It should be about my view of myself."

"Okay, profound moment there. Does that mean we're back to being kissing friends?"

"Oh come here."

Ten minutes later, they went into the marquee. It was packed with people who had taken part in the sponsored ride. Joe, yesterday's barman, was serving food. "Well, how's the head?"

She laughed. "No more shots for me."

"That Rachel is crazy when she gets going. Herself and Jay are in a heap today." He laughed as he passed her a bowl of vegetable soup.

She smiled and turned to see where they were. "Come on, Donagh. Let me introduce you properly to Rachel."

Monique could see Rachel's shocked expression as she walked across to join her, then it turned into a huge smile.

"Donagh, meet my best friend in the world, Rachel."

"Hi Rachel." He smiled.

"I thought I was your best friend. I met you first," said Jay, standing up. "We've met a good few times in Jack's place. Good to see you. I was just getting a beer, want one?"

"Sure, I'll join you."

"Oh Monique, you have so much to tell me. I'm thrilled for you." Rachel hugged her. "You deserve the best of everything. And let's face it. He is gorgeous, not as nice as my Jay, of course."

Monique laughed. "Nobody compares to our Jay. Let's meet tomorrow because I need to tell you so much. I'm so sorry I have been so in my own head since Garvan left. You and Jay have been so good to me but I did not realise how much I was blocking you out."

"Monique, I'm your best friend. I always will be. I understand that everybody needs space to figure things out for themselves. Hey, here come the two lover boys."

"Oh Rach, you are the best."

Rachel winked at her.

Kate found Richard outside the marquee talking with Geoff. "Lads, this might not be the time or the place but I'd like to suggest something to you both."

"What is it?" asked Richard.

"We've all seen the work Donagh has done in the adventure park, and in Sophia's kitchen. I'd love to offer him a job in Butterfly Barn USA."

Both Geoff and Richard looked at her and then at one another.

"Kate, did you consider he might not want to leave here?" asked Richard.

"I don't mean forever. He can create an adventure park over there and maybe help on the rest of the building work. There is no work for him here at Butterfly Barn until the spring. He could come until then."

"That sounds like a better plan. We could offer him a good package for his skills and make it worthwhile for him." Richard looked at Geoff. "What do you think?"

"Sounds great, but take a look over there." Kate turned around. Monique and Donagh were walking towards the stables; she was linking him, and laughing.

"Your brilliant idea has just been ruined by the master of us all – love." Geoff laughed.

"Don't you mean – sex?" said Richard, ducking to avoid Kate's punch.

Monique lay in bed. "Yesterday was the beginning of the rest of my life," said Monique out loud, and she startled when she heard another voice.

"That is the best news I have heard in a long time, Monique Chevalier," said Nora, from the open bedroom door. "Now, tea or coffee?"

"Oh Gran, thank you. Thank you for always being here for me. Je t'aime."

"I love you too, pet. We are going to have a fantastic New Year in

France, Monique. I just know it. I think we deserve the full Irish breakfast to celebrate. I don't know how I feel about that continental breakfast business."

"You are so right, Gran. About both!" For the first time in a very long time, she felt light and free. "I'm meeting Rachel at ten in Bonita's so I will have a mini breakfast."

She showered and changed. After breakfast and a great chat with Gran she drove to Bayrush Beach to meet Rachel.

She sat in one of the back booths of Bonita's. She was nervous about telling her about her uncle and the château. But then she thought of Sophia – nobody treated her any differently.

She waved when she saw Rachel.

"Hey Mon, the window seat is free," said Rachel. It was their favourite seat but Monique had chosen the back booth for its privacy. It must have shown on her face because Rachel just slid into the seat.

"Okay, have you ordered yet?" asked Rachel, her face was filled with concern.

"Not yet."

"The usual?"

Monique nodded. Rachel got up. Moments later she was back with a latte for herself and an Americano for Monique.

"Okay, I'm listening," said Rachel.

Monique began to talk. She didn't stop through another coffee.

"Okay, I need air," said Rachel, finishing her second latte. "Let's go for a walk on the beach."

They walked along the wooded trail towards the golden sandy beach. The beach was empty; even on a winter's day Bayrush Beach usually had walkers or surfers around.

"They must know we need the space today," joked Rachel. "So continue." She listened as Monique continued her story and then stopped in her tracks.

"You kissed him that long ago and you never told me! I need to sit down." She found a flat rock and sat down. "I'm stunned. But I'm also hurt. All of this has been going on and you didn't tell me anything?"

"Oh Rach, I still should not say I helped Donagh. It is confidential. Please, you must understand." Rachel nodded her head. Monique continued. "I wanted to tell you about the beach and going back to his bedroom."

"What? You slept with him and never told me!" Rachel hopped up.

"This is crazy. I tell you that my uncle is a count and lives in a château and you are more concerned about Donagh and me."

"Of course I am. That's great and all about the castle or château or whatever it is. Well, I don't really think it's great because I don't want you to leave. But that's just me being selfish. I just think that you and Donagh are perfect together. Actually, Jay thinks so too."

"Rach, I nearly slept with him in Paris."

"OMG, you were in Paris with him!" Rachel's face was incredulous. "And I was worried you were staying in too much with Nora."

"I'm sorry, Rach."

Rachel smiled. "I'm so happy for you, Mon. Come on, let's walk to get some heat into us." She hooked Monique's arm as they walked down the beach. Monique told her about visiting her parents' grave. They were nearly back to the entrance by the time Monique finished talking.

"You need to talk more. Bottling up all that stuff is not good for anybody. I am so glad that you visited your parents' grave and spoke to Nora. These are important things. Now I'm not saying that I wouldn't love a trip to a château."

"Come here," said Monique, giving her best friend a huge hug.

Breaking away, Rachel smiled and said, "What are we going to do with you?"

"I do not know. I was hoping you would tell me."

"No, you weren't. Everybody needs to talk, Mon. By talking you find your own answers. You know in your heart what's best for you. You might make a wrong decision but then you'll just have to make a different one."

"True, I think I know what I need to do."

"And if someone tells you what to do you'd probably do the opposite. My poor mother still doesn't get that." Rachel laughed.

"Thanks for being my friend."

"Mon, he's a good guy."

Monique looked into Rachel's sincere green eyes and said, "He is. We plan to meet in June no matter what is happening in our lives."

"As I said, you need to do what is best for you."

"Let's go out tonight."

"Do you know that is the first time you have asked to go anywhere since Garvan left last June."

"I had not realised."

"We'd invite you, but you never suggested it. I'm glad the old Monique is back. Then again, you were snogging the most handsome guy within a fifty-mile radius besides my Jay. Why would you want to go out?"

Monique burst out laughing and slipped her arm into Rachel's as they walked back along the beach.

"Rach, I feel a whole lot better."

"Told you, talking is good."

Sophia sat in the sunroom reading. But she couldn't concentrate. She could hear Eoghan talking with Donagh in the kitchen.

"So when is the kite-surfing exam coming up?" asked Eoghan.

Donagh yawned and then answered. "The Wednesday after New Year's Day."

"I can nearly see your tonsils with all that yawning. Are you not getting enough sleep?"

Sophia could feel her irritation rising.

"Huh," she said, not realising she had said it aloud. Donagh was living it up while Monique was clearly broken-hearted. She could no longer tolerate his behaviour. At the wedding, he had treated Monique like one of his floozies. Well she had enough. She put down her book and marched into the kitchen. "I am an upfront person and I have to tell you Donagh Mullally that I am so cross with your behaviour. I accept you are somebody who attracts a lot of female attention but that does not mean you can mess with people's lives."

She paused. Both Eoghan and Donagh gaped at her. Then Eoghan looked from her to Donagh and back again. "I'm sorry, pet. But I'm a bit lost here. What are you talking about?"

"You were there, Eoghan. You saw what he did."

"What did I do?" asked Donagh, confused.

"The song," said Sophia.

"Oh yeah, the song," said Eoghan. "Well, I agree with Sophia about that."

"About what?" asked Donagh.

"I didn't think you should have brought that lovely girl to the wedding and, well, it looked to me – to us – that you were singing to Monique. It's not on, son," said Eoghan.

She watched as Donagh scratched the stubble on his chin. She shook her head. She might as well be talking to the wall. Then he scratched his head.

"Lads, let me get this straight. You both think I am seeing, dating, going out, whatever with Evie?"

"Yes," they both chorused.

"Do you mind telling me where I find the time to date anyone? Evie is one of my best friends. She came to the wedding as a favour."

Sophia found that very hard to believe. It certainly hadn't looked that way to her.

"Oh," said Eoghan. "Well I suppose that explains it. Sit down, pet. Will you have a cup of tea?"

She sat down but she did not intend to let it go. Eoghan took out a mug for her and poured her tea. He even began to look for biscuits. The tension was palpable.

"Is the song about Monique?" Sophia decided to cut to the chase.

"Yes."

Sophia sat with her chin resting on her hands. What could she say? To her surprise, Eoghan spoke. "Do you love her?"

"Yes, but she wants some space. I don't blame her. I'm not up to much. I'm only, well, I'm not an engineer, for God's sake."

Sophia's head sank further into her hands. She had thought that she and Eoghan had trouble communicating but these two were the pits. "What are we going to do?" she said.

"Well, at least you're not kicking him out of the house. He has an exam next Wednesday."

She smiled.

"I'm leaving as soon as I get my qualifications. Monique and I have planned to meet in June. She needs space and I need some time to prove I can make something of my life."

"Donagh, you don't need to prove yourself to anyone, least of all Monique. She loves you," said Sophia.

"How do you know?"

"You'll just have to believe me. I have an idea."

"I think I need something stronger than tea," said Eoghan. He went to the drinks cabinet and took out a bottle of Hennessy's and three glasses.

"I just need to make a call," said Sophia. She went back to the sunroom and picked up her cellphone. "Kate, do you have ten minutes to drop by on your way?" She paused for Kate's answer. "Great, see you then."

She went back to join Eoghan and Donagh.

"So?" Eoghan raised his eyebrows.

"Kate and Richard are on their way."

"I thought they had already left. Aren't they staying in Dromoland Castle tonight?"

"They are. Thankfully I caught them in time. Where are you thinking of travelling to, Donagh?"

"I'm heading to the Canary Islands. It's a winter sun destination and I can pick up bar work at night and teach surfing by day. I want to earn as much money as I can. I'm prepared to work day and night. A friend has offered me a sofa bed for a couple of months, so it won't cost much to live there."

She was impressed by his resolve.

"Eoghan knows my ambition is to have a surf school of my own. It's a long-term goal but one I know I can achieve one step at a time. I just didn't allow for falling for someone like Monique. She deserves the best and well you know my story."

My God, she thought, who had destroyed him? His self-worth was so low he couldn't see the talents that oozed from him. There was nothing he couldn't achieve. He had been cast aside because he had a specific learning difficulty. It made her mad. She heard Kate and Richard coming along the hall.

"Thanks for coming over. I promise I won't delay you from your honeymoon."

She saw Kate looking at the table with the brandy bottle and glasses. "Looks serious, what's going on?"

"Who's driving?" asked Eoghan, getting up.

"Richard, but tea is grand for me, thanks, Eoghan."

"I'd like to offer Donagh a job at Butterfly Barn USA. We could definitely use someone with his skills set."

"Brilliant idea," said Kate, looking at Donagh.

"I'm, well, I'm stunned. And yes, I'd love it, as long as I can come back here for the first Sunday in June?" said Donagh.

Richard shook his hand. "It's a deal."

"Okay, I'm delighted, thrilled actually. But didn't I see you and Monique together last night?" Kate asked.

"It's a long story." Donagh smiled.

"We're okay for time. We'll have that cup of tea now, won't we, Richard?" said Kate.

Richard smiled and patted Donagh on the back. Sophia was so pleased. She hoped both Donagh and Monique would find a way to be together. In her eyes they were perfect for each other.

Monique was riding Jasper to Miller's Point. It was the second week of January. So much had happened in such a short space of time. She had travelled with Nora to France for New Year's. They had a wonderful time with Philippe and Eric. Nora had spent hours with Madeline at her house and they had taken long walks together around the lake. Monique had seen a huge shift in her gran. It was as if Nora had finally found a sense of peace that only Madeline could have provided. The French woman had been so kind to her mother and then to her gran. She had brought her and Nora to visit places her mother had loved and to meet friends who had known her parents. The trip to France had also finally allowed them to talk about the past without falling to pieces. It had been a therapeutic experience. She had promised Philippe that she would visit again soon and so had Nora.

Her heart raced every time she thought of Donagh; she had missed him so much when she had been in France. How was she going to live through the next few months without him? He was leaving today. They had gone through Donagh's educational psychologist's report with Kate because she had offered to help Donagh with his reading and writing while he was in America.

With each passing day, she began to feel stronger and more alive. She had also made some decisions. She planned to finish the term with her group, which would bring her to the middle of May. She loved the work and the experience would be good for her CV. After it her only other plan was to meet Donagh again.

She had offered to drive him to the airport today but he had suggested they say goodbye at Miller's Point. She hopped down and opened the gate. When she saw him in the distance under the hill, she smiled.

Donagh watched as the black horse galloped across the field with Monique on its back. Her long brown hair flowed behind her. Jessie would go crazy if she knew Monique was riding bareback and without a helmet. But he was thrilled. It was another memory he could store of her to get him through the next few months.

"Good morning," she called. "Ride with me."

"Are you nuts? Why do you think I walked here?"

But she gave him that look he couldn't resist. He stood on a boulder and climbed on behind her. He held her around her waist as the horse began to trot and then canter. It was an incredible rush, moving in rhythm with her and the horse. No matter what happened he would always love her. She slowed Jasper to a walk along the trail towards Miller's Point. He pushed her hair back and nibbled her ear. She laughed. He began to hum the air of an Italian song his mother used to play over and over again. He loved the melody but had no idea what the words meant. To him it sounded like a man trying to tell a woman how much he loved her.

"It is beautiful."

"Ear nibbling or the song?"

"Both."

"How about this?" He kissed her neck.

"Do you want us to fall off?"

"No, but I want us to hurry up and get to the top."

She laughed again. He loved the sound of her laughter. When they reached the place where she tied up Jasper, he took her hand and walked to the top of the hill. It was a cloudy day. It looked like rain clouds were building out over the sea. They sat in the same spot. He put his arm around her.

"So," he said.

"The song you hummed is called 'Caruso.' It is about the great opera singer's love for a woman he is leaving because he is dying."

"You are so beautiful and clever. How can you want to be with me? I have nothing."

She turned into him and began to kiss him passionately. Then she whispered, "Make love to me."

It was the second time she had asked him. But this time, he kissed her back and then held her face in his hands and said, "Monique, when we make love it will be the right time for both of us. There is a lot of world out there that you and I haven't experienced. I know who I want to be with but you don't, not yet. I'll understand if you find what you're looking for with someone else. I'll just live in hope that you won't."

Tears ran down her face. She never had been so sure of anything in her life but she knew he needed the time as much as she did. She wanted to be an equal going into this relationship, not the insecure girl she had been for so long. He wiped her tears with his thumbs. She rested her head on his shoulder again and they stayed like that until it was time to say goodbye.

Chapter Eighteen

*I*t was the end of May. Monique could hardly believe the term was over. She put the last portfolio on top of the bundle. They were ready for submission to an examiner. There was a great atmosphere in the room. She had loved every minute of her work. Watching faces light up when they achieved some success in what had haunted them for years. She had met so many interesting people over the past few months. It had opened her mind even further. Literacy and numeracy affected people from all walks of life. She wished there wasn't such a stigma to it.

"Thank you all, I have had a wonderful time working with you."

"Well, Monique, I for one am very glad I found the courage to come in that front door," said Rory, a man in his fifties, who had worked as a gardener most of his life. He could identify every plant or tree but he hadn't been able to spell or write. "It's been more than learning to read and write. I've made great friends here in the group. I'm really going to miss it. Thanks for all your help."

"I won't miss ya, boy," said Shane, who was Rory's buddy in the group. She smiled. From the first day, they had hit it off.

"I wouldn't worry about you. I've have enough of you too," said Rory, slapping him on the back.

"I'm looking forward to the numbers class in September," said Lucy, a girl in her thirties who had been sent to a special school because she had a severe speech problem. They had thought she wasn't very bright. Monique had been heartbroken over her. Lucy was very clever and had improved immensely in the small group. Her speech and confidence had come on too. Everybody could understand her and she loved that the group had been so patient and had given her time to speak.

"I wish you all the very best of luck and have a great summer."

"We have a little something for you," said Maeve, a lady in her sixties. She handed her an oil canvas of Bayrush Beach. "We know how much you love it here."

"Thank you so much. It is so beautiful. I will treasure it especially because you painted it, Maeve."

"Ah come 'ere, we chipped in too," said Shane. "There's a bottle of wine to go with it. Since you're French."

She laughed. "I will miss you all."

When the last person left, Monique shut down her computer and began to pack up. The past few months had been a rollercoaster of emotion. She spoke to Donagh on Skype every night. She could hardly wait to see him in sixteen days but first she had planned a trip to France. She was excited and apprehensive about the future. She had better hurry or else she'd be late. She planned to meet Rachel for a bite to eat at Murphy's.

Grace put a cup of coffee in front of Jessie. "I'd love a holiday."

"Get over it, you've had a holiday of a lifetime. Honeymooning in Aspen, no less!"

"That was five months ago. Oh but it was fantastic. I'll never forget the view from the living room."

"Enough, I'm turning green with envy."

"But still, I'd love even just one night away with Jack – on our own."

"Well, that's what you get for 'putting the cart before the horse' as your mother put it."

Grace laughed. When Richard had offered them the keys of his cabin, they hadn't expected it to be a huge house with an indoor pool in the basement with a sauna, jacuzzi and steam room. They had brought the kids on honeymoon and the whole experience was one she would never forget. At night they had been happy to sit in front of a great big log fire from where they could see the lights of Aspen twinkling beyond the glass wall which ran the length of the room. Richard had even organised a tour coordinator who had arranged a crèche for Lily and a camp for Finn while they took ski lessons. It had been incredible.

"But I'd still love one night of no little bodies in our bed."

"Okay, I got the hint. I'll take them," said Jessie, going over to pick up Lily who was sitting on the floor playing with blocks. "Come here, you little dotey. Show me how you are taking your steps." Lily squealed with delight as Jessie swung her around. Then she placed her next to the sofa. Lily balanced herself as Jessie held out her arms. Lily took a step and dropped to the floor.

"She's getting there," said Jessie. "She's only eleven months."

Grace watched Jessie cuddling Lily. She loved Jessie so much. She wished her babies were here to play with Finn. They would have been just a few months older than him. Would they have grown up as friends like her and Jessie? It must be so hard for Jess, but she always said her babies were irreplaceable. She had confided that she had stopped trying to have another child. Grace had noticed a change in her over the last few months. She was doing what she had written in her song. She had finally accepted her babies were angels by her side.

"Finn, stop throwing your toys. You're supposed to play with them not break them," said Grace, picking up a toy tractor that had just lost its front loader.

"Maybe I might withdraw that offer."

"Too late."

They both laughed.

It was getting late when Donagh put the final touches to the wooden sandpit he had built. The weather was getting steadily warmer. When he had arrived in the Hamptons at the end of January, it had been minus five degrees. At first he had thought it was the craziest decision he had ever made. He worked nonstop. If he wasn't roofing, he was painting. He had even tried landscaping. And every night he spoke to Monique. She was his last thought before sleeping and his first when he woke. He had found what he hadn't known he was looking for – in her.

He was so lost in his thoughts that he was disconcerted when he heard someone calling his name. He looked around. It was Kate. She was walking towards him with two glasses in her hands.

"For you," she said, handing him a pint glass filled with Coke and ice.

"Just what I needed, thanks." He took a big swig of Coke. "Beautiful."

"Hey, it's perfect. The height will suit the kids in wheelchairs."

"Or little ones who are not," said Donagh. "They love standing and building castles and stuff. So it works for everyone."

"True. I know you are a recluse these days. All work and no play. But Richard is away in the city tonight so I thought you might drop in for a bite to eat. I've got ham and cabbage. He hates the smell of the cabbage. But an Irish boy, like you …"

"Love it. Yeah, what time?"

"Whenever you're ready!"

"I'll be over shortly so." He handed her back the empty glass and picked up his tools. Just over two weeks left. He smiled when he looked back towards the main house. It was ivy clad and surrounded by mature, manicured gardens. It was one of the oldest mansions in the area. The Wynthropes had been one of the first families to build such a place. Renovations were nearly complete. Richard had decided to provide five-star guesthouse accommodation along with self-catering units in the courtyard that had previously been quarters for the estate workers. He was staying in one next door to Richard and Kate while they waited for their house to be completed. They had opted to build at the other side of the property nearby but far enough for some privacy. His favourite part of the project had been building the barn. It was like the ones he had seen on TV as a child, all redwood with white trim. Sophia was determined to stick with the name Butterfly Barn, so they had great fun planning the build and how it would look inside.

He opened the door of the converted outhouse. He noticed his mother was online, so he clicked and her face appeared.

"How is Oisín today?"

"Much better, thank God. The specialist is pleased with his progress. The medication we changed to is definitely better. We've had fewer episodes these last few months."

"How are you, Mum?"

"I'm good." She always said she was good. But he was never convinced.

"Are you happy, Mum?"

"As happy as I can be. Oh Donagh, I know he's made life difficult for you, but in his own way, he loves you."

He looked into her eyes, a reflection of his own. "How can you say that after everything he has done to us, to you, to me, to Oisín."

"Donagh, he has given you everything you ever wanted."

"But isn't that it, I never wanted things, I just wanted … Ah forget it."

"He's sorry. Since you left, he sees that he was wrong. He just … he did to you what was done to him. He thought by being hard on you, it would make you strong. And in some crazy convoluted way, it did. But he lost you in the process."

"Mum, do you still play that Italian song?"

She nodded and looked down.

"Why?"

She looked up and said, "I play it to remind myself that he loves me and all of you when he behaves as he does. Your father thinks he has to be the best at everything to be someone. Donagh, please remember that life should really be about being the best version of you. Please think about what I said. Don't make the same mistake. I love you, we all do, and we always will."

"I have to go." He had a lump in his throat and he didn't want her to see his unshed tears.

He pulled up a pair of swimming shorts and ran towards the ocean. He needed space. He swam until he was exhausted.

He was grateful Kate had invited him over later. He needed company after that call. He took a shower. What had his mother been trying to tell him? Didn't she realise that he had nothing? He stopped and wiped the condensation from the mirror. He looked at his reflection. "I am just like him?"

He tried to Skype Monique but the internet was acting up again. He went next door. "Kate, is your internet down too?"

"Why do you think Richard went to the office? It drove him crazy yesterday. It kept going down."

"I'll try Mon from here later."

"Make yourself useful and set the table, will you?" said Kate, taking a pot from the cooker.

"Sure," he replied. He loved being around Kate. It was hard to believe she was married to a billionaire and she was getting excited about a ham and cabbage dinner.

"Oh, the smell of home," said Kate. "Well, maybe not your home. You're posh. But certainly mine."

He laughed. "My mother was partial to cooking it too. Okay, not very often I'll admit."

"I couldn't believe it when I saw cabbage at the farmers' market." She laughed. "Get yourself a beer. There's Miller in the fridge."

"Just like home eh. Cheers." He twisted the tops off two bottles and sat down at the little table.

Kate dished up spuds, ham and cabbage. "Are you excited about moving in to the new house?"

"I actually can't believe Richard agreed to live here while it was being built."

"It's a come-down from the penthouse, alright." Richard had surprised them with VIP tickets to the Knicks game at Madison Square Garden. They had gone on a pub-crawl after it and he had stayed at the penthouse.

As always, time flew when he was with Kate. There was never a pause in the conversation. He helped her clean up.

"I hope the smell will be gone by tomorrow," said Kate, laughing. She opened the patio doors wide to let in some fresh air. It was a lovely spring evening. They sat outside.

"It's so beautiful here. The first time I saw the house, it reminded me of the one in the movie *Sabrina*."

"Ah Kate, I can't say I've seen it." Donagh stretched his legs in front of him.

"Harrison Ford was it in. I loved that movie. I really am living the dream."

Donagh picked at the sticker on the bottle. When he didn't answer, she looked over. She was staring at him.

"What?" he asked.

"Talk to me. How are you really doing?"

"Do you have all night?"

"Yeah." She laughed. "Actually I do. Grab a couple more beers from the fridge, Donagh. Sorry I'm being lazy."

"Will do! If I have a hangover in the morning I'm going to blame you, sunshine," he said, going inside.

She laughed and called after him, "I've been there. Thankfully I survived. A couple of beers or a glass of wine now and then is my quota. My problem was drugs."

"Really? I didn't know." He sat back down.

"It's not something I'm proud of. But that's for another night. Tell me about you, Donagh, the real you."

He pulled over another deckchair with his feet and stretched them out on it. She sat across from him and did the same. He began to talk. It was like someone had pressed a button and he couldn't stop. He talked about what it was like growing up. When he was really young he remembered spending hours in his father's workshop watching him making cabinets. His father had brought him with him when he priced carpentry jobs. But everything changed when he was ten years old; his teacher called his parents in and told them he found reading and writing difficult. She offered extra help. Later that evening, he had overheard his father shouting at his mother, saying that no son of his was going into the dunce's class.

"Oh Donagh."

"And that was it. As far as he was concerned, I was useless. When I started to play guitar and keyboard, I bugged him even more. I'll never know why. Then one day I heard him ask my mother where she got the footstool she was using. She told him I had made it. He never said a word about it until two weeks later, at the dinner table. I can still hear his voice: 'You're starting a carpentry apprenticeship with Jimmy Phelan tomorrow.' He hadn't even told my mother. She objected because I hadn't even done my Junior Cert. He just said, 'What's the point? He'll fail anyway.'"

He shifted in the seat. "Kate, do you know what bothered me most?"

"What?" She was sitting on the edge of her seat.

"He did it at the dinner table in front of my four younger brothers."

"Donagh, I'd like to march over and give him a piece of my mind."

"My biggest fear is that I might turn out like him."

"That won't happen."

"The day I heard Monique on the radio changed my life. I got the last place on the literacy weekend. This past year has been a whirlwind. I have dyslexia. I just learn in a different way. I'm not thick or stupid. Do you know for someone who talks so much, you're a great listener, Kate Fitzgerald?"

"Thank you for trusting me, Donagh. Isn't it wonderful that Sophia, Eoghan and Monique helped you?"

"And you too, Kate. This place is going to be fantastic. So many lives can be touched in a positive way."

"I really hope so Donagh. Another beer?"

"Sure, go on."

Kate got up. "When I come back I want to hear all about you and Monique." When she came back, she handed him a beer and sat back down.

"Have to admit from the first time I saw Monique, I was caught. I didn't know it at the time. I looked on her as a bit of a challenge. She was the first girl in a long time who, well, I don't want to sound big-headed, but she didn't offer it on a plate."

"You're a gas man, Donagh Mullally. You didn't have to oblige so much."

"Ouch." He laughed.

"I won't pretend I didn't hear about your reputation." Kate smiled. "We all do stupid things. You're not even near my league. Go on. Sorry I interrupted."

He told her about the learning sessions in the house and how much he had looked forward to them and then the night she had walked in on them. "I'm glad you did."

Kate nodded.

"It's different. She's different." So he told her about the beach incident and staying in his room and meeting her in France and going to Paris to visit her parents' grave and the hotel suite.

"And did you, you know, do it in the hotel suite?"

He paused. He didn't want to betray Monique and talk about the accident and her scar.

"She was going through an emotional time."

"It must have been so hard for her. I can't imagine life without my mother."

Neither could he. Kate's phone rang. It was Richard.

"I'll check the internet connection to see if it's back up," said Donagh, going inside.

He smiled when he saw Monique's face. She was talking out of sync which sometimes happened when the connection was bad.

"How did your last day go?"

She held up the painting. He loved it. She told him she had been out with Rachel. "Donagh, I am going to France on Monday. I would like to spend some time getting to know my family over there."

"That sounds great," he said, but the first Sunday in June was sixteen days away. He had been counting them down. Was this her way of letting him go? She must have seen the disappointment in his face.

"I'll be back for our date."

"That's okay. I thought you were trying to tell me something."

"Donagh, I have never been so sure of anything in my life. You once said you could live in France. Do you still feel the same?"

"Yes, definitely."

"There is so much more I need to tell you face to face."

"Ah Mon, don't do this to me! Now I'm worried."

"I promise I will tell you everything when I see you. No more secrets."

"Okay, see you tomorrow online. I'd better get back to Kate or she might start talking to herself. And we already know how crazy she is."

Monique laughed and blew him a kiss goodbye. He smiled but drew the line at blowing a kiss back.

"Mon is going to France."

"Did you meet her uncle when you were there with Geoff?"

"God, no, we were busy checking out sites. She's planning to check out job prospects over there." He took a swig from the bottle.

"How do you feel about that?"

"I loved it there. Sure, it's a surfer's paradise."

He stayed a while chatting about Bois Saint Etienne and his impression of the place and about how he would love to own his own surf school either in Bayrush or France.

Grace sat at her kitchen table with Monique who had her laptop open. She listened as Monique spoke passionately about how extensive the literacy problem was both in Ireland and in other countries. They were surrounded by paper. A mixture of internet sources and CSO statistics, British studies and American studies on literacy.

"Why, oh why, did I start this?" Grace put her head in her hands.

"Are you writing fact or fiction this time?" asked Monique.

"Fiction but I like to get some facts before I launch into something."

"You have to speak to people who are living with this challenge. Find the real stories." She pointed at the papers spread across the table. "These are proof that the western world has a literacy issue and if countries who historically have provided an education system have difficulties then what about the countries with no education system?"

"You are so right."

"Grace, you write about people and their experiences. That is why I can relate to your books. Most of us have felt like some of your characters at one time or another. If readers are interested in an area that you write about, they can follow it up. You can provide links from your website."

"Monique, I'll boil the kettle. Let's have a cuppa and you can tell me how Donagh is doing."

Grace heard a cry on the baby monitor. "I'll just check on Lily."

Monique was making a pot of tea when Jack arrived in.

"Boy, did I time that well?"

Monique sat with Jack at the kitchen table. He was on a high. A horse he had bought that Jay and Rachel were training was due to race at the weekend. It had performed well on the gallops that evening.

"Jay is a natural jockey and Rachel is just so perceptive around horses. She can just see something in them and knows how to bring out the best. So enough about me. How's life with you?"

"Good. Jack, how is Garvan getting on in Dubai?" He hadn't answered her calls or texts. His mother had even crossed the street to avoid her.

"One phone call and Garvan had his old job back. He was promoted recently too."

"That's good." She looked down.

"Monique, Bayrush was never enough for Garvan. My brother and I knew that. Marie does too. She just needs someone to blame."

"I feel so guilty."

"Well don't. Staying together for the wrong reasons would be worse."

"I'm glad he's doing well over there."

"He's living the life he wants. You need to do that too."

"How did you know, Jack?

"Know what?"

"That you loved Grace?"

"I knew it from the first day I saw her. She was a fifteen-year-old with an attitude. But Monique, we put an awful lot of water under the bridge before we found one another again."

"You still found her though."

"If you love Donagh, don't do what we did. I wish Finn was my biological son. I wish we didn't have to send him to France in the future for holidays with his dad or fit in visits to Dirk's mother here. Life is complicated enough. I want him to know how loved he is by everyone but I'm always afraid I'll be the one he resents when I have to say no. I'll always just be his stepdad."

"Sorry about that, Mon," said Grace, coming back into the kitchen. "Finally a cup of tea."

"It's well cold now, Gracey. I'll make a fresh one," said Jack.

After another long day at work, Donagh came out of the bathroom and saw a Skype notification pop up on his laptop. With just a towel around him, he clicked the key. Butchie and Pepe's faces looked out at him. It was great to be able to chat to the lads for free. They were both in great form. Butchie asked if there might be any summer work for him. He had just finished college. Donagh told him he'd check it out. "The American girls would love you here."

Pepe laughed and pushed him. "Butchie, you might finally have some luck with the ladies."

"Funny, ha, ha. You're no James Bond."

"He does have a look of Will Smith, though," Donagh grinned.

"Oh give me a break. I'll have to listen to that for a week."

His mobile rang. It was Kate. "Sorry lads, I have to go. See ya." He disconnected.

"Donagh, can you drop in this evening? I want to run something by you."

"Okay."

"Make it late, like nine-thirty or so. I want Richard all to myself for a while. Last night was the first night we were apart since we got married. And although I enjoyed your company and all, well ..."

"I get the picture. Just don't give me the details." He laughed.

At about nine-thirty, he knocked on their door. He heard giggles. Jeez, he obviously hadn't given them enough time. He turned to walk away when the door opened.

"Come in, mate. Sorry about that." Richard's hair was sticking up and his T-shirt was inside out.

"I'll come back tomorrow night."

"Come in, Donagh. We could be at it tomorrow night too," shouted Kate, from the bedroom.

"Told you, Richie. You are a lucky man," he muttered.

Richard made to punch him in the stomach and handed him a beer at the same time. "I hear you're trying to get on the property ladder?"

"Yeah, I'm saving hard to get a deposit together. I really appreciate the chance you have given me. The money I'm earning is going directly into the bank at home. It costs me hardly anything to live here. I don't go out. Kate feeds me most of the time. I want this, Richie."

"Okay. Kate said you mentioned both Ireland and France. I suggest that you do a cost analysis on both. Cost of land, labour etc. and do some market research. Type of clients, weather conditions, competition etc. Then make a decision. If you bring me some well-researched figures, I'll certainly look at being an investor on the project. I say, clearly an investor because it will be completely your venture. I will act as a banker and as such I need to be paid back with interest no matter what. Let me add, I have absolute faith in you, Donagh."

He was stunned. He looked from one to the other.

"I appreciate your offer. I promise you'll get every cent back with the agreed interest. Thanks, Richard, and you, Kate, for giving me a shot at this." He put out his hand. Richard shook it.

"I need to speak with Monique. She will be a huge part of any decision I will be making."

"Of course," said Richard, getting some more beers from the fridge.

"Kate," Donagh whispered. "He knows about my problem and he's still prepared to invest in me."

"It's not something to be ashamed about. You are a fantastic person; lots of people have the same problem and have achieved incredible things. You are doing something about it."

Richard came back and passed him a beer.

"Cheers."

Kate sat with her feet up taking a well-deserved break. Richard was due home soon. Richard had suggested they postpone the opening day for a few weeks. They had been working at a crazy pace since their honeymoon. She had agreed. So she had come up with an idea for Donagh. She sat outside in the shade sipping iced tea.

Donagh came out to join her.

"Why don't you change your ticket and go to France?"

He sat down. "Yeah, maybe I'm killing time here, Kate. Everything is pretty much done, except to help you move into the new house."

She gave him a look. "There are movers for that."

"Oh, excuse me." He laughed.

"Ah, it would be a fantastic surprise for Monique. Also it will be easier to research sites and costs locally."

"I know a great guy called Thierry. He'd have local knowledge about what is happening."

"Let's take a look at flight availability."

Monique came out of the en-suite bathroom. She walked across the huge bedroom to the window. An antique burgundy armchair was placed beside it. She sat in it and looked across the vineyard towards the lake. She wondered what he was doing. The melody of his song played in her head. She had heard him strum it so many times. Just little pieces when she'd watch him work on it on the jetty in the far distance. Sometimes his voice would travel on the wind. He'd strum, stop, hum, and sing into the voice recorder. She used to wish he had meant it for her. She hummed it and then began to sing it.

She walked down the stairs. The library door was open. Philippe saw her and waved at her to join him.

"Eric has left for Bordeaux. He is planning an art exhibition."

"Oh, I thought he was a curator."

"Yes, he worked as a curator in Amsterdam for the past thirty years or so. But now that we can both live here, it seemed crazy to continue commuting to Amsterdam. He has been painting for years. I think it is time for him to do what he loves. He has been offered an opportunity to exhibit."

"Does he have enough work completed?"

"Just about but he will say no. Artists are never happy with their work. I'm sure he will give you a peek at his studio. We converted one of the outhouses to give him peace and space."

"That is fantastic, Philippe. Can I ask your advice?"

"Of course, my dearest.

"I would like to find work here using my degree."

"Oh Monique, that's the best news. I hoped and prayed that you would make this decision. I have followed your progress for years."

"How did you know about me?"

"Through my solicitor, I requested him to keep me informed about you."

"Oh."

"But you must understand, you are very important to me. Although I could not be in your life, I wanted to make sure that you were cared for and safe."

"It is all still surreal."

"Shall we take a stroll around the estate? I want you to see a working day. Always, it has been weekend or holiday time when you visit."

Donagh's flight landed in Bordeaux in the early afternoon. Kate had hardly given him time to think about coming here. He had booked a room at the Hotel Pilate and he planned to ring Monique when he was actually in Bois. He went to the car hire desk. Within twenty minutes he was driving the VW Golf out of the airport heading south for two hours.

He had trawled the internet with Kate looking for estate agents in the Gascoigne Region. He had set up a couple of viewings of both sites and properties. It was amazing how much they had organised in a night. He had also contacted Thierry and had arranged to meet him tomorrow morning.

His phone rang. It was his mother. He looked for the next safest place to pull in. He hoped there was nothing wrong at home. He took the next exit off the main road. His mind was working overtime. What if something had happened to Oisín?

He pulled into an entrance to a field and called her back.

"Mum, is everything okay at home?"

"Yes, it's just …"

"Don't tell me something has happened to Oisín?"

"God, no, he's fine. It's just I need to tell you something. It has been on my mind constantly. It's just that, well, I didn't want to betray your father."

"Mum, what is it? What's the matter?"

"He can't read. He thought by pushing you the way he had been pushed it would make you strong. Since you left he has … he's devastated. You're so like him. You can do anything, fix things, build things, play guitar. You have so much ability; he didn't want anyone to call you stupid like what had happened to him. That's why he works so hard. He's always trying to prove himself."

"Mum, I'm not like him." He hung up. He turned the car around and rejoined the road to Bois Saint Etienne.

Chapter Nineteen

Sophia heard Eoghan's pager go off. Oh no, she thought. There must be an emergency at sea. Her heart thumped.

"Have to go." He kissed her and left. She watched from the sunroom as he got into his jeep and drove away. Eoghan had promised not to go out in the boat again. The guidelines said fifty-five was the upper age and Eoghan was fifty-nine, but he had found some small print that said if he had a yearly medical he was good to go until he was sixty. Of course, Eoghan had been delighted with that discovery, but she wasn't. The ocean had taken enough from her so he had promised he would take more of a back seat.

She was edgy. Her phone rang.

"False alarm. It was some kids caught on the rocks by the tide. The cliff rescue sorted it. Now that Butchie, Pepe and a few more new volunteers are here, I decided to run a training session. Pepe is proving to be a natural helmsman."

"I'll see you later. We'll go out for a bite to eat."

"I'll look forward to it."

She opened the door and wandered down to the end of the garden. The sun glistened off the ocean. It was a perfectly clear day. She had nothing to worry about so she decided to visit Grace and the kids.

Monique walked with Philippe around the courtyard. The place was full of activity.

"When did you open the restaurant?"

"At the beginning of the month. We have so many plans for the place. My father wouldn't allow change, Monique. Both Eric and I have a vision for this place. Take a look, the views would inspire even lesser mortals like me to paint. I believe we can attract people to come to stay at the château. The upkeep of it is incredibly expensive. Thankfully, the vineyard runs at a profit. But we see no need to live in this huge place alone. Maybe you will live here too."

"Philippe, I am meeting someone very special to me in Ireland soon. I will have a clearer plan for the future then. I am honoured that you feel this way about me. But I cannot make a decision yet."

"His name is Donagh Mullally?"

"How do you know about Donagh?"

"Your grandmother told me. She asked me to take good care of you while you are here. I hope we can be part of your life too."

Her phone rang. She smiled and held it up to show Philippe who it was. He smiled and went to speak to a staff member.

"Hi Donagh, you are up very early. It must be only 6 a.m. in the Hamptons." She was thrilled to hear from him.

"You will never guess where I am."

"Are you back in Ireland already?"

"No, I am at the Hotel Pilate."

She was stunned. "Oh my goodness, I will be there in a few minutes." She hung up. Philippe rejoined her.

"Monique, you are shaking."

"Donagh is here."

"But this is wonderful." He smiled. "Tonight will be a celebration."

"Philippe, you do not understand. I have not told him about this." She threw her hands in the air.

Philippe looked confused. "But is this not better? He loves you as you are."

"He does not think that way. He is ambitious and complicated and so many other wonderful things. He thinks he has to prove himself just because my ex-boyfriend was an engineer."

"What does Donagh work at?"

"He is a carpenter."

"I see." Monique couldn't read Philippe's reaction. Was it approval or disapproval? Maybe Donagh was right – people were judged by their occupation. Well, it did not matter to her. She ran to the car.

"Monique," called Philippe. "Please bring Donagh to meet us. He should not judge us and I shall not judge him."

"Thank you, Uncle." She got into the car and drove the fifteen minutes to Bois Saint Etienne. She saw him standing outside the hotel. Her heart flipped. She pulled up and he climbed in. He leaned over to kiss her. She kissed him back, briefly. She began to rejoin the traffic.

"Okay, so maybe you don't like surprises!"

She turned to him. "We need to talk." She parked at the beach car park and got out. The beach was quiet, unlike her mind. She walked hurriedly towards the ocean.

"Wait up!" said Donagh. "Monique, if I'd known you'd react like this I wouldn't have come."

"I just did not expect you to come here."

"Look, if you've met someone else, just say and stop all this shit."

She turned around. "I have not."

"So just tell me then."

"You will be … I do not know." She felt like being sick. "Count Philippe Chevalier, my uncle, lives in Château Vieux De La Lac here in Bois St Etienne."

"You are not serious!" His blue eyes flashed with a mixture of confusion and bewilderment.

"You see. Just as I thought. It should not make a difference."

"But, Mon, it does."

"Why? I am still me."

"I'm talking about building a surf school and a little place beside it for us."

"I would live in a shed as long as I was with you."

He gave her a disbelieving look. "Come on Monique, give me a break. Why didn't you tell me? We talk every day!"

"I wanted to tell you in person."

"Then why didn't you tell me that day at Miller's Point?" he asked, his beautiful eyes fixed intently on hers.

"I told you I was messed up and confused. I needed time to figure things out. I did not know about him until a few months ago."

He seemed to soften. "Look at me," he said. "I love you and I always will. I can't help it. It's just how it is."

He took her hand. She pulled it away.

"Donagh, you confuse me. I do not understand. What does 'it's just how it is' mean?"

"I'm only twenty-six years old and you're twenty–three. I didn't plan to feel like this about anyone yet. I hoped that someday I might have something to hold somebody like you."

"Donagh, you believe you have to provide for me. I just need someone to love me."

He sat down on the sand. "I spoke to my mother today. She told me my father can't read and that I am just like him. I've been acting the same way. I am him."

She sat beside him and pulled him close to her. "Oh Donagh." She stretched over and ran her hand along his jaw. "I love you.

He reached over and kissed her. "That's the first time you said it."

"Come, meet my family," she said. They walked hand in hand back up the beach.

She rang Philippe to tell him they would be at the château in twenty minutes. She drove through the gates of the walled estate along the winding road toward the château. When it came into view, she stopped to see Donagh's reaction.

"Wow."

"It is very beautiful. You will see the lake soon."

Both Philippe and Eric were standing in the forecourt.

"Which man is your uncle?" asked Donagh.

"The man with the peppered grey hair. Eric is his partner."

"Business partner?"

"No, life partner."

"Oh," said Donagh, getting out of the car. Monique was already out and had run into her uncle's outstretched arms. Then she turned to introduce Donagh.

"It is a pleasure to meet you, young man."

"Hello, eh, Philippe," said Donagh, shaking his hand and then Eric's. "How's it going, Eric?"

She noticed how self-conscious and awkward Donagh was.

"It's some job. The place is just fantastic."

She relaxed when she saw that both Philippe and Eric were smiling.

Philippe led Donagh towards the vineyard. "Come on, let's give you a tour."

Donagh's jaw dropped when he saw the vineyard. There were coaches and private cars in the parking area and tourists milling around. He followed Philippe and the others into the huge stone building. It housed a wine-tasting area and cellars to the side of it. The restaurant was bustling with people.

"This is amazing," said Donagh.

"Let me show you the outhouses. I believe you were in America converting outhouses and building barns. Maybe you will come here to do some work, non?"

"How do you know about that?" asked Monique.

"Your gran, of course. We speak regularly. We are family now."

She smiled.

"I'd love to but we have a lot to talk about first," said Donagh, taking her by the hand. She hugged him and planted a kiss on his lips in front of the two men.

Philippe laughed. "Je pense que l'amour est dans l'air. Let's go and celebrate."

"What did he say?" asked Donagh, looking from Monique to Eric.

"He said, 'I think love is in the air.' Come my friend," said Eric, leading Donagh towards the château.

"It sounded a whole lot better in French."

Eric laughed.

Kate couldn't believe her eyes when the coastline she loved so much appeared. "What a surprise!"

"We've waited long enough for our honeymoon, what's another few days! I thought it would be nice to pay a visit on our way to Paris," said Richard.

"You're just so cool." He was sitting opposite her. She wanted to open her seat belt and jump into his arms but the private jet was about to land at Waterford airport. "Oh Richard, I love you."

He smiled across at her and said, "I love you too."

She was so grateful for the life she was leading. "I can't wait to see Mam. Can you imagine what she'd say if she saw this?

"We'll bring her and Nora to the opening of Butterfly Barn. I'll send the jet for them."

"OMG Richard, she would love that." Kate paused. "Richard, on this visit I'd like you to meet Marilyn, my eldest sister."

He looked at her quizzically. "I've met her lots of times."

"I mean, properly. We've had a difficult relationship over the years, and I suppose I've been thinking about her so much since our wedding. She was the eldest and I think she saw more of what was happening in our family than the rest of us. She was the one who had to leave school early to go to work because Dad left and there was very little money. She looked after us when my mother could hardly get out of bed those first few months. I blocked out all those memories and I didn't show her the respect she deserved. She was so angry with me for turning to drugs. I let her down and when Grace helped me find my way back, I stayed angry with Marilyn for judging me. I never saw it from her point of view. Every time I looked at Marilyn my guilty conscience would lurk."

"Wow Kate, that is powerful."

"Art therapy has a lot to offer, Richard. Come on, before I start crying."

He opened his seatbelt. "You're just amazing." He kissed her.

As Richard drove out of the airport in the direction of Rose Cottage, she called Jessie. "Have you heard anything from Monique?"

"Yes, she sent a text. Donagh has met her uncle."

"How did that go?"

"I've no idea, but, well, there's a story. I couldn't mention it before now."

"There always is. Go on, tell me."

"Monique's uncle is a count and he lives in a château in France."

Kate paused. If it was anybody else, she would be thrilled, but Donagh was different. She had no idea how exactly he would react to that news especially since Monique hadn't told him.

"Interesting times ahead, I'd say."

Donagh was glad he had dressed in a pair of chinos and a shirt, crumpled as they were from travelling through the night and driving. He had never imagined that Monique's uncle would host a banquet for them. He hadn't a clue what people were saying. Madeline, a woman in her sixties, and another younger woman called Mimi kept smiling at him.

"Okay, I think we need to speak English as Donagh is at a loss," said Philippe. "I apologise but you know how we French love to only speak French."

Donagh smiled. He held his tongue in case he said something out of the way.

The older woman reached across to him. "You are très … how you say?"

"Handsome," said Mimi.

He felt foolish. What was he supposed to say to that?

Monique winked at him. He smiled.

"You have good teeth," said the older woman.

"Ah, here is the next course," said Philippe, grinning in his direction. "Escargots."

He wasn't sure what that meant but everybody looked at him. He took a big slug from his glass of red wine.

"Snails," whispered Monique.

"Look Mon, I'm mad about you and all that but it's just not happening. I am not eating them." He thought he had whispered but he was overheard and everybody burst out laughing.

"No, Donagh, not tonight. We will break you into French cuisine gently."

"You got me there, Philippe." Donagh grinned and Philippe laughed. They were so welcoming. He began to relax. He spoke to Eric, who had grown up on the coast in Holland and loved the sea. He was excited about living so near the coast again. Henri, Monique's cousin, was a professor of some sort based in Bordeaux. Donagh figured he was in his early thirties and seemed friendly enough too. And Rosario, the housekeeper, joined the table to eat with them. Donagh liked that. The Count didn't act like Donagh had imagined he would.

"I can tell you about the best surf areas along the coast," said Henri.

"That would be great, thanks." He was beginning to feel the effects of the wine and jet lag.

"Donagh, I hear you are a musician. Will you play something for us?" asked Philippe.

"I will sometime when I have a guitar." But Eric disappeared and moments later came back with a classical Gretsch guitar.

"Wow!" said Donagh, getting up to admire it. Eric handed it over.

"Really?" said Donagh, taking the beautiful instrument from Eric.

"Of course, play us some Irish tunes."

Monique sat beside Philippe listening to Donagh play guitar.

"He is very good. Does he play professionally?"

"No, surfing is his passion."

Donagh began to strum the melody that was so familiar to her. She looked over. Their eyes locked as he began to sing.

I see your face across a crowded room …

There was complete silence in the room. When he finished there was a burst of applause.

"I have never heard that song before," said Philippe, clapping his hands.

"I wrote it for Monique," said Donagh, still looking at her. She got up, went over, and kissed him in front of the whole room.

Everybody cheered.

"I'm a bit on the tipsy side," said Donagh, passing the guitar back to Eric. "I don't want to damage it."

Eric laughed and began to strum. "I am not sure I can follow that."

Donagh smiled. "Cheers Eric, but anyone who owns one of them can play guitar. Go for it."

Eric began to play. She rested her head on Donagh's shoulder. Eric played guitar beautifully. After a while Donagh asked him if he knew "Caruso".

"Of course."

She saw Eric exchange a glance with Philippe. They were so in love even after all their years together. Eric began to pluck the guitar,. The sounds of the evocatively beautiful melody filled the room, and to her surprise her uncle began to sing in Italian. She looked at Donagh. She had never felt so contented in her life. Donagh's lips were stained with red wine and she could see he was definitely feeling its effects.

"Philippe, Eric, that was so beautiful," she said when the clapping ended. Eric began to play again. She did not recognise the air. This time Eric began to sing in French. He sang as though only he and Philippe were in the room. The song was about acceptance of difference and of all kinds of love between people. It was beautiful. When it ended, she asked what it was called.

"La Difference," said Philippe, holding up his glass of wine in a toast. She held up hers and so did Donagh.

"That was incredible. But lads, I'm done. I need a taxi." His words were slurred. There was still a full glass of wine in front of him. Eric had been topping it up all evening.

"There is a very big room upstairs. I'm sure you will both fit in it," Philippe grinned.

"Philippe, I was just sayin' … what was I saying again?"

Monique laughed. "I think he needs sleep," said Monique, helping Donagh up.

"Good night, my dearest and young Donagh. It has been a great pleasure to meet you."

"Good night, Philippe. Night all," said Donagh, wobbling towards the door. "Where am I goin'?"

"He will get used to the wine yet," Eric smiled.

"No offence, lads, but I'm never drinking that stuff again."

They all laughed as she guided him out the door and up the stairs to her room.

"Jeez, this is some place. Only I'm seeing two of everything."

She smiled, holding on to him as they climbed the sweeping staircase.

"Look at that chandelier."

She opened the door and he saw the big four-poster bed. "Oh come here," he said as he threw himself face down on it. She laughed and went to the bathroom.

When she came out he was snoring in exactly the same position he had landed. She didn't try to move him. She placed the top cover over him and climbed in beside him. Within minutes, she fell into a contented sleep.

She woke to the feel of his arms around her. Sunlight streamed through the long windows making diamond shapes across the huge room. She turned towards him. He was still on top of the duvet fully clothed while she lay underneath it with just a vest top on.

"How's my beautiful girlfriend this morning?" he asked. His lips were red and his hair was tousled. He looked both funny and gorgeous at the same time.

"So I am your girlfriend. That is presumptuous of you!"

He laughed. "Well, you'd better be. I've chased you long enough. My God, I travelled halfway across the world to be with you."

"You should see your lips." She grinned.

He laughed. "It's my head I'm worried about. It's thumping. I swear Monique, never again am I drinking that stuff. Give me a pint of Guinness any day." He hopped up and went to the en suite. "I look like a clown," he called. She heard him turning on the shower. If only she was brave enough she would get in with him. Oh God, she thought. Knowing her luck, she'd probably trip on the soap or something silly. Instead she got up and pulled up a pair of jeans. She sat in one of the antique chairs near the window and gazed at the view. She remembered the first time she had sat in the same spot. How much her life had changed in such a short time. He came out of the bathroom with just a white towel wrapped around his waist. Her breath caught. He was incredibly beautiful.

"Why are you dressed?"

She blushed. He came closer and took her hand in his. She stood up and he began to kiss her. First her forehead; she closed her eyes and took in the freshness of him as he kissed her eyelids, and down along her cheek. He pushed back her long hair; his bare touch sent shivers through her. He began to kiss along her shoulder and up the nape of her neck. Her body tickled in anticipation. She turned to him. His lips found hers. He kissed her so passionately; she matched him. She was finally where she was always supposed to be, at one with him. He swept her off her feet and they both fell into the bed. He laughed as his towel fell away. He opened the top of her jeans and traced his fingers to the part of her she hated so much. He pushed up her vest top and pulled it over her head. "Now I can see you, you are so beautiful. He bent his head and traced kisses along her scarred side and then his hands touched her breast for the first time. She had never felt anything like this before. The anticipation was almost too much. This time she prayed there would be no interruptions. She was ready to give herself to him completely and totally.

Sophia made scrambled eggs; she added smoked salmon and some herbs. Eoghan was coming around to it. He still much preferred a fry-up for breakfast but she was working on him. He had gone to get the newspapers. She looked out from the kitchen towards the glass wall of the extension.

The sky was filled with great sweeps of dark grey clouds ready to burst any minute with rain and the winds were getting worse. The forecast had been wrong. A storm was definitely brewing. Their house was perched on the cliff and was inclined to get the worst of the wind but still she hoped the fishing vessels were tied up and that holidaymakers would not take any silly chances today.

"Hi honey, I'm home."

She smiled. That was his line no matter how much Donagh joked with him about it.

"It's wild out there," said Eoghan, taking off his coat. "Sometimes these summer storms are worse than winter ones."

She saw him check his pager. Her heart sank.

"It's days like today that I wish you'd retire from the sea rescue and let some of the young guns take over." She handed him his plate.

"Thanks, pet, it looks delicious." He put the plate on the counter.

"I can see you making faces." She laughed.

"If I promise to give up the sea rescue, will you promise I won't have to eat this anymore?"

She laughed even louder. He gave her an amused look. "I'm kidding. It's lovely, really. The lads are good, just not very experienced yet. Thankfully, there hasn't been any big drama this year."

Yet, she thought. It was only May. She changed the subject.

"I'm looking forward to this evening, are you?"

"It will be great to get us all together in the one room. It will be the first time since the weddings." He smiled. "What's for dinner?"

"I decided to keep it simple – roast beef and all the trimmings."

"Perfect, with your carrot, turnip and parsnip speciality, I hope. And your tiramisu. Oh, I'm eating it already."

"You love your food, Eoghan Forrester."

"I do, girly. I'll peel some spuds and prepare the veggies."

"Great, I'm hoping to finish Grace's book. She's asked me for feedback before it goes to the editor."

They chatted over coffee about so many things. She looked across at him and thought how lucky she was. Her life couldn't be any better. It would be perfect, if only his daughters would contact him. It was a subject he'd never bring up. She'd dearly love to send a letter but never would.

She had been thrilled too that Richard and Kate had surprised them with a visit. It was a perfect excuse for a gathering. Rachel had offered to babysit Finn, Lily and Sam. So there would be eight plus Nora and

Molly; it would be the first time they were all together since the wedding. She was really looking forward to it

Monique browsed the swimwear rails at the surf shop. Over breakfast, Henri had given them the names of the best areas to go surfing. Donagh had suggested they surf before setting off for the rest of the day to meet the estate agents. Thierry had called to say he had a job that had run over and he would not be able to meet Donagh. Monique was glad. She would have him all to herself.

She held up a bathing suit. Donagh looked over and made a face. She looked at him questioningly. He came towards her and browsed the racks.

"What's wrong with these?" he asked, pointing to a rail of bikinis. She looked down at her side.

"So what? You're beautiful, Monique." She turned away from him to hide the tears in her eyes. He came up behind her. "What's wrong?"

"Nothing, I just remembered something."

"Is it the accident? Oh God, I'm sorry. I shouldn't have said anything. You should wear whatever you're comfortable with."

It wasn't the accident she had remembered. It was a time when she had gone shopping with Garvan for their first holiday together. She had picked up a bikini. He had made a face and then picked up a bathing suit. She had never worn a bikini since because of that moment. Garvan had never acknowledged her scars nor had he ever touched them.

She walked back to the rack and picked up a pretty bikini that had caught her eye. She smiled and went to the counter to pay. She asked to use the changing rooms while Donagh hired the boards.

On the beach, she took off her T-shirt and dropped her shorts. "Last one in is a rotten egg."

He ran after her, caught her, and swung her around in his arms. He carried her into the ocean and dunked her. She emerged spluttering, splashing and laughing. She tried to catch him but he was too fast. He dived into the next wave.

She had the most fun she had had in a long time, ducking, diving and generally fooling around in the sea. Donagh swam over and wrapped his strong arms around her. The water had slicked back his hair and his blue eyes danced. "Let's get the boards."

They waded back to the shore and picked up the abandoned surfboards. "I'll just run through the basics."

"No need, you can just catch me as I fall." She ran into the water, laughing.

*

Donagh watched as Monique caught a wave. He started whooping when she managed to get to her feet but then fell over. He couldn't believe what had happened between them in less than twenty-four hours. He had never felt so happy in his life. The weight of the world had lifted off his shoulders. He didn't know what was going to happen next but nor did he care because together they would figure it out. He wanted to hold her in his arms forever. She fell off again and came up spluttering.

"I am getting worse not better."

"Just wait a sec." He ran into the shore with his board. He left it on the beach and ran back out to her. "Now let me teach you." He showed her where to place her body on the board and he explained how to catch a wave. He relished touching her and being with her. She kissed him at every opportunity and he couldn't get enough of being with her.

"This is better." She laughed. "Your lips taste of salt." She kissed him again.

He pulled her down under the water still kissing her. She broke away first and came up gasping for air. "You are such a joker."

He laughed and climbed back onto the board. He perched on it, bobbing on the gentle swells. "Hop on." He pointed to the spot in front of him. He helped her up. She rested her back against his chest as they floated together. He would remember this day forever. After a while, he asked, "Are you hungry?"

"Only for you." She laughed. "I have always wanted to say that. It is so ..."

"Corny. But I do love when you say I 'ave and use French words. It's just so sexy."

"I will use them more often. You will have to learn French, ma chére."

"And so I will, ma chére." He nuzzled her neck.

"You like my neck."

"I like all of you."

"Corny."

"Ha, ha. Let's go to the patisserie and buy some food for a picnic. We can dry off on the beach and get moving."

Fifteen minutes later, he watched as she sat on a grassy bank eating olives and some bread rolls. She had seen Orangina, the soft drink of her childhood. She took a swig of it.

"Does it taste as good as you remember?" She nodded and smiled. He wondered how he would have coped if he had been orphaned. Then he thought of his mother. He hadn't rung her back. "Mon, I have to ring my mother to apologise. I was rude yesterday. I hung up on her."

"That would be nice, Donagh. I will get dressed."

His mother answered on the first ring. He apologised and promised to call over as soon as he got back. It was time he cleared the air with his father. No matter what way it would turn out. His mother had been caught between them for too long. She told him she loved him.

"I love you Mum. There is someone special I want you to meet when I get back."

"I'll look forward to it. Is she American?"

"No Mum, I forgot to mention it but I'm actually in France."

Chapter Twenty

Monique had the map and real estate brochures on her lap in the passenger seat. It was late afternoon; the sun was still beating down. They had viewed a good few sites, but none had really caught their attention. She was so glad the car had air-conditioning. "The next site is right on the beach front with a small village set beside it. It is within walking distance of four campsites and there is a village school. It does not have a surf shop in the area."

"All sounds good but we'll have to see what the real estate guy says. I wonder are there further developments planned for the area."

She looked at his side profile and thought what a good businessman he would make.

Donagh parked. She got out of the car, and walked towards a beautiful, wide golden sandy beach. There was a wooden walkway leading down towards the wet sand.

She saw children and adults playing at a mixture of activities along the water's edge, ping pong, sand boarding, and building dams. There were also body boarders in the surf but no surfers around.

"I hope surfing isn't banned here," said Donagh.

"Surely not, the beach stretches for miles."

"Fingers crossed Mon, I have a good feeling about here."

So did she and it was only twenty kilometres from Château Vieux. They walked back towards the car park and spotted the estate agent. He was the only person wearing a suit. He spoke French so Monique translated.

"There is already permission to build a surf school and shop on the site," Monique translated.

"Why is there already permission?" she asked in French.

"The owner ran out of money, he is getting a divorce." She translated for Donagh.

"Poor guy," said Donagh. "Ask him about permission to surf and kite-surf on the beach in case that was the problem and not a divorce."

She listened and translated again. "The town council has granted permission because of the length of the beach and they are keen to attract more tourists to their village. Those four new mobile home and camping parks were only completed last year."

"All sounds good. What do you think, Mon?" he asked.

"It doesn't matter what I think."

"Of course it does. I don't think you've been listening to me at all," he said, coming closer to her. She glanced at the real estate guy as his phone rang. He walked away to take the call. "Monique, I went to America to earn money for a deposit. Every penny I've earned there is in the bank along with my savings. I want a future for us. I'm serious about this. I can teach in the summer and I can work carpentry jobs in the winter. Also I can contact the local school and offer surfing lessons to them. I've always managed to find work."

Before she had a chance to answer, he rang Richard.

"Calm down, Donagh. Take some time around the place. Collate your research, look at all the costs and email me some details when you're finished. How long has it been on the market?"

"Only since last week, Richie."

"You are reminding me of the buzz I got from finding the first property I ever bought."

"Has anyone else seen it?"

"Yes, Monique is with me."

She sat on the grassy bank, overlooking the beach. She had stopped listening. Eleven months ago, she had sat on a grassy bank on a beach across the sea, when Garvan had dropped the bombshell that he was moving to Dubai.

Her life had changed so much in such a short space of time. There had been some desperate lows but also some incredible highs too. She could never have imagined that she could love someone so much. It was easy to get caught up in the whirlwind that was Donagh. She watched him on the phone to Richard. The estate agent had finished his call and was waiting for Donagh at his car. Donagh's body language had changed on the call. He walked towards the agent and shook hands with him. She wondered what decision he had made. He hadn't come back to talk with her first.

He walked towards her and sat down on the grass beside her. "Richard told me to take my time. I also realised I didn't wait to hear what you had to say."

"Donagh, we are young. We can travel the world together. I can teach English or French. You can teach carpentry, surfing, building so many things."

"It's beautiful here but I think you are right. I was so caught up in trying to prove myself. To me that means owning something, like a business of my own, but I've enjoyed working in the Hamptons. If you are with me even better, it doesn't matter where we go."

"When Garvan asked me to move to Dubai, I was afraid to leave both Gran and Bayrush. I have realised, Bayrush will always be my home but that does not mean we cannot experience new places together. In my heart, I think Bayrush is where I will want to live eventually."

He took her face in his hands and kissed her. "I want to be wherever you are. Let's just enjoy the rest of the day and night."

"How about some pizza? It smells lovely." She got up and slipped her hand into his. Not once today had she felt conscious of her scar. Her hair was ropey from the salt water, she had no make-up on and yet for the first time in her life, she actually felt beautiful.

She sat opposite Donagh outside the pizzeria under the canopy. The sun was going down on the ocean and she was looking forward to a lifetime of adventures with the man who sat across from her. He was attempting to speak French, but even the Italian waiter laughed at him.

"You as bad as me at French. Speaka the English." The waiter laughed.

"What's a guy got to do to get some support around here?"

The waiter patted him on the back and threw his eyes up to heaven. He looked at Monique and said, "Noa hope for him."

She laughed but nothing could be further from the truth. There was all the hope in the world for both of them. When the waiter left, she leaned across the table and took his hand. "I love you, Donagh Mullally."

"It's back to Hotel Pilate after this. I want you all to myself."

"Mais oui."

"I don't know what that means but it sounds good."

"It means 'but yes.'"

"Always sounds so much better in French."

Sophia was about to dish up the main course when Eoghan's pager went off. He smiled reassuringly at her and excused himself discreetly. Kate picked up the bowl of potatoes and placed them in the centre, while she carved the beef.

"I love when you do dinner like this," said Kate. "It reminds me of when I was younger at home."

"Eoghan likes to do it this way when we have a crowd. Stretch or starve, he says." She watched the door anxiously. Minutes later he came back in.

"A fishing vessel with six men on board is in trouble. The coastguard and sea rescue have been called. It's a red alert. I'm sorry, love, but I have to go," he said, kissing her on the cheek.

"Please be careful, Eoghan," she whispered into his ear.

"Please God, I'll be back in time for the dessert," he said, heading out the door.

"Take care out there, Eoghan," called Richard after him. Then he looked across at her. "He'll be fine, Mom. He's experienced."

"He's doing this for years and nothing has ever happened. It might even be a false alarm again," said Grace.

"You're both right. Let's enjoy the dinner while it's still warm." She tried to sound upbeat. Eoghan wouldn't be the man he was if he didn't do this work.

But try as she might Sophia could not concentrate on what people said. Dessert was over; she had kept a plate of dinner for Eoghan. She wrapped cling film around the tiramisu. She checked her mobile discreetly; still no call.

"So Kate, they are in France together, have any of you heard how it's going over there?" asked Grace.

"Yes." Kate began to tell them about Donagh finding a site for his surf school. Sophia half listened. She had been delighted to hear that Donagh and Monique were together. But they were young which did concern her. Then she thought of Bill. She had only been twenty-one when they had met and she had spent thirty-five good years with him. She glanced at her cell again willing it to ring. This was his third call-out since they had become a couple. When they were friends, he had often been called but he would have told her about it after the event, filling her in on what had happened.

"Sophia?" She startled at the sound of Kate's voice.

"I'm sorry. Did I miss something?" But then her cell rang. When she saw his name appear she jumped up. "Oh, thank goodness."

She listened as he spoke and then clicked off.

"He'll be home in a few minutes." She looked around the table at the anxious faces looking at her.

"What about the fishing boat?" asked Richard.

She shook her head. "The search has been called off for the night."

"You should tell him how you feel," said Grace.

"I have. But somebody has got to do it and they need volunteers who are prepared to be on call and risk their lives for others. There are not that many people prepared to make such a huge commitment."

"But he's not getting any younger," said Jack.

"You try telling him that. Sophia is right. It is hard to find people with that kind of skill and knowledge of the sea. I'll be honest, I don't think I could do it," said Geoff.

"Donagh's friends, Butchie and Pepe, have signed up and I know Donagh wants to get involved if he comes back," said Sophia. She heard the front door opening. She put Eoghan's dinner into the microwave. "Let's say a prayer the fishermen will be found safe and well."

When Eoghan came in she walked towards him and held him in her arms. "I'm so glad you're home."

"It all begins again at first light, love. It's heartbreaking for those families."

"It's eleven o'clock," Donagh muttered into her ear. "I need food."

She stretched languorously in the bed and turned away from him to get up. He started to nuzzle her neck. "Stop," she laughed. "Or else we will never get out of here."

He pulled her back down. She squealed and then said, "Mmmm, do that again."

An hour later she walked down the stairs. The hotel receptionist whom she had met on her first visit smiled at her when she saw her with Donagh.

Monique blushed and said, "Salute."

So did Donagh.

She looked at him and smiled.

"What? I'm practising my French."

"Let's go to the patisserie in the square. You can practise your French there."

"Hold your horses, girl. It will take me all day to order."

She walked up the street, holding his hand.

After ordering, they sat outside in the shade. It was a fabulous day.

"I could get used to this weather," said Donagh, as he buttered his croissant.

Monique felt like pinching herself. It was still so hard to believe that they were planning a future together. Last night had been fantastic, fabulous, everything she had ever dreamed of and more. Donagh's phone rang.

"Hi Geoff, how's it going?" He smiled across at her. His smile disappeared. Oh no, she thought, something awful has happened.

"Geoff, when? It's Eoghan, he's missing. Monique is with me. I'm putting you on speakerphone."

"I'm so sorry to ring with this news but I know how close you are and you'd go crazy if I didn't tell you and Monique."

"What happened?" he asked.

"A fishing vessel went missing last night. When there was no contact they called in the emergency services late yesterday afternoon. Conditions were too bad to continue so they had to halt for the rest of the night. Eoghan came home; he was worn out. As it happened we were at his house for dinner. Anyway, the search resumed this morning. Seemingly, they had enough crew and someone suggested Eoghan stay home."

"But he didn't like that, I'll bet," said Donagh

"Yesterday had wrecked him and there were enough young guys to go out."

"So what happened?"

"He and two others went out in a smaller rubber inflatable boat. Unfortunately it capsized. The other crew members managed to get onto the overturned boat and were rescued by the helicopter service. But the current pulled Eoghan away. He is still missing.

"What about the fishing boat?"

"It had a problem with its radio and managed to dock in Kinsale at around 10 a.m. which is around the time Eoghan went missing. The coastguard are on red alert and every boat in the communities of Bayrush, Kilowen, Dungarvan, Youghal and the other nearby ports are out searching for him. Volunteers are walking the coastline in case he …" Geoff's voice cracked.

"We're on our way. What time is it, Mon?"

"12.30 which means 11.30 at home."

Donagh could hear the wind catching the phone. "I'm walking the cliffs here as I speak. I promise I'll keep you posted."

"We'll see you as soon as we can. And thanks for telling me. Eoghan is …" His voice cracked.

"I know how much he means to you and to us all. I'll see you soon."

The phone went dead. Monique put her arms around him. Donagh's face had turned pale under his tan. She was crying.

"They better find him. I only know him a short while, but …"

"I know," she said, holding him close.

Then he gathered himself. "Okay, I need to get my things from the hotel."

"I will check flights and I must ring Philippe to let him know we are leaving." Donagh paid the bill and they ran down the street towards the hotel. While he checked out, she rang Philippe. He told her to come at once to the château. He promised to have a solution by the time they arrived. She told Donagh, but he wanted go straight to the airport.

"Please, just trust him. He said we must go to the château."

"I hope we are not wasting valuable time."

She ran to the car with him and he drove off at speed towards Château Vieux De La Lac.

True to his word Philippe had arranged a helicopter to take them to Bordeaux where he had secured two seats on the next flight to Dublin. Monique asked Rachel and Jay to pick them up. They arrived in Bayrush at eight o'clock Irish time. Philippe had pulled so many favours to get them there.

One of the offices of a fish storage unit on the dockside had been turned into a headquarters for the rescue mission. When she saw Sophia's ashen face she wanted to cry but she had to be strong. She put her arms around her.

"Thank you for coming back," Sophia whispered. "Oh Monique, what are we going to do?"

Monique never felt so helpless in her life. She had no words. Nothing would sound right. She just squeezed her tighter.

From the corner of her eye, she saw Richard leading Donagh out to the corridor. She sat with Sophia, Grace, Kate and Jessie.

"What am I going to do if ..."

Grace cut across Sophia, and taking her hand, she said, "He's still here, Sophia. He's fit and he loves you so much. He has so much to fight for."

Donagh listened intently to Richard who had brought him outside.

"The weather is getting worse and we only have two hours' daylight if we're lucky."

"Okay Richard." He spotted Butchie at his jeep. "Butchie, do you have a map in there?" he asked, walking towards it. Butchie got it and spread in out on the bonnet. "Richie, show me where the helicopter rescued the crew."

Richard pointed to an area on the map.

"Do we have any idea about the currents or wind directions?"

"Yes, from that information they are concentrating on this area," said Richard.

Donagh looked at Butchie. "Are you thinking what I'm thinking?" Butchie nodded.

"Richie, I think Eoghan will try to get to Everest Rock. It's the nearest piece of land and based on the currents and wind direction Eoghan could use it to his advantage."

"They are reporting swells of three to four metres high and a wind force fifty to sixty knots," said Butchie.

"Eoghan will still see the rock," said Donagh.

"But isn't it very dangerous? Surely he won't try to get there. He could be smashed against it," said Butchie.

"He needs to get out of the water. His drysuit will protect him to some degree but any prolonged time spent in the water at a temperature of ten degrees could bring on hypothermia. There are caves on it where he could shelter from the worst of it. That's what I would try to do. We need your father's rubber inflatable and Pepe to helm it."

Richard threw his eyes to heaven. "No you don't, let's just tell the professionals. Look it was enough that Eoghan took the boat out. I'm not letting you do something stupid."

But Butchie was already on the phone to Pepe.

"If he's on that rock I'll find him. That old dog is a survivor. Eoghan has dived around here many times."

"I thought it was off limits."

"That's what makes it even more attractive to us."

"Donagh, I'm not letting you risk your life."

"I'm doing it with or without your help."

He turned around and saw Monique standing there. She followed him as he walked to his van to see what equipment he had.

"Donagh ..."

"Don't say anything, Mon. I have to do this. If they find him there when the storm is over, I'll never forgive myself for not trying to rescue him. You join the land search party. They will stay going for as long as they can. I promise you. I will be fine."

When the news first broke that Eoghan was missing Sophia had contacted Eoghan's eldest daughter. She told her what had happened. She added that she accepted that neither she nor her sister wanted any contact but that she would never forgive herself if she didn't tell them.

Emma had said she would come immediately but her sister had moved to Australia. Sophia thanked her and hung up. She was too upset to get into any kind of conversation. She was angry that they hadn't contacted him. She had done her bit.

The door opened again. Her heart lurched. A blonde girl came in with a man behind her. Sophia noticed everybody looking confused wondering who these people were. She stood up. "Emma?" she asked, noticing the same eyes as Eoghan's looking at her. The girl nodded and began to cry.

Silent tears. Sophia put her arms out and the young girl walked into them. "I just hope I'm not too late."

One of the search coordinators came in. "I'm sorry to say …" There was a communal intake of breath. "But there is still no news." There was an audible sigh of relief. He must have realised what he had done. "Oh I'm sorry to have upset you."

"I'm Seán," said the young guy, beside Emma. He put out his hand to shake Sophia's. "I'm just going outside. I need to make myself useful. Will you be okay?"

Emma, nodded and said, "We'll be okay together, won't we?"

A tear trickled down Sophia's cheek. She couldn't lose him. Oh please God, don't take him. You have to meet your daughters, she pleaded. It couldn't be happening again. The sea had taken her daughter-in-law Heather and her little grandson, Billy. They had never recovered their bodies after the aeroplane crash. When those thoughts hit her consciousness, her stomach lurched. "Excuse me." She rushed to the toilet where she threw up. She sat on the downturned toilet seat and made a decision. She went to the basin to wash her hands and caught a reflection of her face. She hardly recognised the image that looked back at her. Her life force was leaving her. She turned and walked out.

"I can't just sit here waiting. I'm sorry," she said. "I'm going out to find him."

Grace got up immediately. "Let's go. I'm going stir crazy sitting here too. We can join the land search, Sophia."

Kate, Jessie and Emma followed them outside to get jackets.

"It will be bright for at least two more hours," said Kate.

Donagh and Butchie joined Richard who was speaking to the coastguard. Butchie was already suited up. Both he and Pepe had been on the sea rescue boat searching all day. A replacement team had come to relieve them. Donagh listened to get an update on the weather. He did not intend to discuss his plan with the authorities. They would be obliged to try to stop him. "There's a very real possibility that Eoghan might have made it to that rock. But the helicopter has circled it a couple of times. They have body heat analysis on board and nothing has shown up. It's very difficult to access it by sea especially in these conditions. There is no sign of the weather abating," said the burly officer.

Donagh left Richard talking to the coastguard. Butchie followed him. As soon as he was out of earshot, Donagh said, "Butchie, ring Pepe and tell him I can't launch from here. They'll see me."

"What do you mean *I*? I'm going with you."

"Butchie, maybe it's not such a good idea." But Butchie was already on the phone telling Pepe to meet them at Laddies Slip.

Donagh opened the van. He had filled his waterproof backpack with a survival blanket and a basic first aid kit. He hoped that if Eoghan had made it to the rock he hadn't sustained an injury. For a brief moment, he thought he must be crazy. "Butchie, we need some flares."

"I'll get my hands on some."

Donagh took some climbing ropes from Butchie's jeep.

"Donagh, it will be impossible to climb in the drysuit especially as they are connected to the rubber boots."

"Right, we'll wear rain gear under the drysuit and take hiking boots in the bag."

"Where are you going to get a dry suit?"

"Surely one of the boys has one I can borrow."

"Donagh, are you crazy?"

"Don't think about it too much. I'm sure one of the lads will give me a loan of their equipment."

"Good luck with that."

"Forget it. Just sort the flares and don't look for a few minutes."

Donagh walked away and headed straight for the sea rescue building. It was open. Five minutes later, he was completely togged out with a drysuit, full life jacket, helmet and head lamp.

"Problem solved, let's go."

"You are nuts and I am even worse to go along with you."

"There is a great man's life at stake. I know they are doing their best but I have to do this. I'd prefer to do it on my own."

"I'm coming with you. The auld fellow will never speak to me again if anything happens to his RIB."

"Your father would forgive you anything."

"We'll need this too," said Butchie, throwing in a hand torch.

Donagh's phone bleeped. "Pepe is on the way. Okay, he can drop us to the rock and go straight back. I don't want anyone hanging out in that longer than they have to," said Donagh, nodding towards the sea. The waves were crashing against the pier, sending spray high into the darkening sky. Even the fishing boats tied up in the harbour were tossing around as though they were weightless.

He was about to drive away when Richard came running towards him, waving. Donagh's heart lifted – they might have found Eoghan.

"Don't do this," said Richard. The rain pelted down on him and the wind nearly blew him off his feet.

"If we find him, I'll send up two flares, otherwise I'll send up one and that's to tell you to send the helicopter to get us off that rock," shouted Donagh. He drove away before Richard had time to reply.

He drove in silence to Laddies Slip. Donagh figured Butchie must be as lost as he was in his own thoughts. It might be the craziest thing they were ever going to do. He rationalised that they had all the survival equipment they needed. Between them they had years of experience of the sea, but one wrong move and they could all perish.

Pepe waved at them. He had the boat ready to launch. In the corner of his eye, he saw Geoff coming towards them. Donagh signalled to them to get into the back of the van. They needed to make a plan and it was too wild outside.

"Firstly Geoff, go home. You are not coming out in that."

"We need a fourth man," said Pepe. "What if I have a problem getting you off or something happens on my way back? Think Donagh, the rules are nobody gets off the boat. We are breaking all of them."

Donagh paused. Pepe was right. "Okay, but you just drop us and head straight back. We'll dock at the point we used the last time we went snorkelling over there. Remember?"

"I'll reverse in and Geoff can drop the anchor over the bow. You two climb off the back and we'll get out of there straight away."

"Exactly, don't hang around or take any unnecessary chances. I'll flash the torch to let you know we're safe. And you do the same. Keep a watch for flares. One will mean we need to be rescued, and two flares will mean there'll be three of us. Then call in the helicopter to get us off."

"Fair enough."

"Any questions?" Three faces looked back at him.

"Let's get the flock out of here," joked Butchie. They all smiled. They needed something to lift the intensity in the air. They packed into the orange rubber inflatable boat and set off.

Sophia, Emma, Grace and others walked the beach. People had brought dogs to help. They planned to search every piece of coastline for thirty miles.

"People are so good," said Emma, pulling up her hood as the rain began to beat against them. Sophia had missed what she said. Emma's words had been wiped away on the wind. The freaky thing was the last time she had walked a beach in similar circumstances, the sea had been calm and the sun had been shining yet the authorities had still been unable to recover, their bodies.

She began to cry as she battled on against the rain and wind. She had stopped trying to keep her hood up a long time back. "Oh God, why? She screamed silently inside. She felt a hole where her heart used to be. "Why, oh why?" He had promised last night when they lay in bed together that this was the last time. He had held her face in his hands and promised her.

Monique had joined Rachel, Jay, Jack and some of the lads from Bayrush Stables searching on the cliff top. They had brought dogs in the hope that they might sense something. They kept them on leads because the terrain was so dangerous only people who knew the cliff tops well were on them. The wind howled and the sea pelted against the rocks throwing up spray. She walked towards the edge and looked down just as a huge wave smashed against the rocks. She puked there and then. Rachel came running over to her.

"ARE YOU OKAY?" shouted Rachel as the wind roared around them. Darkness was descending and Monique had an ominous feeling in the pit of her stomach.

"Donagh is out there." She wasn't sure Rachel heard her. So she roared it again, pointing towards Everest Rock, "Donagh is out there looking for Eoghan."

"Oh God," said Rachel, dragging her away from the edge of the cliff. "You'll be blown in too. It's dangerous."

Rachel put her arm around her and guided her towards the rest of the group. It looked like a decision to call off the cliff top search was imminent.

"Don't tell anybody else, Rachel. There is enough to worry about already."

Rachel just nodded.

Sophia saw Molly and Nora with members of the bridge crowd and some of the bingo women coming towards them. She couldn't believe their generosity of spirit to come out on such a horrendous night. They had walked the quay and harbour areas. All of them must be afraid of what they might find but they still searched.

Donagh and Butchie sat in the middle of the boat, with Geoff at the nose and Pepe at the helm driving. The boat sped over three metre high waves. Donagh held on for dear life. He was one of those people who liked to be in charge. He had never been a good passenger. He felt like puking. As they got nearer Everest Rock, Donagh signalled the way. Pepe turned the boat and began a reverse manoeuvre to get as close to the rocks as possible to jump off. Dusk was setting in along with big black clouds and pelting rain.

"Geoff, drop the anchor," shouted Pepe. "Slack, slack. Get ready boys! More slack, Geoff. Go Donagh."

He hopped out quickly and managed to make it to the rock. "Thank God," he muttered, but just as he turned around, he saw Butchie slip and fall into the water. "Jesus Christ," Donagh roared, throwing the rope he had around his body to Butchie. Thankfully, Butchie caught it.

"Cut the anchor rope," roared Pepe to Geoff. Donagh knew what Pepe meant. If the boat hit Butchie, it could smash him against the rocks. The best thing was to get the boat away as quickly as possible. Donagh pulled the rope with all his strength. He could see a big swell coming in. Pepe had the boat going at full throttle towards it. The boat disappeared over the top of the wave.

Donagh could only hope the wave would wash them both further inland and that the lads would make it over without capsizing. He roared, "Hold on tight." He prayed the rope wouldn't get caught in the rocks.

The wave hit. He went underwater and was tossed and turned by its power. He was completely at its mercy. Then he felt the water dragging him backwards. He prayed like he had never prayed in his life.

The wave had thrown the two of them up onto a stony piece of cove. Thank God they had both worn helmets. Butchie was conscious but disoriented. Donagh grabbed him and pulled him to his feet, rushing before the next wave hit. There was always a sequence.

"You okay?" he roared. Butchie nodded. "Tie the rope around you. Follow my lead. If we can make it up there, we'll be safe from the worst of it."

Chapter Twenty-One

Grace heard a siren going off. Her heart lifted until she heard the Coastguard Officer say, "The land search is off. Please contact any friends and family and tell them to go home. The weather is worsening but we'll need all the help we can get again in the morning. Thank you, thank you everybody for all your help."

She led Sophia back to the building they had been waiting in. People talked about the great community spirit around them. She overheard Jack talking to Richard on the phone.

"Jack, I need you and Geoff down here. I'll explain when you get here." She felt the boys were hatching some kind of plan of their own.

"I'll be there straight away. But Richard, Geoff went out on the boat with Donagh."

"Oh my God, are you all crazy?" said Grace.

Jack clicked off the phone and pulled her aside. "Keep your voice down and don't tell anyone, especially Jess."

Grace nodded. She was sick to the pit of her stomach.

As soon as Donagh reached a safe point high on the rock, he stopped and took out his torch. He flashed it and waited. Nothing.

"I hope they made it back," said Butchie.

Donagh said nothing. He'd never be able to live with himself if anything happened to Geoff and Pepe. The realisation of what he had done hit. He had put all their lives at risk. He flashed the torch again. He waited. And again.

"What are we going to do?" said Butchie.

Donagh went to take out the flare. "We'll put this up. Richard is watch …"

"Look, a light," shouted Butchie. "They're okay."

Donagh let out a sigh of relief that came from his toes. The rain had stopped momentarily but black clouds still loomed, making it darker than usual. He checked his diving watch; it was 10.30 p.m. Eoghan had been missing just over twelve hours.

From the tidal records at the time Eoghan went overboard, Donagh figured that he was more likely to be on the other side of the rock. But there was no way they could have attempted to access the rock from that side. The worst of the weather was hitting it. If Eoghan had made it here, Donagh figured he'd have tried to get to the cave higher up on this side. There was much to be hopeful for. Eoghan had been wearing a drysuit and a life jacket. He was experienced and cool-headed.

"We need to stash these drysuits somewhere safe. Follow me and stay close, Butchie." Donagh shouted to be heard above the sounds of the sea and winds. He didn't want to get into even more trouble for losing them.

Sophia sat in Eoghan's chair next to the fire in his cottage. People were milling around but she couldn't engage with anyone. She remembered being put into a car and driven back to the the house. Everything felt like it was out of reach.

"Sophia, I've made soup. Come over to the table. You need to eat something," said Kate.

She began to object but that would take too much energy. Instead she followed Kate.

Grace poured the soup.

"Do you think I should contact my sister?" asked Emma, quietly.

"I'm sorry," Sophia replied; she didn't want to be party to this.

"Excuse me," said Kate, leading Emma away towards her boyfriend. Sophia overheard Kate say, "I think you have quite a decision to make and I'm sorry but it's really not fair to involve Sophia at this time."

"Thank you, Kate. You're right," said Seán.

"You are very welcome to stay here and have the guestroom."

Kate was wonderful, thought Sophia, but what would she do if Eoghan didn't come back? Her body began to shake and then she lost consciousness.

"Eoghan, E O G H … A … N …" Donagh's voice was hoarse from calling and the wind whipped it away as soon as it left his mouth. But it didn't stop him. Maybe, just maybe, it would carry to Eoghan wherever he was. So he kept calling.

His left foot slipped; he grabbed a piece of rock. "Fuck that was close!" He barely managed to find a foothold. He looked down. Waves pounded against the rocks below him. Ten metres more and he would be at the cave. He took a deep breath and kept moving forward. He pulled himself onto the ledge of the cave. Butchie came in behind him. The disappointment he felt was almost overwhelming. There was no sign of

Eoghan. It had all been in vain.

When Sophia came around, she was lying on the couch with an unfamiliar face looking at her.

"We got the doctor," said Grace, holding her hand.

She felt groggy, had she been given something? She was drifting. "I hope you haven't given me any sedatives. I want to be awake when he gets back. Oh Richard, he will be back, won't he?"

"Mom, the doctor hasn't given you anything. I know how you feel about them. You're just tired; close your eyes for just a while. I'm here." Richard's voice was so reassuring she did as he asked.

"Look Donagh, it's time to send up one flare while we still have a chance of getting off this rock," said Butchie.

Donagh sat on a boulder in the shelter of the cave. He was exhausted but his adrenaline was still up. He did not intend to give up. He took a swig of water. "I know it's a lot to ask but can we just try to get to the other side? Even just to see if there is any trace of him. It would be crazy to give up now. We can come back here after and wait it out for a rescue."

Butchie peered out the cave entrance. "The storm is getting worse. Let's get moving so that we can get back here if needs be."

"Thanks, mate," said Donagh. "You'll never know how much I appreciate you doing this. He's an incredible man ..."

Butchie slapped him on the back. "Let's get a move on."

They began to climb again. They were just ten metres from the top when the rain abated again. He prayed the wind would die down enough to let them get over the ridge without being whipped out to sea.

"STAY LOW, CRAWL ON YOUR BELLY, OKAY?" he shouted to Butchie, making signs to his stomach. He waited for a momentary break in the wind and then roared, "NOW." They both began to crawl over the top. He hoped they wouldn't lose any gear. It was their only protection from the elements. Luckily they made it over. However, the waves and wind crashing against the rock was far worse than Donagh had anticipated.

Rachel caught Monique's eye and nodded towards the door leading to the living room. Monique followed her into the empty room.

"Why won't you tell anybody where Donagh is?"

"Oh Rachel, I can't think straight. Richard knows but there is no point in causing more anxiety. He is gone back to the harbour."

"I heard him say he's meeting Geoff and Jack down there."

"I cannot stay here any longer. I am going crazy."

"Have you eaten?"

"Non."

Rachel led her back to the kitchen. She ladled soup into a bowl and stood over her, making her drink it. Monique took a mouthful and had to rush to the toilet.

She retched but nothing came up. "My God, why is this happening? Why?" She leaned against the back of the door and slid to the ground. She began to cry. In an effort to stifle the sound, her body racked silently. She had never felt so much pain. It just wasn't fair.

She heard a knock on the door. She stood up and opened it. She was tired of holding everything in. It was Gran. Nora came in and closed the door.

"Rachel told me. Oh Monique, I am so sorry." She put her arms around her and Monique just wept in her arms. Then she turned back towards the sink and ran the tap. She splashed water on her face. "Gran, I have to go to the harbour. I cannot stay here. I really do not want the girls or Sophia to know. They will worry even more."

"Do what you need to, Monique. I won't mention it."

Donagh made his way down the other side as far as possible with Butchie. It was getting too dangerous to continue. He knew of another smaller cave that would provide limited shelter. To go any further would definitely be risking their lives. He signed toward Butchie to continue parallel instead of downwards. Butchie followed. He pointed towards the cave.

"E O G H A N nnnnnn," Donagh called; his voice sounded desperate to his own ears. He had been using the head torch to climb. But he wanted to show Butchie where he was heading to so he took out the hand torch from the backpack. He shone it in the direction he intended to go, looking back towards Butchie.

"Look!" Butchie shouted. He turned and saw something orange. Excitement and fear filled him at once.

"EOGHAN H HHhh," he shouted again but there was no movement. He climbed frantically across, slipping and sliding in his haste, hoping it was Eoghan. "Butchie, it's him. Thank God."

When Donagh finally clambered up to the small cave, the relief was huge. Eoghan's breathing was very shallow but he had obviously been well enough to get himself up this high. "We're here. You're safe now. We'll get you off as soon as possible."

Eoghan blinked.

Donagh figured hypothermia was setting in. The sea, wind and the cold had done its damage. He also had a nasty gash on his forehead.

"Are you hurt anywhere else?"

Eoghan shook his head slightly.

Butchie took out the flares and the survival blanket. Donagh wrapped the blanket around him and began to treat the gash on his forehead. Butchie set off two flares.

"Butchie, we'll sit either side of him, our combined body heat will help."

"Good idea, we'll wrap the second one over us too."

"They won't be long, Eoghan," said Donagh, reassuringly. "I'll stand out on the ledge in ten minutes' time. The heat sensor on the chopper will pick me out." Donagh checked his watch again. It was one 1.10 a.m.

"We're snug as bugs in a rug, eh?"

"Can't … wait … to … say …" Eoghan's words were laboured he was finding it so difficult to breathe.

"Hi honey I'm home." Donagh smiled and took out some energy bars and water. As soon as Eoghan's breathing stabilised he'd get them into him. The glow from the head torches gave a psychological feeling of warmth. "You're going to have some story to tell after this."

Eoghan attempted a weak smile.

"You've been missing approximately fifteen hours."

Monique was in the car with Richard when they saw the first flare and then a second one. They both jumped out of the jeep and danced around in the pouring rain. Pepe came rushing towards them too. They were all hugging and jumping up and down.

Richard ran towards the makeshift headquarters, shouting. She ran behind him. Jack and Geoff followed and then Jack picked her up and swung her around.

"He did it. James Bond would be nothing on him," Geoff shouted above the wind and rain.

"And Butchie too. Batman and Robin." Richard laughed.

"Guys, you sound really cheesy," said Monique, beaming.

"We need to inform the helicopter rescue," said Richard.

They ran up the stairs to tell the man in charge what they knew.

Monique sat beside Richard as he drove back up the cliff towards the cottage. They were both soaking wet. The high she was on had abated. They weren't sure if the helicopter could fly in these conditions. Pepe and Geoff opted to stay at the harbour. Monique was overcome by the friendships Donagh had. It was unbelievable what he and Geoff had done. His other friend, Butchie, had risked so much too and they still weren't out of danger. As they approached the top of the cliff, Monique could feel the power of the wind against the jeep. The night was becoming increasingly horrendous.

"I honestly don't believe it will be safe to fly in these conditions. I hope they have found some shelter."

"Richard, we have to be positive going inside. Let's just tell Sophia they are safe and we just have to wait for a break in the weather. Which is the truth."

"You are right. Come on." He got out of the car. She opened the door and the wind nearly blew it off its hinges. Richard had to run around to push it closed.

They burst in the front door, followed by Jack. She allowed Richard do all the talking. "They found them!"

"Them?" asked Sophia.

"Mom, Donagh and two of his friends took a boat out to Everest Rock along with Geoff. Donagh figured from the tidal currents that Eoghan might have made it out there."

"Oh my goodness, that rock is dangerous to access on a good day, even I know that. Oh Monique, thank God," Sophia said, putting her arm around her.

"I will kill Geoff McGrath when I get my hands on him," said Jessie.

Everybody laughed but it was cautious laughter. None of them knew the full extent of how difficult it would be or how long it would take to get them off that rock. At least they knew they were alive. She could breathe again and so could Sophia.

"Monique, you need to get out of those clothes before you get pneumonia," said Nora.

"Go to my wardrobe," said Sophia.

Monique smiled – Sophia was back to herself. Everything was going to be okay.

"I'll put the kettle on. Now we can have a cup of tea and actually taste it," said Molly, going over to the kettle.

Kate put the soup back on the cooker.

"Lads, take off those wet jackets and Richard, go and borrow some of Eoghan's clothes."

"Oh, it's all about Richard," said Jack, nudging Grace. "She couldn't care less about me."

Kate laughed. "I suppose you'd better look for something for Jack too."

Kate had suggested that everybody should try to get some rest. Emma and Seán had gone to their room. Sophia had fallen into a fitful sleep on the couch. However, the rest of them remained sitting around the kitchen table, waiting. An hour had passed. The high they had been on had abated. Anxiety was setting in. Nobody said it but it was almost tangible.

"Pepe said the helicopter can operate in all kinds of weather," said Richard, attempting to sound reassuring. His words were only spoken when his mobile phone rang. Sophia woke immediately.

"We're on the way," said Richard. Kate rushed to the guest bedroom. She knocked on the door. Emma and Seán came out immediately.

"Follow us to the hospital, Seán. They'll use the landing pad there. Kate, ring Geoff just in case they haven't heard."

She dialled Geoff's number. He told her they were already on their way. Everybody ran through the rain to their cars.

From the emergency department window, Monique watched as the helicopter descended on the hospital grounds. It was an incredible sight to witness the search light shining in their direction. It was actually quite scary-looking. They still didn't know if any or all of them were injured.

"I contacted his father," Richard whispered to her.

"Donagh's father?" she asked incredulously.

"Yes, he needs to see the man he raised," said Richard, looking straight ahead. She glanced up at his side profile. Richard never ceased to amaze her. She bit her lip to stop her tears. Jack, Grace, Jessie, Geoff, Nora and Molly had all gathered waiting. Gran put her arm around her.

The helicopter set down on the pad in the hospital grounds. She held her breath as the doors opened. Two figures stood out of it, wrapped in silver survival blankets. The back door dropped to the ground and she presumed it was Eoghan being rolled out on a stretcher. The emergency staff rushed Eoghan in. Monique looked towards Sophia. Richard was reassuring her and Grace held her at the other side. Much as Monique wanted to rush into Donagh's arms, she didn't. Donagh went to Sophia immediately.

"He's going to be fine. He's suffering from hypothermia. His breathing is shallow. They'll check him over completely, Sophia. Being taken up on a winch is a terrifying experience. It must have been worse for Eoghan being stretchered."

"Donagh, I'll never be able to thank you enough," said Sophia, hugging him.

"It's thanks to these guys. Butchie, Pepe, meet Sophia. And of course, we couldn't have done it without Geoff too."

"How's it going?" said Butchie, shaking her hand.

Sophia smiled and said, "Good, thanks to all of you guys."

"Come on, let's get you two inside. We need to check you both over," said one of the nursing staff.

"Just a sec," said Donagh. He put his arms around Monique and swung her around.

"Thank God you are home," she said when he put her down. She kissed him. After a moment, he broke away. He was smiling at her and then his face changed. She followed the direction of his gaze to a man and woman in their early fifties.

"I can't believe *he* is here. I'm going to have to listen to his shit again. Telling me what a stupid thing it was to do. I know it was reckless. But I don't need to hear it from him." He ignored them and began to follow Butchie. Monique stopped him. His mother smiled gratefully at her and came over.

The poor woman put her arms around Donagh and when she pulled away Monique could see the tears in her eyes. His father's face was ashen. He put out his right hand. Donagh took it. His father pulled him a little closer. It was all the encouragement Donagh needed. He hugged him and his father held onto him for what seemed like an age. When they broke away, Monique heard him say, "Well done Donagh, that was a very brave thing you did."

Donagh took her hand and said, "Mum, Dad, this is Monique, the love of my life."

"Hi Monique, I'm so pleased to meet you." Her voice was so warm and friendly, Monique liked her instantly. She smiled at his father. It would take her longer to figure him out.

"I hate to break things up, but we do need to check over the hero of the day," the nurse smiled.

Donagh grinned and followed her. "Back shortly."

Sophia sat in the Accident and Emergency Unit, waiting. Emma paced up and down. A door opened and Donagh and Butchie came out. They had received the all clear. Another door opened and the doctor said, "Can I speak to Eoghan's next of kin?" Sophia looked at Emma.

"That would be us," said Emma, taking Sophia's arm.

"He's going to be fine," said the doctor. "We'll need to keep him in for observation for a day or two."

"Thank you, Doctor," said Sophia. "Can we see him?"

"Of course, but not all of you." He looked around the nearly full waiting room.

"Yeah, we get it, Doc. Let's get out of here," said Donagh. Everyone began to leave except Richard, Kate and Emma's boyfriend.

"Thank you all again for your support," said Sophia. Grace, Jessie and Monique hugged her. Donagh winked and she smiled. She was so grateful to him.

"Do you think he'll want to see me?" asked Emma anxiously as the crowd left.

"Your father loves you and your sister very much. He will be thrilled to see you. Come on."

"We'll wait here," said Kate to the two men. Sophia linked Emma as they followed the nurse into the restricted area. The nurse drew back the curtain and when Eoghan saw his daughter, his eyes lit up. He had an oxygen mask on and wires and tubes attached to him.

"Oh Dad, I'm so sorry. Thank God you are safe."

Eoghan held up his arms as best he could and Emma leaned into them. He caught Sophia's eye and smiled.

"No more, Eoghan Forrester. Or else I am moving out."

Jessie strolled down the lane towards Butterfly Barn. A week had passed since Eoghan's accident. Thankfully, he was out of hospital and recuperating well under Sophia's watchful eye. The whole episode had scared everyone.

She was meeting Monique at the yard to ride out for the last time together before Monique and Donagh left for Butterfly Barn USA. She was so excited for them both. Seeing Monique with Donagh for the past week had filled her heart. Monique was the daughter she never had and like all children there came a time to let go. She remembered setting off with Geoff to Australia all those years ago – the excitement she had felt had been incredible. There was so much to experience in the world; she was delighted Monique had decided to spread her wings. Bayrush would always be her home. When she reached the yard, Monique had tacked up the horses.

"Hey Jess."

"Ah, thanks for tacking up Jessie's Angel."

Monique smiled. "I know she's your favourite even though you like to think you do not have one."

"You know me too well." Jessie laughed as she got on the horse. Monique was so right. Jessie's Angel had brought them such luck at the start of the Butterfly Barn journey.

"Any news from Kate?" asked Monique, trotting along beside her on Jasper.

"Yes, she loved Paris. They finally managed to have a honeymoon although it was shorter than they had anticpated. She is so excited about the opening day of Butterfly Barn USA."

"Oh Jess, I can't wait, and I'm so delighted you are all coming over for it."

"It's thanks to Rachel and Jay we will be able to. They offered to look after things both here and over at Oak House."

"Sam is so excited about his first trip on an aeroplane."

"We really do need to get a life," Jessie laughed. "Geoff and I travelled the world together and since Sam was born the only holidays we take are a few days here and there."

"Well I hope that's going to change."

"Tell me about the course Richard suggested you take."

"It's called equine therapy. Seemingly it is very beneficial to people who have suffered trauma. It's about caring for the horses, and building trust not just riding them. I cannot wait."

"Wow, it will be wonderful to get a recognised qualification around something we've been offering here."

"So true, I hadn't heard of it before."

Jessie smiled as they trotted side by side. She couldn't think of a better person than Monique to train in that area. "Monique, it is amazing how so much good comes from horrific events. I believe that everything happens for a reason. It used to annoy me when people said that. I was so angry when my when my baby boys died. I could see no light."

Monique stretched out her arm and touched Jessie's shoulder. "I think I understand. I might never have met you or be living this life if, well, you know what I am trying to say."

"Come on, Mon. Let's canter to Miller's Point. I just need to feel the wind in my hair," said Jessie opening her helmet. She tossed it on top of the hedgerow. "Rules are made to be broken." She shook her long, curly red hair out of its hair tie.

"I do not believe you, Jessie McGrath, after all of the years of preaching about health and safety," said Monique, taking off hers too.

Jessie led the horse through the open gate. "I'll deny this ever happened," Jessie laughed as the two horses took off. "Woo hoo," she shouted, above the sound of the horse's hooves thumping along at a gallop.

"You are crazy but I love you."

Jessie grinned at the sight of Monique beside her. Her long chocolate-brown hair flowed in the wind and her eyes were alight. Jessie could feel a lump forming in her throat. She was going to miss her so much. "Me too," she said.

A week later, Kate rang her mother's mobile. Molly was constantly misplacing her mobile phone and then she'd never ring back. Grace always said it was because Molly couldn't justify making a call. Kate had laughed because she was the one who paid the phone bill for that very reason.

"Mam, are you sitting down?"

"Why would I want to sit down – I'm too busy to sit in the middle of the day. Tis well for the likes of you to be telling me to 'sit' down." Kate threw her eyes to heaven and sighed.

"Okay, Richard is sending the jet over for you, Nora, Butchie, Pepe and whoever else in the family might like to come to the opening of Butterfly Barn USA."

"Oh Jesus, Mary and Joseph, I am sitting down. That would be … oh my God." There was silence on the other end. Kate was terrified; she had given her mother a heart attack.

"Are you there?"

"Of course I'm here. Where else do you think I am?"

"Oh Mam, what are you like?"

"Where do you think you get it from?"

Kate laughed. "So you have three days to round up whoever else wants to come. Sophia and Eoghan are arriving here this evening."

"Isn't Grace already booked to travel with the McGraths on Friday?"

"That's right. Richard just thought it might be a nice surprise for you and the family. And he wants to include Butchie and Pepe for all they did for Eoghan. Please say you'll come."

"Oh Kate, tell Richard thanks a million. I can't wait."

"Ah Mam, you'll love it here. You might even stay a while eh?"

"You never know, I just might."

Grace sat beside Jack as he drove into the town of Southampton on Long Island. It was exactly as she imagined, colonial and tree-lined, with fabulous boutiques, restaurants and art galleries. She couldn't wait to wander along the main street as soon as they got settled. The traffic hadn't been too bad. She had heard it was horrendous at weekends, but who could blame people for wanting to visit such a beautiful part of the world.

"Didn't the kids travel really well?"

"Absolutely, it's hard to believe we'll be celebrating Lily's first birthday here."

Grace smiled and glanced behind. Finn's blond hair fell in his eyes while he slept. "Look at you, you're wide awake." She stretched her arm back and squeezed Lily's chubby little legs. Her baby daughter chuckled back at her. "You little dotey."

"I'm glad I'm following Geoff, saved us the bother of setting the sat nav."

"Oh wow." Grace's eyes widened as Jack drove through the gates of the estate. Nothing could have prepared her for the beauty of the place. When the car stopped, she jumped out and ran to hug her sister who was standing in front of the huge house.

"It's incredible, Kate."

Meanwhile, Jessie got out of her car and was standing with her mouth wide open. "I'm speechless."

"Well, that makes a change," Kate laughed. "Come on, I'll show you all around."

On Saturday evening as the sun went down, Sophia sat on the beach surrounded by all the people she loved and cared about. She glanced at Eoghan, who was attempting to melt marshmallows at the campfire on the beach. Everybody milled around chatting and eating from the wide selection of food brought in by the caterers. She had spared no expense on this celebration.

She smiled and looked out across the ocean. The sky was streaked with hues of purple, yellow, red and orange. She thought of her beloved Bill; she truly believed he was looking down on her and that Heather and Billy were with him. Tears filled her eyes as she thought, I hope I am making you proud.

The sound of Donagh's guitar playing brought her attention back. People began to gather around the campfire as a singsong began. Eoghan came back and sat beside her. He put his arm around her. "Just look at the mess I made of that." He laughed. "How come it always looks simple on the telly?" He held up a burnt marshmallow.

She laughed and leaned into him as she listened to the voice of Monique's uncle sing "Caruso". She had invited him and his partner, Eric, as a surprise for Monique. She looked across at her. Monique's face glowed in the light of the campfire and Sophia couldn't help noticing how Donagh couldn't stop looking at her. They were so in love. She glanced at his parents who were sitting together listening as he played. That had been another surprise. She had wanted them to see the work Donagh had done here in Butterfly Barn USA. She was so very, very proud of him and grateful to have Eoghan beside her because of his bravery.

Everybody clapped for Philippe.

Grace came over with Lily on her hip. Sophia stretched up her arms to take her from Grace.

"Hey little girl. One year old today." Sophia kissed her chubby cheeks.

"And what a way to celebrate it," said Grace, sitting down on the rug beside her. "It's idyllic here."

"Grace, the first Christmas after Bill died, Richard and I came here, just the two of us. It was the loneliest time of my life. You're right it is beautiful here, but people are what make a place special. I am so glad we met that day on the aeroplane. Did you notice that tomorrow is the fourth anniversary of that day?"

Grace nodded. "I did."

"Serendipity."

"I never believed in that kind of thing until what happened to Jessie and meeting you."

"And it's still only the beginning."

Grace laughed as Jessie came over to join them. "Oh Jess, who knows what's in store for us next?"

THE END

Acknowledgements

Hello again! I'd like to start by thanking my husband, Michael, for his unwavering support and belief in me. Without him none of this would be possible. Thanks also to our daughter, Aisling, who makes us smile every day and is a gift; and to our son, Eoghan, who brightens our world. They are three incredibly patient people.

Please bear with me while I share some of the incredible things that have happened since the release of my first novel, Butterfly Barn.

Who knew that a self-published book that I had originally intended to launch in an art gallery would become the manager's choice and reach number one in original fiction in the Book Centre, Waterford, and stay there for six weeks? Thanks to Maeve Ryan, Nellie, Catherine, John and all the staff at The Book Centre. Or that Ireland's two book wholesalers would take stock of the book, making it available in every bookshop across the country? Thank you Lucy and Catherine in Eason Dungarvan for supporting Butterfly Barn from the beginning. Or that it would be downloaded as an ebook in so many countries around the world.

All of this is thanks to the people of Waterford who believed so much in the characters and story that they told their friends and family from near and far about it. When my friend, Siobhán and her partner, David, went to Paris, they took a photograph of Butterfly Barn under the Eiffel Tower. That photo became a catalyst that readers engaged with. Photographs of the cover of Butterfly Barn continue to flow in from all over the world. It has been on trains across Asia, perched on a hill on Sark Island, in Capetown under Table Mountain, in the snow in Norway, Sweden and Finland, on the top floor of a government building in Singapore, on beaches all over the Med, rallying in Monte Carlo, in Israel, Iceland, all over the USA, UK, Australia and Canada, on cruise ships and even on a butterfly farm in Spain. The list is endless and was only possible thanks to all of you, readers out there. I love opening my emails and social media to see where the next one will come from.

One reader, Jenifer Coady Murphy, went to Bermuda and when a freak wave ruined her friend's iPad and Butterfly Barn survived, they decided to share the story with the owner of the Bermuda Bookstore in Hamilton. Guess what! The lady actually ordered stock. Butterfly Barn has sold out in Bermuda!

Thank you, all so very much. It's a testimony to how far and wide Irish people travel and how very supportive you all are.

Every day I am heartened by the emails and messages I receive, especially about Jessie. Sometimes I wonder where I found the courage to write Jessie's story but I'm glad I did. I remember thinking if just one person can find some peace reading it, then it will be worth it. I never anticipated that so many would.

On a lighter note, nor did I anticipate the number of women who would ask me where was I hiding the real Jack Leslie. It is so lovely when readers stop me in the street to talk about Grace, Jessie and Sophia, as if they are real people, and tell me that they can't wait to know what's going to happen next. It's thanks to all of you that I am able to continue writing. I hope On Butterfly Wings leaves you wanting more. Or if you are new to the series, you might want to go back and find out how it all started in Butterfly Barn.

Huge thanks must go to my editor; Grace Wells. She has been an inspiration to me and many other writers here in the south-east of Ireland. Thanks to Margaret Organ, Waterford City and County Arts Officer, for her unwavering support and encouragement over the past number of years. I'd like to thank Artlinks for their work in supporting writers both in the form of bursaries and guidance. I am delighted to be a member. I am very grateful to Waterford City and County Council for their support and for ordering copies of On Butterfly Wings for visiting dignitaries to our beautiful county. I was so honoured by this gesture.

Thanks to Jane Cantwell from the Waterford Library Service for ordering copies of the Butterfly Barn Series. I could never have imagined the Library Service in Ireland would support the books in the way it has, or that Trinity College Library would have copies along with every university in the country, including our own Waterford Institute of Technology.

Without the love and support of so many people in my life, I couldn't do this. My parents, Nancy and Paddy Galvin, mean the world to me. They have always encouraged me and have been solid in both the good and bad times. My parents-in-law, Siobhán and Eugene Power, have also been a steady, caring influence in my life. Thanks to my brother, Alan, and my sister, Yvonne, who was one of my beta-readers. Thanks for being my sister and especially for taking the early-morning phone calls. To my sisters-in-law, Fionnuala, Edel, Siobhán and Eleanor, for spreading the word, and to Úna and Isabel for also taking on the role of beta-readers. Issy, as always you're a star.

Speaking of beta-readers, huge thanks must also go my mentor and friend Patricia Daly, Síona Stokes, Deirdre and Agnes Power, Karen Tomkins, Catherine Kavanagh, Gráinne Delaney, Denise Keogh and Rose Butler. I have met many wonderful new people and become reacquainted with some old friends on this journey. From a publicity perspective, without support from Matt Keane at the Munster Express and WLR FM, Karen Tomkins of WLR FM and Ireland's Own, Timmy Ryan of WLR FM, Marie McCann of WLR FM, Suzanne and Brian Walsh of Nationwide RTÉ, Darren Skelton and Catherine Murphy of Waterford News and Star, Paul Dower of Waterford-in-Your-Pocket, Kieran Foley of the Munster Express, Pat Carroll of Yougal Community Radio, Rose Butler and Norman Graham of Tramore Community Radio and Eimear Ní Bhraonain of KCLR FM, it would have been impossible to spread the word about Butterfly Barn. It was like a snowball effect and I will be forever grateful to each one of you. I'd like to thank Buddy Cuddihy and Paul Tuohy for their advice, they know what I am talking about and if there were errors they were mine.

Chenile Keogh from Kazoo Independent Publishing Services makes my life as a self-publisher easier. It's a pleasure working with both her and editor, Robert Doran. Thanks so much to you both. Thanks to Vanessa O'Loughlin at Writing.ie and to Andrew Brown of Ardel Media for the book covers. Thanks to my good friend and photographer John Foley, who took the author profile photograph and many shots of locations around the county featured in the Butterfly Barn Series. Huge thanks to Kieran McCarthy, who designed my website and provided me with an unexpected video of my first book launch, which I will treasure forever. A well-deserved thanks goes to Síona Stokes for guiding me through the fog that is social media. Thanks to Dave at Design Print House who looks after all the flyers, posters and print work. Thanks again to Claire Spencer Bowman for designing fabulous displays for both books. Thank you all so much for your incredible talents. The lovely thing about writing books is all the great new people I get to meet. One of those people is radio presenter and broadcaster Karen Tomkins. Karen has been a great support to me and I am honoured that she agreed to launch On Butterfly Wings.

Thank you to all my friends on social media, in particular Facebook, without your support Butterfly Barn would not have spread so far and wide. On Twitter, I've met some fantastic people who are following their dreams and helping others to follow theirs, Peter, Bernadette, Sally, Traci,

Jagdeep and Justin come to mind in particular. Thanks guys, it's continues to amaze me how the world is becoming a smaller place.

For twenty years, I have lived in a little place called Ballyduff, the kindness and support I have received over that time has been incredible. When the path wasn't always smooth, neighbours called, I never felt alone, the sense of community that some would say is missing in Ireland of today, is still alive and well here. The people of Ballyduff/Kilmeaden have supported me beyond anything I could have imagined on this mad adventure, especially Bobby and Noreen Byrne, Mary Cuddihy, Andrew Bridgett, Micky Joe Morrissey and of course, Linda Spillane, writer of the Ballyduff Community notes, I am very grateful to you all for your help.

And finally, great big thanks to Mary and William Harrington, Siobhán Millea, Deirdre Power, Fiona Redmond, Noeleen O'Neill, Siobhán Power, Roseline Dalton, Denyse Keogh, Denise Ryan Sherman and David and Ann Veale, for being great friends to us on this roller coaster called life.

Love and best wishes to you all,
Karen.

Also available in this series

Butterfly Barn

Sheets of rain beat against the windscreen as a wiper began to break loose from its rubber band. The shrill ring of Grace's mobile added to her frustration. She had left it in her handbag, which was lying on the floor on the passenger side, too far to reach. She was already running late, and pulling over could mean the difference between making the flight to New York or not.

It was probably Dirk and she really didn't want to talk to him. Why couldn't he understand that this was her dream? Yesterday morning when the cruise liner docked in Bayrush Harbour, it had been the best feeling. All of her hard work had been worth it. But then Dirk had started on about setting a date again ... Why couldn't she commit? She was wearing his ring. She was already in deep – three and a half years and a house together deep.

"Stop," she said out loud, surprising herself. "Focus on what's ahead. JESUS!" She narrowly missed the bumper of the car in front. The sooner she got to the airport the better.

What if the call was from Eoghan, her business partner? A great deal depended on the meeting she was to attend later. Maybe he'd forgotten to tell her something? He was supposed to be with her but had woken earlier with an ear infection and couldn't possibly fly. At sixty years old Eoghan was in excellent health but today it had let him down. It meant she'd have to make the pitch of her life, alone! The nearer Grace got to Dublin Airport the worse she felt. Nerves mixed with excitement filled her.

Waiting at the traffic lights on the dual carriageway, she looked into the rear-view mirror. "If it's to be it's up to me," she said, trying to quell the many doubts she had about herself. She looked across towards the lane beside her and sure enough, there were two lads in a minivan grinning at her. Thankfully the light changed so she stuck her foot to the floor, laughing.

Grace had sent an email explaining about Eoghan's sudden illness and had asked if they would agree to him making a conference call. The time difference meant she'd had no reply, but at least they'd be aware of the circumstances. Eoghan was an expert at all things nautical while excursions and activities were her areas. If they could sign Pal Pacific to their books it meant they could stay in business. If not, well ... that wasn't a thought she could afford to have!

Sophia sat in the back of the taxi. The radio was playing one of her favourite songs, "The Way We Were". Barbra Streisand's voice said it all.

"What time is your flight luv?" asked the driver, breaking her reverie with a thick Dublin accent that she knew so well from her many trips.

"Oh not until one-thirty, I've got plenty of time."

"Well you certainly got the weather until now," he said nodding towards the window as the rain bucketed down. "The best we've had in years! What part of America are you from?"

"New York."

"The Big Apple! Me and the missus went there a few years ago. In the good times. Sure I couldn't get her outta the shops. I got lost in that Macy's more times."

Sophia smiled, noticing two twinkling brown eyes looking at her through the driver's mirror. The way he spoke about his wife saddened her. She would never be Bill's missus again.

"So, were you here long?" He seemed determined to keep chatting.

"Just four days this time."

"Oh, so you're a regular. Well, is there any Irish blood in ya?"

"None."

"Jaysus that makes a change! I don't think I ever had an American in the taxi that didn't have a drop in them." He paused, obviously waiting for an explanation.

"I'm an original then." This seemed to stop him in his tracks. He fiddled with the radio and changed the channel. Sophia looked out the window and wondered would the emptiness she felt inside ever leave her. The taxi driver was nice but she'd had enough of idle chatter.

*

Sitting in Mr Morrison's waiting room in Bayrush, Jessie could feel her heart racing. She looked across at another couple; the woman seemed to not have a care in the world as she browsed through VIP magazine. Jessie could feel Geoff shifting uncomfortably in the seat beside her, a sure sign he was just as nervous as she was. She picked up a magazine and flicked through the pages, anything to distract her.

"Did you see the match last night?" asked Geoff, directing his attention to the fellow sitting across from him beside a heavily pregnant woman.

"Ah stop, it'd break your heart," the guy replied. Their voices became a background noise to Jessie's nerves. She turned the magazine page and saw a picture of a mother kissing a chuckling baby on its cheek. Its beautiful round eyes seemed to look straight into Jessie's heart. She was terrified. Twenty years together and they had been blessed with six-year-old Sam. She was afraid to think about what had happened four years ago.

"Mr and Mrs McGrath," announced the secretary, breaking Jessie's thoughts. She touched her tummy and felt so grateful for the little life inside. She was so looking forward to seeing the baby for the first time. She knew it would just be a blob on a monitor but it would be their little, long-awaited blob, and she was looking forward to showing Sam the print-out. He was so excited. "Only another twenty-eight weeks to go," Geoff had told him this morning at breakfast.

Jessie heard the rain outside and hoped that Grace would make it safely to the airport. All her hard work was paying off. If the deal went through Grace could finally make wedding plans. Just then Geoff looked at her and gave her that sweet, private smile he saved for her. She relaxed; he was right to smile. She had made it to twelve weeks. Their dreams were coming true.

Jack Leslie looked out of the aeroplane window. They were circling over Dublin. The view was incredible, even on a rainy day. He had loved Dubai but since the shock of finding out about Lynda's betrayal, he hadn't been functioning properly. He'd never suspected a thing. He had actually thought they were trying for a baby. What a fool she'd made of him! Women, he was finished with them, devious, conniving and cold. The jolt of the aeroplane touching the tarmac bought him back.

"Fáilte romhat go hÉireann, and thank you for flying with us today." He loved the sound of the Irish accent. He had missed it. Over the years he had been back and forth for holidays. But could he actually live in Ireland again? Or did he even want to?

"Miss Grace Fitzgerald, travelling to New York, please report to the Aer Lingus customer service desk immediately!"

Oh no, thought Grace as she weaved her way through the June holiday crowds. She joined the queue at the desk. Her mind was working overtime. What could it be? *Oh please God it's not Jessie; stop being such a pessimist*, she told herself. Grace was so anxious about her best friend's scan. Please God everything would go well for her this time. Grace was virtually hopping from one foot to the other; she was already short on time. She settled herself and continued waiting her turn.

"I'm terribly sorry," said the perfectly made-up ground hostess. "We actually have a small problem with the flight to New York. It is overbooked but we have taken the liberty of upgrading you to our premier service."

"Oh my God, that's fantastic. Thank you so much. I'd better get a move on or I'll never get through security."

"Here is your boarding card and have some champagne on us. Enjoy!"

"Thanks a million," Grace said, picking up her hand luggage and rushing towards the security gate.

After passing through security she made her way along the series of corridors to the gate, thrilled to be travelling first class. She could hardly keep the smile from her face. Eoghan not being able to travel had been such a blow. Being upgraded certainly made up for it.

Standing on the moving sidewalk she looked through the glass wall dividing the arrivals from the departures. "Oh my God. Jack!" she said out loud, spinning around and nearly tripping over her carry-on luggage and crashing into the woman behind her.

"I'm so sorry," she said, completely flustered.

"No probs, whoever he is … he's very cute! Don't you think you might be heading in the wrong direction?" The woman laughed.

Grace smiled but the man she had taken for Jack had been swallowed in the crowd so she couldn't be sure it was him. "An old friend," she said, taking the handle of her carry-on and pulling it off the moving sidewalk. The woman smiled too knowingly for Grace's comfort so she decided to walk along the corridor instead.

Jack Leslie had been such a good friend when she had badly needed one. She had seen his wedding photograph in the local paper nine years ago. He had looked so happy her heart had nearly broken all over again. Underneath the photograph it had said he was living in Dubai and that the dark-haired girl beaming beside him was from Chicago. What's wrong with you, Grace? Focus, she told herself, shaking her head from side to side as if willing all her issues and concerns away.

www.karenpowerauthor.com

14340494R00162

Printed in Poland
by Amazon Fulfillment
Poland Sp. z o.o., Wrocław